Léopold's Wicked Embrace

Immortals of New Orleans

Kym Grosso

MT Carvin Publishing
West Chester, Pennsylvania

Edited by Julie Roberts
Cover design by Cora Graphics
Formatted by Polgarus Studio

DISCLAIMER

This book is a work of fiction. The names, characters, locations and events portrayed in this book are a work of fiction or are used fictitiously. Any similarity to actual events, locales, or real persons, living or dead, is coincidental and not intended by the author.

NOTICE

This is an adult erotic paranormal romance book with love scenes and mature situations. It is only intended for adult readers over the age of 18.

ACKNOWLEDGMENTS

I am very thankful to everyone who helped me create this book:

~My husband, for encouraging me to write and supporting me in everything I do. I love that we can laugh and learn on our journey. I look forward to reading you more naughty passages from my books and getting your feedback. You are the most amazing husband and father, and not a day goes by that I'm not grateful for your support.

~My children, for being so patient with me, while I spend time working on the book. You are the best kids ever!

~Julie Roberts, editor, who spent hours reading, editing and proofreading Léopold's Wicked Embrace. I really could not have done this without you!

~Cora Graphics, for designing Léopold's sexy cover.

~Romance Novel Covers/Jimmy Thomas, for shooting the custom image for Léopold's cover.

~Polgarus Studio, for formatting Léopold's Wicked Embrace.

~Claire, for helping me to correctly translate and utilize French phrases within Léopold's book.

~My dedicated beta readers, Denise, Elena, Elizabeth, Gayle, Julia, Julie, Kassie, Katrina, Leah, Maria, Rochelle,

Sharon, Stephanie, Sunny, and Tanner, for beta reading. I really appreciate all the valuable feedback you provided.

~Gayle Latreille, my admin, who is one of my biggest supporters and helps to run my street team. I'm so thankful for all of your help!

~My awesome street team, for helping spread the word about the Immortals of New Orleans series. I appreciate your support more than you could know! You guys rock!

❧ *Chapter One* ❧

Léopold's lips curled in restrained amusement. If it weren't for the acrid smell of burnt flesh emanating from his silver-cuffed wrists, he might actually enjoy schooling the wolves in what it meant to fight with a thousand-year-old vampire. When he'd made the decision to confront Hunter Livingston, Alpha of the Caldera Wolves, he'd fought the desire to kill the leader without hesitation. It was true that the death of adults came as naturally to him as piercing the skin of a delectable human on a warm summer night, but even Léopold had hard limits. It was only yesterday that he had pried the small infant wolf out of the arms of the lifeless woman. The sight of the helpless child had shaken him to his core. He'd many times witnessed children die during his lifetime, but the loss of an innocent life never got easier to stomach.

An eye for an eye; he'd considered penetrating the cold walls of their den and ripping out the Alpha's throat without mercy. Yet he'd known his friend Logan, Alpha of the Acadian Wolves wouldn't approve. Nor would Logan's beta, Dimitri. After he'd saved the Alpha's mate, Wynter, it appeared a bond had been forged between him and his newfound friends. Ever since Dimitri had made the long trip with Léopold to Yellowstone to retrieve Wynter's frozen blood, the two had grown closer. Out of respect for Dimitri, he'd grant the Alpha the opportunity to explain before he killed him.

Earlier in the evening, he'd approached the den peacefully, allowing the distrustful wolves to cuff his hands. The sting of the silver was worth enduring for the pleasure he would get from draining the Alpha. Unlike younger vampires, Léopold stood calmly, easily enduring the bite of the poison. His eyes scanned the room, taking in the sight of the growling wolves who'd gathered to watch their Alpha. Had he been any other supernatural being, he should have been concerned. Yet anger flowed through his psyche, not fear.

His patience wore thin as he observed the Alpha transforming into man. Hunter Livingston rose from a crouched position. Reaching above the fireplace, he snatched a silver claymore off the wall. The air in the room crackled with tension as he deliberately stalked toward his prisoner. He growled and his eyes locked on Léopold's. Sweat dripped from Hunter's forehead as he sliced the sword through the air.

Léopold's face remained impassive as the blade seared a trail of blood in its wake across his abdomen. He gave a devious smile a second before he launched himself at the Alpha. The snap of metal was the only sound alerting the wolves that the vampire was freed. Léopold rushed the tall wolf, smashing him against the stone wall. Clutching his right hand around Hunter's neck, he applied pressure with his other until the weapon clanked onto the floor. His fangs descended, scraping against the rough skin of the Alpha's shoulder.

"Where is the child?" the Alpha sputtered, surprised by the vampire's strength.

"Let me be clear, Alpha. It is I who will ask questions. And it is I who shall grant mercy. Nod, if you understand." Léopold fought to keep his rage at bay. Answers would be forthcoming before he sated his desire for revenge.

Dimitri heard the commotion and immediately sensed danger. He exited the shower and tore off his wet towel. Transforming to wolf, he ran toward the source of the melee. As he rounded the corner, he couldn't believe his eyes. Léopold had Hunter jacked up against a painting. Hunter's eyes glowed red; his claws were embedded into the vampire's arms. The pack wolves growled but didn't attack. Even though Léopold wasn't wolf, his attack on their Alpha was seen as a challenge, one that had to be fought alone. But Dimitri knew that whatever was going on had nothing to do with a challenge to Hunter's role as Alpha. He charged the pair to break up the fight, shifting back to human in the process.

"Jesus Christ, Leo. What the fuck are you doing?" Dimitri placed his palms against their chests in an attempt to separate the dominant males. "Alpha. Hunter. Please stop."

"The child," Hunter spat out, never taking his eyes off Léopold.

"Yes, the child," Léopold hissed in return. His fangs descended, readying to strike.

"Fucking stop it. Both of you. Whatever's going on, it's not what it seems. Leo, release him," Dimitri commanded.

Dimitri knew that both the Alpha and vampire could kick his ass, but he wasn't about to let them kill each other. The vampire's gift of life to his Alpha's mate had secured his friendship with Léopold. But he'd known Hunter his whole life, and he'd stake the ancient one before letting him kill the Alpha.

Upon hearing Dimitri's words, Léopold reined in his anger. In doing so, he was taken aback by his own acquiescence. *Since when the hell do I listen to anyone, let alone a wolf? It's official. I've gone soft.* He'd known that the past few days with Dimitri had changed him. It was as if someone had pounded a crowbar into his cold dark heart and poured in warm honey. *Goddammit, this is exactly why I don't have friends.* He'd freely chosen his solitary life, made a deliberate choice to keep both humans and supernaturals alike as mere acquaintances. It was true that he was close to a few vampires that he'd sired, but they weren't friends. Rather, they were relationships borne out of necessity and respect. A growl brought him back to the situation. Resigned to the fact that he needed the Alpha alive if he were to get answers, Léopold tossed Hunter to the ground.

"Fucking wolves," Léopold grumbled. He glanced up to Dimitri and gave him a look of disgust, realizing his friend was once again naked.

"Get over it, asshole," Dimitri growled in return, raking his hand through his hair. "Goddammit, Léopold. Whatever the fuck your problem is, you could have come to me. I realize this concept may be foreign to you, but use your fucking words instead of killing first."

Léopold rolled his eyes at the admonition and shook his head. He didn't want to admit that the wolf was right. But trust wasn't something that came easily to him nor was he used to having someone who would willingly help him.

"And you," Dimitri gestured toward Hunter, who'd pushed up off the floor. "I told you I came out west with the vampire."

The Alpha limped over to the bar and began pouring himself a scotch. He threw back a shot of the amber liquid and slammed the glass onto the bar. "Yes you did. But you didn't tell me everything."

"Blake, take the pack for a run. I'll be fine. Now go," Hunter told his beta. He wasn't about to have this discussion in front of the entire pack. Hunter waited only a few seconds after they'd gone before crossing the room to slam the door.

"Would someone like to tell me what the hell is going on?" Dimitri grabbed a throw blanket off the couch and wrapped it around his waist. He could have cared less if his nudity bothered the vampire, but it was winter in Wyoming. Even indoors, his human form couldn't take the bone-chilling temperatures.

"Last night is what happened. Ask the Alpha." Léopold sighed, staring into the flames that blazed brightly inside the stone hearth. Ironic that even though a mere lick of a flame could easily bring about his demise, he was still attracted to its warmth.

"Last night you were supposed to get the blood that Fiona had buried. Did you take care of it?" Dimitri's eyes darted back and forth between Léopold and the Alpha, who'd already started pouring himself and his guests another drink. "Come on, what the hell am I missing?"

"Un bébé. A girl." Léopold turned to stare into the eyes of the Alpha, who was handing him a glass. He took it, downed the caustic drink and sighed once again.

"What have you done with her?" Hunter seethed.

"A baby? You took a freakin' baby?" Dimitri jumped to his feet and grabbed Léopold by his shoulder.

Léopold's lips tightened in rage, and he seized the wolf's wrist. "Yes, I took the damn baby. She would have died."

"So she's alive?"

"But of course she is." Léopold shrugged him off, turning to Hunter. "Why, Alpha? Why would you allow a human to take the child into the woods? Had you ordered her death?"

"Are you fucking kidding me?" Hunter yelled.

"What? Did you not deem her to be perfect?"

"We'd never do anything to harm a child," the Alpha retorted.

"Really? 'Cause I just found one of your pups in the woods. Nearly dead, in fact. Don't tell me that wolves haven't ever tried to kill a child, one they didn't want in a pack. You know it's been done. Exposure. That's what they called it in ancient Rome. An illegitimate child. A sick child. Tossed aside to the elements, they were. A barbaric practice seen in other cultures as well." Rage coursed through Léopold, and he fought to remain calm. "Did you send the human out to do your dirty work? Where are the child's parents? How could you let this happen?"

"I didn't fucking know!" Hunter screamed as he began to pace wildly, rubbing the back of his neck.

"So you deny involvement?"

"I swear to the Goddess that I did not order this…I did not know. I would never do something like that. She's just a baby," Hunter fought back.

"Is she yours?" Dimitri asked.

"No, I'm not even mated."

"Just askin'. But how the hell does one manage to get a pup away from its mama, anyhow?" There was no wolf more protective than a mother.

"Ava's mother is dead. Ava. That's her name. Her mama, Mariah, died during childbirth." Hunter blew out a breath, rubbing his eyes. "She was a gentle hybrid, but Perry knew how frail she was when they'd mated. She could shift, but she couldn't take the cold, couldn't keep up with the pack either. Once she got pregnant, she deteriorated. The pregnancy was rough. And when she gave birth to Ava…" Hunter's voice trailed off, unable to continue.

"What of the human doctors? If she was hybrid, surely they could have helped her?" Léopold inquired.

"She wouldn't hear of it. Beside, her labor came fast. With the blizzard, it could have taken hours to get her there anyway. She hemorrhaged. And Perry, well, he was despondent. With the loss of his mate, he couldn't take care of himself, let alone a baby. Two days after she was born, he went missing. Of course, we searched for miles, but he'd gone. As for Ava…ya know I'm a bachelor. But I took care of her anyway. Hired nannies… I don't know how it happened…why it happened…one of them just took her." Hunter's cheek quivered in the lie.

Dimitri, sensing the untruth, got up off the sofa, approaching the Alpha. "Hunter, what the fuck happened? You and I know that wolves wouldn't just let someone take one of their own, a baby, and walk out of the pack. You can tell me…him too. That vampire over there," he gestured to and locked eyes with Léopold, "he saved the pup. You can trust us."

Hunter sighed and licked his lips in indecision. They'd all known the child wouldn't be all wolf, yet no one had suspected the origins of her human side.

"The baby, she's special. Yes, she's at least half wolf. But Mariah, we didn't know what she was. We all assumed she was human and wolf."

"What are you trying to say?" Dimitri put his hand on the Alpha's shoulder to comfort him.

Hunter raised his gaze to meet Dimitri's. "I can't explain it. Ava has this strange energy about her. I could almost handle that, but then I felt something…something worse."

"What the hell did you feel?" Léopold asked, growing concerned for Ava's safety.

"Something dark was out there. No, it was more than that. Something evil. Hell, I don't know what it was."

"A witch?" Dimitri offered.

"I don't know. I mean, come on, guys; we're in the middle of the wilderness out here. It's not like we're in New Orleans. What the hell would someone be doing practicing dark magick in the middle of Yellowstone? It doesn't make sense. Besides, this was more like something watching…waiting. I don't know, it could've been nothin'. I can't explain it. If I didn't know any better…" He shook his head, unwilling to share his thoughts. Even to him, his suspicions were ridiculous.

"Say it, wolf. I need to know," Léopold insisted.

"There were times when her energy felt so strong. I actually thought I saw her skin glow…like a firefly. And things in her room…would be moved."

"Moved? What do you mean?"

"Like objects. Like a stuffed toy. Her pacifier. I never saw her do it but I think she may be able to move things. Like call them somehow." Hunter pressed his hands on the bar and bowed his head, embarrassed to look at their faces. What he was saying made no sense, he knew. "Goddammit, I know it sounds crazy but I'm tellin' you that she's not just a hybrid."

"The baby glowed?" Dimitri laughed.

"I told you it was crazy. Even if that pup's part wolf, she's something else…something besides human."

"Then what is she?" Léopold considered that he'd best call her caretaker as soon as possible. He'd seen all kinds of supernatural beings during his long life. He may not have liked Hunter, but that didn't mean what the Alpha was saying wasn't true.

"I don't know," Hunter admitted. "So Devereoux, I've laid out my cards. Where'd you take the baby?"

"I shall tell you where she is, but let me be clear, I'm not returning the baby to your pack until her safety is assured. The fact that a human nanny was able to steal her from your home and drag her into a blizzard is outrageous. Given that you have so many security measures, one can only assume that the human didn't do this on her own." Léopold eyed the Alpha, walked to the overstuffed chair and sat down, shifting his feet onto an ottoman. He raised an eyebrow at Hunter, who stood silently contemplating his words. "That being said, you don't need to worry about her being with pack. She's with Logan."

"Logan? How the hell did you get a baby to Logan so fast?" Dimitri asked.

"Why would Logan take Ava?" Hunter questioned, doubting the vampire's words.

"He owes me a debt."

"Must be some hell of a debt if you got Logan to watch her," Hunter said with a shake of his head.

"That it was," Dimitri confirmed. "Léopold saved Logan's mate, Wynter. I was there when she died…almost died. His blood runs through her veins."

"Since when does a vampire give his gift to a wolf?"

"Doesn't matter, Alpha. Just know that it does, and she's alive. I went to Logan last night. It's no business of yours as to how." Léopold shot Dimitri a knowing look. He'd show the wolf soon enough. "It wasn't as if Logan had much choice, but he agreed. And Wynter was more than happy to take the baby. She may not have known it before, but she's very nurturing. They know it's not permanent. But they will care for the pup, and she'll be around a pack."

Hunter quietly considered what had happened. He had no explanation for how the nanny had taken Ava from his well-secured home in the middle of the night. And he couldn't be sure if he'd only imagined the dark force he'd felt or if the pressure of losing two wolves and caring for a baby had skewed his senses. While he cared for Ava, he was not her father. He'd merely been foster parent and he'd known that he'd eventually have to find her adoptive parents.

"I agree that Logan is well suited to watch the child, but we still don't know about the baby…what she is. Her mother, Mariah; I didn't know her very well but I know she'd lived in both New York City and New Orleans. Maybe if we could find Perry or track down a relative, they could help us figure out if Ava has any special abilities."

"We're leaving for New Orleans tonight," Léopold informed them. "Tomorrow, we'll meet with Logan to make sure the child is safe."

"I'm going to search Perry's house tomorrow and see if we can find any clues to Mariah's background. I don't understand why someone would want to kill her baby. It makes no sense," Hunter said.

"People kill for all kinds of reasons, Alpha. Spite, love, anger, jealousy…sometimes people kill just for fun. It is a wonder at times there's anyone left on the Earth," Léopold pondered. "I, myself, prefer to kill for revenge. And the next person who attempts to harm Ava will die. I can assure you of that."

Hunter went to his desk, pulled out a piece of paper and wrote down Mariah's and Perry's full names. He extended the note to Léopold. "Perry's local. He met Mariah in New York last year. But I remember him telling me that she hadn't lived there very long. I don't think she even ran with a pack. You know how the hybrids can be...they like to lay low sometimes. Even though he'd mentioned New Orleans, she may not have been there very long either. I don't have an address or anything else to go by."

"She's never been part of the Acadian wolf pack. Maybe she was just passing through or stayed with a friend?" Dimitri suggested.

"We'll find her family and her friends. And we'll find Perry, too. I don't give a damn if the wolf had his heart torn out all over the floor, a man doesn't just walk away from his child," Léopold replied with disdain.

Dimitri didn't answer the vampire, hesitating to agree with him. While the loss of a wolf's mate was devastating, there was no excuse for leaving one's offspring. Dimitri caught Hunter's gaze, expecting the Alpha to argue with Léopold. Instead, deafening silence hung in the air for several minutes until Hunter responded.

"Listen, I don't condone what Perry did and he's not welcome to return, but I agree with the vamp. We've got to find him. Ava deserves better." The buzz of Hunter's cell phone drew his attention away. He clicked it off and took a deep breath. "I'm sorry gentlemen, but I've gotta take this in my office. I'll just be a few minutes."

As Hunter retreated out of the living area, Léopold addressed Dimitri. "Time to go, wolf."

Dimitri rolled his eyes, recognizing the patronizing tone of Léopold's statement. "Yeah, I need to get dressed, first. How the hell did you get here anyway? I told you I'd find my way back to the cabin. Even if you drove the main highway, you'd be hard pressed to make it up Hunter's driveway tonight. Did you walk?"

Léopold smiled coyly at Dimitri. It had been so long since he'd had a friend and now he was about to clue him in on a little secret. Léopold approached him with a small chuckle, closing the distance between them.

"What's so funny?" Dimitri stood with the blanket wrapped loosely around his hips, confused as to what Léopold found so amusing. The hairs on the back of his neck pricked as Léopold raised his hands as if to embrace him. "Come on, man. Let me go get dressed and we can get the hell out of here. We can call the airline on the way back to the cabin and…"

"Ah, mon ami, have I told you how much I've enjoyed the past few days?" Léopold set his palms on Dimitri's shoulders.

"What? Yeah, okay. Good times and all, but we've got to get going." Dimitri cocked a worried eyebrow at the vampire. His gut told him something bad was about to happen; something very, very bad. He looked from side to side at Léopold's hands. Their heavy weight warmed his bare skin. A whisper fell through his lips. "What are you doing, man?"

"First, know that it's going to be okay."

Dimitri nodded, attempting to remain calm.

"Second, we aren't taking a plane."

∽◈∙ *Chapter Two* ∙◈∽

Dimitri hit the floor with a thud, his head barely missing what he recognized as a heavy wooden spindle from a four poster bed frame. His eyes flew open and he realized he was in a strange room, but he wasn't alone. Léopold lay next to him, grunting in pain.

"What the fuck did you just do, Devereoux?" Dimitri yelled, unable to gather the energy to get up off the carpet. Confusion fogged his mind as he tried to figure out where he was and how he'd gotten there. A deep rumble of laughter interrupted his growing state of panic. *Damn vampire.* "Jesus Christ. Are you trying to kill me?"

"Yeah, I thought it'd be better not to tell you. You might not agree otherwise. Much faster than a plane, no?" Léopold continued to laugh as he attempted to push up onto his elbows.

He glanced over to Dimitri who was laid flat out on his back, naked as a jaybird. Very few knew of his ability to materialize and very rarely had he pulled someone through with him. But he needed to get back to New Orleans as fast as possible and flying in a plane would have taken hours. Unfortunately, he'd had to bring the baby last night and hadn't fed in a few days. Exhausted, he clasped his hands onto the side of the mattress and used it as leverage to hoist himself off the floor and onto the bed.

As he rolled onto the soft comforter, he groaned in agony. Reaching across his chest, he fingered the torn fabric and ripped open his shirt. The crusty line across his abdomen provided evidence that he hadn't fully healed from the Alpha's blade. The rush of adrenaline must have kept him from feeling the pain, but now the sting tore across his chest.

"Merde," he coughed.

"What the hell is your problem, vampire? Travel arrangements not up to your standards?" Dimitri spat out, trying to get his bearings.

"Don't tell me you're not impressed, wolf. It's a cool trick. Don't try to deny it." Léopold took a deep breath and blew it out.

"Now you see it, now you don't. You'd better fucking tell me what you just did. I feel like you scrambled my brain. Not cool."

"Ah, stop complaining. You'll feel better in a few minutes. Just look at it like shifting. It's a kind of magic, sort of. Or one could say it is the temporary reorganization of mass and energy. Perfectly safe, I assure you."

"Yeah, well, it may be safe, but you could have told me. A little warning might've been nice."

"And you would have agreed?" Léopold choked up blood and his eyes fluttered.

"Probably not, but shit, Leo," Dimitri huffed. He was loath to admit it but Léopold was right; he was beginning to feel well again. He sat up and noticed Léopold sprawled out on the bed, looking unusually pale...even for a vampire. A nasty scab lined his chest. "Hey man, what's wrong with you? What happened to mister, oh so powerful ancient one? You do remember that vampires heal themselves, don't you?"

"Mon ami, even I have my limits. I need to feed. I flashed back here last night with Ava and now again with you. If I can get my phone out..." Léopold kicked off his boots with his feet and began to take off his jacket, searching the pockets. "Where is my damn phone?"

"What're you doing?" Dimitri stood and stretched, looking at his hands, feet and groin, checking to make sure everything was in working order.

"Arnaud."

"Who's Arnaud?"

"He's my, uh, you know, assistant."

"Like your Renfield, huh? Maaassster," Dimitri joked in his best Transylvanian accent.

"He's not sired or bonded, smart ass. But he is well paid. He was supposed to bring me a donor, and you, some clothes. I just need to lay here a minute...find my fucking phone."

Dimitri laughed. "Looks like the great one is definitely loosening up. First the hot tub. Your liberal use of the f bomb hasn't gone unnoticed either. There's hope for you yet."

"What can I say? You're a bad influence." Unable to find his phone, he threw his jacket to Dimitri, who effortlessly caught it mid-air. "Find my cell."

Dimitri quickly rummaged through all the pockets of the parka. "Nothing. You said, Arnaud is supposed to be here? And by donor, I assume you're talking about a human?"

"Oui. Some are paid, some are volunteers."

"Volunteers, huh? You got em' lined up waiting for you to suck their blood? You must be good," he joked as he made his way toward the door.

"The very best," Léopold replied with a smile. But as soon as Dimitri left the room, he moaned, gritting his teeth together. Damn, he needed his sustenance. He should have known better than to try to transport again without feeding but he'd be damned if he spent another minute in the Alpha's home when there was work to be done. He stared at the ceiling, weighing his options. Sure, he could drag his sorry ass downstairs and catch a cab to a local blood club. But the donor should have arrived already. Within minutes, he heard Dimitri returning down the hallway. The distinctive sound of a singular set of footsteps told him that he was alone.

"No one's here yet. But hey, look at this." Dimitri gestured to the dresser which was covered in an assortment of new clothing with the tags still attached. "Jeeves must've gotten one thing right. You mind?"

"Please do. If I have to look at your naked ass one more second, I think I'll bite my own arm."

Dimitri laughed, ripping open a new package of boxers. He quickly put them on and went to look through the large pile of jeans. He was about to ask how Léopold's manservant would know his size, more than a little creeped out that some personal assistant was trying to dress him, when he heard a hiss from the bed. He sighed, knowing that his next idea was probably not the smartest thing he'd ever proposed, but damn, he felt a little guilty that the big guy had brought him all this way, sharing his 'special travel skill' and now the vampire was having trouble even sitting up in bed.

"Hey, Léopold. How about we take a cab to one of those clubs? What's the name of that place? Mordez?"

"Soon enough. I just need to rest a bit before I go anywhere."

Dimitri crossed the room and sat on the bed, taking in the listless state of the vampire. He observed that Léopold's eyes were now closed, and the wound had started bubbling apart. Before he could stop himself, he'd made the suggestion.

"I'll feed you."

Léopold's eyes flew open, meeting Dimitri's. "What?"

"You heard me. Come on, let's do this thing. You can bite my arm, right?"

"I don't know…I can't ask this of you. The donors, they come to me freely."

"Yeah, well, so do I. Come on. You did this for Wynter. You had her back, I have yours. It's no big deal, right? I mean, it's not like you're going to have some weird bond to me."

"No." Léopold gave him a small smile. "No bonds. No sires or anything. But still…"

"The faster you're on your feet, the faster we can go try to find connections to Mariah's past."

Léopold's lips tightened and he looked away.

"Ya know I'm right. We can't waste any more time. You didn't fly me all the way out here to lie around, did ya?"

"No, but I don't think this is a good idea."

"Well let me put it this way…At some point, possibly very soon, whoever wanted that kid dead is going to realize that she's still very much alive. Then they're gonna go after her again. And since she's staying with Logan, I don't want them going after my Alpha and his mate. So let's go. Come on, just take a little, enough to get you by until we find your donor."

"I won't need much. Your blood; it's strong. You're wolf," Léopold admitted.

"There ya go, then. Let's get to…what do you need here?" Dimitri sat on the bed and considered how best to feed a vampire. *What the fuck am I thinking? Too late now.* He sat cross-legged, and then changed his mind, lying onto his back.

Léopold grew amused at his friend's insistence. Not that he didn't appreciate the offer, but he wasn't accustomed to needing anyone. Dimitri's blood, given in friendship, felt all too intimate, making him uncomfortable. Yet the lancing pain to his gut reminded him of his dire situation. He shifted onto his side, cradling Dimitri's arm in his hands. Slowly he lowered his head to the wolf's wrist. The aromatic scent of blood called to him as he found the strong beating pulse.

"You're sure?" he asked, locking eyes on Dimitri's.

"Yeah, I can take it. Do it now, before I change my mind." Dimitri glanced away as if someone was about to give him a needle.

Without hesitation, Léopold's fangs extended, striking the wolf's arm. He closed his eyes, allowing the pungent flavor to coat his tongue. Deliberately, he suctioned the life-sustaining fluid, releasing his own power into Dimitri's body. Léopold, grateful for the gift, would cause the wolf no pain, only pleasure. He knew Dimitri would resist, confused by his reaction to the bite. Léopold clutched the wrist to his lips, watching as his friend's body bowed off the bed.

As soon as Dimitri felt the pinpricks, his body flooded with unexpected warmth. The tug of Léopold's lips sent a rush of blood to his cock. *What the fuck is happening?* He wanted to rip his arm away from the vampire, but he felt paralyzed to fight. Desire washed over him from head to toe and before he knew what he was doing, his own hand had reached to grip his shaft through the fine cotton shorts. Stiff as a board, he stroked himself, attempting to relieve the pressure. *Goddess, this feels wrong on so many levels.* His mind screamed at him to move, to struggle, yet his lips parted, releasing only a moan.

Léopold licked the wounds he'd caused, and released Dimitri's arm. Thoroughly energized, he sat up, and stared down at Dimitri, whose face had grown tight in both arousal and anger. Léopold laughed, and rolled off the bed. He watched in amusement as the wolf attempted to launch himself off the mattress but fell backwards, clutching himself.

"Fuck me." Dimitri shook his head at the realization of what he'd just said. He quickly took his hand off his groin and glared at Léopold. "No. I didn't mean that. Don't touch me."

"You're fine," Léopold assured him. He glanced in the mirror and finger-combed his hair back into place.

"This," Dimitri gestured to his erection, "is not funny. Goddammit, I need to get laid. Not that you aren't pretty, Leo, but you're not my type. Shit, look what you did."

"You may recall that I told you that feeding from you was not a good idea. But I must admit, your blood is fine. Very tasty." A broad smile broke across his face.

"Really, Leo? What the hell, man?"

"Sorry, but there aren't many choices when it comes to a bite, you know. Would you have rather had pain? I'm not a sadist by nature, but if you'd preferred it…"

"No." Dimitri pushed himself up so that he was sitting on the edge of the bed. His painful erection was finally starting to subside.

"Well, then, you have to admit that it didn't hurt. Go get a shower, see to your need. I'd love to help you but I'm afraid you're not my preference either, wolf."

"Really, so you give hard-ons but no blow jobs? Lucky me. For the record, if I ever am dumb enough to suggest this again, would you please just say no?" Dimitri hobbled over to the bathroom door.

"Hey wolf," Léopold called from the doorway.

Dimitri lifted his gaze to him. "Yeah?"

"Seriously, Dimitri. I appreciate you helping me. I should've paid more attention. I let myself get run down. It won't happen again."

"No problem."

"You need to know that it has been a very long time for me…this friendship thing. This isn't something someone like me does." *Or deserves.* Léopold's eyes darkened and his tone grew serious. "These few days have been quite the adventure, and I suspect there is more to come. I must ask, however, that you keep what you experienced tonight to yourself. Not the bite but the travel. Logan knows as I couldn't hide it from him when I showed up in his house last night. But no one else. It's a special ability…one I'd prefer others not know about. Understood?"

"My lips are zipped." Dimitri sensed sadness in Léopold. As wolf, with his pack, he was never truly alone. Perhaps he underestimated the loneliness that plagued the vampire.

"Well, then…see you downstairs in a few. I've got someone I want you to meet," Léopold commented as he left the room.

Laryssa Theriot carefully controlled her heartbeat and breathing in an attempt to convey indifference. For the past week, she'd felt the energy. She couldn't be sure but suspected a child of her lineage had been born. So rare, she'd never experienced the warmth, the calling of another whose power was so strong. Yet as soon as she'd indulged in her excitement, acknowledging the fact that someone else like her existed, a cold chill had rolled over her skin, emphasizing the reality of her situation.

Sitting at the bar, she crossed her legs, the tight black leather pants caressing her thighs. There was no way she'd ever wear a skirt in this place. Like the humans, she'd be vulnerable to suggestion and the sexual excitement the vampires could induce with a mere look. She kept her eyes low, glancing around, taking in the auras of the supernaturals. If necessary, she'd invoke her powers to protect herself from danger. She'd gone to great lengths to hide herself, to blend into the magical background of the French Quarter. After nearly thirty lonely years, she'd grown weary of concealing her true nature. The cloak of evil that she'd recently felt brush across her face had reminded her she'd never be safe, freedom to be herself would remain elusive. It hadn't been the first time she'd felt it nor would it be the last.

Laryssa pushed down her sunglasses, shielding her emotions further from the prying eyes of vampires and humans alike. The bartender regarded her for a moment, noticing that her glass was still half full with wine. She'd needed the alcohol to take the edge off her nervousness. *Show no fear.* The supernaturals would detect the smallest infraction of a loss of control. Increased heartbeat. Sweat. Rapid breathing. So many years in hiding had taught her well to mask her abilities. Like an actor in the grand theater, she played her part, meticulously attending to every last detail of her role, a dominant biker chick, looking for nothing more than a drink. Tomorrow, she'd return to her unassuming job in the Quarter, selling antiques, coming and going as she pleased on assignment. But tonight, she looked as if she was the predator; cold, calculating and ready to catch her prey.

She scanned the room, noting the usual spectrum of auras. Excitement. Hunger. Desire. Jealousy. She nervously tapped her fingernail against the glass, waiting for her friend, Avery, to arrive. Avery was the only soul in New Orleans who knew her secret. She'd been her savior, helping her to hide. After sensing the dark ones, she speculated she'd need a stronger witch to find a spell to ward off the evil. The mere fact she could sense it meant it knew she existed as well. She needed someone to better shield her powers, to keep her safe from the hell that sought her soul. Yet the thought of a new child weighed heavily on her shoulders. If what she suspected was true, she wasn't the only one in danger.

A shuffling of patrons alerted her to a new arrival. She turned to face the bar and glanced in the mirror to observe the commotion. Struggling to keep her composure, she lifted her eyes to the reflection. Both men and women appeared captivated by the dark haired, well-dressed man who'd entered the room. The air thickened with palpable arousal, auras flickered to red, with fangs descending in response. The stranger stopped to take in his surroundings, looking over to the bar. Laryssa lowered her lips to the rim of her glass, attempting to look uninterested.

As soon as he glanced away, her eyes were once again drawn to him. He was tall, at least six-four, his lean muscular build carefully concealed underneath his form-fitting black suit. Strikingly handsome, he smiled with a cool arrogance that told her he was a vampire. And he wasn't a neophyte; quite the opposite, he exuded the confidence of a master. He laughed at something his friend said and winked at a passing waitress. The rugged good-looking fellow who accompanied him looked out of place next to the debonair vamp. Casually dressed in jeans and t-shirt, his forearms were painted in tattoos, the stubble of his day-old beard darkened his jaw. She'd be surprised if he was anything other than wolf, as his aura shone in relaxed blues. Like the magnetic attraction of polar opposites, the odd pair seemed inseparable, and she wondered about their connection.

Her curiosity seemed to get the better of her as she swiveled her stool to catch a glimpse of them leaving. Unconsciously, she tugged at her short black wig, pressing a stray hair back underneath it. Her breath caught as the vampire stopped in his tracks and turned to stare over at her. Her traitorous heart sped up slightly in response to the way his gaze caressed her body. Laryssa crossed her thighs together as warmth spread throughout her chest. Like a blushing schoolgirl, she felt the heat rise in her cheeks. Hastily, she spun away from the sight of him, but not before his eyes locked on hers and she caught his broad smile in the mirror.

She wasn't sure if it was his stare or her own confusion, but as she tried to tear her eyes off him, the slippery leather seat gave way. Her cheeks flushed in embarrassment, her hands flailing to reach the bar top. Expecting a hard fall onto the stone floor, she cringed, anticipating the pain. Air rushed from her lungs as strong hands wrapped around her shoulders, jerking her upright. She grasped her sunglasses that had fallen down her nose, revealing her emerald green eyes to her rescuer.

Léopold felt somewhat guilty for throwing the human off her game. As soon as he'd entered the bar, he'd spotted a woman dressed in black leather. Leather in Mordez was hardly unusual, but this woman looked tightly wrapped, like a Christmas present waiting to be opened. He observed the way she tugged at the ends of her short black hair, as if she was pulling a baseball cap down over her face. Interesting, he thought. Try as she may to blend into the supernatural crowd, her vitality licked at his senses the second he sniffed the air.

Although he hadn't come to play, the way her pulse increased, if only for a second, told him she was aware of his presence in the room. He didn't have time to get distracted, but when he noticed her tottering on the barstool, he rushed to her side. Catching her right before she landed on the ground, a rush of desire slammed him as the swell of her restrained breasts grazed his chest. Léopold felt her quiver underneath his touch, but she quickly recovered. He caught a glance of her captivating green eyes right before she shoved the black glasses onto her face, shielding her from his gaze.

"Careful, pet," he told her.

"I'm fine…really," Laryssa stammered.

"But of course you are," he chuckled at her defensive posturing.

Léopold was about to engage her further when he heard Dimitri call his name. *Merde, cock-blocked by the damn wolf.* He was starting to regret the day he'd become involved with the whole lot of mongrels. He nodded to Dimitri, who was staring at him as if he'd grown a second head.

"Take care, mon petit lapin," Léopold commented as he grazed the back of his forefinger down the side of her cheek.

"I'm fine," she repeated. Laryssa had hoped the vampire would leave her alone. Quite the opposite, he'd positioned himself within inches of her body, invading her personal space. His leg brushed hers, and she took a deep breath, her mind warring between sliding her hand down his thigh or running out the door. Lost in her own confusion, she heard someone call out toward their direction. Out of the corner of her eye, she observed his sexy pirate-looking friend give a wave. Refusing to acknowledge the lash of sexual awareness that he'd left on her skin, her fingers tightened around the stem of her glass.

"I'm afraid I must go. Be safe, mademoiselle. This is no place for a single human," he warned.

Léopold hesitated but a second before returning to Dimitri. While nonchalantly guiding them through a sea of bodies, he stole a glance back to the girl, wondering who she was…what she was. Her scent was like lilies on a spring morning, sweet and fresh. But it was her energy that alerted him that perhaps he was wrong about her. When he'd touched her cheek, her smooth skin sizzled underneath his, and he'd detected something otherworldly. Yet he could tell she was neither vampire nor wolf. A witch, perhaps? Maybe, but the look of innocence and fear in her eyes worried him. She didn't belong in Mordez, and his curiosity about her stood to distract him from the entire reason he'd come to the club. He shook the feeling off as he spotted the person he'd come to meet, making a beeline toward him. Lady Charlotte Stratton.

Laryssa breathed deeply, forcing her physical response into submission, all the while despising the way she'd lost control of her equilibrium. Not only had she broken character, she'd fallen like a dumbass, totally distracted by the sexy but dangerous stranger. His touch had scorched her skin through her jacket, leaving her tingling in his wake. As her eyes caught his, she struggled to slow her pulse, to control the power that could easily spill into the room, revealing her true identity.

Although Laryssa had never met the vampire before, a sense of familiarity and desire had washed over her. There was something about him, something driving the rapid fluttering in her stomach that made her want to jump into his arms. The rush of lust threatened to push her into a panic. She forced herself upright, stiffening her spine, and ratcheted down her foolish and dangerous response to him. *Goddammit, I almost revealed my identity.* The warmth inside her was shaken cold when she felt a tap on her shoulder.

"What?" She spun around to see her friend, Avery, smiling broadly, a hand to her hip. Glancing over to where she'd last seen the handsome stranger, she saw nothing but customers quietly engaging in private conversations, but the smirk on Avery's face told her she'd witnessed the embarrassing spectacle.

"Smooth move, girl," Avery laughed and took the seat next to Laryssa. She held up her hand to the approaching bartender, in an effort to get his attention.

"Please tell me you didn't just see what I did?"

Avery laughed harder, nodding.

"Yeah, just call me Princess. Nothing but grace. God, I'm an idiot for coming here." Her face reddened.

"It was kinda funny. But what was really interesting was watching the most powerful vampire on the east coast catch you like a football. He's hot, I'll give ya that. Smokin'." The bartender approached and she cleared her throat. "I'll have two Sazeracs, please."

"What did you just say? Oh sweet Jesus, please. Who was he? No, don't tell me. I don't want to know." It was best she didn't know who he was. If she knew, she'd be tempted to Google him, look him up or otherwise stalk him. She shook her head. This was so unlike her. The man had her rattled and he'd barely even spoken to her.

"Hey, it's not that bad. You did make a nice recovery. His name's Léopold Devereoux."

"How do you know him?"

"I don't really know him, but he's visited the coven house a few times to see Ilsbeth. I heard that he's some kind of a billionaire philanthropist. Rich but deadly. It's rumored that he likes to kill with a smile."

"Nice."

"Well, I suppose you could still date him. Samantha, one of the new witches; she married one…a vampire. Luca. Kade's his maker and Léopold is the grand mac-daddy of them all."

"Shit, shit, shit," Laryssa muttered under her breath.

"Look on the up side." Avery took the drink from the bartender and sipped it up through a pink cocktail straw.

"What could that possibly be?"

"Samantha doesn't seem to be afraid of Léopold. I've seen her with him."

"Yeah, why's that?"

"Apparently he saved her…once upon a time. Long story."

"Does he have a girlfriend?" *Why do I care?*

Avery laughed. "No way. That one there is the epitome of a playboy. He's here often enough…a different woman every time. And he's kinky as hell."

"Kinky, huh?" Laryssa took a deep breath and tried to tone down her interest in the subject. If she let her mind wander, imagining what sorts of things he did in Mordez…no, she wouldn't let herself go there. "Well, he may be hot, but it's not like I'm lookin' to get involved with anyone."

"Go ahead and tell yourself whatever you want, honey, but I know you. That man had you all seven ways to Sunday flustered. Not that I blame ya. I mean, he is seriously a fine piece of man candy."

"Stop it, Avery. Not happening. Anyway, we didn't come here to talk about my sex life."

"Or lack of one?" Avery teased.

"Yeah, that's about it. Seriously, we need to talk." Laryssa looked over her shoulders to make sure no one was listening and lowered her voice. She knew that despite her whispers, the supernatural could hear her and she'd need to remain cryptic.

"No problem. I mean, I'm sorry we couldn't meet at your place but I'd already promised Mick I'd meet him tonight." She shrugged, and swiveled her head toward the dance floor, searching for her boyfriend. "It's date night."

"Does he know? You know you can't tell him."

"Come on, Lyss. I'm not stupid, okay. He doesn't know anything about you. What's going on?"

Laryssa put her arms around her friend in an embrace, and whispered into her ear. "I need help. I need you to up your wards. If you know what I speak of, nod your head."

Avery's face dropped in concern. It'd been years since Laryssa had asked for her help. Her eyes darted from side to side, taking in the vibe of the room before she quietly nodded.

"It isn't safe to talk…not here…not anywhere. I just need you to do what you can, okay?" Laryssa took a sip of her wine and sighed.

"We should've waited until tomorrow to talk. You can come to the coven," Avery suggested. She wasn't comfortable discussing this issue out in the open with so many wolves and vampires within hearing distance.

"No, this couldn't wait. I needed to see you. I need to know that you'll help me." Laryssa couldn't stand the waiting. "I can feel them."

"Do you feel it here?"

"No." Laryssa scanned the room. She'd instantly recognize the dark presence that haunted her outside her home, the heavy feel of the air. Dead, stale pressure pounding into her lungs. Here, the air was tinged with sex and excitement, lust and hunger, but no darkness.

"Listen, Lyss, I'm not discounting what you've sensed, but maybe things aren't as bad as you think. Someone could've been cooking up some black magick just to try it out...you know, things are always a little funky in the Quarter. It's just the way down here," Avery assured with false bravado. She didn't want to worry her friend, but there wasn't a whole lot more she could do to protect her on her own. She'd need the help of her sister witches to provide anything else than she'd already done. Inwardly she shrugged, knowing that her spells had only been temporary.

"I just...I'm not sure how to describe what I feel. Something's off." Laryssa spied Mick approaching and changed the subject. "Hey, I don't want to keep you any longer. Just, uh, stop by my store, tomorrow, okay?"

"I'll do my best." Avery nodded. "I'd better go find Mick, now. If I don't stay with him, the leeches will come crawling out of the woodwork."

"Looks like he found you."

Laryssa pressed her lips together in a tight smile as Mick surprised Avery, wrapping his arms around her waist. Her friend jumped in surprise, giggling in recognition. *Maybe someday*, Laryssa thought. But as things stood now, she knew that she'd be lucky to survive, let alone find love.

It wasn't as if Laryssa hadn't dated. She'd always purposefully chosen humans, since they were considerably safer than supernaturals, and thankfully, clueless to the existence of her kind. She thought about her last boyfriend, David, who in their final argument, had described her as frosty the snowgirl. Despite their uninspired and utterly vanilla encounters, she'd tried to make their relationship work. Granted, he'd been good on paper, someone her parents would have approved of; responsible, held in good standing in the community, well off and practical. So she'd continued dating him, afraid to admit her clandestine, carnal fantasies even to herself. The sex they'd had was like eating bologna sandwiches for lunch. It was okay to eat every now and then, but hardly nutritious or satisfying.

They'd both known the deal, but still, she'd been surprised when he'd finally broken up with her. The past two months since, she'd become entirely too familiar with her purple plastic friend. Regrettably, while he brought relief, the little fellow was no substitute for the intimacy she craved.

Lady Charlotte, the proprietor and owner of Mordez, glided across the dance floor with the grace of a ballerina. Dressed in a dark satin purple corset and matching mini-skirt, she stretched out her hands toward Léopold, beckoning him to come to her. Her long straight black hair was pulled high onto her head in a ponytail. While she looked as if she were in her mid-twenties, she was several hundred years old. The influential vampire, neither sired to Léopold nor Kade, had been rumored to have been a pirate who'd come to enjoy her fortune shortly after the war of 1812.

"Léopold, darling," she crooned over the blaring music.

"Lovely as always," Léopold said with a brief bow.

"Still the sweet talker, I see. This way."

Lady Charlotte gestured to an exit behind one of the bars, and they followed her. As the door slammed, a dull vibration was all that remained of the music. After a dizzying climb up a spiral wooden staircase, they entered a large living room. In the corner sat an oversized mahogany desk and red velvet chair. A sectional u-shaped red leather sofa faced a set of clear French doors that led to a balcony, overlooking the entire nightclub. Charlotte flipped a switch and a small gas lit fire pit blazed to life, instantly warming the room.

Léopold, familiar with his surroundings, strode into the room. "Char, this is Dimitri LeBlanc. He's beta of…"

"Acadian Wolves," she finished Léopold's sentence, slinking up to Dimitri. She flipped her hair, and smiled seductively at the wolf. Her voice grew husky as she let her palm fall onto his shoulder. "Yes, I know who you are."

Dimitri smiled in return, carefully removing her hand and placing a kiss to the back of it. "A pleasure to meet you, Lady Charlotte."

"A gentleman," she commented with a wink to Léopold.

"He's smooth with the ladies," Léopold responded, his voice dripping with sarcasm.

"Clubbing with the wolves these days? My, my, Léopold. Things are changing." She went to the bar and pulled a bottle of aged rum off the shelf.

"Let's just say Dimitri is a special wolf, one worthy of my loyalty and friendship."

"You are a suave one, Leo. You'd better stop with the compliments… they'll say we're fallin' in love," Dimitri jibed. After the blood donation and the set of blue balls he'd nursed, all he wanted to do was go down to the dance floor and find a she-wolf to fuck. But no, here they were in the lair of the very knowledgeable but dangerous Lady Charlotte, and the damn vampire still hadn't explained why they were there. Considering it'd been a long shitty day, he gladly accepted the drink she offered.

"Where's your Alpha, Dimitri?" Lady Charlotte filled another glass and then handed it off to Léopold.

"Logan? He's home with his mate. I'm taggin' along with the big vamp here." He shot Léopold a look as if to say, 'What the fuck are we doing here?'.

Léopold simply smiled and fell back into a chair, making himself comfortable.

Charlotte raised an eyebrow at Léopold and promptly took a seat on the sofa across from him.

"Léopold, you know I love seeing you, but I assume you need something." She crossed her legs and cocked her head knowingly.

"Oui. We both know you have the pulse on this town. I'm looking for someone. Someone special."

"Aren't we all?" she laughed.

"This is a serious matter. I'm not sure who I'm seeking, but I'm looking for someone with certain powers."

"This town is crawling with supernaturals. Frankly, I'm surprised you're coming to me. Kade practically runs this town. Between him and Logan, they could find whoever you are looking for."

"I've already talked to them both. Logan doesn't know and neither does Kade. Neither has heard of the one I'm looking for."

"And who's that?"

"I'm looking for a being who can move objects." Léopold raked his fingers through his hair, reluctant to share too much information about the child.

"A witch?"

"I don't know…maybe. We all know the most powerful witches can make things move but in all my years, it's always taken a spell of some sort. This gift…from what I can tell, involves pure telekinesis. No magic." Hunter had told him that he'd suspected the child had the ability to move objects. Witch or not, a baby wasn't capable of spells.

Charlotte gave a small smile, waiting to see if he was serious.

"It's possible no one knows what kind of supernatural we are looking for. We only know a few of their powers," Dimitri added. Taking a cue from Léopold, he held back information about why they were asking. He knew damn well that if Hunter didn't know what the child was, then it was likely no one knew. Hell, Léopold of all vampires should know. He'd been on the Earth nearly a thousand years, and while Charlotte was a mover and shaker in New Orleans, he couldn't imagine she'd have the answers they sought. He had to suggest something else, something to brainstorm. "Or it could be a hybrid. Maybe a new kind of supernatural."

"Man or woman? Bigger than a breadbox?" Charlotte laughed as she said it, noticing the scowls that crossed their faces. "Come on. Seriously, look at this from my point of view. A vampire and werewolf walk into a bar…"

"This isn't a joke," Léopold snarled.

"Okay, fine. No joke. How the hell am I supposed to know what you are talking about here? Telekinesis? That's all you've given me."

"We don't have much to give." Dimitri rounded next to her and sat down, sighing in frustration. This was not turning out how he thought it was going to go. He stared over to Léopold who pushed out of his chair and approached the French doors, appearing deep in contemplation.

"Forget it, Char. Let me ask you this. Have you noticed anything dark in town over the past few days?" Léopold practically choked on the question, realizing how stupid he sounded. Darkness in New Orleans? The town was the epicenter of both worlds, good and evil. Yet Hunter had told them about the presence he sensed. Léopold shook his head, realizing that he needed to disclose more information. "When I say dark, I don't mean the usual. I'm talking, well, evil…from hell."

"Demons?" she asked in a whisper, not wishing to conjure trouble.

"Yeah, anything like that? Hell hounds, a demonic trace on anyone here in the club, rumors of rituals," Léopold continued, keeping his back to Charlotte, scanning the club through the glass.

"Léopold, I'm not sure what you are looking for or why, but if we're going down this path, I'd appreciate a little more information. Whatever you tell me, I'll keep it confidential. I swear it. But let's not speak more of demons. You know as well as I do that we don't want to attract the evil to us. I may not be a witch or psychic, but even a human can call on hell."

Léopold stood silent a minute, deciding how much information to divulge. "A wolf named Perry. A she-wolf named Mariah. She was a hybrid. Have you ever heard of them?"

Charlotte bit her lip and her eyes honed in on Dimitri. "Let me get this straight. You're asking me if I know a couple of wolves?"

"They aren't ours," Dimitri offered. He wished Léopold would turn around and give him some indication of how much he wanted to share with the vampiress.

Damn it all to hell, what could it hurt to tell her where they were from? "They belong to Hunter Livingston. But they've been here in New Orleans. No one in our pack knows them. All we know is that they've been to the city, but at no point did they check in. But Hunter says they were here."

"Well, now, this is interesting, boys. Sorry to disappoint, but I've never heard of them. And as far as evil, it's been the same ole, same ole. Nothing terribly out of the ordinary." Charlotte blew out a breath and took a sip of the golden liquid in her glass. "I can't say I've heard of pure telekinesis. But the witches...they must know. Have you tried Ilsbeth?"

"I don't think the person we're looking for is a witch, but I'll be calling on her. She may be able to do a spell to help us find the supernatural we seek. I wanted to start with you first because..."

Conversation stopped as a tall lithe blonde entered the room, carrying an iPad. Charlotte quickly approached her and accepted the tablet.

"Camera five. Situation has been handled, my Lady." Focused on her task, the newcomer pointed to the screen.

"Excuse me gentlemen. This is my assistant, Lacey." Charlotte crossed to the staircase, readying to leave the room. "She'll attend to your needs."

Lacey wore a see-through mesh mini-dress, which left little to the imagination. Her black lace panties and rosy nipples were clearly visible through the netted fabric, catching the attention of Dimitri. Clearly in need of female companionship, he smiled and stood to greet the alluring woman.

"Hello, cher. I'm Dimitri," he said.

"Yes, I know who you are. Beta of Acadian Wolves." Lacey smiled.

Avoiding contact with the wolf, she made her way over to the French doors and opened them. A wave of music rushed into the living space, and she pranced out onto the balcony. She closed her eyes and her hips began to sway. Léopold watched as the siren on the ledge crooked her finger at the beta. Dimitri shot him a knowing smile before he joined her, sweeping her into his arms.

Normally, Léopold would enjoy watching the erotic dance of a man and woman sensually moving to a driving rhythmic beat. He'd revel in the excitement, knowing that eventually they'd make love. Perhaps in public or in private. He may even join into a threesome given the right circumstance. But not tonight.

While he found Lacey attractive, his mind drifted to the leather clad woman who'd fallen off her barstool. Perhaps after he finished with Charlotte, he'd call on the lovely little rabbit whose scent reminded him of home. He smiled to himself, slightly confused as to why she held his interest. It wasn't as if she was his type. No, he generally liked his women assertive and ready for sex, ones who weren't looking for a commitment that he'd never give.

Léopold sighed, attempting to dismiss the feelings that had been creeping up on him over the past week. He'd only made one vow in his life to a woman, his wife. At the young age of nineteen, they'd married. Then, the day he was turned, reborn as vampire, he'd sworn he'd never love another. Women were mere distractions in the adventure he called life. In all his years, not once had guilt arisen as he liberally used humans for blood and sex. But ever since saving the Alpha's mate, he'd found himself reminiscing about his first life, the last time he'd felt anything...felt love, alive. Yet every time he allowed himself the indulgence of remembering his wife, a flood of memories of his last hours as a man slammed his psyche, reminding him why he'd never love again. No, love brought nothing but pain, death and despair.

Thoughts of Ava wrapped around his heart, draining his libido. He had to find a clue as to what she was so that he could protect her. He wouldn't allow another child to die under his watch. He could still hear the sound of her cooing as he'd held her tight against his chest. It was as if her own energy had meshed with his, cleaving open the terrifying past he'd worked so hard to keep sealed tight. By the time he'd gotten her to Logan's, he'd felt the bond forming and he cursed it. Ava had clutched on to his fingers, smiling at him as he rocked her softly. Even though she couldn't talk, he knew the connection between them was as real as a father to daughter. When he placed the infant into Wynter's loving arms, a tear ran down his face as he turned away to materialize back to Wyoming. Goddess help him, he'd keep the child in a New York minute if she weren't wolf. He knew it wasn't right for him to raise a wolf. No, she needed to be with her people, her pack. And she sure as hell deserved better than the cold-hearted bastard he'd developed into over the years.

The sound of Charlotte's voice jarred him out of his silent contemplation and he turned to find her still clasping the tablet. A devious smile crossed her face. She'd found something.

"Well, my old friend, you're one lucky fellow."

"Ah, mademoiselle, there's no such thing as luck. Destiny? Perhaps. Fate? Maybe. But I believe we make luck. Besides, you know the universe won't fight with me for long. She owes me." Léopold let it go at that. He wasn't about to share why, but as far as he was concerned, the universe was a diabolical bitch who owed him a debt, one far greater than she ever could repay.

Charlotte offered the iPad to Léopold, stealing a glance at Lacey and Dimitri, who appeared to be lost in their own world.

"Hit track twenty-seven. Interesting little fight we just had in the bar."

"And we missed it?" His thoughts immediately flew to his little rabbit. *Is she okay? Still here?*

He tapped the screen; a grainy black and white video began to play. Anger licked through him as he watched the scene, his eyes widening in disbelief. A large vampire approached the woman in leather, wrapping his arm around her neck, flicking off her sunglasses. As he hoisted her off the seat, her feet began to flail on the floor. With one hand, she clutched the banded arm around her neck and attempted to elbow him with her other arm, but her attacker refused to let go. No one intervened or attempted to dislodge the man. She struggled helplessly as the others told him to release her. What Léopold saw next both amazed and thrilled him. It happened so quickly, he was surprised Charlotte had caught it. He looked to her and back to the screen.

"Telekinesis, no?"

"I think you may have found the being you seek. A woman no less? Play it in slow motion. I almost missed it, but after you'd asked me if I'd noticed anything strange, well, it was remarkable that a human was able to best that asshole. My suspicion was confirmed. I don't know what she is, but she's no human."

Léopold replayed the video, ignoring Charlotte's commentary. Second by second the frames passed and he observed how his little rabbit, held tight by the beast, had glanced over to the bar. A knife that had been used to cut lemons and limes sat on the edge. With the naked eye, it would have appeared as if the object had been within her reach. It was only a few inches, hardly enough movement for anyone to notice. But on the slow motion video, it was clear the knife had slid to her. As her hand wrapped around it, she immediately brought it to her assailant's neck. Locating his carotid artery, she pierced the skin right beneath his ear. If she'd pressed any harder, he'd have bled out, but very smartly, he released her. As she fled, bouncers pounced, taking him to the floor and cuffing him in silver.

"Gotcha." Léopold smiled at Charlotte.

"You do realize that the witch could have caused it."

"The witch? The blonde spitfire yelling at the vampire?" He pointed to Avery on the screen.

"Avery Summers. She's a regular. Belongs to Ilsbeth's coven. The big guy behind her is Mick Germaine. Warlock. Also runs with Ilsbeth's witches. From what I've seen, they're a couple. But your little dominatrix-looking girl, she's new. I've never seen her before."

"Tell me she paid with a credit card. I need a name."

"Sorry, darling. No name, but I do have a way to find her."

"The witch?"

"No, it would take too long. Besides, I doubt she'd tell you…well, not willingly, anyway."

"Stop with the games. If you don't have a card and you haven't talked to the witch, what's her name? Do you know how to find her?"

"Ah, do you doubt me?"

Léopold smiled at her. This is why he came to Lady Charlotte.

"Track thirty-five." Charlotte grinned smugly as Léopold tapped at the screen.

"Well, now, that is surprising." Léopold licked his lips as his rabbit hopped onto a motorcycle that had been parked across the street and took off like a bat out of hell. *Hell.* He sighed, shaking his head. She'd piqued his arousal, but damn it all, she'd better not be some kind of fire-breathing demon. She smelled way too good for that. Pulling his mind away from the memory of her scent,

Léopold tapped again on the screen, freezing the image of the bike and used his fingers to enlarge the photo until he had a clear shot of the license plate.

"Welcome to my world, mon petit lapin," he growled. He memorized the numbers; he'd find her by the morning and she'd be his.

⇽❧ *Chapter Three* ❧⇾

Léopold sat in his black Lamborghini outside LT Antiques. The candy-apple-red Harley had been registered to a Laryssa Theriot. Through the painted glass window on Royal Street, he watched a man arranging knick knacks in the window, and he couldn't help but wonder about his relationship to the girl. Was he an employee? A family member? A husband? The thought of her with another man caused a tick in his jaw. He shook it off, aware that it didn't matter either way. This afternoon, he'd get answers.

He half wished he'd brought the wolf with him today to help him focus on his target. Last night, he'd reluctantly left him to Lacey, figuring Dimitri needed a little female loving to offset the awkward feeding situation. When he'd left Mordez, he'd given fair warning that not a single hair on his mongrel friend was to be harmed while he was there or there'd be hell to pay; more specifically, death. Lady Charlotte, while powerful in her own right, knew better than to go against his wishes and had guaranteed the wolf's safety. Dimitri had promised he'd only stay briefly and then go to Logan's to check on Ava.

As Léopold opened his car door and breathed in the cool winter air, his determination to protect the infant grew stronger than ever. He'd called Kade in the middle of the night, unapologetically waking him and Sydney. Sydney had agreed to run the license plate number for him. They'd planned to meet at Logan's later in the day to discuss the best way to keep Ava safe from whomever, whatever had tried to kill her. Léopold refused to leave her security solely in the hands of wolves. No, his people would be on the case, ensuring that nothing happened to her while he investigated.

Léopold confidently approached the storefront and entered. The distinct musky odor of times gone by filled his nostrils. But there was another scent, one far more delicious and enticing that caught his attention. *Laryssa.* As he passed through the crowded aisle of chairs and tables, he noted the feminine nature of the store with its pink floral stencils along the edge of the ceiling. A collection of crystal chandeliers illuminated the ancient treasures. As he made his way past an enormous armoire, his eyes lit up with excitement. Perched precariously on a step ladder, his little rabbit was hanging a mirror on the wall. He quietly observed as she toyed with the wire backing, carefully adjusting the frame so that it hung straight.

His eyes roamed over her body, and he smiled, realizing that she'd been wearing a wig in the club, which had hidden the thick brunette curls that danced to the middle of her back. Gone were the tight leathers, replaced by a form-fitting pencil skirt that accentuated the curves of her hips and bottom. A pink cashmere sweater clung to her shoulders. She'd casually pushed the sleeves up as if she'd been working for quite a while and Léopold couldn't hide his amusement at the transformation. While he certainly enjoyed the way she'd looked last night, he admittedly favored this softer, feminine attire. He sniffed into the air, catching a hint of mandarin with notes of coconut. She smelled fresh and warm, as if she'd just stepped out of the shower. Shocked at his reaction to the mere sight of this woman, he silently rolled his eyes. It had taken all of fifteen seconds to lose focus. Willing his visceral attraction to Laryssa into submission, he cleared his throat, hoping to get her attention.

Intrigued, Léopold observed her with both interest and annoyance as she fumbled with the mirror. He heard her say that she'd be right with him, and sought to offer assistance when she began to topple off the third step of the ladder. A loud scream filled the air just as he caught her in his arms. He wanted to be angry, but all he could feel was the softness of her breasts under his hands. Instantly, he hardened as her back pressed against his chest. He wished he could stop but before he knew what he was doing his nose was buried deep into her hair. And he'd been correct about the citrus, definitely mandarin.

Léopold loosely held Laryssa, indulging both his curiosity and desire to touch her. *Goddess, what is it about her?* He couldn't help but notice how well she fit against him. Merde, he needed to get this conversation going. But of course she'd fit against him. She was a female after all. Any female would feel good against his body, but it was as if her body melded to his, making him harder than he'd ever been. He moved his legs, unwilling to let her feel the way she'd affected him. His burgeoning erection painfully pressed against the zipper of his pants and he cursed. Setting her onto her feet, he forced his hands away from her and took a deep breath. Never. He'd never feel this for a woman. He'd never let it happen again.

Laryssa had heard the customer behind her, but the damn mirror wire wouldn't seem to catch right. It kept slipping and she cursed under her breath, hoping she wouldn't drop it. If she could just hold it up a minute longer, she could get it to hang squarely on the wall. She fingered the hook that she'd just renailed into the wall and then moved her thumb over to the thin metal string. With a final shove upward, she attempted to flick it into place. But as the wire caught, it sliced into her flesh. A sharp sting threw her off balance, and her pumps began to waver. *Shit. Not again.*

"Oh my God!" Laryssa squeaked as she fell backwards, fully expecting to crack her head open on one of the many sharp-edged desks that sat adjacent to where she'd been working. As she felt strong male hands slide up under her ribcage, grazing her breasts, she gasped. She wasn't sure whether to thank the stranger or call the police, but as she turned her face to try to see him, she immediately recognized her rescuer.

"It's you," she stammered, clutching his arms. Laryssa giggled nervously, realizing how once again she'd foolishly fallen in front of the sexy vampire. And like last night, he'd caught her. She couldn't believe how clumsy she'd all of a sudden become. She tried to relax and find her footing, but her heart was beating so fast that she could barely think. *What is he doing here in my shop? How did he find me?*

Like a story book flipping pages, her mind whirled until she remembered what she'd done last night at the club. She'd fought off the asshole who'd grabbed her at the bar. The feel of his hands around her throat had forced her fear into overdrive. The knife had only been a few inches away, but still too far. Desperation had taken over as her power surged, calling the blade to her fingertips. Jamming it into his neck was as instinctive as breathing. Kill or be killed, she'd always choose the former. She'd run into the alley, refusing to discuss it with management. The only one who knew her was Avery and there was no way her friend would have divulged her identity to the vampire. She'd be more likely to turn him into a three horned sheep before she'd squeal. The only way the vampire could have found her would have been if he'd followed her home.

A brush to her breast reminded her that she was still being held upright by him, and Laryssa felt her face grow red. Arousal licked over her skin. Cautiously, she rooted her shoes on the floor and turned around, steeling her nerves.

"I'm so sorry," she said.

"My pleasure, mademoiselle, but I suggest you avoid heights in the future."

Surreptitiously, she stole a glance at him, which reminded her how incredibly handsome he was. His short dark hair was perfectly coiffed. His white dress shirt hung casually over the waistband of his jeans. Laryssa forced herself to look away, trying not to stare at the masculine features of his face. Straight nose, square jaw and perfectly kissable lips… lips that were smooth talking and way too articulate, teasing her with every word he spoke. Beads of sweat broke out across her forehead. It felt as if someone had turned up the heat, her skin was on fire. She noticed his eyes were no longer on hers and had dropped to her chest. They lingered only a second, and then he met her gaze and smiled. She looked downward and noticed that several buttons had come undone in her fall, revealing the edges of her white lace bra. *Could this day get any more embarrassing?* Laryssa's fingers shook as she buttoned her sweater.

"I'm so sorry. I just…you just…I just…" *Great, first I'm a klutz and now I can't speak.* She bit her lip, paused and then took a deep breath before starting again. "Thank you for catching me."

"Again." Léopold watched her as she adjusted her clothes, wishing to rip the rest of the pearly buttons from their fragile seams. But he refused to let the beast within take what it wanted. No, he'd find out what the hell she was before showing her his true nature. "Yes, thank you…again." She smoothed down her skirt, trying to pretend she hadn't just fallen into his arms and let him feel her up in the process. *Business, think business.* Her pulse slowed and she willed herself to appear nonchalant.

"We met last night, remember?" he pressed. Léopold smiled and ran his hand over the colorful marquetry in rosewood that scrolled through a seventeenth century secretaire. Interesting that she could deliberately control the flow of her blood. It further piqued his concern about her species. What was she?

Laryssa's eyes met his, widening at the confirmation that he knew exactly who she was.

"Yes, yes I do. But I'm afraid I didn't catch your name." *Vampire. Big bad vampire.* Laryssa watched intently as he fingered the furniture, trailing his thumb over the symmetrical scenes as if he was caressing a lover.

"Lovely." Léopold flashed his eyes to hers.

"What?" Laryssa realized that he was toying with her, purposefully trying to make her nervous.

"I said, it's lovely. The neoclassical architectural structures. The white marble top. Doré bronze mounts."

"Is there something specific I can help you with?"

"You get directly to the point?" Léopold had intended to play with her a bit, throw her off her game. Yet his little rabbit wasn't frozen in the field like he'd anticipated. No, she rebounded nicely, and now stood confidently like a wildcat, poised to attack.

"I don't really have time to waste. So yeah, I'd like to know why you followed me from the club. And I really want to know what you are doing in my shop."

Léopold merely laughed and crossed the room to admire a chair and matching settee.

"Circa 1775?"

Laryssa walked over and placed her hand on the elegant Louis XVI chair. "Yes. How did you know? It's a very special piece. It has the mark of Versailles Palace on it."

"Indeed." Léopold sat in the chair, wrapping his fingers around its arms. "Nothing but the best. Fit for a king."

"And I suspect you'd like being a king." She put her hands on her hips, waiting for him to respond.

"Ah, a king I never was. But I've dined with kings, and I can assure you that while they enjoy the extravagances of the rich, they often lose their heads. Easy come, easy go."

"Why are you here?" Laryssa brushed her hair back, attempting to regain her composure. "Are you looking for something specific?"

"Oui, pet. But not an antique. While I do enjoy shopping, this is hardly the time." Léopold lost the smile, allowing his eyes to pierce hers. "So I shall get to the point. What are you?"

Laryssa lost her ability to rein in her pulse and her heart began to fiercely pump hot blood through her veins. Her lips tightened, and she clenched her jaw. How dare he ask about her? What the hell did he want from her anyway? Dear God, she had enough issues with the darkness on her tail and now he was asking about her origins.

"What do you mean, 'what am I?' I'm the owner of this store. Does that answer your question?" Laryssa asked, her voice growing louder. "Who are you?"

"Léopold Devereoux. That's who I am. I can be your angel or nightmare, depending on the day. So listen up. What. Are. You?" Léopold didn't make a move. He sat completely still, anticipating her answer.

"Get out of here right now. I don't have to tell you anything."

Laryssa realized she'd made the classic mistake of turning her back on a predator and within seconds, she found herself backed against the wall. A mixture of fear and arousal flared as he pressed his body against hers. His hands caged her, and he'd effectively pinned her to the wall without ever restraining her arms. She breathed deeply, inhaling the clean male scent that surrounded her, and she sagged against him. *Please God, don't let me be attracted to him. This is wrong.* Even as she told herself that he was nothing but trouble, she could feel the heat grow between her legs.

"What are you?" Léopold whispered into her ear. His lips brushed her hair and he resisted the urge to kiss her.

"Please...I can't tell you," she begged.

"Laryssa...there's a child." Léopold knew no other way to be than honest. He'd swear her to secrecy if he was wrong and she wasn't aware. Deep in his gut, he knew she was the being he was looking for, the one who'd help him save Ava.

"Oh God. It's true then," she breathed into his chest. Her fingers rose to clutch his shirt. *How can he possibly know about what I sensed? A baby? One born like me?*

"You must help me, mon petit lapin. Tell me what you are."

"No. I can't." He couldn't possibly know what he was asking of her. They'd kill her. Hell, he'd kill her. She shook her head but didn't release the fabric curled into her fists.

"You must." Léopold's hand snaked up toward her throat. His mind warred against the urge to fuck her. At the same time, his frustration grew; her determination to withhold information was maddening. The child could die if she refused to help him. He wouldn't let it happen…not again.

"No," she whispered. Laryssa froze under his touch. As his fingertips grazed her collarbone and his thumb settled into the hollow of her neck, she closed her eyes, pressing her forehead into his chest. On fire with fear and the hot need growing in her belly, she relaxed into him, desiring the submission he sought from her. He could break her neck like a twig, but she sensed that he wouldn't hurt her. It was irrational, she knew.

"How can I trust you? I don't know you." A hot tear escaped her eye.

"Tell me, pet. And while you're at it, I'd like to know why you don't fear me." Léopold fingered her throat, holding her fully exposed to him. His fangs snapped down, both in anger and hunger for the woman in his arms. Her breath warmed his shirt, and he rocked his hardness into her belly, letting her feel what she was doing to him. He fisted his other hand into her long hair and pulled her head backward, revealing the smooth skin of her neck. *Was she crazy? Why wasn't she scared of him? She should be screaming, not aroused. Goddammit, she was making him insane.*

"I…I know…you won't hurt me."

"And how do you know this?" He pressed her further against the wall, and she released a small moan.

"I don't know…I just know you won't."

Léopold bent his head forward, grazing his fangs across her delicate skin. He didn't draw blood, but earned a small squeak from her lips. He swore that if she didn't tell him within the next thirty seconds, he'd taste of her blood.

"Please, don't," she cried. "The child."

"Oui, the child," he repeated. In the heat of the moment, he'd lost sight of why he was even there. Having her in his arms had become all that mattered, taking her, dominating her.

"I need to be able to trust you. You can't tell anyone…please," Laryssa pleaded.

"I swear it to you. Now tell me," he breathed. Before he could stop himself, he dragged his tongue from the hollow of her neck up to behind her ear. She tasted like the sweetest tropical fruit. For the love of the Goddess, he had to have her. He settled his teeth once again against her flesh, but didn't break the skin. It was pure torture and pleasure all at once.

"I...I can do things. Move things...by thinking it."
She made the decision to tell him this much, but it was
too soon to trust him with all her secrets. Still, her
instincts told her that she needed to seek his protection.
She released his shirt and wrapped her arms around his
waist, pulling him toward her.

Not much could shock the ancient vampire, but the
feel of her hands around him made him go stiff. *What
kind of game is she playing?* She'd just admitted that she
could invoke telekinesis. Immediately, he released her,
breaking away from the sumptuous vixen who threatened
his sanity. Her look of surprise, then disappointment
jarred him further. Instead of running, she fell down into
one of her antique chairs and wrapped her arms around
herself as if she was missing the feel of him on her skin. He
spun around, plowing his fingers through his hair, taking a
cleansing breath, willing his erection to subside. *What the
fuck is going on with her? With me?* She must be some kind
of witch to have this effect on him. He needed to get it the
fuck together and damn soon. He thanked the Goddess
that Dimitri wasn't with him to bear witness to his idiocy.

"You're a witch?" He bit out, and turned to face her.

"No, not a witch. Listen, Léopold." She lowered her
eyes, shaking her head and pressing her fingers to her
forehead. "I want to trust you. I need to trust someone,
but I can't tell you everything. Not yet. I'll say this much,
the child you speak of...I've felt her. I can't say how, I just
did. But I'm alone. There's no one like me."

"What do you mean you're alone? Surely there must be others."

"No. Just me. I wasn't born this way. I've only met one other person like me, but she's not here. Not in the city. We don't keep in touch."

"But how did you know? About the child? Or this other person?"

"How do you know when you're around other vampires?"

"Scent. The power. I feel it."

"And I feel it too. Like a hum over my skin, in my mind."

"Did someone infuse you with this magic?"

"It's not magic."

"It has to be magic. I've seen it happen with witches and vampires. What are you?"

"It's not important. What's important is the child." *And living. I really like living.*

"What else do you know about the child?"

"Nothing. I just could feel her." She dropped her head into her hands unable to tell him anymore. The dark ones were going to kill the baby. And her. Worse, she wasn't sure how to stop them. Avery had been her only hope of hiding. But the evil was growing stronger. "You need to protect her."

Laryssa's voice sounded desperate and Léopold grew gravely concerned. He slowly approached and knelt before her. She kept her head lowered, refusing to look at him.

Léopold put a hand on her knee and with the other, cupped her face until her gaze met his.

"You can trust me. I can help you. But you have to let me in."

Laryssa's eyes began to water. She didn't want to cry, but the warmth of his voice surrounded her in a shroud of security. His piercing eyes had softened, revealing the heart of a protector, a man who felt deeply, perhaps more so than she ever thought possible. She hadn't felt safe in so very long. And here he was offering her trust. She wanted so badly to be able to rely on someone other than herself.

"The dark ones. They're here," she whispered.

"What are you talking about? Who's here?"

"I've seen them…their black eyes. Like angels of death."

Léopold cared, he really did. Clearly she believed what she was saying. But he was skeptical of what she was telling him.

"Ma chérie, it's not that I don't believe in evil. I've seen it first hand, but…"

"Hollow eyes…well, they're not really hollow. They're black, so dark…it looks like there's nothing in the sockets. And it's not just them…there's someone driving them, someone leading them. I know it. It's like they just stand there. Waiting." Laryssa knew it sounded crazy, she really did. But she'd seen them.

"Waiting for what?"

"I don't know. Maybe for someone to give them orders." She looked up and caught his gaze. He didn't believe her. She sighed and shook her head. "I'm telling you the truth. There's something out there."

Léopold paused, trying to think of the diplomatic words that eluded him. It wasn't as if he didn't know that someone had tried to kill the child. The Caldera Wolves Alpha had told him that he'd felt a dark presence. Léopold considered the possibility that perhaps the infant carried the evil within her, but dismissed the idea as soon as it surfaced. No, there had to be another answer. And as crazy as Laryssa sounded, she was his only lead at this point.

"I've lived a long time and seen all kinds of terrible things." *Many done by humans.* "But I've never heard of the beings you describe."

"But they're real," she protested, her eyes begging him to believe her.

"I'm not saying they're not. I'm just saying that I haven't seen them."

"But you don't believe me."

"Someone tried to kill Ava."

"What?"

"I told you she was in danger. I found her in the middle of Yellowstone. There was a blizzard. The nanny tried to kill her, but I saved her. Now she's here."

"In New Orleans?" Her heart began to race.

"Yes. She's safe…for now." Léopold let his hand slip down to the chair, but not before he slid his thumb over her quivering bottom lip. "I think you should meet her."

"You need to get her out of here…away from them. They'll find her….if they haven't already," she insisted.

"Are you sure you could tell if she's like you?" Whatever the hell Laryssa was, she was holding back, denying him the truth. Supernatural, she admitted as much. He needed more if he was going to save the child. He didn't necessarily believe that she'd seen what she thought she saw. But if someone had tried to kill Ava and she and Ava were somehow related, it wasn't a stretch to think that someone was after Laryssa, too.

"Yes." Of course she could tell if they were the same. But if the two of them were together in the same room, she couldn't predict what would happen.

"You're coming with me now," Léopold told her. This was utter bullshit. If she wasn't going to tell him everything, he'd put her and the infant together, see what happened. He wanted the wolves to meet Laryssa. If Ava's mother had been wolf, maybe they'd be able to sense shifter in her.

"No."

"What do you mean, no?" Incensed, he shook his head. First she lets him practically strangle her and now she was going to refuse him? The woman was certifiable. She obviously had no idea who he was or what he was capable of.

"Uh, I think you heard me. I thought vampires were supposed to have bionic hearing or something like that," Laryssa replied, worried that it could be dangerous for both her and the baby if they got together. "Are you hard of hearing? Or just hard headed? No, don't bother answering. The bottom line is that I don't think it's a good idea for me to meet the child. Not only that, I can tell you don't believe me. So there's no way I'm leaving my shop in the middle of the day to go off with you. But I'm going to hold you to your word. You promised not to tell anyone what I am. I may not look like much but if you don't keep it quiet, I'll….I'll…well, I don't know. But I will be really mad and trust me…I can take on a vampire if I need to."

"Are you seriously threatening me? Me?" Léopold's voice grew louder. That was it. Not only was she crazy, she was as mad as a hatter. "Listen to me, pet. You will come with me. I'm not asking you. I'm telling you. You really don't understand who I am, do you?"

"I'm not your pet," she protested under her breath. Laryssa heard Mason in the back room moving boxes, hoping he hadn't heard their conversation. Thankfully, he usually listened to music through his headphones when he was sorting the items. She hadn't told him about her abilities and didn't want him involved. Keeping her voice lowered, she continued. "You need to keep it down. And yeah, I know who you are. If you remember, you just told me. I also know that you are a pushy vamp who thinks he can order people around. And guess what? I'm not one of those people. I just sat here and told you what I knew and you don't believe me. So believe what you want, but I'm right about what's happening in New Orleans. You don't need to protect me. I can protect myself. I'm still alive. I think you should leave."

Laryssa was shaking by the time she got finished ranting. Exhausted and frightened, she needed to go call the witch. The vampire couldn't help her. She doubted anyone could. As she pushed past Léopold, he grabbed her wrist.

"Let me go." Like a power plant, the electrons began to hum, slowly building in her system.

"No. I need you."

"I said. Let. Me. Go."

No longer able to control it, Laryssa's eyes flew to a settee. Calling on her ability, she hurled the large piece of furniture across the room at Léopold, nearly grazing his head. Laryssa gasped, aghast that she'd nearly hit him. Immediately, fatigue slammed into her and she bent over at her waist, trying to catch her breath. Even though it wasn't a surprise that she'd be drained from using her powers, it had been years since the last time she'd moved such a heavy object, and she never imagined that it would be so intense.

"Point taken, mon petit lapin." Léopold jerked to avoid the projectile, but he stood firm, refusing to leave. He was about to yell at her for trying to smash a fine antique, when he noticed her slump in response. Curling his arm underneath hers, he gently set her onto the floor. He knelt, brushing her hair from her eyes. "What's happening to you?"

"I'll be fine. I just need a minute." She wanted to shove his hand away, but couldn't summon the energy to argue. Regret poured through her at the thought that a piece of the wood could have staked Léopold. She hadn't intentionally meant to hurt him. She'd just wanted him to stop pressuring her, to let go of her arm. "I'm sorry. I didn't mean to…oh God, are you hurt?"

"No worries, I'm fine. That was very impressive, but you'll have to do a lot worse to hurt me. Are you really going to be okay? I've never seen anyone move an object so swiftly."

"It was an accident. I can't always control it. I was just so mad. You wouldn't stop."

"I wouldn't let you go."

"No."

"I may never let you go after that little display. You're a strong woman, that's for certain." *A woman who could defend herself against the likes of him?* Well, damn, that was a major turn on if he'd ever felt it. He laughed softly. "Now can we discuss why you won't go with me?"

"Because I don't know what will happen. No, that's not true. What I suspect will happen is that our energies could be like fireworks. People will notice. The dark ones will notice. It's not a good idea. Neither of us will be safe."

"I promise you that I'll keep you safe." Léopold gently took her hand in his. He meant what he said. Even if he didn't believe her, he was confident he could protect her.

"But you don't believe me…why would you protect me?"

"Because it's what's right. Ava. The baby. I can't let anything happen to her. I won't just sit by and fend off another attack. I have to find out who's doing this so she can live a normal life."

"She'll never live a normal life," Laryssa sighed. Ever since she was turned, life had been far from the warm and loving upbringing she'd once known. Now she was a freak, one who'd grown accustomed to her solitary existence.

Léopold's heart constricted. Whatever had driven Laryssa to conceal her abilities had not been kind to her. Her shame was apparent, and he struggled to understand it. Life as a vampire was not always easy by any means, but it did have its perks. He'd chosen not to get close to anyone, selectively turning only a few humans over the years. Kade was the closest thing he had to family, and it had always been enough. But now? After bonding with Logan and Wynter? The wolves had brought forth an upheaval in his desire to be alone.

"The child. I need you to save her. I don't know how. But you're all I've got. Please." Léopold's voice softened.

"Is she yours?"

"No, she's at least part wolf. I cannot raise her." *But I want to keep her as my own.* He'd never admit it to another soul. If things were different…if he weren't such a self-centered asshole, he'd beg the wolves to raise her as his own. He deserved a lot of things in life; money, accolades, but the privilege of raising Ava, a chance at love and family, wasn't one of them.

"Why? Why do you care what happens to us?" It made no sense why a vampire would put his own life in danger to protect her or the child.

"Because she's important to me. She's innocent. She didn't ask for this when she was born into this world. She's in my charge now. I won't fail her. I won't fail you, Laryssa. Please. Please help me." Léopold inwardly cursed at how pathetic he sounded. Dammit, he should just drag her by the hair into his car and make her do what he wanted. Never in his life had he begged. He should resist the temptation, he knew. Yet looking into her soft green eyes, he could not.

Laryssa took a deep breath, studying the vampire. She knew she'd regret her actions but there was a part of Léopold that she wanted to know. He cared about the baby. An ancient vampire willing to protect the life of one human child seemed unbelievable, yet the truth shone in his eyes. And now that he'd held her in his arms, she craved his touch. It was stupid and foolhardy, but she couldn't deny her body's reaction. He was dangerous and altogether arrogant, but the way he talked about the child only made her want to get to know him more. As he dangled the key to the treasure chest in front of her, revealing his feelings for the child, the only word on her lips was 'yes'.

If something happened to the baby, she'd never be able to forgive herself. He said he'd protect her. As she stood and brushed off her skirt, she gathered up the strength she needed. God help her, she'd go with him. She'd meet the child, and do whatever she had to do to help him save the baby, hopefully saving herself too.

"I'll do it." She gave him a small smile, driven out of uncertainty, not happiness.

"Merci, ma chérie. You will come with me now, no?"

"I need to do a few things and close up here before I can leave. Can you give me an hour?"

"I will send someone for you. Please don't disappoint me. I'm trusting that you'll be here."

"I will." Laryssa sighed as he turned his back and walked out the door. She prayed she'd made the right decision.

Léopold smiled to himself as he left her shop. Relief swept over him as he entered his car. Triumphant for only a minute, he reflected on how close he'd come to losing it, to biting her. He couldn't remember the last time he'd been so terrified. His little rabbit called forth emotions he never wanted to feel again. He cursed, dismissing it as lust. It had to be. After all, he hadn't been with a woman in over two months. It had been in Philadelphia with a pair of lovely twins, if he recalled correctly. A lack of sex was a perfectly acceptable excuse for his behavior, he thought. Still, he couldn't risk emotional involvement with Laryssa.

He'd introduce her to Ava and gain her assistance in protecting the baby. He still wasn't sure what she could offer. But something in his gut told him that she was far more important than he could imagine. No matter her powers, she'd underestimated his ability to get what he wanted. Confidence swept through him. Not only would he save Ava, he planned on stripping Laryssa of all her secrets. What was she? And what other powers was she hiding? He was a patient man, determined and perseverant in all tasks. He'd rally every bit of self-control he had, ignoring the desire for Laryssa that grew inside him. It would serve only to distract him. *Mon petit lapin, enjoy your reprieve, for you will reveal yourself to me. And how sweet it will be.*

Chapter Four

Laryssa knew it had been a bad idea to acquiesce to the vampire. But as she glanced over to the imposing wolf in the driver's seat, her anger grew hot. She wasn't sure if she was madder at Léopold or herself for actually looking forward to seeing him again. Like a schoolgirl, she'd hurriedly closed up her shop, nervously fixing her hair right before she locked the door. The wolf seemed pleasant enough, but he was incredibly muscular, almost scaring her with the sheer size of him. She crossed her arms and pulled at her sleeves, willing her nerves to abate. Stealing a glance at the attractive beta, she jumped when he caught her.

"I won't bite, cher." Dimitri chuckled as she gave him a tight smile and looked out the window. He was beginning to think Léopold's nickname for Laryssa was right on target. *Rabbit?* She certainly was skittish when he'd arrived. Sensing her irritation, he reasoned maybe she'd kicked it up a notch, acting more like a feral cat at this point.

He still wasn't sure why Léopold hadn't brought her himself. Why send him to pick her up when it was clear Léopold had showed interest in her last night? He had a suspicion that the vampire was avoiding her, which was disconcerting considering he wasn't exactly the kind of guy to avoid anything, unpleasant or otherwise. Dimitri would never forget the way he'd deliberately challenged the Caldera Wolves Alpha, effortlessly pinning him against the wall in his own home in front of pack members. Surreal as it was, Léopold had let him go, only caring about the baby. It was a paradox he couldn't wrap his head around, but it served to remind him that no matter what kind of friendship they'd forged, he really didn't know Léopold that well.

Dimitri's mind drifted to his Alpha and how the baby had taken over their household. After only twenty-four hours of caring for Ava, both Wynter and Logan had become exceedingly watchful of her. It was as if the baby had set off both their biological clocks. Wynter was demonstrating the fierce protectiveness of a new mama wolf around her cubs. Dimitri laughed to himself, thinking how insane it was that not only had he watched his Alpha change a diaper but now they were hosting a party for the very supernaturals they'd pretty much avoided over the past hundred years. Fangs and fur didn't usually mesh well. Just as he was leaving Logan's home, an entire crew of Léopold's vampires had arrived.

Dimitri could sense Laryssa's fear, and it made him uneasy. It wasn't as if she didn't have reason to be seriously concerned about her safety. She could be in danger of being attacked if she didn't cooperate. Laryssa's unwillingness to disclose her abilities, what she was, didn't bode well. Léopold told him that she could move objects. He'd seen the tape, but he also knew there was a lot of witchcraft in New Orleans, and they weren't all like Glenda from the Wizard of Oz. No, these folks weren't into ruby slippers, butterflies and fluffy bunnies, magick ending in a happily ever after. The witches and mages he'd known were more about skinning the rabbit and eating it with a fine wine. Dimitri prayed Laryssa didn't pose a danger, that she wasn't part of whoever was behind Ava's murder attempt.

Glancing at Laryssa, he had to admit that she hardly looked the part of a bad witch. Her shiny brunette curls complemented her light pink sweater, making her look more like a librarian…a curvy, sexy librarian. She kept crossing and uncrossing her legs, revealing just a hint of her thigh, as if she couldn't get comfortable. Shit, no wonder Léopold liked her.

As Dimitri's eyes roamed over Laryssa's body, and when his eyes met hers, he noticed she was staring back at him. He smiled, well aware he'd been caught. Well, how the hell was he supposed to react to having a beautiful woman sitting next to him? He was a red blooded wolf, after all. Léopold was the one who'd asked him to pick her up and bring her to Logan's. All was fair in love and lust, he thought to himself; however, his smile faded when he realized she was frowning at his ogling. *Smooth move,*

Romeo. He considered that maybe instead of undressing her with his eyes that he should try engaging her in conversation. Perhaps he would have better luck than his friend discovering what she was and if she held interest in the baby.

"So, you run an antique store, huh?"

"Yeah," she responded cautiously.

"How long have you been in New Orleans?" He'd known the store had been in existence for at least two years, but he wasn't the shopper in the pack. No, he'd leave that honor to his Alpha.

"Um, around six years. You?" She'd lived in the city for several years but her business was just starting to prosper.

"My whole life." Nearly a hundred and fifty years. "Well, to be honest, I used to live in the back country most days, but Logan prefers the city. Where'd you come from?"

"Las Vegas. Ohio, originally."

"Why'd you move to New Orleans?"

"I just needed a change. Las Vegas was fun, but too hot for me," she explained. *Too dry.* The idea that she thought she could live in the middle of a desert had been born out of denial. That and desperation to escape Ohio, her former life. Laryssa looked out the window, trying to hide the sadness that washed over her face. "Besides, I love it here."

Dimitri sensed that she was blurring the truth. At most, she looked to be in her mid to late twenties.

"Your family? Are they from Ohio? Do they live here with you?"

"No," she responded curtly. She didn't want to discuss her family or her lack thereof. Sure they were alive. They just didn't want *her* in their lives and hardly cared to keep in touch.

"Okay, I get it. Don't want to talk about it, huh?" No, he didn't get it, but he got the message, definitely not a pleasant topic. *Interesting.* But was she related to the baby? Léopold had only told him that she'd admitted having supernatural abilities, that she'd flung an ottoman at him. He would have paid to see that. "So, Léopold tells me you've got some power to your punch."

"I can't believe he told you that. It was…it was private." Laryssa snapped her eyes onto the handsome wolf in disbelief that the vampire had told him what she'd done. "I knew better than to trust him."

"Hey, it's okay. I'm the only one who knows." *Him and his Alpha.* Dimitri hadn't meant to upset her, but now that he was in for a penny, he might as well go for the pound. "Léopold said you think you're in danger too. He told you that we're trying to find out who tried to kill Ava, right? It sounds like you might know why."

"Yeah, I know a few things, but not much. But I told him I didn't think this would be a good idea to get us together. Our energy," she pleaded. Her eyes brimmed with moisture. She was so tired of hiding, of being alone. "I don't know what will happen. I don't want to attract attention."

"What do you mean?" Dimitri pulled the car into the driveway, lowered the window and opened the biometric security pad. He pressed a button, which extended the retinal scanner and waited for the green light. A buzzer clicked and he turned his head to address her. "Whatever it is, Laryssa, you're not alone. Léopold's committed to protecting Ava and now he seems pretty intent on keeping you safe as well."

Laryssa shook her head, unsure whether to trust him. Completely defeated, the pressure of keeping secrets had caught up with her. "Our energy. Well, I guess Léopold told you that I can move things. But that energy is unstable." She blew out a breath and bit her lips, trying to think of how best to explain it. "My ability is strong when I use it. I've learned how to keep it hidden, but it's powerful enough that I still can use it." *To live. Not die an early death.* "And Ava. Well, she's more like a spotlight at the Saint's stadium at times. When she was born, I could feel it all the way across the country. I'm just afraid that if we are together…"

"You'll blow the grid?"

She laughed. "Yeah, something like that."

"And it's like some kind of siren to these folks you're worried tried to kill Ava?"

"I don't know if they feel it, the humans. But there are others…they'll know we're here."

Dimitri pulled the car into the port and switched it off, deciding to warn her about who was waiting for her inside.

"Listen, cher. I'm not sure if or when you'll be ready to trust Léopold and me with what's going on with you, but I've gotta tell you, even though we haven't shared information about you with anyone else, Léopold's friends are here."

"Is this Léopold's house?" Laryssa asked in almost a whisper. She looked at the beautiful three-story corner home and glanced to the pool. She'd been so busy talking and worrying that she hadn't realized he'd turned off the car. Her heart began to race at the thought of seeing Léopold again. She was angry with him for telling the wolf about her powers, but at the same time, there was no denying the heat and attraction she'd felt when he'd held her. She rubbed her arms, remembering his touch.

"No, this is my house. Over there, the carriage house is mine. And the main home belongs to our Alpha."

"Alpha? As in Alpha of Acadian Wolves?"

"Yeah, and like I just mentioned, a few of Léopold's friends are here."

Her eyes caught his. "Vampires?"

Dimitri smiled, trying to put her at ease. "Yep. No need to say more. And for the record, I feel the same way."

"But you're friends with Léopold?"

"Well, yeah, but that's, uh, different." *Different. Unusual. Odd.* Dimitri laughed to himself, realizing that he really was starting to consider him a friend. "We're tight. But I don't know his friends, so stay close. Got it?"

She nodded quietly. Instead of waiting for Dimitri to open the door, she pushed on the handle, but it slipped from her hands. She raised her eyes and her breath caught at the sight. *Léopold.* Before she could help herself, she'd placed her hand in his outstretched palm. God, he looked magnificent. If she hadn't known he was a centuries-old vampire, she would have sworn he was a high fashion cover model.

Her gaze fell from his captivating black eyes to the hard lines of his jaw, eventually landing on his soft lips. Spellbound, she wondered briefly what it would feel like to touch them with her fingers, kiss them. Her face grew hot and she knew she'd looked for a second too long. Her eyes darted to his, and a broad smile broke across his face. *He knew. Oh God, how could she let herself think for one second that fantasizing about a vampire was even close to a good idea?* Hell, it wasn't at all safe; she knew that as well as anyone.

But there was something about him that drew her to him. Like a comet hurling toward the sun, she let him pull her up out of the car, into his arms, and she quietly gasped as his lips brushed her cheek. She closed her eyes, pressing her hands to the fabric covering his chest. For a second she considered sliding her fingertips downward so she could feel the ridges of his abdomen. Enclosed within his wicked embrace, her world stopped, and she realized her life would never be the same.

Léopold knew he should've waited inside the house for Laryssa, but he'd felt her presence as soon as she'd arrived. It had nearly killed him to ask Dimitri to pick her up, but after his fiery reaction to her, he resisted the urge to see her. He'd met hundreds of beautiful women throughout the years, had sex with nearly as many, but he'd long protected his heart from love.

The insidious torment of his wife and children's deaths had nearly killed him. It had ripped through his body and soul, breaking him down to a skeleton of a man. Truth be told, he would have welcomed the loss of his own life. Their violent murders left him questioning not only God but his own humanity. Ironically, his oath to protect his king and God had caused her demise, and yet it was what drove him to keep living afterward, leading to the ultimate death of his mortal life.

As a knight for King Capet, he'd been sworn into service, earning his place in the nobility. During the snowy winter of 988AD, he'd taken up arms in a Parisian skirmish targeted at the weakened king. He'd known the monarch held little power outside the boundaries of his domain, yet he'd held faith that the new leader would unite France. Gallantly he'd fought, successfully defending the king's territory, only to find out that his own home had been a casualty of war.

Returning from the battlefield, he'd trod into his estate, discovering the aftermath of the attack. His family had been slain. Falling to his knees, he'd submitted to his grief, taking in the sight and smell of death. The blood-splattered floors. Their rotting bodies. The maggots and flies that had somehow managed, even in the cold heart of winter, to proliferate. Despite their decomposed states, he'd gathered his wife and children into his arms, screaming a cry of despair into the night.

The very next day, he'd rejoined his brotherhood in what was supposed to have been a celebration of their victory. Drinking himself into oblivion, he languished in his grief. The loss had stolen any sense of self-preservation. So when a fight had broken out at the inn, he readily threw himself into the brawl. Thirsting for death, he'd fought mercilessly and welcomed the final blow that struck him down. Dragged into the alleyway by a benevolent stranger, Léopold spent his last mortal moments lying on his back in the gritty rubble, crying aloud, the name of his wife and children on his lips. Quintus Tullius, a mercenary loyal to no king, had taken mercy on the young warrior that night, gifting him with immortality. Léopold, despite his wish to die, had been reborn. Vampire. Quintus had stayed until morn, only to inform Léopold that he'd been turned. For a sire he was not. While he'd saved Léopold from certain death, he had no desire to mentor another of his kind. Without regret, he'd left Léopold to fend on his own, never having contacted him again.

Over the centuries, Léopold had learned how to compartmentalize the pain, to shove it deep down, disassociating from the horrific nightmare. Most days, it was as if it hadn't happened...until now. Deliberately, he'd avoided relationships, keeping acquaintances and other immortals at a distance. Saving Wynter had been the impetus for his reversal in fate. Watching Logan and Wynter, their love and commitment splayed open, had driven a wedge into his icy demeanor. Perhaps he should have let her die, but in the heat of the moment, he'd breathed life into her. Like dominos, his actions had triggered the memories of his past, leading him to Wyoming, continuing to help Wynter by finding her blood that could have been used to hurt the wolves.

He'd also grown entirely too close to Dimitri in the past few days. *He cared.* And caring was something Léopold generally didn't do. Caring meant feelings. Feelings meant pain. Pain was something he delivered as punishment, not endured. The ancient warrior was far too battle hardened to go soft, yet that is what he feared had happened. Yet there was no undoing what he'd done, saving Wynter, befriending Dimitri. However small, the experiences had pierced his heart and mind, cleaving open a path to emotion. Now within just a week's time, he'd saved a pup and become infatuated with a woman he barely knew.

Looking down at Laryssa, he couldn't help but wonder if she'd felt the shiver of excitement that he'd tried to suppress. So wrong, but undeniable, he simply smiled at her. Shutting out the unsettling thoughts, he released her from his embrace.

"Laryssa."

"Léopold." Laryssa, shaking, looked down to her hands, which he firmly but gently held in his. Léopold's voice wrapped around her like a blanket, calming her racing thoughts. It was as if she could feel his power connecting with her own, filtering it so that she'd relax. She shook her head disbelieving the warmth that ran through her body. There was no way he could touch her energy, let alone control it. She lifted her eyes to meet his, searching for answers that didn't come.

"Ma chérie, don't fret. It'll be all right. You okay?" Léopold asked. Goddess, the woman charged him like no other. She hadn't been lying about her energy. His fangs itched to pierce her creamy flesh, tasting her essence as he fucked her mercilessly. It was wrong, he knew. He had to leave her alone. If he didn't, she'd only get under his skin further, driving him mad with emotions he swore he'd never feel again. As if he'd touched a hot pan, his hands fell from hers. The less he touched her the better, he thought.

"Um, yeah," Laryssa stammered, embarrassed that she'd held onto him like a child. She wrung her hands together, confused that she'd felt a tinge of rejection at the loss of his touch. He must have thought she was either insecure or pathetically weak.

"Come this way," he gestured toward the door. "I'm not sure if Dimitri told you but there're quite a few people waiting to meet you."

"But you said...you promised you wouldn't tell anyone," Laryssa sighed. She gazed into his eyes searching for the truth.

"I didn't tell anyone else," Léopold said with his hand on the sliding glass door.

"You told the wolf," she countered. *Did he think she was an idiot?*

"Ah well, he doesn't count. And the others? They only know that I'm bringing someone who's helping me find information about Ava. They don't know what you can do or what you are. But then again, you haven't told me what you are, have you?" he challenged.

"Point taken. But why doesn't Dimitri count?"

"He was at the club last night. He's seen the video. So he's in on your little secret. He just hasn't had a personal demonstration like the one you gave me." He smiled and raised an eyebrow at her, reminding her how she'd thrown the settee at him. *What a fiery little thing, she is.* "You're ready now, no?"

"No. Yes. No. Ugh, look what you do to me." She took a deep breath and then stilled as he leaned his head toward hers. *What was he doing? Was he going to kiss her?* She closed her eyes as she felt his warm breath on her ear.

"And what do I do to you, mon petit lapin?" Léopold resisted the temptation to go any closer and waited for her response.

"You...you..." He was too close to her, much too close. She couldn't think about anything but wanting to touch him, to sink her body into his.

"Oui?" Léopold smiled, thoroughly enjoying making her nervous, putting her on edge. But when he scented just a faint touch of her arousal, he regretted what he'd done. Slowly, he dragged himself away.

"You make me...I don't know...I'm flustered. Please, Léopold, let's just go in," she said, both relieved and disappointed that he hadn't kissed her.

Léopold turned to open the door and then stopped and faced her. He didn't owe the woman anything, but he was nothing if not forthright. "They're going to know."

"What?"

"They're going to know you're supernatural. I don't know what you did in the club to hide it, but you're projecting. If I can feel your energy, well, they'll know, too."

She sighed and bit her lip. Oh Lord, he was right. Being around Dimitri and Léopold had made her drop her defenses. It just felt so good not to hide it, to go around concentrating on keeping the hum of her aura to an unnoticeable, human level. Anger surged through her as she thought about being dragged into this situation and she quickly realized that she wasn't mad at Léopold. No, she was mad about being in danger, about being turned. The constant watching and concealing, she couldn't take it anymore.

"I don't care," she stated, looking directly into his dark eyes. She hated to admit the truth of it, but there was something about him she trusted. Moreover, she wanted to trust, to finally have an ally. *Why not go for broke?* "I'm not ready to tell you everything about me, so I'm sure as hell not going to tell whoever's behind that door. But I'm tired of hiding. And if you keep your word about my safety, then that's good enough for me. So let's do this thing, okay?"

"As the lady wishes." Léopold smiled at her bravery. Even though her heartbeat revealed her fear, she intrepidly stepped forward.

The delicious scent of Jambalaya floated in the air as they walked into the kitchen. Instead of being attacked by fangs and wolves, smiles greeted them. Dimitri came in behind Laryssa and put his hand on her shoulder. He guided her over to the stove, where a petite lady with frizzy blonde hair busily stirred a pot.

"Hey, gorgeous," Dimitri said, kissing the woman's cheek. "Laryssa, this is Wynter, my Alpha's mate. Where's the big guy?"

"Hey, yourself. Logan's touring the house with Kade. He'll be out in a few." Wynter dipped the spoon into the pan, lifted it and blew off the steam before tasting her creation. As she did so, she caught the look of surprise on Dimitri's face.

"What?" Wynter asked. She suspected that he was worried about Logan allowing vampires in his home. "It's all right. Sydney's with him."

"Okay," Dimitri reluctantly agreed. Dimitri had heard that Kade Issacson kept his vampires on a tight leash and his fiancée, Sydney Willows, was a hard-nosed police detective, who'd recently transferred to the Big Easy.

"They're double checking our security. You know…for the baby." Wynter wiped her hands on her apron and smiled at Laryssa. "Welcome to our den. Sorry it's a bit crazy in here, but we've got us an impromptu party going on. That little lady over there is the cause of the fuss. I know I should be upset with Léopold, but I just can't be. Ava's just so sweet. Like sugar."

Laryssa looked into the family room and saw a couple cooing over a baby. *Ava.* The handsome man wrapped his arm around the red-headed woman, and they both made faces at the little girl then looked lovingly at each other. She couldn't help but think that Dimitri and Léopold had overreacted in warning her about the vampires. They appeared happy and caring, a far cry from the bloodthirsty monsters she'd been expecting.

"She's adorable," Laryssa agreed, feeling drawn to the infant. Ava's tiny energy pulsed like a siren. Overwhelmed with emotion, knowing another one of her kind actually existed, she took a deep breath.

"Can I get you something to drink? Wine? Water? Sweet tea?" Wynter offered, jarring Laryssa from her thoughts.

"Tea would be great. Thanks." Laryssa, disoriented, dug her fingernails into her palms, trying to focus.

"Come," Léopold told her as he took her hand in his. He could tell she'd been as captivated by Ava as he'd been. He guided her over to the baby, intent on introducing her to everyone. "Laryssa, this is Luca Macquarie."

Laryssa nervously smiled. Luca nodded coldly and stood to greet her. She briefly shook his hand. His eyes were cold and dark, and she knew instantly that she'd been wrong about her initial impressions. Death lurked beneath this man's skin. His aura swirled in red and purples, dominance and compassion sliced through the colors.

"And this," Léopold approached the baby, but Luca moved to block him. Before he could protest, the woman stood with the baby and pushed in front of him.

"Hi, I'm Samantha. Please excuse my overprotective fiancé. He seems to think everyone is a danger, but he forgets that I can take care of myself." Samantha smiled up at Laryssa, holding the baby.

Luca's eyes softened and he put his arm around her. "Just taking care of you, darlin'. You can feel it, can't you?"

"But of course I can. She's very strong." Samantha smiled at her, knowingly. "Come sit. Léopold told us that you may be able to help us protect her."

Protect the baby? Laryssa tensed and glanced up at Léopold, who had perched himself above her, sitting comfortably on the arm of the sofa. His lips curled in approval, never taking his eyes off of her. Laryssa felt her heart begin to race. What was he thinking? He shouldn't have faith in her. She hadn't promised him a thing, only that she'd meet the child. Laryssa had barely succeeded in keeping herself hidden, safe. How the hell was she supposed to help them?

As if he'd read the impending dread stirring in her belly, he placed his hand on her shoulder. The tingle of his touch seared through the thin fabric of her sweater. A sense of calm settled over her, leaving her even more confused. What was he doing to her? She searched his eyes for understanding, but he merely looked away to Ava, who gurgled happily at her caregivers.

Laryssa wasn't sure how much to disclose to Samantha. She seemed nice enough, but she suspected that she also wielded powers. Although Laryssa didn't have great knowledge about supernaturals, she'd never heard of a vampire bearing children. Even if she could trust her, Laryssa wasn't used to others discussing her energy. Anyone who'd known about her abilities had shunned her, afraid of what she could do. The strangers had no reason to trust her. She considered her options and decided to partially disclose why she was there.

"I don't know if I can help." She looked again to Léopold for reassurance, and he simply gave her shoulder a squeeze. It would have to be enough. "I felt her...I could feel her being born. And now..."

The baby squealed, and grabbed a pacifier from Samantha's hands.

"That's right, sweetie. See? She feels you, too."

"May I suggest that we get to the bottom line? What are you, Laryssa? And why would anyone want to harm this baby?" Luca asked. He and Léopold had never seen eye to eye, and he grew annoyed that Léopold had involved vampires in wolf business by bringing Ava to New Orleans, putting them all in danger.

Like an insect pinned to a mounting board, Laryssa struggled silently, her thoughts flailing in distress. Revealing herself was not part of her bargain with Léopold. She reached inside herself for the diplomatic words that would both cease this line of questioning and appease the vampire's curiosity.

"Léopold asked me to come here to meet the child, to see if we connected. Do I know who tried to kill her? No. I have no direct knowledge of who did this. In fact, I literally just met Léopold last night." It was the truth. Sure, she had her suspicions. But that was all she had. There was no hard evidence of anything.

"Why is she here, Devereoux?" Luca demanded. He remained seated but his brow furrowed; he looked like a caged animal ready to attack.

"She's here because I asked…" Léopold began, but was interrupted by Laryssa.

"I'm here because unlike you, I can feel her. And when I say feel, I mean she's putting out energy."

"So what? All humans do that. Or wolves in this case," Luca countered.

Léopold watched intently, altogether peeved at the insolent vampire who challenged him, but his anger was tempered by the way his little rabbit had turned into a tigress, not just defending herself but him as well.

"It's not just some kind of heartbeat or pulse or anything like that. It's pure, clean energy. The kind that electrifies the night sky and can move objects. I don't know you very well, so I don't plan on sharing my life story with you, but suffice to say, there's a chance Ava's like me."

"What exactly are you?"

"Don't you mind what I am. You aren't here to protect me. You're here because of Ava. I'll do what I can to help but make no mistake, the only reason I'm helping is because Léopold asked me and I'm doing it for Ava."

Laryssa realized she'd raised her voice at Luca. Silence cut through the room like a knife and her face heated as she became aware that everyone was staring at her. She caught Dimitri's eyes and he began laughing. *What the hell was so funny?* She took note that Léopold wasn't laughing, but he was smiling.

"Luca, dear. Leave poor Laryssa alone," Samantha said sweetly but firmly. Still cradling the baby with one arm, she cupped his cheek. "You'll catch more flies with honey. Be nice. We just met Léopold's friend, and you're giving her the third degree. I can tell she isn't a danger. And she's right about the little one. Ya'll may not be able to feel it. But I can. She's very special. Little Ava here, is humming her own tune."

Luca opened his mouth, about to disagree, when Logan walked into the room with Kade and Sydney. As much as he wanted to argue the point further, he didn't want to upset his lovely pregnant wife-to-be.

"Hey, you're missing all the fireworks." Dimitri jumped up and clapped a hand on Logan's shoulder.

"Yeah, I heard some yelling going on." Logan's eyes shot to Léopold. "Why am I not surprised?"

Léopold laughed. While it was true that Logan was paying a debt by watching Ava, he could tell that it hadn't been that much of a hardship. When he'd first arrived, both Logan and Wynter had been fawning over the baby, looking like a picture perfect family. The Alpha and his mate would be wonderful parents, but they all knew the danger the child represented.

"Come, mon ami. Let's discuss our plans for keeping our petit bébé safe," Léopold suggested. "Sydney. Meet Laryssa. She has…how should I say? Similar abilities to Ava."

Laryssa noticed the blonde detective right away and knew she'd been identified.

"Laryssa? Laryssa Theriot?" Sydney approached her and held out her hand.

Laryssa stood and greeted her. "Hello, detective."

Léopold raised his eyebrows, surprised that they knew each other. *How did Sydney know Laryssa? Had she been in trouble with the law?*

"Laryssa here, volunteers on diving assignments. One of the best I'm told," Sydney explained. "We met on a case. Unfortunately, the search and rescue didn't turn out so well."

"The calls on the river are never good news." Laryssa shook off the compliment, fully aware of why they thought she was a good diver. After hours of searching, they'd called off a rescue but she'd stayed on in the murky water, finally finding the missing kid. She shuddered, remembering how the teen had lain listlessly at the bottom, the body stuck under debris.

"A woman of many skills, I see," Léopold noted, giving Laryssa a look that told her he intended to find out more about her.

"Well, we really appreciate your help." Sydney sat down into a chair, and a man came up behind her, putting his hands on her shoulders. "Sorry, I forgot to introduce you to my fiancé. This is Kade. He heads up the vamps down here. They're a wily bunch. I could hear Luca all the way upstairs. A real troublemaker."

Laryssa almost laughed at the casual way the detective talked about the vampires. Luca cracked a small smile at the comment, revealing to her that they all knew each other well.

"I'm Logan," the Alpha said, grabbing his mate for a kiss.

"Hi," Laryssa managed. This was the Alpha of the Acadian wolves? He looked more like a love strewn puppy than a ferocious leader of the pack.

"Les tourtereaux," Léopold shook his head. "Come, sit. Time for business."

Laryssa gave him a puzzled look, not understanding his French.

"Lovebirds," he translated. "It appears the mates can't keep their hands off each other."

She smiled in understanding, but a twitch of yearning for that kind of relationship flitted through her heart. Between the Alpha and his mate and the other couples, she could see the love in their eyes, causing a twinge of jealousy. The odds of finding a man who'd accept her were exceedingly low. Even her family had tossed her out on her ear.

A hand on her shoulder reminded her why she was there, and she gazed up into Léopold's eyes. As if he knew what she was thinking, he brushed the back of his fingers down her cheek and gave a small smile. The gesture caused her to blush, and as much as she wanted to look away from him, she was mesmerized by his eyes.

Léopold was aware that he couldn't keep his hands off of Laryssa. In a day, the subject of his search had gone from a suspect to the object of his desire. If it had been any other woman, he'd already have fucked her, leaving before the bed grew cool. But his little rabbit affected him in a way that was entirely too intense. Not only could he feel the power pouring out of her skin, he was certain he'd been able to reciprocate, calming her when she'd grown anxious. The crease in her brow had smoothed as soon as he'd touched her. Goddess, he'd have to have her soon. Pretending he could deny himself was becoming increasingly difficult as the minutes passed. He hoped like hell that if he assuaged the need, the passing fancy would cease like the wind. For now, he needed to concentrate on why he'd brought her here, why he'd gathered his trusted men along with Logan's. Protecting Ava was paramount.

"Logan and I would like to discuss how we're going to keep the baby safe," he began. "They tried to kill her once."

"And we can't risk another try on her life," Logan added.

"Which is why we're going to take shifts watching over her. It's best we keep her in one location, here with Logan and Wynter. Ava's wolf. She needs to be with pack," Léopold asserted.

"Laryssa can't stay here, though," Samantha commented. "Whatever's after the baby is probably after her too."

"I'll take care of Laryssa. But I need everyone here to work with Logan on the schedule, at least for a few days until we find and eliminate the threat," Léopold told them.

"Everyone except Samantha," Luca said.

"Oui." Léopold nodded.

"Hey, just because I'm preggo doesn't mean I can't help out with the baby. It'll be good practice," Samantha protested.

"No way, darlin'. Too dangerous." Luca placed his hand over her belly.

"But, I…"

"For once, Luca and I are in agreement. Even though I've seen your magic do some damage, we don't want to risk another baby's life." There was no way Léopold would let Samantha stay with the Alpha. He ignored the rolling of Samantha's eyes but was glad she didn't argue. With both Luca and Léopold against the idea, she didn't stand a chance of winning. "What you can do is talk to Ilsbeth. Find out what kind of wards you can set on this place so that she's better hidden."

"Avery's set wards at my place," Laryssa added. "But I'm not sure they're working right. That's why I met her last night, to see what else I could do. She said she'd have to talk to Ilsbeth."

"It's important that we keep Ava under wraps. That means the fewer people who know she's here, the better," Léopold said. "Kade's bringing in two of his people to keep guard."

"Dominique and Xavier," Kade confirmed.

"You sure about Xavier? He was pretty tight with Étienne," Logan asked. Although it had been a few weeks, Logan couldn't shake the memory of the vampire who'd nearly killed Wynter.

"He's a man of honor. You have my word that he'd never hurt Ava," Kade assured them.

"Jake and Zeke also know. They can be trusted." Logan also had seen his fair share of traitors within his pack. Fiona had been a trusted she-wolf who'd plotted against him and tried to kill his mate.

"But no one else can find out the child is here, got it? You're going to need some kind of excuse to keep the pack away," Léopold suggested.

"Wynter and I can come up with something. To be honest, I've been trying to keep the house just for us anyway. They all know we just mated…been kind of busy, ya know. Really busy up until our little visitor arrived." Logan smiled at Wynter, enjoying the blush that painted her cheeks. "Besides, if the pack wants to get together socially, they've got plenty of places to go besides my house. And meetings are held at the pack house. I think we'll be good."

"What about the girl?" Luca asked pointedly, annoyed that Laryssa still hadn't been candid about her abilities. "We've established that she feels energy or she *thinks* she feels it. She's got some kind of special skills. But we haven't seen a damn thing."

"By girl, I assume you're talking about Laryssa? I'm pretty sure she's a woman. All woman from where I'm sittin'. How 'bout showin' a little respect, fang boy?" Dimitri growled. Vampire or not, he was ready to deck him if he said one more derogatory thing about Laryssa.

Luca, duly chastised, stared at Léopold, waiting for an answer.

"Macquarie, I recall a time not too long ago when I saved your ass. So I suggest you take heed of the wolf and watch your words carefully. Laryssa will be staying with me." Léopold suppressed the grin that lingered behind his impassive tone. The shocked expression that Laryssa wore had not gone unnoticed. *Well, I can't tell her everything.* After all, she was keeping secrets as well. And he planned to find out every last one. The only way he could do that was to spend time with her. "We'll go see Ilsbeth. Her spells are nice, but the witch is often more valuable for her information. I suspect she'll have knowledge about why someone would try to kill Ava and possibly even who that person is. Laryssa can explain best what she is, and she will be fully disclosing that information to me soon." *Whether she likes it or not*, he thought to himself.

"So now that that's settled, anyone have anything else they want to lay on the table? I admit we don't have much to go on here, but we've got to find whoever is behind trying to kill the child." Léopold instinctively reached for Laryssa's hand. He wasn't just worried about Ava. No, he had to keep them both safe.

"I'll take first watch. I'm off duty tonight and I want to go over the exits and entrances one more time. We've gotta make sure this place is sealed up tight," Sydney advised. "I can call in extra support from the station."

"I don't think we should go there yet. We don't know if the threat is human or not. No offense, detective, but we can't trust others. This is pack business now. We take care of our own," Logan told her.

"You sure, Alpha?" Kade's eyebrows drew tight.

"Let's just see where Léopold gets with Ilsbeth first. If she thinks we need to do something else to keep Ava safe, we'll do it. The last thing I need is cops crawlin' around here. If anything, we'd call in P-CAP, and I'm not crazy about that idea either." P-CAP, the Paranormal City Alternative Police, was a supernatural-run sector, but Logan didn't trust them, given it was comprised mostly of vampires. He knew that Kade had been involved with them, but if they were in on what was happening with the child, there'd be no way to keep the information about her contained, secret from the rest of the pack.

"We'll hold off on P-CAP for now, but if things heat up, we're going to need backup and Syd can't do this on her own," Kade concluded.

"I hear ya, but if you want this kept under the radar, we've gotta keep this between us. As it stands now, pack is gonna wonder why my place is vamp central. They all know Léopold saved Wynter, so they're okay with him being here. The rest of you…well, I'm afraid that'll take some explaining."

"As long as Sydney's wearin' a badge, she can always make up some excuse about being here. It's not like we don't have crime on the streets," Dimitri noted. "A human officer is welcome. The second you start bringin' in more supes, badge or not, the wolves are gonna know something's not right."

Ava started to cry and Samantha stood, rocking her back and forth.

"Sounds like someone's hungry," Wynter said. "Let me get her bottle."

"Sydney stays tonight with the Alpha and his mate. Any other comments? Suggestions?" Léopold was met with deafening silence. They all knew it wasn't the best plan but they didn't know the danger that was coming for them. Léopold stood and crossed the room, extending his arms to Samantha. "May I?"

"Of course." The witch kissed the fussy infant's forehead and gently placed the baby into Léopold's waiting arms.

Léopold knew they were all watching him, astounded that someone who they perceived to be the hand of death had the capability to show mercy and compassion toward a child. He ignored their stares and focused on Ava. None of them would be able to fathom the excruciating, churning memories that flared within him. The warmth of

Ava's tiny body spread through his hands, spearing grief through his dark heart, cleaving it open where he'd sealed his painful past. When he looked into her blue eyes, a spark of healing gave way to hope. *Could I ever have what was stolen from me all those years ago?* He closed his eyes for a second, imagining that his ability to love could be resuscitated, renewed.

As he lifted his lids, he caught Laryssa's insightful gaze. Was it possible that she'd felt his pain? That perhaps he couldn't hide the darkness of his past any longer? Goddess, no. He couldn't afford to acknowledge the sliver of faith he clutched to like a thread at the end of the rope. Awkwardly, he blinked and turned away, trying to avoid the erupting feelings that clutched at his chest. An expert at cloaking his emotions, Léopold smiled at Ava. None of them would find out what lay deep in the recesses of his mind. Like an actor, he'd pull off the grand façade and protect Ava. Then as soon as it was all over, he'd leave for another city, resuming his empty but immortal life.

⊷⊱· *Chapter Five* ·⊰⊶

Aa Léopold rocked the baby, Wynter and Laryssa stood in the doorway, observing from a distance. They'd set up a crib inside their master bedroom so they could watch over the infant at night. Wynter quietly closed the door to the bedroom so that she could talk to the stranger who'd come to their home.

"Can I talk to you a minute? Um, this is kind of hard to ask, but what's going on with you and Léopold? I mean I thought he just met you. It just seems like there is something there…something more," Wynter stammered, unable to find the words she needed to articulate her concerns. She had no sire relationship to Léopold, but the man had saved her life; his blood ran through her veins. Like her connection to her mate and the pack, it was as if she could sense how Léopold was feeling, which at the moment felt like torment.

"Well, yes. We met last night but it was just…you see, I fell off a stool. I was waiting for a friend and he was there when it happened. And he kind of caught me…both times. I actually fell twice. It was kind of embarrassing." She rubbed her hand over her eyes, wishing she could crawl into a hole. "You're friends, right?"

Wynter laughed. "Yeah, I guess we are friends. You know Laryssa, as much as I only have eyes for my Alpha, I won't deny that Léopold is a really good looking guy. But he's also dangerous. Very, very dangerous," she whispered. "Listen, I'm not going to tell you what to do, but just be careful. I saw the way you were looking at him and…"

"I wasn't looking at him like anything. It's just that he's the only one I know…really, that's all it is," Laryssa lied.

"He saved my life."

"Sorry?"

"Léopold. He saved my life. I was dying…died. He gave me his blood."

"You're a vampire?"

"No. I'm a wolf. But I do have a few side effects from what he did."

"But he saved you? That doesn't sound so dangerous to me."

"Yes, but…" Wynter didn't want to discourage her as much as warn her. "Just be careful, okay? Léopold is not to be messed with. He's one of the most powerful vampires around."

"In New Orleans?"

"Ever, from what Logan tells me. Look, I know he's very smooth and cultured, but he's lethal. Just don't forget it, all right?"

"Okay." It didn't take much for Laryssa to believe that Léopold was dangerous. Even Avery had said as much. But after her interaction with him today at the shop, not only was she desperately attracted to him, she was certain he wouldn't hurt her. Her ability to throw a large piece of furniture at him hadn't undermined her confidence that she'd be able to hold her own if she was wrong.

"Sorry, I know it's none of my business, but I just felt like I had to say something." Wynter had seen, too, how Léopold had been looking at Laryssa. "I'm sure he'll be fine with you. I mean, just look at how he is with Ava. It's unbelievable really. I've never seen him that way with anyone…so gentle. I guess maybe I didn't know him that well, but I never thought I would have seen Léopold Devereoux taking care of a baby." She shook her head in disbelief and cracked open the door.

"He seems so at ease, doesn't he?" Laryssa commented, knowing Léopold probably heard every word they'd spoken.

"Yes, he does. God help me, it really makes me want to have pups," Wynter confided. "I have to go check on things downstairs. Will you be okay here?"

"Thanks, yeah, I'll be fine," Laryssa assured her.

Quietly, Laryssa pushed open the door, and caught sight of Léopold, who was softly singing a French lullaby to the child. She contemplated what he'd told the others…how she'd stay with him. Was he crazy? If she stayed with him…no, no she could not even go there. In the little time she'd spent with him, she'd already told him so much, too much. Like a geyser, the secrets she'd kept buried for so long had begun to spew forth. She wanted to trust him, to tell him everything. But she couldn't. Going to his home was simply not going to happen, yet the words of protest failed to emerge from her lips. She told herself the reason she didn't argue the point was because she hadn't wanted to stir up more trouble with that nasty vampire. But her gut told her it was because she didn't want to say no. She wanted to say yes. Yes, to everything that was Léopold.

Slowly, Laryssa approached Léopold, as he rocked in the chair, the infant finally asleep against his shoulder. Kneeling before him, she rested her hands on his thighs.

"Elle est belle. She's beautiful, no?" Léopold commented. Speaking softly to the infant, he continued. "Mon petit bébé, we shall keep you safe and sound."

"She's so sweet. It's hard to believe someone would try to kill a baby. Sick. Really sick."

"Einstein said, 'the world is a dangerous place to live; not because of the people who are evil, but because of the people who don't do anything about it.' So much evil exists. It's a wonder people even get up in the morning."

"We're going to stop this…whatever, whoever did this."

"That we will, Laryssa." Léopold pressed up out of his seat and gently placed Ava on her back in the crib. Pulling up the blanket, he felt Laryssa's hand on his shoulder. "I've lived hundreds of years. Like immortals, evil never dies.

It's almost as if we know this when we're born. Even the newborn babes cry as they're birthed into our world."

"I don't know, Leo. I do believe that there's something bigger than all of us." Unconsciously, if not out of comfort, Laryssa noticed she'd touched Léopold.

"The Goddess? Oui. But hell, I believe, also exists, spawning the evil in both men and supernaturals. It won't have her."

"Evil? Babies aren't born evil."

"That's not what I mean. I mean that whatever is after her is evil, and it can't have her. I swore it tried to kill her that night in Yellowstone. With all I've seen, it makes no sense. There's something bothering me about this...the creatures you've described."

"No eyes."

"If they are real..."

"They are."

"If they're real, I've never seen anything like them. But then again, I've never met anyone like you." He smiled and captured a lock of her hair in his fingers.

Laryssa took a deep breath, slowing the pace of her heartbeat. She was certain he'd heard her talking to Wynter. She sighed in embarrassment. He was so out of her league.

"You are really good with her." She changed the subject, turning her gaze to Ava. "Have you always been good with babies?"

"We've got to go. It's getting late and you need to rest before we see Ilsbeth in the morning. You should get something to eat downstairs," Léopold suggested. Hastily, he strode across the room, away from both Laryssa and the crib and put his hand on the door handle. He didn't want to discuss his feelings about children with anyone. Foolishly, he'd let his guard down around Laryssa.

"What?" she asked, startled by his change in tone. *Is he angry with me?*

"I said we need to go," he responded coldly. Like a vault, he'd successfully closed his heart and mind shut from Laryssa.

Wynter opened the door, surprising them both. "How's she doing?"

"Ah, Wynter. Thank goodness you're here. We can't leave Ava unattended, not even for a minute. Laryssa and I are going to get going. We need to stop at her home to get her things." Léopold was grateful for the interruption.

"I see you got Ava down. I think I'm gonna take a nap while she's sleeping. I'll tell you, you sure seem to have the magic touch with babies, Léopold. Who would've thought? Big bad vampire is a softy," Wynter sang in a baby voice while tucking in the sides of the blanket, making sure Ava was comfortable, and didn't catch the look of disdain that washed over Léopold's face. "Well make sure you get some of the jambalaya I made. There're bowls out on the countertop. Or you can take some with you to go."

"I'm really not hungry…." Laryssa started to say, upset with Léopold's apparent shift in mood.

"I'll make sure she eats something," Léopold replied and gestured for Laryssa to leave the room. "Come, pet."

"Not a dog," Laryssa snapped, walking past him toward the steps.

"Excuse me?" he asked.

"You heard me."

"I never said you were an animal." He knew full well why she was angry with him. It was better this way. As much as he wanted her, he could never give her what she needed.

"Yeah, right. Next time, I suppose you'll blow a whistle. Better go find a breeder if you're lookin' for a pet."

Léopold snorted in response, but didn't let her see the small smile that he couldn't keep from curling upward. She was a little spitfire, one he knew was going to give him a few burns before the week was done. Damn, he wished he could keep her in his life, but it'd never work. It was better to keep her angry than aroused. Once this was all over, he could leave her with little fallout.

They'd ridden in virtual silence from Laryssa's apartment. She continued to bite her tongue as they pulled into the gated driveway of his enormous lakeside mansion. Struggling with her feelings, Laryssa found it difficult to understand how she'd let the charismatic vampire take over her life within the past twenty-four hours. When she looked into his piercing dark eyes, it was as if he'd reached into her chest and stolen every ounce of self-control she'd ever had. He made her want to do things, very naughty things…to him, with him. She'd never responded so viscerally to any man, let alone a supernatural. Instead of remaining cool and collected, controlling her energy and her body's reactions to him, she'd lost her concentration. She'd let him arouse her, and then anger her, freeing her power, exposing her abilities for the first time.

The way he commanded the others within the Alpha's home left her in awe. They'd both feared and respected him. But it was how he revealed his gentility with Ava that stole her heart. She wasn't stupid. She suspected that he'd killed over the centuries. An immortal didn't live as long as he had without doing so. Yet he fed and rocked the baby as naturally if he was her father. The simple act divulged more about Léopold than anything else he'd said or done. Beneath his hardened exterior, goodness resided. The anger he'd expressed when she'd asked him about having children was preceded by a brief flicker of grief in his eyes. He may not have intentionally shown it, but the fact he couldn't look at her told her that he was hiding something, something that was so painful that he'd reacted like a hurt animal. What Léopold didn't know about her was that she wouldn't accept his refusal. Perhaps she wasn't thinking with her head, but she was determined to get to know her beautiful vampire.

Like it or not, Léopold Devereoux would learn to open up to her, to trust her. There was no other way she could justify revealing her true nature to another soul. She needed to know that Léopold was worthy of her secret, not just seeking to protect Ava. If he was simply after her powers, she'd still help him, but she couldn't risk becoming intimate with him. It would be nearly impossible to resist his charms, she knew, but she sought more than just a roll in the hay. If she gave him her body, she'd have a difficult time protecting her heart.

Laryssa's thoughts were interrupted when Léopold opened the car door for her. *A perfect gentleman*, she thought. So many years on this Earth had certainly taught him about the finer things in life. She ran her fingers over the soft leather seat one more time before exiting. As she reached for her overnight bag behind the seat, Léopold's hands brushed over hers.

"Allow me," Léopold told her, easily lifting it.

"I can carry my bag," she protested.

"Well of course you can, but I insist. You're my guest. This way." Without arguing further, he walked up to the front door and flipped open a biometric security pad. "I usually park in the garage, but since you're here with me..."

He didn't finish his sentence as he twisted the doorknob, gesturing for her to go ahead of him. "I don't have many people over, but you'll be comfortable."

"It's lovely," Laryssa responded, trying to act nonchalant as she entered his home.

It wasn't as if she hadn't toured a Garden District mansion, but Léopold's home was spectacular. A large foyer with a circular staircase led directly into a great room. Spacious and contemporary, cathedral ceilings gave way to a wall of floor to ceiling windows. The kitchen, with its white cabinets and white marbled countertops, separated the area with a large breakfast bar. Modern cream-colored leather sofas offset the dark cherry floors. A two-story white stone fireplace climbed the far wall.

Laryssa couldn't help but think how ironic it was that Léopold's home was so airy and open yet he himself was quite the opposite, mysterious and enigmatic. She wondered if this was how he saw himself or perhaps it was how he wanted to be. Reflecting on his caring behavior with the child, she knew there was more to him than his role as protector and leader. As she entered the great room, she supposed that although the décor was understated, it presented a flair for the dramatic. As she took in the room, she noticed, however, that it also appeared impersonal. Unlike her tiny apartment which was decorated with pictures she'd taken on vacation and places she loved, aside from a few pieces of art, there was nothing to indicate who lived here or what they did. His home was like a floor model, modern and inviting, but still not quite finished.

As she approached the windows, she couldn't help but press her hands against the glass. *Water.* Its call was undeniable. Before she had a chance to ask about the lake, lights flickered outside, revealing a large rectangular Olympic-sized swimming pool with a semicircular wading pool with fountain. Multicolored lights sparkled within the azure water, appearing to dance in the night.

Magnificent as it was, it was the prize lying beyond the pool, waiting for her, that captured her attention.

As she tried to contain her excitement, exhaustion washed over her. She felt drained, in need of its healing. If she didn't tell Léopold soon, she'd have to sneak out into the night air to find the restorative liquid. Like air, she needed the lake's water to survive.

"You like to swim? You're welcome to use the pool while you're here," Léopold commented, watching her out of the corner of his eye.

"Swim?"

"The pool. You're a diver. One can only assume you like the water if you dive on a regular basis," Léopold said, taking the takeout container he'd brought from Logan's. He walked into the kitchen, setting it into the microwave. Léopold worked in the kitchen, all the while aware of her every move.

Laryssa's reticence hadn't surprised him during the drive. He'd driven her to it after she'd asked about him having children. His response had been meant to silence her, and now that he'd done what he'd set out to do, he found he missed the sound of her voice. He'd turned on the outside lighting, thinking she'd caught a glimpse of the pool area. But she seemed preoccupied with something else altogether. *This woman, this creature, what was she?*

She was clearly lost in her thoughts; he observed how she was bent toward the window, her hands spread against it. Her pert bottom peeked at him through the pair of skin-tight jeans she'd changed into at her apartment.

Léopold shifted his legs as his dick hardened at the sight of her well-rounded ass. He inwardly groaned, picturing himself peeling them off then driving into her from behind while her firm breasts pressed onto the cold glass.

Merde, I shouldn't have brought her here. Léopold shook his head in disgust with his lack of discipline. True, he needed to get laid, but not with her. His instincts told him that there was something about Laryssa that would shake his carefully constructed world, and that simply could not happen. He wouldn't let himself fall any deeper into her spell. Pulling out his cell phone, he tapped out a text to Arnaud. Food and a fuck would solve his problem. If he didn't sate his hunger, it wouldn't be long before he had Laryssa stripped bare, with his cock buried deep inside her.

The microwave beeped, thankfully distracting him from the tempting thought. He reached in and pulled out the bowl, setting it on the counter.

"Sit."

Laryssa turned her head toward him and glared.

"Sit please," he replied with a sarcastic tone. "Come pet, you need to eat. See? It's Wynter's jambalaya. Smells delicious."

"Are you always this bossy?" Laryssa asked, irritated that he continued to give her orders. She considered telling him to go to hell but her stomach rumbled, reminding her that she truly was hungry "Can't you just say, 'your dinner is ready?' No, I get, 'sit.' Listen, Leo, if you plan on keeping me here, I'll repeat it once more...contrary to your belief that I'm some kind of a dog or servant, I'm neither."

"I can see quite clearly that you aren't. As for being 'bossy' as you put it, I am the boss, no? It is what it is. You cannot change the moon or the stars, nor can you change the man." Léopold sighed. *Oui, maybe I am an arrogant prick. Little rabbit better get used to it, though, because I'm not changing for a woman, especially one who won't be in my life very long.*

"Why am I not surprised that you'd compare yourself to the universe?" she huffed and sat down at the breakfast bar. She looked down and saw that not only had he heated her food, he'd given her a neatly folded cloth napkin, utensils and bottle of water. She closed her eyes and tried to quell the pang of guilt for calling him bossy. Despite his cavalier attitude, he was trying. "Thank you. It smells great."

"Would you like wine?" Léopold selected one of his favorite reds from a wrought iron rack on the wall.

"No thank you," she answered, picking up her spoon.

"Oui, I do think you need some wine. This is a lovely Pinot Noir I picked up in New Zealand a few months ago." Léopold proceeded to retrieve a couple of glasses from the cabinet and opened the bottle. After pouring a generous portion, he slid the glass in front of her and smiled.

Laryssa watched as he completely ignored her answer. *Did he not just hear me say 'no'? But of course he did.* Despite his actions, there was no denying how incredibly sexy she found his confidence. Acquiescing to his suggestion, she shook her head and picked the glass up, taking a sip. As the dark fruity flavors coated her tongue, she closed her eyes, enjoying its excellent pairing with her meal. It had been a God awful day, and she relaxed as the delicious nectar began to take the edge off. Her eyes snapped open and she silently swore. *Damn him. Did he have to be right about everything?* The soft rumble of his laughter filled the room and she knew she'd been caught.

"Good, no?"

"Okay, yes, the wine is wonderful. And even though I said no, and you ignored me, you were right about it. What about you? Aren't you eating?" Laryssa could've smacked herself right after she asked such a fatuous question. *Food for vampires? As in blood.* It wasn't as if she was volunteering, but as she watched his mouth break into a broad smile, she couldn't refute that she desired his lips on her skin.

"Brave one, mon petit lapin." He held his glass up to the light and swirled it. "I do love the finer culinary delights of humanity but I'm afraid only sang will keep me alive. The wine is delectable, but it doesn't suffice."

"And the food…real food?"

"Real food?" Léopold laughed and placed his drink on the counter before catching Laryssa's eyes. "It's all a matter of perspective. Blood…warm blood from a living human is what I require…crave."

"You don't scare me," Laryssa said, willing her hands not to shake.

"It's not my intention. You asked. I'm answering. A simple conversation. Besides," he returned to his wine. "I don't kill to eat. I do, however, prefer live donors. I can afford it, so why not?"

"As in people?"

"It's who I am. There's no denying my nature." Léopold circled around the bar until he was behind Laryssa. He set his glass next to hers and slid his fingers down through her hair.

"But why not just get bagged blood or whatever that stuff is they have at Mordez?" Laryssa asked but didn't really care. The second he touched her, she lost her concentration, falling back into his hands, but stopped short of purring like a kitten.

"Why should I when I can have what I really want? When I want. How I want it," he whispered into her ear. His hands fell to her shoulders. "If you could have what you want, wouldn't you take it? Relish the experience. Just be who you are. No living in fear or shame."

Laryssa could feel her muscles melt as he massaged her neck. *Oh dear God, I'm never going to be able to deny him. What was he saying? Did he ask what I wanted? That's an easy answer; I want him.* Ah, but it was that small detail about telling him who she was that was going to be a bit of an issue.

"I don't know what that's like," she managed to say. Losing herself in his touch, she moaned. "I want to be free, but I can't."

"Tell me what you are, ma chérie. Free yourself."

"Quid pro quo. Tell me why you got upset with me. I asked if you'd always been good with children and you shut me down."

Léopold released her and walked across the room, gazing out the windows. Laryssa jumped up from her seat, following him.

"Oh no you don't. Not again," she scolded. "You expect me to tell you everything about me, but I ask a simple question, and you get angry. Well, I've got news for you. I'm not laying it all on the line unless you do the same. You want me to trust you with something that is really important to me, but you won't even tell me why you're so good with a baby that I'd think you actually had one."

Léopold had a family? A child? Laryssa knew instantly the minute she'd pressed the issue, and he'd gone as stiff as a board. *But why hide it? Were they missing? No, they were dead.*

Léopold said nothing as her words fell through the air, tearing open old wounds. The woman made him crazy. He should have just left her in that damn antique shop. She hadn't given him any reason to think she could really help him protect Ava. He'd never needed anyone, yet he was acting like he needed her. He contemplated grabbing his car keys and driving her right back to the French Quarter where she belonged. He was about to walk over to the door when he felt her hands on his back.

"I'm sorry," she whispered.

"There's nothing to be sorry for."

"Really, I'm sorry. If you'd just told me…"

"Like you've told me what you are and how you got that way?" he snapped, turning to face her.

"That's different. You don't understand. I don't tell anyone. There's been no one. Don't you get how badly I want to trust you? You don't even know, do you?" Laryssa countered. She looked to the floor, wringing her hands. "I can't just tell you what you want to know. I want to tell you but we need to have trust. Bossing me around isn't trust, Leo. I need more."

"More? I've brought you to my home. There are things about me you don't know, Laryssa. I've lived a long time."

"Yes, but when two people are building a friendship, a relationship…" Laryssa cringed at the use of the 'r' word but whether it was romantic or not, it was what she required in order to tell him the truth.

"Relationship?" Léopold threw his head back and wiped his eyes. "I cannot deny that I'm attracted to you, but a relationship? No, I don't do relationships. I'm not who you need. And my past is dead and buried…where it needs to stay."

"I'm sorry for upsetting you, but yeah, I do need to have a relationship with you if I'm going to just tell you everything about me. I get that you have a past, but I have one too, and unlike you, I'm not some ancient badass. I'm just trying to survive. And I'm all alone. I can't do this. If you can't trust me…I don't know." The effects of the wine weren't nearly enough to calm her; moisture filled her eyes.

Léopold saw her tears threatening to spill, and while he'd generally ignore if not enjoy the sight of fear and pain in another being, it felt as if he was absorbing her torment. *Why does she need me to show her my trust?* He didn't want to do it. It was a bad idea, but she looked so defeated and he really didn't want her to go.

"I was a father." Saying the words out loud for the first time in centuries was surreal. He hadn't said them since he'd been turned.

"Leo," Laryssa's voice cracked. He'd trusted her. She closed the distance between them, wrapping her arms around his waist.

"Rosamund. She was four. Maiuel, he was only a bébé…" It felt so foreign to say their names yet it was as if it was only yesterday that he'd held them in his arms. He could hear his daughter's voice calling for him, *'père'*. "It was so very long ago…" Léopold closed his eyes, his face tensed. *Why was he talking about this?*

"It's all right. I'm so sorry," Laryssa cupped his face in her hands. "I shouldn't have pressed it. I just wanted to know you…"

When his eyes flashed open, the look of grief quickly turned into one of passion. With the exception of Dimitri, there'd been no one he'd shared anything personal with, let alone the death of his children. Laryssa had not only stirred his desire, but had renewed his memories and connections to the human world. It was as if her brief presence in his life had begun to strengthen the delicate fibers that remained of his compassion. He couldn't bring himself to take her blood, but with her in his arms, he could no longer resist her body.

As his mouth captured hers, Léopold knew it was wrong. He didn't deserve her, but couldn't stop as he tasted the sweet innocence on her lips. Self-restraint slid away as he immersed himself in her, his lips deepening their luscious kiss. Reaching into her mane and taking command, he wrapped his fingers around her locks, and held her in place. He needed to have her, be in her. He'd regret it, but as she responded to him, giving herself to him, he couldn't stop. With a gasp, he pulled his lips from hers and began to trail kisses down the delicate skin of her throat. Hungry for more, his other hand slid up her belly, pushing up her shirt until he'd found the swell of her breast. She moaned at his touch, encouraging him. More, they both needed more and fast. Léopold pulled down the lacy fabric of her bra until her swollen nipple released into his fingers.

"Leo, please," she begged.

"I want you," he breathed against her neck. Léopold leaned into her, his rock hard erection jutting into her. "Do you feel that?"

"Yes," she responded breathlessly.

Léopold grasped her chin with his hand, until her hooded eyes met his. "This," his fangs snapped downward and he bent his knees, pressing up into her with his cock, "is what you do to me. You make me lose control."

"You don't scare me," she responded and licked the crook of his neck.

Is there nothing I can do to deter her? Goddess almighty, this woman would be his downfall. He knew it as sure as he was standing there next to her. Léopold gave in and kissed her passionately, allowing his fangs to nick her tongue. A monster, he was. She needed to know he wasn't safe. He'd hurt her just like he'd done to his family.

Laryssa sensed Léopold's hesitation. He'd shown her his teeth to frighten her, and a small part of her was scared. But an even bigger part of her yearned to have his fangs pierce her skin, possessing her, in every way possible. As his tongue moved inside her mouth, she sucked and breathed, letting her own tongue brush over his sharp teeth.

"Off," was all she heard before he'd ripped the fabric of her shirt over her head.

"Stay still," he ordered, holding her upright. He glided his hands over the smooth skin of her back and he turned her body once again, this time so that she was facing the window. With a flick of his wrist, he slipped the hooks out of the eyes and her bra fell to the floor. "Much better, pet."

"No," she protested at the name he'd called her.

"Now." Léopold reached his hand around her neck, and gently but firmly held her in place. His other hand found her breast. "This is what I've wanted to do to you. Lovely."

Laryssa didn't fear his restraint of her body, but instead embraced it, focusing solely on the touch of his fingers as they kneaded her flesh. She wanted to scream and tell him to stop calling her that name, yet it was as if he was playing her like a grand piano. The music resonated throughout her entire being, making her dance to the rhythm he created.

"Léopold," she breathed, seeking more than he gave.

"Patience. You're so soft and ready, aren't you? But you play with fire, no?"

"What do you mean?" She tried to move her head but he tightened his grip, softly stroking the skin beneath her ear.

"Quid pro quo. What are you?" Léopold breathed against her skin, brushing his lips to her nape.

"I can't," she insisted.

Léopold laughed, frustrated, aroused by his little witch. She may not have been magical but she wielded a sexual spell over him like no other woman he'd met. After confessing the names of his children, she thought she could get away without meeting the terms of their agreement? There was so much he would teach her, if he'd let himself indulge. But he couldn't have her, he knew. In this moment, however, she owed him the truth. *Quid pro quo.*

"Oui, you will," he assured her. Sucking the lobe of her ear into his mouth, his hand fell from her breast and she moaned in protest. Slowly, he teased his hand over her belly, downward.

"Please."

"Qu'est-ce que tu veux?"

"I don't understand," she cried in frustration. *Why is he torturing me?*

"Please what?"

"I can't...I can't say."

"You are a stubborn one. So determined yet so fragile. Like the silk of a spider...you're strong but delicate. Both tough and ductile, you fight against what you are but strain to conform to what society expects of you. But what you must learn, Laryssa," Léopold paused before gliding his fingers under the seam of her jeans, "is that even a spider's web can be tested." His fingers slid through her slick folds, grazing her hooded pearl until he heard her moan. "Ah, yes, the web, while strong, it can be tested, flexed. The energy it can absorb is extraordinary in nature, but not limitless."

Laryssa's pussy ached with heat, pulsing in anticipation of his next stroke. She struggled to move her hips into his hand but he gently squeezed her neck, reminding her who was in control. Her core contracted as he pressed a finger against her entrance and she knew then she would give anything to be with this man.

"I'll tell you, just please....touch me."

"Like this?' He plunged a long thick finger into her, licking her neck as he did so. He kissed along the bottom of her cheek, wanting so badly to taste her lips again.

"Ah," she cried. "Yes."

"Or like this?" Léopold strummed the pad of his thumb over her clitoris, pumping another finger into her wetness.

"Yes," she cried. The tendrils of an orgasm lingered beyond her reach. She couldn't move, couldn't touch herself. She could only wait for him to give her what she desired. Her chest heaved a breath as he flicked over her swollen clit a second time.

"Tell me what you are, everything you can do. No relationships. Just give." He pressed two fingers up into her, eliciting another moan of pleasure. "And take."

"I'm so close...please, Léopold. Not now...just make me feel." As he stilled his fingers, she groaned.

"Yes, you are...so close to getting what you want. I desire you, but we cannot be. I'm not the man for you. Pleasure I can bring you easily, but anything more will cause you nothing but pain."

"Stop talking," she demanded.

"You want it so badly, don't you? I can feel your flesh quivering around my fingers, sweet, sweet Laryssa," he grunted as he ground his cock into the swell of her ass. If she didn't tell him what she was within the next two minutes, he knew he'd completely lose control and take her right there on the floor. Once they made love, he feared he wouldn't be able to let her go. No, he needed information, not complications. He had to break her, get her to tell him how she came to be, what she was. "Tell me now and you can have what you seek, mon lapin. What are you? I can feel it...you want to give in to me...so just tell me. I can't promise you anything but my trust and protection."

As his fingers pumped in and out of her, driving her higher and higher, hurling her toward climax, she could barely hear him speaking. *Trust? Give in? What is he saying?*

"I can't tell you now…please, don't stop," she breathed, resting her forehead against the cool window pane. "It feels so good. Oh my God."

"Tell me now or we stop."

"What?" Laryssa quivered, her orgasm teetering on the edge. She shook her head, refusing to tell him.

"Tell me!" Léopold grunted as his seed began to seep from the tip of his hardness. *Goddammit, this woman is impossible.* Before he had a chance to press her further, the doorbell rang, interrupting them. "Saved by the bell?"

"What?" Disoriented, Laryssa shivered. Falling off the precipice of ecstasy, her orgasm fell out of reach as Léopold pulled his hand out of her panties. *Why was he stopping?* She'd heard the familiar sound of a buzzer. Was someone at the door? She tried to compose herself, reeling from the loss of his touch. She felt him lift her arms, draping the hole of her shirt over her head.

"Dinner's arrived, I'm afraid. Get dressed," he told her as if he'd ordered off a menu and was sitting in a restaurant waiting for his meal to arrive.

"Seriously?"

"Quoi?" he said, smoothing down the fabric. He bent down, grabbing her bra off the floor and brought it to his nose and sniffed.

Coming to her senses, Laryssa twisted away from him. A mixture of disappointment and embarrassment coursed through her, as she realized that she'd let him restrain her. Worse, he'd deliberately baited her, arousing her, bringing her so close to coming and then stopping. Her eyes flared in anger, as he smiled at her with a knowing look. He wanted her to know what he'd done.

"Get away from me." She brushed his hand off her arm.

"A pity, no? So close, yet so far away." He extended his arm, her bra dangling from his fingertip. She snatched it and clutched it to her chest.

"I wasn't that close," she lied. "How would you know anyway? I could have been faking it."

"You don't wear deception well, mon lapin. Besides, I was referring to the fact that I was so close to finding out the truth....de vous. You'll tell me. That was our agreement. I share, you share. I'm afraid you now owe me." Léopold circled her as she stood as still as a statue. Coming up behind her, he felt her jump as he pressed his lips to her hair. "And I intend to collect right after I'm finished."

"Finished doing what?" She heard a door opening, and Léopold paid her no heed as he moved from behind her toward the foyer.

"Excusez-moi. The door...I must attend to our guests," he called out, leaving her behind.

Cautiously following him, Laryssa moved to where he'd put her bag and snatched it up into her arms, concealing her unrestrained bosom. From across the room, she could see a man and a woman push through the entryway. She didn't recognize them from earlier and wondered who they were, what they were doing here. Panic rose in her throat at the thought that Léopold had lied to her, told others about her and her abilities. She watched pensively as Léopold guided the female into the foyer, toward the great room.

"This is my assistant," Léopold told Laryssa, nodding to the strange man who politely smiled at her. "He's brought dinner."

"Hello," she managed to say in a soft voice, but didn't extend her hand.

"Bonjour mademoiselle. Or should I say bonsoir as it's getting late, isn't it?"

Laryssa forced a small smile. Her eyes darted to Léopold, as he escorted the blonde guest over to a chair. The woman appeared to glide across the floor, her heels clicking a soft staccato on the wooden planks. Laryssa silently gasped, noticing that the woman had a mask tied to her face, blocking her eyesight. *What the hell is going on?*

"Um, why is she wearing a blindfold?" Laryssa couldn't contain her curiosity.

"No worries," Léopold cajoled, appreciating the look of worry on Laryssa's face. "This is Sophie. She's quite comfortable, I assure you."

"But…I thought you said your assistant was bringing dinner…we already…" Laryssa's face turned white as her words trailed off into silence. Her brain slowly put together the pieces of the puzzle. No, Léopold would not do this. Not in front of her.

"Arnaud."

"What?" she asked.

"Arnaud. My assistant's name is Arnaud. And while you've already had dinner," Léopold stood behind the woman and put his hand on the top of her head as if he was petting a cat, "I have not."

Laryssa could feel her blood pumping, fear and loathing tearing through her. *Is he serious? Of course he's serious. He's a vampire. Bloodsucker. Parasite.* She bit her lip, trying hard to fight the tears. Only a few minutes ago, she'd almost made love to him, knowing what he was capable of doing, secretly hoping he'd pierce her skin, drinking in her essence. With disgust, she watched as the woman calmly untied the belt that cinched her trench coat, and shrugged out if it, baring her skin. She wore a black satin slip and nothing more, the hem inching up her thighs.

Laryssa's face heated as her anger simmered. She'd heard the rumors about how vampires ate, their bite inciting the most spectacular orgasms. She'd been foolish to think for one second that she could actually have a relationship with Léopold. Unlike her, he'd proudly confessed who he was, what he was. Behind his debonair and seductive exterior, a cavalier man stood before her, no apologies given. *Why didn't I listen to him? How could I have been so stupid as to misread the attraction as something more than what it is...lust?*

Léopold knew this would be the result when he'd texted Arnaud, telling him to bring him a donor. It wasn't as if he hadn't done it a million times. The donors, male or female, were always blindfolded. Sometimes just for the ride to his mansion, sometimes for the entire time until they returned to their residence. Regardless, they were never privy to the whereabouts of Léopold's mansion.

His home was his refuge, the location of which he only shared with Arnaud. He'd planned on inviting Dimitri eventually, once they returned from Wyoming. In a lapse of judgment, he'd brought Laryssa here. For every hour he told himself that he needed to be done with her, get her out of his life, he grew further unable to deny his hunger for her. He reasoned it was purely a physical attraction, but when she insisted on something more, a connection to assure her of his trust with her secret, he'd broken a million of his own rules. First he'd brought her to his sanctuary, and then told her about his children.

Convinced if she saw him in his true light, she'd understand that they could never have a relationship, he'd asked Arnaud to bring the donor, a female for good measure. The look of hurt and distrust in her eyes should have been cause for celebration, for victory. But the joke was on him, because the only blood he wanted was Laryssa's. Not only had he maliciously caused her distress, denied her an orgasm, he was now taunting her with another woman. Conflicting emotions vacillated inside of him for only a minute, before he'd decided he'd done the right thing.

This was who he was and he wouldn't hide it, wouldn't conceal his true identity. Long ago, before he'd been turned, he'd been a gentle man, caring to his wife and children. Hardworking, a knight for the king. But that man had died with his family. The trifling of decency and compassion within his soul could not compete with the savage animal within. No woman would ever love the beast he'd become.

Laryssa hadn't told him what she was, but he could sense the purity within her. Her humanity thrived, and she'd crave a man who cared only for her. She deserved more, not the selfish individual that she lusted for. He told himself that by hurting her, showing her this side of him, she'd give up illusions of friendships, relationships and connections. Their liaison must be based on finding who tried to hurt the baby. No more, no less. But as he spied a tear trailing down Laryssa's cheek, he questioned his motives. Was he feeding out of hunger or protecting his own heart, one he would deny existed?

"Arnaud, please show Laryssa to the guest room," Léopold stated and then gave her a smug smile. "Unless you wish to stay and watch?"

Laryssa glared at him. The man had to eat but it was as if he was being cruel on purpose, taunting her after withholding her orgasm. Yet he had every right to eat or fuck whoever he wanted. It wasn't as if she'd offered to give him her own blood. No, she'd taken pleasure from him, knowing she wouldn't tell him everything. She had no right to the jealousy that swelled inside her. She held Léopold's gaze as he sat next to his donor, who was proffering her arm upward to his nose. She hated him. She lusted after him. None of it mattered because he would do whatever he wanted.

Léopold absorbed Laryssa's stare. It was as if he could feel his lips on her skin, but the woman he held in his hands wasn't her. For every second of anguish he caused to Laryssa, he felt it tenfold, denying and relinquishing his own desire for her. She'd never want him once he demonstrated how cold he could be, his nature. Descending his fangs, he never took his eyes off of her as he licked the inside of the woman's wrist, detecting her pulse.

"Can I take off the blindfold?" Sophie asked.

"No," he told her.

"Do you want me to lie down? I've missed you."

"Do not speak. It's your blood I seek, nothing else," Léopold claimed. While he'd used and had sex with her before, it was all part of their feeding arrangement. Like any other donor, her purpose was merely nutritional. But after meeting Laryssa, he wondered if he'd ever be able to make love to another woman.

"Come, mademoiselle. Let me take you to your room while monsieur has dinner," Arnaud politely suggested.

"Uh, yes, I think that would be a good idea," Laryssa stammered. A sick sense of relief washed over Laryssa as she observed the interaction. *Did the donor expect him to have sex with her?* Perhaps, but he'd refused her, and it appeared as if he was truly only using her for her blood. Sophie placed her hand on Léopold's thigh, and Laryssa thought she'd vomit. The only thing stopping her was the touch on her elbow, distracting her from the scene.

"Yes, a very good idea," Arnaud asserted.

Laryssa gave Léopold one last glance as Arnaud escorted her out of the great room. A long hallway led to two doors, one on the left and one on the right. She caught sight of a second staircase which appeared to trail downward.

"Mademoiselle, this room here is the guest room." Arnaud opened a solid oak door and flipped on a light switch. "The master's room is across from yours."

"The stairway? Where does it go?" she inquired right before they walked into the room. Water. She needed to get out to the lake.

"There's a billiard and exercise area downstairs. Leads out to the pool. You're welcome to a swim, if you want. I can unlock the back sliders for you."

"Swim? Uh, yeah, that would be great." Laryssa glanced around the room. Like the rest of Léopold's home, it was stark white except for a Blue Dog painting that hung on the far wall. Its captivating yellow eyes seemed to follow her. She'd seen the brightly colored canines so many times when she'd passed the gallery in the Quarter but it was the first time she'd seen the artwork in someone's home.

"You a George Rodrique fan?" Arnaud asked, sidling up next to her.

"Yeah, I love it. His work's amazing, huh?"

"Yes, indeed. Monsieur loves his pieces as well." Arnaud walked away, opening the door to the bathroom. "The towels are in here if you decide to go for a dip. I'll go downstairs now and see to the lock."

"Do you live here?" Laryssa asked, glancing at Arnaud. She wasn't sure why she asked other than interest in what sort of person would work for Léopold. She laughed silently, thinking he must have the patience of a saint.

"Me? No. My boss prefers solitude. Besides, when he's in the city, I live just down the street. But I'm available to him twenty-four seven when he's home."

"Home?"

"New Orleans."

"He travels often?"

"Sometimes," he hedged. "He also prefers his privacy. If there isn't anything else I can get you, I need to attend to a few things before I take Sophie back."

Sophie. Laryssa's breath caught, realizing that for a brief second she'd almost forgotten where she was. That and the fact Léopold was with another woman…dinner. As much as she wanted to pump Arnaud for information about his little 'feeding' arrangement, she could tell she'd already crossed the boundary of what he was willing to share about his employer.

"No, I'm fine. Thanks."

"You're very welcome, mademoiselle. Now if you'll excuse me, I'll see to the door."

As Arnaud left the room, Laryssa admired the painting, thinking about how many times she'd considered purchasing a print. She'd often thought of keeping one in her tiny apartment but had decided she wouldn't see it nearly often enough and had decided to display one in her shop so she could enjoy it all day.

Her store, she thought with a sigh. After closing early, she'd forgotten to call her assistant manager to make sure he opened it tomorrow. She reached for her cell in her pocket and realized that she'd misplaced it. Rummaging through her overnight bag, she remembered she'd put the phone in her purse which she'd left in the kitchen. *Dammit*. As much as she loathed seeing Léopold feed, she needed to keep her business running in her absence.

Laryssa discreetly peeked around the corner, glancing down the hallway. Not seeing Arnaud, she kicked off her shoes and quietly padded toward the kitchen. Sneaking around in a dangerous vampire's home was probably not the best idea she'd ever had, but curiosity bit at her, wondering if Léopold did more than *eat* his dinner. As she tiptoed through the foyer into the kitchen, she eyed her purse. By the time she'd snatched her bag off the stool and turned around, movement caught her attention. *Léopold.* His black eyes pierced into hers, while he held the woman's wrist to his mouth. Sophie writhed and moaned his name aloud, much as Laryssa had done when he'd pleasured her earlier. Except unlike Laryssa, she was most definitely climaxing, enjoying the sexual titillation his bite offered her.

A fresh rush of jealousy seized Laryssa's chest at the sight. Unable to watch for a second longer, she ran out of the room, dropping her purse along the way. She stumbled into the guest room, tearing at her clothing, until she wore nothing but her panties. Remembering she'd forgotten to pack a swimsuit, she grabbed a towel out of the bathroom closet. She wrapped it around her as she took off out of the room and down the stairway. Hot tears ran down her face, embarrassed and hurt that Léopold could bring another woman to orgasm after what they'd done together. The splash of reality, that he truly was just using her for her abilities, slapped her. But she'd been so tired of hiding. Even though she'd been scared, Léopold, with his dashing looks and provocative personality, had seemed like he'd be the one person she could finally entrust with her secret. Bathed in confusion and shame, she fumbled through the darkness, guided toward the outdoor lighting.

As she grasped onto the sliding glass door, she yanked at it, easily pulling it open. While she should have been impressed with the elaborate outdoor pool and lounges, it was the vapor from Lake Ponchartrain that drove her onward. Following the patio, her feet eventually touched down upon the cool, dew-covered grass. Even though the yard was pitch-dark, she spotted a small light coming from a dock down by the water. She put one foot in front of the other, quickening her pace until she was awkwardly running, holding the towel in place. No one could stop her from reaching her asylum, she thought. But as she approached the water, the light flickered off, and she heard a low growl. Red eyes glowed in the distance.

"Who's there?" she yelled into the night. Laryssa had never seen the eyes of the dark ones before, yet this had piercing ones that felt as if they were drilling into her gut. The heavy menacing presence she'd felt over the past months was undeniable and all too familiar.

"Laryssa," it snarled, coming into her line of vision. "It's time."

"Time for what?" she asked, terrified at the answer. As it came into view, her chest began to heave as she fought for breath. The creature, covered in black scales, took the shape of a man. Horns curled from its skull, and its blood-red lips drew up in a sickening smile. It extended its claws, stretching and balling its fists.

"Did you think you could avoid me forever? Since you died, you've been mine," it asserted, stepping closer.

"I don't know you." Laryssa's feet inched backward toward the water's edge, but she never took her eyes off of the menacing creature.

"Don't lie!" It snarled, licking its tongue over its lips. "Your soul's mine."

Laryssa frantically began looking around for a weapon. The exhaustion of using her powers earlier had left her weak, but adrenaline could help her to summon it. In the darkness she saw nothing but a boat hanging off its dry dock. Her eyes darted to a log that had washed up onto the sandy beach. It was a small piece of wood. Slowly, she began shuffling toward it, hoping she'd have enough energy left to move it.

"Do you value your life?"

"Get away from me."

"There's nowhere you can go now. Did you really think the vampire could protect you? He has no wards to protect you, little Lyssa."

"What are you?" she asked, focusing on her target.

"Don't you recognize me? It's been many years, I know, but you owe me your soul. And I'll have it."

"You're crazy."

"Sweetheart, you've always belonged to me. But I'd be happy to take little Ava too, if you'd like."

"Fuck you!" she screamed. *How the hell does this thing know the baby's name?* "You'll never get her."

"Oh, I'll get whatever I want. You. Her. And the Tecpatl."

"Tecpatl?" she questioned.

"One week. Bring me the Tlalco Tecpatl or I take the infant."

"I don't know what you're talking about."

"The dagger. You own it, and I must have it."

"Please leave me alone. I can't do this."

"Remember your death, Lyssa? My sweet embrace, taking you home. That bitch stole you, made you into what you are. And now, I'll take you back. We'll be together. I can please you."

The scaly beast transformed into a man. Devilishly good-looking and muscular, it took its cock into its hands, stroking itself. Laryssa felt her lungs cave at the sight. This demon wanted to mate with her? Keep her as its concubine? Shaking, she looked to the broken branch that had washed ashore. If she could gather enough energy to beckon it, she'd have a chance of making it into the water.

"No, no, no, no…" Laryssa repeated, trying to focus on calling forth her power.

She tried to ignore the sight of its growing erection, but found it difficult as the vision of it began to waver from human to demon, and back again. The putrid stench of ash and musk filled the air, making her cringe. It laughed as a greenish fluid began to seep from its hands. The surge of electricity pushed through her cells, singeing her fingertips. As she made her first attempt to bring the makeshift weapon into her hand, the beast lunged at her, its claws extending forward.

"Your skin tempts me. Show me your flesh, little whore," it roared, swiping its talons at her towel.

Laryssa screamed as its red-hot barbs scraped across her chest. The searing pain and horror provoked her power, commanding the log. As it flew into her hands, she swung it at the creature's head, cracking its lip open. The beast snarled and bared its teeth at her but before it had a chance to attack, she jerked her knee up into its aroused groin. Crumpling to the ground in agony, it released a high-pitched wail. Laryssa gasped for breath, faltering down the bank until she reached the water's edge.

"One week," it screeched at her.

Terror brushed her mind as she reached to the gash on her chest. Falling onto her hands and knees, Laryssa crawled into the lake. Letting her body sink into its curative depths, she closed her eyes. Water rushed into her nose and throat, reminding of her of who she was, what she sought to hide. Deliberately she opened her mind to its curative waters, taking in its energy, healing her wounds.

The positively charged ions danced from one molecule to another infusing their energy within her chest, into her bloodstream. As the vital force permeated every cell, her skin began to glow, casting a dim aura around her entire body. Over the years, she'd learned how to control it, retaining the full effect of the water and its illumination. Careening her own strength into focus, she compelled her light. If the creature came at her in the lake, she'd kill it. How she knew she could do so, she wasn't certain. But with every breath of the cold fluid, in and out, the energy built and her confidence in her ability escalated in tandem. Floating down into the lake bed, she rested in quiet apprehension, waiting for her enemy to strike.

·❦· *Chapter Six* ·❦·

Léopold immediately stopped feeding after Laryssa had witnessed Sophie in the throes of her orgasm. Remorse, a distant emotion that he'd long buried, burned through him. It wasn't as if he was ashamed to feed off a human, to be nothing more than he was, a vampire. But he'd deliberately hurt Laryssa, aggressively discouraging her from seeking companionship from a man who wasn't capable of reciprocating.

"Leave it on. Arnaud is going to take you home," Léopold told Sophie, noticing that she'd begun to adjust the blindfold, attempting to see, obviously sensing his discontent.

"But I thought we would…"

"We would what? Have sex? We have a contract through the agency, Sophie. I pay for your services as a donor only. If and when I decide we are to go further, it may proceed. The blindfold stays on. We're finished with our business."

"But you always want to…"

"Tais toi. Not another word. We aren't dating. What happens between us is merely a completion of the food chain. Pay per bite, as you will. If you aren't able to live within the confines of said agreement then I suggest you contact the agency when you return."

"You're a bastard," she huffed, fumbling to adjust her negligee.

"Oui," he responded, unfazed. As soon as she left, he'd request that she no longer be sent to his home. As a result of the pleasure he gave, the donors, both male and female, too often began to develop unhealthy expectations as a result of their exchange. Sophie had become increasingly demanding over the past weeks. Léopold met eyes with Arnaud, who was tidying up in the kitchen. "I'm finished. Please get her out of here."

He felt like an asshole for taunting Laryssa with his donor. He'd specifically chosen Sophie, aware that her physical attributes would draw Laryssa's ire. While there was no denying her outer beauty as defined by societal standards, her lack of personality dulled her allure. No, it was Laryssa who drew his fascination. Léopold reasoned it was merely chemical attraction, driven by pheromones combined with the practicality of the situation, that must be driving him mad with desire for his little rabbit. It amused and impressed him that she'd thrown a piece of furniture at him, standing up for herself, undaunted by his dubious reputation and the reality that he could kill her within seconds. He knew he could have shaken it off, called her foolish for doing so. Whether she'd been conscious or not of the explosive power she was capable of harboring and utilizing on a whim, she'd almost clocked him with the ottoman. But it was her caring nature, selflessly agreeing to walk into the Alpha's den and further, challenging Luca that had displayed her true intrepid nature.

Yet, the woman frustrated him beyond reason. Why wouldn't she just tell him what she was, so they could leverage her abilities? It seemed the prudent and rational thing to do. She was driving him insane with need, and forcing him to extreme measures.

Léopold walked over to the windows, glancing down toward the pool. He'd heard the door slam and known she'd gone swimming. Scanning the veranda, he searched for her lovely body, expecting to see her plotting to inflict torture on him or perhaps a slow miserable death. But instead of finding her brooding on a lounge chair, he saw nothing but the calm blue water shimmering back at him. Where was she?

Panic gripped his chest as he spied fiery red eyes near the dock. The horned creature transformed into a naked man, but he immediately recognized it. A demon? Merde, it had been centuries since he'd seen one out in the open. He cursed as he caught sight of it stroking its dick as Laryssa defensively clutched a towel to her body. The barbarian was jerking off in front of her? Jesus almighty. Léopold readied to materialize to them, and saw the creature lunge toward Laryssa. She flailed a branch at it, and then kicked at its gonads, leveling the beast into the grass. Léopold's heart dropped as she fell screaming to her knees. Enraged, his fangs lengthened and he disappeared into thin air, transforming, intending to kill the beast. But by the time he reached the dock, the demon had dissipated. A revolting smell of rotting flesh lingered in its wake.

"Laryssa!" Léopold screamed out into the yard, unable to find her. Met with silence, he scanned the area, but saw nothing. He raked his hands through his hair, devastated at the possibility that Laryssa had been abducted. A roar of frustration tore through his lungs. He pulled out his cell phone, intending to call Dimitri, when he caught a glimpse of the lambent glimmer rolling through the black waves.

"Laryssa! Laryssa!" he yelled, kicking off his shoes.

Léopold dove into the brisk, murky water, exploring blindly with his hands. Unable to find her, he surfaced, gasped for air and called her name again. Returning into the depths, he plummeted deep into the nebulous reservoir. His body troweled through the vegetation in darkness until a luminous aura appeared. *Laryssa.* Léopold could hardly believe what he was seeing. Her entire body was emitting a fluorescent gleam and her chest moved up and down as if she were breathing on land. Like a firefly, she was lit up, glowing from her forehead over the pale skin of her abdomen to her toes.

He reached for her, concerned that she was dying. As his hand brushed her cheek, her eyes flashed open in alarm. Léopold wished he could somehow communicate that he was attempting to help her as she began to claw at his face and kick her legs. He tried to secure her arms, but she easily slipped out, swimming upward and away.

A touch to her face startled Laryssa's bioluminescent meditation. Renewed terror surged through her mind at the thought that the demon was in the water. Her glow faltered as she used all of her energy to escape. Temporarily unable to see, she shoved at the creature. Frantically swimming, she crested up into the night. The water in her lungs spewed forth and she gasped for breath. She treaded water, swiveling her head side to side in panic, searching for the horned demon. *How did it get in the lake?*

A blood-curdling scream released from her lips as it, too, broke through the watery cloak. It clutched at her arms, and she instinctively brought her knees to her chest and then extended her feet, kicking its chest. Unable to get traction in the aqueous environment, her feet slid downward. She twisted her body, squirming to free herself from its grip. Its hands held tight, and she heard it call her name.

"Laryssa," Léopold grunted as she continued to thrash. Goddess, the woman was strong. "Laryssa, stop," he commanded in a strong, dominant tone. "Enough. It's me. It's Léopold."

"Léopold?" she croaked, forgetting how angry she'd been with him. *Not a demon.*

"Oui. You're safe," he lied as they drifted further away from the coast. Perhaps the demon was gone, but he knew that Lake Ponchartrain could be a dangerous place for even the most experienced swimmers. Besides the treacherous tides and currents, the basin was littered with trees, logs and even glass.

"Is it here?" she cried.

"The demon is gone," he assured her.

Exhausted and relieved, she sagged into his arms and rested her forehead against his chest. It was gone.

"You saw it?" she whispered against his skin.

"Oui, I saw it. Come, let's get inside, ma chérie. It's cold."

Using one arm to paddle, Léopold brought them to the dock. By the time they reached it, Laryssa had begun to shiver uncontrollably and wasn't speaking. Léopold held tight to her, pulling her up the steps with him.

"I can walk," she stammered through chattering teeth. Laryssa wasn't sure what was happening. Normally she never got cold. She reasoned it was the shock of the demon that had done this to her.

"I've got you," Léopold insisted, easily lifting her into his arms.

He cursed, realizing that she was naked save for her panties. Cradling her against him, he knew his own body heat wouldn't sufficiently warm her. He was soaking wet as well, laden down with sodden clothes. He should have asked her before he transported them into his bedroom. But she'd never agree, so he'd made the decision without explanation. Léopold was not surprised when she began mumbling into his chest, complaining about what he'd done. He placed a kiss to her hair, intending to explain to her later about his special ability.

"What did you do? Where are we? Please…" Nausea rose in her belly. Laryssa looked around and realized that Léopold had moved her somehow…without walking. "How did you do that?"

"A conversation for another time, love. Take a few deep breaths. You'll feel better in a minute," he assured her, refusing to put her down. "No time for walking, I'm afraid."

"I don't feel so well," Laryssa slurred. She clumsily pushed at his chest. *How did I get in the house?* Confusion and fogginess blanketed her brain. She swallowed and her breath quickened.

"You're a bit hypothermic is all. Nothing severe, though. Let me look at you." Léopold noted her glassy eyes and the pale color of her skin. Her lips were slightly grayish but not blue. He snatched the comforter off the bed and wrapped it around her.

Reluctantly, he set her into his bed so he could get undressed. He stripped, throwing his lake-soaked clothes aside. Walking into his bathroom, he started a lukewarm shower and then returned to her side.

"How're you feeling?" He asked, gently bending down to eye level.

"Help…help me," she stuttered.

"It's gonna be okay. Easy now." Léopold carefully scooped her up in his arms and took her into the bathroom.

"What're you doing?" she asked, aware of the warmth caressing her skin.

"You're just a little cold from the water. Not surprising given that you were under so long." He unraveled the bedspread, dropping it onto the floor.

"I don't get cold."

"Yeah, you do," Léopold disagreed, stepping into the spray.

"I can go in any water," she insisted. "No matter the temperature."

"See that? You're starting to warm up already," he said, ignoring her comment. He bit his lip, resisting the urge to ask her, 'How's that workin' out for ya?' Yeah, not so well. She could go in any water? What the hell was that supposed to mean?

Part of him wanted to scold her. But he knew in her current state, it wouldn't help the situation. Glancing down, he couldn't avoid noticing how incredibly beautiful she was. Her swollen breasts pressed against his own naked skin, her pink nipples beaded into ripe tips. Goddess, what he would give to take one into his mouth, teasing it further into hardness. He closed his eyes and took a deep breath, willing his dick into submission. *Jesus Christ, already, the woman is suffering and I'm thinking about sex?* He knew it was wrong, but his passion was scarcely controlled.

"Léopold," she whispered, tilting her head upward so that her eyes met his. "I think I can stand. Please."

"Careful." Slowly he let her slide out of his hold but kept his hands on her waist.

"Warmer."

"Hmm?"

"The water. Can you make it warmer?"

"Oui." Léopold reached around her, turning the spigot to the right.

"Ahhh," she purred. Laryssa began to remember what had happened by the lake. *Demon. Rejuvenation. Léopold.* But no matter how hard she racked her mind, she couldn't figure out how he'd brought her to the bedroom. She glanced down to her skin. Realizing she was nude, she covered her breasts with her hands.

"Don't," Léopold told her softly. He reached for her shoulders and slid his hands slowly down her arms, bringing her hands to her sides.

"But I don't have any clothes on..." Her voice was weak. Embarrassed but fatigued, she let him guide her.

"Oui. Nor do I. But we're as we were meant to be. Nous sommes naturel." Léopold let his hands fall to her hips and hooked his thumbs over the sides of her panties. With great patience, he tenderly but deliberately dragged them downward. His lips passed mere inches from her bottom as he bent to remove the dripping undergarment.

"I can't..." she began.

"Don't fret, ma chérie. Let me take care of you," he breathed into her ear.

"No one cares for me." She shook her head, still looking down.

"You're wrong. You have me."

Laryssa exhaled heavily as his breath warmed her ear. Whether it was out of need or defeat, she believed his words as truth. Tendrils of steam poured into the air as she nodded in acceptance.

Léopold removed his hands from her skin and reached for the loofah and soap. Laryssa went to turn her head to see what he was doing when his voice stopped her movement.

"Stay," he directed with a smile, aware that she'd be none too happy with his command.

"I'm not a..."

"Oui. I know, ma chérie...not a dog." He laughed. "You're a woman. A beautiful one at that. Someone who needs lessons in trust, I fear. Will you allow me that much?"

Laryssa didn't answer. The man was incorrigible. Simply unbelievable. But as he swirled the sponge over her back, she sighed, conceding that he was right.

"Yes, yes, I'll trust you. Oh God, that feels so good."

Léopold didn't respond. He merely smiled, continuing to brush his fingertips over her slippery breasts, gliding them across her belly. Dipping further downward, he slid the loofah over her mound. His left hand massaged her shoulder, sloshing the bubbles down her back and into the crevice of her buttocks. Craving her touch, he pressed into her, his cock settling against her silky skin. Léopold dropped the sponge into its wall holder and reached with both hands to deposit a dollop of shampoo into his hand.

He heard Laryssa gasp as he fingered the solution into her hair, frothing it throughout the wisps of her mane. Working from underneath, he tended to her scalp.

Laryssa shuddered in arousal, angry that she could feel this way for a man who'd treated her the way he had. Only earlier, he'd pushed her away, almost enjoying the way he'd played with his food in front of her. She tried to imagine the donor moaning on the couch, Léopold's eyes boring into her. But as quickly as the picture came to her, it faded as he ground his hardness into her ass. Confusion swept through her. She hated herself for how much she wanted this man to touch her and was almost glad he'd finished soaping her skin. But as soon as his hands reached the nape of her neck and began to gently caress her hair, she melted, losing her fight to remain angry with him.

"We need to talk." She couldn't go on like this, naked with Léopold, craving his touch, without discussing what happened. Laryssa knew she'd risk making a fool out of herself, sharing how she felt, but the words began to spill out of her mouth before she could stop them. "Listen, Léopold, I don't know what's going on between us. One minute we're kissing and the next you withdraw. That woman…God, I must be an idiot. I mean the way she was dressed. You can call her food or whatever the hell you want, but I'm a woman and she wasn't gussied up just for dinner. She was practically wearing nothing for Chrissakes. But kissing you and touching you, it felt so good. I haven't been with someone in a long time but you're like this super-old vampire guy and I'm like…well, I'm not a vampire. And you know I haven't been completely honest with you."

Léopold smiled, knowing she couldn't see his reaction. Articulating was an art, he supposed. And given she'd just been thrust into his world, had an encounter with a demon and almost drowned, he assumed he should cut her some slack and let her get whatever she needed to off her chest. He wanted to hear what she was, after all, and he knew she was precariously close to taking a leap of faith.

"It's not like I get naked with every guy I meet and jump in the shower with him."

"I should hope not." He stifled his laughter.

"I was so mad at you. I have no right…I know that. I mean you have to eat. But you…she…and we'd just…you know what you did to me," she sighed. "And what you didn't do."

"Ah, that." This time he did laugh just a little.

"Were you going to sleep with her? Do you have sex with all your donors? I know we just met but I can't do this with you. What I'm trying to say is that there is something about you…about us. God, I know I must be crazy. We just met but I was thinking if we could get to know each other better we could…"

"Make love," he suggested, continuing to wash her hair.

"If you hadn't stopped upstairs, yeah, I guess that could've happened. But you want to know what I am. And there are things I want to tell you. I want so badly to trust someone. I've been alone forever. Well, I've had friends but that doesn't really count. The only person who really knows is Avery, my friend from the club. And now that thing…"

"The demon?"

"Yes. That."

"You can say the word. It is what it is. When you described the eyeless dark ones, I wasn't sure what you were talking about. Now a demon. Well, I haven't seen many but I have seen them before. Nasty lot."

"I don't want to say it. If I say it, it'll…" Maybe she'd watched the Exorcist too many times or maybe it was her lapsed Catholic upbringing, but she didn't want to say its name. It was as though if she acknowledged it, she'd be asking it to show itself. "I don't want it here."

"Saying the word demon won't bring it to you. What does worry me is why a demon would show itself to you in the first place. It wanted something, I take it? Something besides sex." Léopold had a difficult time erasing the image of the beast touching itself in front of Laryssa, reaching for her.

"Yes," she said softly.

"Do you want to tell me?"

"It wanted me to find something, to bring something to it." She closed her eyes trying to remember what it had told her. She'd been terrified and not exactly taking notes as it threatened her. "It began with a T…Tamo? Teca? No it was Tlalco something. Dammit, I can't think of what it was."

Léopold momentarily stopped moving his hands on hearing the ancient Aztec word, but resumed, squeezing the bubbles out of her hair from top to bottom. He didn't want to alarm her.

"Tecpatl?" he suggested.

"Yeah, that sounds right. Tlalco Tecpatl. Do you know what it is?"

"A Tlalco is a knife. One that was used by the Aztecs." *To perform human sacrifice.* "Tecpatl was one of the Gods they worshipped. I've never heard of such a relic but that doesn't mean it doesn't exist. We're going to have to do some research. I'm not exactly sure why the demon wants it, but whatever the reason, I know it can't be good."

"It threatened to take Ava if I didn't get it. And it wants to kill me." *Keep me.* The demon had said she belonged to it. *Mine.* She shuddered, deciding to tell him about the time constraint instead. "Seven days."

"What?"

"It wants it in a week. Like I can find some ancient knife in seven days," she chortled. "What am I supposed to do? Waltz into the natural history museum and say, 'Hey, you don't know me but could you acquisition an Aztec knife and let me borrow it to give to some demon?' Why in the hell would it need me to get it anyway?"

"My best guess is that it has something to do with what you are," he surmised. Léopold carefully turned her to face him, and brushed the back of his knuckles over her cheek. He waited patiently until she finally raised her eyelids, before tilting her head back into the hot spray. Carefully, he fingered her locks, the bubbles falling away to the floor. His cock jerked as she licked her lips, parting them as if she would drink from him.

"I want to tell you," she responded, returning her gaze to his. Her eyes darted to his chest and abdomen before catching a glimpse of his glorious erection. He was the most magnificent male specimen she'd ever seen, beautiful, every inch of him ripped in muscle. She shouldn't have been surprised by the way his groin had been perfectly trimmed, the enormous length of him straining outward. As she realized what she'd been doing, drinking in the sight of him like she'd been admiring a painting in the Metropolitan Museum of Art, she blinked back up to his eyes in embarrassment. When she caught his gaze, her heart pounded in her chest. Desire washed over her once again.

"It's okay, Laryssa," he said. His voice was low and smooth.

"What's okay?"

"To look." Léopold finally gave in to his own craving, allowing his eyes to wander over her glistening breasts. The water droplets ran down like a stream, a small waterfall spilling off her rosy peaks. "To touch." He reached out to caress her neck, but became alarmed as he moved closer. Four deep grooves sliced across her chest, healed but still pink and tender. His fingertip glided over her wounds. "It did this to you, no?"

"I'm okay now," she piped cheerfully, attempting to hide her fear about what had happened. Laryssa heard him growl in displeasure, and placed her hand over his, sensing his anger. "See? It's almost gone."

"You heal quickly. This is your magic?"

"The water, the lake, it healed me. I can't live without it." *I've tried and almost died.*

"You weren't drowning, were you?"

"No."

"You were glowing."

"Yeah, I was."

"I thought you were dying. I'd told you that I'd protect you. And then when you saw Sophie and ran out...I didn't go after you."

"Did you want her?" Laryssa defensively pulled her hand off of his, expecting him to stop touching her.

Léopold gave a small smile and shook his head. The woman didn't get how much of an effect she had on him, how, in the moment, he only wanted her.

"She's your lover?" she asked, wishing she could take back the question. "I'm sorry. I shouldn't have asked. It's just that...if you want to be with me..."

"She's a donor. If you're asking if I've had sex with her, I won't lie. The answer is yes. But she's not my lover or girlfriend or anything of the sort. I've told you that I don't do relationships but..."

"It's none of my business." She tried to back away, but he inched toward her.

"I want you to know that what you saw today was a physical reaction to my bite. Nothing more. We were created that way. Vampires. If our bite brought only pain, we'd have been killed as a race a long time ago. And for those of us who take mates, wives, we must be able to drink from our partners to complete the bond. Perhaps it's an evolutionary adaptation, but some of us are no different from humans in wanting to find a soul mate to spend our lives with. The bite must bring pleasure, great pleasure if it's to be done during sex, many times a day."

Laryssa swallowed. *Sex many times a day? With Léopold?*

"But my impression is that you don't date. Don't 'do relationships' as you say."

"No, but I must eat. It can be an aphrodisiac."

"Are you going to bite me?" she asked softly, her eyes lost in his.

"No."

"No?"

"You, mon lapin, I could never use for just a meal." Léopold closed the distance between them, his hand sliding over her skin.

"Why not?"

"Because, if I tasted of you, I'd need more. Much, much more," he growled. Léopold felt his cock brush her belly, smiling as his rabbit shivered despite the heat. "If I bite you when we make love, I fear a bond could take place. I can't allow that to happen. It's not fair to you."

"Don't you mean 'if we make love?" she quipped.

"No. I mean 'when' we make love," he breathed, leaning forward so his lips touched her ear. His hand slid up from her chest so that he could wrap it around the back of her neck, spearing his fingers into her wet hair.

Laryssa's heart pounded against her ribs. He tempted her, seducing her into his entrancing web. She wanted him to finish what he'd started earlier, taking it to new heights. But the man was frustrating as hell. He wanted to fuck her but he didn't want a relationship? He'd made it clear that not only did he not date, he didn't engage 'friends with benefits' either.

She found it puzzling how a man like Léopold could be so threatened by intimacy. Built like steel, a mind like a razor, he seemed invincible, both physically and mentally. Despite his immortality, the man had survived the centuries well. The vampire, who'd seen wars and plagues, had achieved unfathomable wealth, deliberately shunned others, appeared to relish his self-imposed solitude. While his words spoke clearly of his wishes to remain isolated, he had revealed his ability to connect with the infant. His eyes had lit up when he'd held Ava, sweetly singing to her and putting her to sleep. Even with the other supernatural she'd met at the Alpha's home, she'd observed his interactions, which appeared natural and uninhibited. Whether he'd admit it or not, he cared about them. But perhaps it was because in at least his mind, those were business relationships. There was no pressure or expectations required so he accepted their company more easily.

Kisses to her neck jarred her back to reality. *Shower. Léopold.* She let her hands roam to his chest, trailing her fingers down his firm pecs. Her nipples hardened in arousal, and the ache between her legs grew painful. The temptation was too great for her to resist. She prayed she could do this, have sex with Léopold and walk away unscathed.

"Don't fight this…us," he said, unsure whether he was talking to her or himself. Léopold gave in to his desires, pressing his lips to the softest hollow behind her ear. He was breaking a million of his own rules, he knew. But this woman, whatever she was, he had to have her…to be in her, to possess her. He heard her sigh in response and grazed his cheek against hers.

"Léopold," was all she managed to say before his lips captured hers.

Laryssa gave in to his intoxicating kiss, wrapping her hands around his neck. She could feel her control slip away as his tongue pressed into her mouth. With a demanding fervor, he kissed her, sucking at her lips, tasting her essence. She couldn't get enough of him, needed him closer. Writhing her belly against his cock, she hoped he'd also lose restraint. In response, Léopold dropped his hands to her ass, lifting her upward until she wrapped her legs around his waist.

"More," Laryssa demanded into his mouth. As her pussy opened against his slippery skin, she pumped her hips against his pelvis, seeking relief.

Léopold merely laughed, but never released her lips from his own. He pressed her back against the tiles, holding her still, ceasing her movement. Tightening his grip on her hips, he slid her upward, then down again, her wet folds brushing his abs.

"Oh God," Laryssa moaned, unable to control his actions. All she could do was accept the pleasure he was giving. Every time he pulled her up and then pushed her down, her clit grazed his skin. The sensation was deliciously arousing yet not enough to bring her to orgasm. "Léopold, please."

"You must trust me."

"I'm afraid to," she confessed. He yanked her up hard against him, putting more pressure against her aching nub.

"I'm going to take you every way I want, my sweet. I don't care what you are. I just need to be so far in you that you never forget this night."

"I'm…I'm a…" She sucked a breath as he let her slide away, losing the contact she needed. Laryssa never thought she could come from just a kiss but when his lips teased at hers, her body lit on fire. The energy rose within her and she let it go. She wanted this man, wanted him to know everything about her. No one had ever commanded her sexuality the way he'd done in just a few short hours. God help her, she had to have him in her life.

"Open for me," he told her as his mouth descended on hers.

Thirst rose and Léopold struggled to keep his fangs from descending. Whatever this woman was, he could not resist her. The thought of his cock and teeth buried deep inside of her flashed into his mind, and his stomach clenched in concern. So many years he'd been alone, and for the first time since he'd been turned, the idea of feeding and making love all at once was alluring to him.

As she sucked on his bottom lip, the only thing that became important to him was bringing her to climax.

"Ah yes," she cried again into his mouth as he jerked her body against his.

"Tell me you want this."

"I need you…now…in me now." She wasn't usually so wanton, but damn, he'd refused her once and she wasn't about to let him back away again.

Losing all control, Léopold bent his knees, sheathing himself inside of her. A primal instinct took over as he waited but a second for her to accommodate his size before pumping out and back into her. Dropping his head to her chest, his lips found her breast. He took her ripe tip into his mouth, then sucked it hard, making her cry with pleasure.

Laryssa's breath caught at the welcome erotic intrusion. With unbridled frenzy, she thrust her hips into his, urging him to make love to her harder. His teeth tugged at her perky nipple, causing a sensation of blissful pain, something she'd never experienced in all her life. As he pounded up into her, he began to grind into her pelvis, caressing her clitoris in rhythm with her own movements. So close to going over the edge of orgasm, she dragged her fingernails down his back.

As Léopold's fangs elongated, he was forced to tear his lips away from her shimmering peaks. He could hear her pulse beating and it drove him into an animalistic fervor. Struggling to maintain discipline, he groaned. Just one sweet taste of her blood, and he'd begin a bond with this woman. Focusing on the feel of her tight pussy around his swollen flesh, he thrust up into her with long smooth strokes.

"Please, harder," she begged, panting for breath. Each slamming surge inside of her stroked the thin line of nerves within her channel. "I'm coming...I need to tell you."

What is she saying? Need to tell me what? Léopold couldn't concentrate, lost inside her. He increased the tempo, frantically pounding his cock into her pussy. He pressed his forehead to the cool tile, refusing the temptation to sink his teeth into her inviting skin. *No blood. No damn blood. Just fuck her and be done.* His fangs pierced his own lip in the process.

"Leo," Laryssa cried into his chest as her climax claimed her. She could feel herself spasming around him, unable to stop the crushing waves of power and ecstasy that rolled over her again and again.

"Fuck, yes, I'm coming. Ah, Goddess," Léopold grunted as he jerked fiercely. Stiffening, he came hard, grateful he'd restrained himself.

A few minutes passed before Léopold released her from his grip, gently sliding himself from her warmth. He glanced up to her flushed face, her wide eyes pinned on his. Despite not tasting of her blood, he could feel a connection to this woman. *Jesus Christ Almighty, this is what I've worked so hard to avoid.* He was a fucking asshole for taking her this way, brutally taking her in the shower after she'd been attacked. The shame in his eyes was evident but he doubted she'd know how he felt. Determined not to share his feelings, he wouldn't tell her. But he owed it to her to make sure she was all right.

"Merde, I'm sorry." He shook his head and stepped backward out of her reach. "Are you okay?"

"Why are you sorry? I feel great," she said truthfully. It had been so long since she'd had sex and for the love of all that was holy, she'd reveled in her orgasm.

By the way he was looking at her, she could tell he regretted being with her already. She sighed and turned herself into the spray, washing away the evidence of their love making. *Screw him. I'm not about to let some temperamental vampire make me feel guilty or ashamed for what I did.* If he was looking for a one-off, then that's all it would be. But she'd be damned if she'd let him ruin the afterglow for her. At least for her, life was too damn short not to enjoy mind-blowing sex.

"It's just that I told you," he began.

"Yeah, I know, I know. You don't do relationships. Got it, big guy."

"You were just attacked. You need time to heal…we shouldn't have done this."

"Hey." She turned to face him and poked him in the chest. "Don't you fucking tell me that bullshit, Leo. You hear me? This…whatever this was…was consensual and felt amazing. God, you have issues."

Laryssa looked around the open-blocked shower and tried to find the exit through the steam. Refusing to spend one more second with this man, she moved to get away from him, and he grabbed her hand.

"Please, it's not what you think. I'm sorry. I just wanted to make sure you were okay. I shouldn't have been so rough when we made love." Léopold embraced her. "You're right. It was amazing...you're amazing."

With certainty, Léopold knew that he'd been so wrong about her. No, his Laryssa wasn't a rabbit at all. She was a survivor and a fighter, unafraid to call him out on his atrocious behavior. He closed his eyes, allowing himself to feel every surface of their skin that joined. She and the intimacy she laid at his feet terrified him more than any demon. For the first time in his life, he wondered if he'd be able to continue to live within his own restrictions.

⊸❦· *Chapter Seven* ·❦⊷

Léopold turned on the heat lamp, guiding Laryssa out of the shower. She took in her surroundings, aware that she'd missed them when he'd relocated them from the lake to the bathroom. Italian architecture echoed throughout the space, with its dark mahogany cabinetry and cream marbled floors. Before she had a chance to walk any further, he wrapped a warm towel around her shoulders.

"Let me," he said in a dark low tone.

"But I can dry myself," she protested.

"I insist," he told her, leaving her no quarter for argument. Placing a bath rug on the floor, he knelt before her, bringing the towel from her shoulders with him so that it trailed down her back.

The act of each soft brush of the Egyptian cotton on her skin was the single most intimate touch she'd ever experienced. Laryssa rested her hands on Léopold's shoulders, reflecting on how they had just made love in the shower. They'd been unleashed, utterly wild with desire. Then he'd grown distant. Despite his apology, it was as if he'd turned off a part of himself emotionally. Yet his behavior continued to conflict with the killer he'd touted himself to be.

"What were you going to tell me when I was inside you?" he asked, caressing the towel down her legs. Slowly, he dried each foot, and then drew the terrycloth up her left inner thigh. He repeated the process on her right leg.

"Naiad. I'm a naiad," she confessed. Relief and concern swirled through her mind, but she was soon caught off guard when he glided his fingertips over her mound.

"I love your smooth pussy. Just a little trail of hair here…very pretty," he commented.

"Um, thanks," she laughed. No one she'd ever been with had ever commented on her lady garden, let alone been on his knees in front of her inspecting it like he was looking at a rare flower. "Aren't you going to say anything?"

"I want to lick you until you can't speak your own name. Shall we give it a try?" He glanced up to her, catching her gaze and gave her a naughty grin.

"Okay. Well that sounds really nice and all, but didn't you just say that we couldn't do this?" She pointed to the shower then to her chest and to him. "Not that I'm disagreeing with you. That sounds pretty tempting to me, but you seem to have a problem deciding whether or not you want to be with me."

"Pas de problème, ma chérie. I want you, don't ever doubt that. It's the bond, the emotions that can form.

Complications and such. I suppose I am wavering. On my knees before you, the only thing I can think of is how much I want to drag my tongue over your pink lips."

"If you don't stop, I'm going to demand it. Seriously, Leo, aren't you going to say anything? After everything I just told you...about what I am and you haven't said one word about it." As much as she wanted to discuss it, the idea of Léopold giving her oral sex was extraordinarily attractive. She grew wet with arousal again and she knew he'd smell it on her.

"Well how am I supposed to concentrate when I'm so close to you like this? You taste sweet, no?" Léopold leaned forward and darted his tongue through her slit, tracing over her beaded treasure until he felt her shiver into his mouth. He licked his lips like a satisfied cat. "Ah, oui. Délicieux."

"Léopold," Laryssa cried. *What is it with this man? He must be well versed in the fine art of torture.* She couldn't decide whether or not to grab his hair, and encourage him to finish what he'd started or slap him out of frustration. But before she had a chance to make a final decision, he quickly patted her pussy dry and had pushed onto his feet, standing before her.

"A nymph, oui?"

"Kind of...I guess."

"Here, put this on." He handed her his bathrobe. "I cannot concentrate on a single word you're saying when you're like this."

"You mean like this?" She smiled and took the black garment from his hands. Refusing to put it on, she draped it over her forearm and put her hand on her hip, giving him a full view of her body.

"Exactly like that. Now, put it on." He wrapped his towel around his waist and walked out into the bedroom.

"You're very bossy for someone who was just on his knees," she commented flippantly.

"You're a bit mouthy for someone who was just screaming my name," he countered.

"Should I give you the pleasure of being on your knees again, I'll try to keep that in mind." She rolled her eyes and put on the bathrobe. "So what? No questions? No 'what else can you do'? Or does the wise one already know all there is to know about naiads?"

"Come sit." He gestured to a double width chaise that curved on both ends. Lined in copper studs, its brown leather appeared well conditioned but comfortably worn.

Wide eyed and incredulous, Laryssa stared at him.

"Please sit," he drawled.

"See? That wasn't so difficult, now was it?" She sashayed past Leo, trailing a finger over his bare chest, giving him a flirty smile. Sitting down into the lounge, she curled into it like a kitten and laid her head back on the cushion.

"You are a difficult woman, no?"

"Oui," she teased.

"We need to talk, Laryssa." Léopold walked over to a large antique armoire and opened its doors. Pulling out a decanter and two snifters he set them on his desk and began to pour them a drink. "I've met a few nymphs, but I've never seen one do what you do. While they're known in mythology to be dangerous, I've never met one that was. Aside from needing water, drawing energy from water, I haven't ever met one who could move objects. Here," he said, extending the glass to her.

With a small smile, she accepted it. She shook her head, amused, but not surprised that he hadn't bothered to ask her if she even wanted a drink. He was aggravating yet undeniably thoughtful.

"Thanks."

"You're very welcome," he replied, sensing her internal struggle with his dominance. "Now tell me, were you born naiad? It's rumored you are created as goddesses of the rivers. Some say the daughters of Zeus. Others? The daughters of Poseidon. I, however, believe mythology to be just that...a myth. The supernatural world, through magic or perhaps evolution has created splinter races."

"I wasn't born naiad. I'm human...or I should say, was human. Raised in a small town in Ohio...just like everyone else."

"How'd it happen?" Léopold sidled up next to Laryssa, wrapping an arm around her.

"I died. Well, I drowned. But I'm pretty sure I died."

"How?"

"I was thirteen. Mom had told me not to go skating alone, but my friend, Lauren couldn't go with me that day. And as you may have noticed, I'm determined when I want to be."

"Stubborn? Really? I don't believe it," he said, his words laced in sarcasm.

"I prefer the term 'strong willed'. It's an asset, you know?"

"Whatever you say, ma chérie. Go on."

"Long story short, I lied. I told mom Lauren was going when she wasn't. It had been at freezing temps for over a week. The ice should've been strong, but as I found out, it was thin near where the creek spilled into the lake. It was stupid of me, I know. But I was just a kid. I can still remember the loud sound, the creaking. And then I saw the crack. The ice began shifting. I tried to skate off to get to the other side, but I wasn't fast enough. It all happened pretty quickly."

Laryssa took a sip of her brandy. It was such a long time ago, but she'd never forget the helplessness as she slipped into her icy grave. Screaming as she plunged into the abyss, she knew no one would hear her.

"I'm not sure exactly what happened. I just remember panicking, scraping at the sheets of ice, trying to get leverage to pull myself out. I really tried so hard to get out, but the longer I struggled...I got so tired. I couldn't think straight and my hands," Laryssa pulled at her fingers, remembering the way the cold had immobilized them, "I remember slipping into the icy pond, unable to hold on and then gasping for air. And once I was all the way underneath the water, I couldn't stop from breathing it in. The water, it just suffocated me."

Léopold put down his drink on the floor and gently took her hands in his, massaging her palms with his thumbs.

"I don't know…it was dark. But then all of a sudden, it was light. Not like how people describe when they are dying with *the* light…you know, the one they say you'll see when you die. This was different. There was no tunnel or anything. Just this bright light and then this woman was there, and she was talking to me like we weren't underneath the water. She told me she was naiad and that she was giving me her gift."

"And then you woke up?"

"Well, not exactly. I mean, the woman, she was so calm and beautiful. I can still remember she had this flowing, fiery red hair and it was kind of fanned out in the water, like these magical little tendrils dancing. I don't remember much after seeing her. Only that just for a second, right before I woke up, I felt this darkness…kinda how it felt tonight. It all was so fast, though."

"Did they find you?"

"Well, yeah. My friend had called the house while I was out, and I was totally busted. When my parents found out that I wasn't with Lauren, they went to the lake, saw my gear on the edge of it but not me. I didn't regain consciousness until I was in the ambulance. I'd been under for nearly an hour and a half. They called it a miracle…at least until I came home."

"Is that when you realized your abilities?"

"You know, it just seemed like a dream. All of it. Dying. Seeing that woman. The darkness. Waking up and then in the hospital, I was just me. I didn't feel any different. But within a week of being home, I started to notice this energy...my energy. I can't explain it but I became obsessed with the lake. I'd sneak out of my parents' house. At first, I'd just submerge my hands. And then one day, a few months later, I became angry about something. I was in my room and instead of picking up a pillow to throw it, I just thought it, like I was going to grab it but I hadn't. It flew across the room."

"That must have been scary, no? I remember how it felt after I was turned. No one had mentored me either," he mused.

"I was scared to death. I thought I was going crazy but I remembered that one word. *Naiad.* I went to the library and researched everything I could find about naiads, which wasn't exactly helpful because as you pointed out, most of what people know is just mythology. Not exactly reality."

"And your parents?"

"They weren't having any of it. They are very, very conservative. Of course, I hid it at first. But when my mom caught me moving things in my room, the next thing I knew they had the priest at the house. They thought I was possessed or something. When they caught me a second time, my mother slapped me across the face, grounded me. And the third time…well, they sent me off to live with my aunt in Chicago."

"How old were you?"

"Fifteen. Aunt Mary wasn't too bad but she wasn't exactly the best role model…drank way too much and brought home lots of strange men. The one thing she did teach me was waitressing. She got me a job at her diner. The day after I graduated high school, I left for Vegas using the money I saved."

"Not much water in the Mojave desert."

"Yeah. I never realized how much of a problem that would be. What can I say? I was young and naïve. I just wanted to get away, to disappear. I knew how to waitress and I thought, 'why not Vegas?'"

"Ah, the lessons of youth."

"In hindsight, I should have known it wasn't a good idea. When I was first changed, putting my hands in a pond or a river was enough to satisfy my need for water. Of course, I tried a pool but that didn't work. It's not part of nature. Anyhow, by the time I moved in with my aunt, I'd begun swimming in fresh water at least once a week. I think she knew that I was sneaking out to Lake Michigan, but she never said anything. It wasn't until my sixteenth birthday that I started to realize that I needed the water in order to thrive. If I didn't go, I'd be exhausted, barely waking up or able to go to school. The longer I went without it, the weaker I'd get. When I got to Las Vegas, though, that's when I learned the hard lesson that if I don't have it, I'll die."

"I imagine a water nymph wouldn't do so well there."

"Yeah, I'm not sure what I thought at the time. Have you ever been to Vegas in July? It's hotter than hell. I'd just turned eighteen and was working in this little all-night diner, staying in a fleabag motel." Laryssa swiped her hand across her eyes. "It was awful. But it was the first time that there was no one to answer to about my 'abilities', no one to make me feel bad about what I was doing. In the end, I only lasted a few months. I had to go all the way out to Lake Mead for my water. I was only going maybe once every two weeks. I knew it wasn't enough, but I couldn't find the time with my work schedule. Also, I think I really just wanted to be normal, so I'd convince myself that I didn't need the water. Denial is a wonderful thing…well, until I crashed. One night I went out to the desert with a friend, I almost died. I should've known. I'd been feeling sick all week."

"A boyfriend?" Léopold shouldn't care, he knew, yet an unfamiliar pain of irritation jabbed at his chest. *Jealousy?* He dismissed it as soon as he thought the word. *Possessiveness perhaps?* Yes, that was more his style. Léopold collected, possessed…*things* that belonged to him.

"No. Yes. Well, it was a guy that I'd seen a few times. You know, we'd fooled around."

"Fooled around?"

"Yeah, you know. We dated. Kissed. I think he may have gotten a little further, but we didn't have sex."

"I see." Léopold remained calm and indifferent. But a fire grew behind his eyes as he thought of Laryssa kissing someone else. *No, this can't happen to me. I don't care who she dated.* As she continued her story, he fought to concentrate, disturbed by his own revelation that he didn't think he'd be able to tolerate her seeing other men, not ever again.

"Where was I?" From her position in his arms, Laryssa was unable to see the look of consternation Léopold wore. Taking a deep breath, she continued. "The desert. By the time we got out there, I was so lethargic that I couldn't get out of his car. I felt myself dying. I begged him to drive me to the lake, to put me in the water. God, I can't imagine what he thought. I was like a crazy woman going on and on about needing water. He had to carry and literally dump me in the lake."

Léopold laughed.

"Hey, be nice." She gave him a small nudge with her elbow. "It wasn't funny. So you can imagine what happened next?"

"I'm afraid to ask." He'd seen the way she'd peacefully lay at the bottom of Lake Ponchartrain, but to a human, she may have appeared dead.

"You saw it, didn't you?" Laryssa turned in his arms so that she could look into his eyes.

"I saw you all right. I thought you were drowning...but you were beautiful. You lit up the water."

"The water. It feeds me energy. I don't know the exact science behind it."

"There's science to being a vampire, witch or wolf?" He laughed.

"Point taken. But you have to remember, and you've got to know what this feels like because you were turned, not born a vampire, there is this human part of me that seeks answers. Not nebulous magic fairy answers. Hard facts."

"I do remember, but I've lived a long time. There are some things in our lives that are better left a mystery."

"Yes, but my glowing?"

Léopold smiled as he recalled the sight of her naked form illuminating the entire lake bed. It had startled him, but also had been a spectacular display.

"From a scientific standpoint, it's bioluminescence. It's found in plants, animals, even insects."

"But not humans," he replied.

"Exactly. The guy, I was with in the desert... I think his name was Scott, well, he completely freaked out. Not only did I go into the water, sinking clear to the bottom, I lit up like a Christmas tree. Twenty minutes later when I re-emerged, he was gone. I knew he'd tell everyone at work, so I hitched a ride back to the motel, packed my stuff and drove cross country to New Orleans. It was embarrassing, but it was also a wake-up call. It sure as hell snapped me out of my denial. Once I got here, I worked for a few months before getting a scholarship to the University. I studied art history. After undergrad, I took on a graduate assistantship, got my masters."

"Lots of water, here, that's for sure."

"Yeah, it's a good place for me. I pretty much stick to the river. It's close. Easy access. I don't get out here too often, but the basin works. Bayou, too. The humidity in the air helps."

"When did you first start seeing the dark ones?"

"Pretty much as soon as I got here. My friend, Avery, the witch I told you about, she was my roommate. I needed to confide in someone. Not only was she supportive, but she began right away creating spells and wards to hide me, my energy. I'd go a few years not seeing any of them and then, 'bam', one would show up in an alleyway. Avery would work her magic and then I'd disappear again...like they couldn't see me. When you saw me at Mordez, I was there to talk to Avery."

"I've never seen you there before," he commented, brushing a hair from her face.

"And you would know this how?" she teased. Laryssa inwardly cringed, thinking of what Léopold did at that place. Sex, blood, dancing and pretty much whatever a supernatural craved could be found there.

"I think you know the answer to that," he replied without apology. Not only did he frequent the establishment when he was in town, he'd engaged in about every activity they had to offer. If he told her what he'd done, she'd really know the beast she'd just made love to. The knowledge of his true behavior would sever whatever attraction they had. For the rest of tonight, at least, he'd save her that anguish.

"Avery said she couldn't help me, that she needed to talk with Ilsbeth. I'm not crazy about her telling the leader of her coven, but I'm desperate. That same dreadful feeling that came over me tonight when I talked to the demon… it's been plaguing me for weeks."

"We should've talked with Ilsbeth today. Unfortunately, she's been out of town."

"Couldn't we FaceTime or Skype?"

Léopold laughed. "High tech solutions to low tech problems. Ilsbeth prefers her meetings in person. She wants to read auras, get a feel for the people she decides to help."

"But she's a witch. What does she know about naiads or demons for that matter?"

"Ilsbeth knows lots of things. I find her a bit of an ice queen, but the woman may be able to help us. She's been around longer than you can imagine and keeps her spoon in many pots."

"Why do you think this demon wants Ava?" Laryssa asked.

"Not sure, but I do know it tried to kill her."

"I've only met one other naiad before. She was here for a convention and came into my store. Her energy was so compelling. I couldn't ignore it. So I confronted her, got her to have lunch with me."

"You're tough, aren't you, pet?"

"She described the same type of experience I had. She'd gone swimming in a lake as a child and drowned. She died." Laryssa paused, trying to figure out how the baby was turned. "This might sound crazy but what if Ava died too?"

"But she was alive when I took her from the snow. Trust me, I know dead, and she was very much alive."

"She could have died before you heard her. Maybe she died and then began to cry when she was touched by the woman who touched me," Laryssa speculated.

"Okay, but she wasn't in water," Léopold replied.

"No, but she was in snow. Snow is just another state of water."

"It's not possible. Even if she had died, we have no connection as to why the demon would target her. The Alpha did tell us that she'd glowed before she'd been stolen, and also said something about an evil presence…like you've described. But we still don't know where the father is, if he's alive or not. We only know that her mother died."

"It's not Ava. She's not evil. I can feel her. She's pure and sweet. Her aura was shining brightly when you held her. A lovely yellow color. I guess I forgot the part about reading auras…I think I was around sixteen when I started noticing the colors," she commented.

"And what does my aura tell you?" Léopold asked.

"Hmm…let's see." Laryssa slowly climbed atop of Léopold, straddling him with her legs. Spearing her fingers into the back of his hair, she tilted her head and licked her lips. "Ah yes, I see it now. Your aura shows that you enjoy telling people what to do. You're dominant in all aspects of your life, expecting everyone to submit to the mighty vampire you know you are. You keep people at a distance, pushing them away so you don't have to feel. You've been hurt, maybe? So you run hot and cold with your emotions…well, mostly cold. But beneath the surface of what we all see, you have unbridled passion in your mind and heart. And you're a highly sexual being. One who craves a certain brunette naiad but won't admit he wants to kiss her, to make her yours."

"You're making this up, aren't you?" In a flash, Léopold had her in his arms and tossed her onto his bed. She landed on her back, giggling.

"I think I could make some extra money in Jackson Square telling fortunes. What do you think?" she laughed.

"You lie, temptress," he growled with a devious smile. Léopold leapt upon her. Placing each of his knees to the side of her waist, he tore off his towel. Effectively immobilizing her hips with his own, he adjusted his semi-erect cock so that it lay heavy on her belly.

"I told you. You don't scare me," she taunted.

Laryssa took in the sight of him, hovering above her like a Greek God. Léopold's ordinarily neatly combed hair was messy and damp. His taut muscles strained as he poised to attack. She knew he'd been careful not to hurt her when he threw her onto the sheets, but he left no doubt that he sought to assert his dominance. Even in play, he was forceful, demanding. Like a feral wolf, he flashed his fangs, stalking his prey. Unable to resist the allure of her sexy predator, she reached her hand upward and traced the tip of her forefinger along his bottom lip.

"You like to play with fire, no?" Clutching the lapels of her robe, Léopold jerked it open, exposing her creamy breasts.

Laryssa gasped as the cool air hit her skin. She closed her eyes and took a deep breath. As her hooded eyes opened slowly, a wide smile broke across her face.

"I want to touch them."

"What?"

"I said I. Want. To. Touch. Them." She extenuated every word before reaching up to his mouth.

Léopold could not believe this woman showed no fear. Hundreds of women had flirted with him, attempted seduction but underneath all their acts, they all bled fear as well as blood. As she trailed the pad of her thumb down his fang, he sucked a breath. *Fuck, what is she doing? Does she have a death wish?* The sound of her sweet laughter filled the room as she plunged her finger into his mouth. His lips captured her thumb like a frog catching a fly. Swirling his tongue over her skin, he smiled until he heard her moan. Only seconds passed before he once again took control.

"Léopold," Laryssa cried as he snatched her wrists and pinned her to the bed. She attempted to move but he'd effectively restrained her. The sensation of being trapped beneath him caused her to grow wet with arousal. But as she tried to move her hips, he applied more pressure, further stilling her movement.

"Going somewhere?"

"Let me go," she demanded. Her back arched as he blew warm air over her nipples. The low rumble of his laughter wrapped around her, promising her pleasure. The bare flesh between her legs moistened, and she was left quivering with need.

"Would you like to read my aura now?" He asked as he settled his chin into the hollow between her breasts. With his eyes on hers, he brushed his lips against her hot skin.

"I don't need to read your aura to know that you'll lose."

"I never lose."

"You'll lose your fight to keep your heart closed." Laryssa tugged again at her arms, relishing the tightness of his grip.

"Perhaps I should gag my little naiad. There are many things you don't know about me."

"There're many things you don't know about me either," she countered. Using her feet, she pressed her hips upward, slowly grinding her body into his. "It's true that I tremble, but that's not fear you detect. It's desire."

"Don't test me, pet. Make no mistake, this isn't play." As he said the words, he prayed it to be true. Her arousal was as fragrant to him as an expensive Parisian perfume. The enticing scent permeated the room, driving him mad. She mocked him. She thirsted for him. He should walk away, leave her alone. But as his tongue probed one of her throbbing peaks, he knew in that moment that he had to finish the game. Like every being in the city, she was his to take.

"Ah, but it is you who errs, Leo. I know full well what I'm doing." *Oh God I hope so. This vampire could break my heart.* His lips on her sensitive nipples. His smooth voice in her ears. His colossal strength wrapped around her like a steel band. It was all too much to resist. Hell, she didn't want to even try. She just wanted to feel and have him feel every shiver he caused.

"You're a brave one. Bewitching." Léopold smiled and captured her breast in his mouth, rolling its tip with his tongue. She moaned in response, and he sucked it hard, careful not to nick her with his teeth.

"Oh my God!" she screamed at the pain. Her core pulsed in response. A hot ache grew in her belly, one that only he could satisfy.

"You continue to surprise me, Laryssa. You sass me yet wish to submit?"

"No," she lied. "It's not true."

"Oui. Your body doesn't lie." Léopold pressed her left wrist into her other, shackling both of her arms, freeing his right hand.

"No, no, no." She continued to deny it, shaking her head. "You don't know me. You don't want to know me."

"You challenge me?" If she only knew how wrong she was. Every second he spent with her would make it more difficult for him to let her go. He wanted to know everything about her from what she liked to eat for breakfast to how many strokes it took to push her over the edge of orgasm.

"It's not a challenge. It's just that...well, you've been clear."

"I thought we already established that I want you very much. Do not change the subject. Look at the way your skin flushes, unable to move. You like this, no?"

"I don't...I can't," she whispered. *Why is he pushing me? What difference does it make if I like it or not?* In the morning, he'd leave her. He didn't want her in his life.

"Shall we see?" Léopold reached between her legs, spreading her slick folds apart. He flickered the tips of his fingers at her entrance, not yet penetrating her heat. As he did so, she cried out his name. "So very wet. Ah, you lie about what you desire...you fancy this, don't you? You do. I think you'll enjoy your submission quite nicely."

"It doesn't matter," she gritted out, panting. She squeezed her legs together trying to assuage the growing pressure but he removed his hand and gave a light tap to her mound.

"No cheating. No coming yet, pet. And oui, it very much matters." Slowly, he glided his fingers back through her slippery lips, avoiding her clitoris. He caught her gaze and gave her a sensual smile. "It was you who read my aura. You started this and now I intend to finish it. My fortune teller thinks I'm dominant, no? I may not be able to read an aura, but your pussy tells me all I need to know. Your body doesn't lie, but I want to hear it from your lips. Tell me, ma chérie, do you want me to dominate you?"

"No...yes. I don't know."

Without warning Léopold thrust a thick finger into her, making her groan in pleasure. He could feel her contracting around him, certain she enjoyed it.

"Oh God, yes."

"So willing and submissive when given the freedom to be so." He yearned to break her, to make her want only him.

"Léopold, please. No more games," she cried as he added another finger. Her satiny flesh tightened around him, anticipating every stroke he gave.

"I don't play games."

"Now it's you who lies," she moaned as he continued to draw out the tension, edging her closer toward climax.

"No games. No lies. Do you, little nymph, wish to submit to me? A fantasy, perhaps?" Léopold speculated that she'd spent so many years hiding not only her identity but her wish to explore her own sexuality. Her ragged breaths grew more frequent as he moved deep within her. Pressing his chest against her belly, he brushed his lips against hers.

"Yes. Oh God, yes!" she screamed as she began to convulse at his hand. Laryssa hated that he knew her dark secret, loved that he wasn't afraid to push her boundaries. Rocked by uncontrollable pleasure, a tear of bliss ran down her cheek.

Léopold slipped his fingers away, driving the hard length of his cock inside her in one swift motion. Without haste, he tenderly made love to her. Releasing her wrists, he braced himself with one hand, so as not to crush her, and with his other, cupped her cheek so that he could gaze into her eyes. The moisture brimming from her lids provided evidence of the implications of what they'd done by having sex. Emotions he hadn't felt in centuries welled up inside his chest. Laryssa was so much more than he'd ever expected. There'd be no meaningless fuck with her. No, if given the opportunity, he'd realize his true desire, which was to know everything about her, to make her his. The sweet pain of his epiphany tore at him, knowing that he couldn't keep her.

"You fascinate me, Laryssa. So very, very beautiful," he confided breathlessly, crushing his lips to hers.

Pouring all of the feelings he'd never confess to her, he kissed her passionately as if he'd never see her again. All of Laryssa's thoughts vanished, replaced with nothing but the vampire who held her in his arms. As he swept his tongue against hers, claiming her mouth, she welcomed the intimacy of his onslaught. Kissing, sucking, tasting of each other, their bodies became one.

As their kiss deepened, they moved simultaneously, slowly increasing the tempo of their rhythm. Léopold's hands glided down her sides, finally reaching her hips. Deliberately, he began to circle his pelvis against hers, stimulating her most sensitive flesh.

"You feel so fucking good," he grunted. .

"So close. Don't stop," she begged, tearing her lips away, gasping for air. Laryssa arched her back, rubbing herself against him.

Léopold rocked faster and faster, brushing back and forth against her clitoris. The spasms of her hot core pulsed around his cock, causing him to suck in a quick breath. She shivered beneath him and he could no longer stop the inevitable. With slamming thrusts, he pounded into her as she cried his name again and again.

Seized in ecstasy, Laryssa surged her hips up to meet his. As her release slammed into her, she stiffened against him, milking every spasm. Her head thrashed side to side, her nails digging into his buttocks. As pleasure claimed her, Léopold gave a loud grunt, erupting deep inside her. Together, they lay motionless as the last quivering pulses rolled through them.

Laryssa curled her body against Léopold as he slowly removed his spent shaft from inside her and brought her up onto his chest. Terrified to look into his eyes, she silently wiped at the tears that continued to fall. *How stupid am I to think that I could make love with someone like Léopold and walk away with my heart intact?*

Powerful and charismatic, Léopold had cut through her defenses as easily as a hot knife sliced through butter. If she stayed with him a minute longer, he'd push her to new heights. Not only would she submit to him sexually, she'd give him her heart. And he'd crush it. With a firm resolve, she vowed to herself that this would be the last time she made love to him. Gorgeous and dominant, he was everything she'd ever want in a lover. But he'd been clear about his intentions from the beginning. They had no future.

Léopold felt her trembling in his arms. No words were needed to tell him what they both knew to be true. Making love had been a spectacular, earth-shattering experience, cloaked in satisfaction but also a sense of loss. It couldn't happen again. Staring at the ceiling, Léopold stroked her hair, hoping it would offer her the comfort she needed to let go. But as he did so, he wondered where he'd get the strength to do the same.

❦ *Chapter Eight* ❦

"Bonjour, mon ami," Léopold commented as he strode into the great room, giving a wave to Dimitri. "See you got my text. Arnaud saw to your arrival?"

"Yeah, got it last night at around four in the morning. You vamps really don't sleep, do you?" Dimitri asked, taking a long draw of his coffee.

"I rest when I need it. Besides, as you know, I prefer the night. Why today's supernaturals wish to walk in the daylight is beyond comprehension. The night is the mother of our strength. Why subject yourself to being the likeness of a human in the sun when you can be a mighty lion by the moon?"

"Well, I'm with you there. I do love a good moon." Dimitri gave a guttural howl and laughed. Some days he couldn't get enough of teasing the vampire. Most days, actually. "Hey, you remember meeting Jake, right?"

"Oui." Léopold rolled his eyes in response to the wolf's incessant howling. He nodded and passed by them into the kitchen.

"Gotcha a café au lait. It's on the counter."

"Merci." Léopold opened the lid of the paper cup and sniffed. "Nectar of the Gods."

"See, he still acts normal every now and then," Dimitri joked to Jake.

"Doesn't seem right, is all."

"I need blood to survive. Coffee, on the other hand, just tastes good. It's not as if I can't appreciate the finer epicurean delights that life has to offer." Léopold circled the table and sat down.

"I've seen some of your so-called epicurean delights and they all look female," Dimitri noted.

"Pleasure comes in all forms," he smiled.

Dimitri eyed Léopold as it occurred to him that his typically well-dressed friend was wearing nothing more than black pajama bottoms. His disheveled state piqued his curiosity.

"Hey Leo, what's with the shirtless look today?" Dimitri glanced at Jake and smiled. "Or is it that maybe Mr. GQ is finally loosening up?"

"He definitely works out a lot. Makes me want to get to the gym," Jake added, giving Dimitri a grin.

"Must be that all-protein diet regimen."

"Fuck you," Léopold laughed. "You do realize that when we're turned as adults, we stay in that form. But yeah, smartass, I work out."

"How'd you get so ripped? What'd you do in a previous life? Let me guess…a body builder? No wait. A lifeguard?" Jake suggested.

"Come on. Just look at him." Dimitri glanced to Léopold. "Too pale."

"A gym trainer?" Jake teased.

"No way. He's an old man. As in really old. Maybe a farmer…workin' the vineyards of France. Or, uh, soldier. Yeah, that's more like Leo. Some medieval black ops badass," Dimitri guessed.

Léopold smiled broadly and shook his head.

"That's it." Dimitri pointed at him. "I'm close, aren't I?"

Léopold sighed, debating whether or not to disclose his former profession. He didn't make a habit of discussing his life as a human. Too many bad memories. Yet, there was a camaraderie that he missed that existed when he'd served in the king's service, one that was similar to what wolves shared. He knew, though they baited him, they sought to create a connection. Dimitri already had his trust, his friendship.

"Oui. A knight. I served under King Hugh Capet. I was a warrior in his service in exchange for a fief, of course."

"Damn, bro, you've been holdin' out on me. I bet you have some great stories." Dimitri smacked his palm on the table in jest.

"Life was hard, very hard. France was merely coming together on its own when I was born. My stories will wait for another day, though. We should discuss today's agenda."

"You see how he does that?" Dimitri asked.

"Does what?" Jake looked to him and then Léopold, who was smiling.

"Avoids the topic. The man is smooth. Still haven't answered my original question, Sir Leo the vamp."

"What was the question?"

"Why aren't you dressed? I wasn't born yesterday. I know you, Leo. You're the most impeccable metrosexual guy I know. And here you are this morning, hair flying all over and half dressed. For the rest of us, totally normal. For you? Not so much. What gives?"

"Nothing at all. I heard you all jabbering about in my house and came to see what the fuss was about." He smiled coyly and raised his eyebrows.

Dimitri eyed Jake and then glanced to Léopold who silently sipped his coffee. He may not have known the vampire very long, but he knew his habits. Something was off. And then it occurred to him that he hadn't seen Laryssa. There was no way in hell that Léopold would be so casual with a woman in the house unless…

"How's Laryssa?" Dimitri asked pointedly. His eyes darted to Jake.

"She's fine," Léopold lied. He expected that Laryssa was as far from fine as she could get. At some point during the evening, she'd broken free of his embrace. She'd curled onto her side, facing away from him. Despite her ability to do so, she hadn't hidden her racing heartbeat. He'd known she was awake yet said nothing. After an hour, she threw back the covers and left the room, without looking back at him. No words. No kiss goodbye. Cold sheets were left in her wake. He should be happy, he knew. It was what he wanted, yet the loss of her bothered him far more than it should.

"You mentioned a demon. Where'd it show itself?" Dimitri asked.

"Down at the lake." Léopold nodded toward the windows.

"It came to you directly?"

"No, to Laryssa. I tried to get there in time, but she'd fallen into the lake."

"What? Somehow it took Laryssa from your house down to the lake?"

"No. She went down to the lake and it appeared to her there," Léopold told him without fully explaining.

"Am I missing something? I thought you said you were going to be with her," Jake interjected.

"I was with her, but then dinner arrived and well, you know…things became awkward. She was supposed to be going for a swim in the pool, not the damn lake."

"Wait a second. Let me get this straight. You bring a hot woman to your house. Then at some point you invite a donor over…aka hot chick number two. So Laryssa takes off out of disgust for your eating habits. Some people aren't a fan of blood," Dimitri conjectured. "Or she takes off because she's not into threesomes. Maybe jealous? Maybe she wanted one of those sex bites, herself?"

"Enough already," Léopold demanded. "I needed to feed. I will not deny who I am just because I foolishly decided to protect some woman. And just because Laryssa is 'hot' as you've put it, that doesn't mean I'm going to become attached to her."

"So you're telling me that when she left this house, she was a-okay with your, uh, naked takeout girl?"

Léopold sighed and stood up from the table. Glancing out onto the lake, he recalled the previous evening, how angry she'd been.

"No, she wasn't. She wasn't at all happy. But that is neither here nor there. What's done is done. She went to the lake and the demon appeared. It's given her one week to find the Tecpatl. The Tlalco Tecpatl to be exact."

"What the hell is a Tecpatl?" Dimitri got up from the table and placed his empty cup in the trash.

"An ancient sacrificial knife used by the Aztecs," Jake answered.

"How the hell did you know that?" Dimitri stared over to Jake in disbelief.

"I'm a fan of Mesoamerican history," he quipped.

"He's correct," Léopold affirmed.

"Human sacrifice. Gory shit," Jake added.

"You wolves do have a way with words," Léopold mused.

"So, how about Laryssa? Is she okay?" Dimitri inquired, still suspicious of the vampire's unkempt appearance.

"It clawed at her, but she fought it off and then it was gone."

"Did you just say it clawed at her? Is she hurt?" Dimitri approached Léopold so that they stood shoulder to shoulder, taking in the landscape. It was the first time he'd been to Léopold's lake house.

"No, she's fine, but…" Léopold didn't finish his sentence.

"But what? Exactly how does someone get swiped by a demon and be fine?"

"She's healed." While she was sleeping, he'd inspected the wound and not a trace of a scar was evident.

"I take it this has something to do with what she does?"

"Indeed, mon ami. But I promised her that I wouldn't tell anyone what she is, so don't bother asking. It's her story to tell. You can ask her when she comes out. My guess is that after that demon showed up, she'll tell you. But I cannot break my oath to her. I've already done enough to hurt her on my own without digging the hole any deeper," Léopold confessed. Turning to Dimitri, he raked his hand through his tousled hair.

Dimitri leaned toward his friend and sniffed. He shook his head, knowing the answer to the next question he was about to ask Léopold. "You fucked her didn't you? I can smell it."

"Must you be so uncouth?" Léopold replied, blowing out a breath.

"You did," Dimitri exclaimed. "Jesus Christ, Leo. Seriously, man. You can have any woman you want. Why her? You ever hear that expression, 'don't dip your pen in the company ink'?"

"Yes, I've fucking heard it, asshole. But she's just so...I don't know, she's just special. Goddammit, I know, okay? I know I fucked up."

"I don't see what the issue is here. I mean have you two idiots ever heard the term 'consenting adults'. What's the big deal?" Jake asked.

"The big deal is that he just fucking met her. And we need her to help us to keep Ava safe. If she's in danger, so is our Alpha. Laryssa was just starting to trust us, trust him, and lover boy here just can't keep it in his pants," Dimitri huffed, taking a seat at the table.

"He's right. There's no excuse," Léopold agreed. "It's not sleeping with a woman that's a problem, it's the fact that I can't...I won't have a relationship. It's not happening. And now that we've made love, well, it adds complications to our situation. Ones we didn't need."

"It would be one thing if you actually cared about anything besides yourself, Devereoux. But you don't. That's the thing. If you fucking hurt her..." Dimitri began.

"Why do you care about her anyway, wolf?" Léopold's eyes narrowed on Dimitri.

"Because, Leo," Dimitri stared at his friend. "She seemed kind of nice. And she stood up to that asshole, Luca. And for some reason, unbeknownst to me, she seems like she might actually care about you. Why is beyond me. And she cares about Ava too, and she has no reason to. We are the ones who sought her out. Now, not only have we upturned her life, we've brought a demon to her...right here to your goddamn house."

"I think we've established that I fucked up. I just said so. Can we just move on?"

"She's okay with one night? Because I know that you never have women sleepover. You've told me as much."

"I told her that I don't do relationships. I can't become involved with her. But you're correct in that we do need her. We need to find that knife."

"This isn't going to go well, you know that, right? I mean, I don't know Laryssa, but I saw the way she looked at you yesterday, and I have a hard time believing she's a one night stand kinda girl. Could be wrong? But damn, it was as if she had 'innocence' stamped on her forehead," Dimitri said.

"Please stop already. Okay?" Léopold tilted his head backwards, closed his eyes and wiped them with both of his hands out of frustration. "I get it. I'm a dick. I shouldn't have slept with her but I did. I can't take it back. I promise you that I'll do my best to repair this...'relationship' I've irresponsibly put at risk."

He choked on the word. *Relationship. No, no, no.* As if it wasn't bad enough that he was developing feelings for Laryssa, now Dimitri had him filled with guilt for what he'd done. Damn wolves. Damn humans. For a moment, he wished he could go back to not caring about his new friend. But no matter how he tried, what was done was done. *Merde. I'm truly fucked.*

Laryssa heard shouting coming from the great room and thought to give them fair warning she was approaching. Dimitri had mentioned her name, and she suspected that whatever they were arguing about, it had to do with her. As curious as she was, she was still reeling from her night with Léopold.

Earlier, she'd gone to take a shower to wash away the memories of her night with him, hoping it'd make her forget the way he'd stirred passion within her. It wasn't as if she hadn't felt his heat mere inches away from her body as they lay in bed. She'd known that even the slightest brush of her skin against his would have broken her resolve to leave. She'd been awake for hours, sensing that he was watching her. But not a word was spoken, nor a caress exchanged. The heavy tension had strangled her, causing her to flee.

The hot spray of the shower had matched the tears that fell down her face. As a vampire, she'd known that he'd hear her. So with every heaving breath, she stifled the sound. Thirty minutes later, she'd convinced herself that her good old-fashioned cry was due to the stress of keeping her secret for so long. Her intense reaction to making love was simply lust, nothing more. She told herself that she needed to think with her head, not what her heart told her it wanted. He'd been up front about his intentions, unbending in his ways. She supposed she'd just have to accept it. She wasn't foolish enough to try to change a man. It'd never work, she knew.

Still, as she stood drying her skin, disappointment washed over her, as she realized he hadn't come after her. The reality of the situation was that she'd just had a one night stand. Whatever she thought she felt, she swore to bury it so deep that she wouldn't feel a thing the next time she saw him.

But as she walked into the room, her eyes flashed to Léopold's and a rush of excitement tightened in her belly. *No, Laryssa don't.* Struggling to get control over her reaction, she averted her eyes to the two good-looking men who sat at the kitchen table. She remembered the tall man with the goatee and tattoos as the person who'd driven her to Logan's home. Dimitri, beta of Acadian wolves. The other man looked as if he was a soldier, with his square jaw and tightly cropped hair.

"Good morning," Laryssa said loudly, interrupting their quarrel.

"Laryssa," Léopold sighed, giving her a small smile.

"Léopold. Um, hi." Hearing her name on Léopold's lips startled Laryssa. The last time he'd said her name with his French accent in that low smooth tone, he'd been buried deep inside her.

Léopold, at a loss for words, let his eyes roam over Laryssa. With only a touch of light pink gloss to her lips and very little makeup, Laryssa displayed an innate beauty he suspected she didn't realize existed. Loose brunette curls fell unrestrained over her shoulders, complementing the tight white shirt that clung to her curves. Her black jeans with matching leather riding boots gave her a contemporary look, tempting him to run his hands over her hips and buttocks. A hungry smile emerged across his face as he wondered if she'd enjoy a riding crop.

He sniffed into the air, enthralled with the ambrosial aroma of her essence that he'd remembered from the night before. Only now she smelled like soap and almonds. Underneath it all, her natural scent remained ingrained in his mind. The urge to taste her overwhelmed him and his gums tingled in response, his fangs begging to release. He glanced to the wolves, who had been watching him like a hawk. Slapped into reality by Dimitri's grimace, he broke out of his spell, and quickly concealed his reaction to her.

"You remember Dimitri and Jake from yesterday, no? Let's see, I have breakfast for you. Arnaud brought it. I'd texted him while you were sleeping. I hope you like fruit. Some pastries. Let me see what he brought." *Merde, I sound like a love-struck fool.* Léopold cringed at how he was speaking to her in front of Dimitri and Jake. Quickly, he rummaged through his refrigerator, retrieving the items he'd asked Arnaud to bring and set them on the counter. He pulled a plate, flatware and napkin out of his cupboards and placed them on the breakfast bar, away from the wolves. "Here you go. Dimitri brought coffee."

"Thank you," she quietly replied. Giving a small smile to Dimitri and Jake, she sat down on a stool and stared at the feast that was big enough for ten people. "There's plenty here. Maybe we should put it all on the table. Would you guys like some?"

"Thank you, Laryssa," Dimitri said, thoroughly enjoying watching his friend squirm. "At least someone here has manners, huh, Jake?"

"Hey, why didn't you serve us? I'd love some mango," Jake added.

"Because if I'd offered it to you first there'd be nothing left for the lady. Dogs get scraps," Léopold countered.

"Hey, hey, hey. No need to get nasty, bro. We brought coffee. Just sayin'," Dimitri teased.

"Yeah, right." The truth of the matter was that Léopold had simply forgotten about the food. As he pulled out extra plates from a cabinet, he glanced over to see her taking a bite of a strawberry and nearly dropped them. The juice dripped down over her pink lips and she caught it, licking her finger.

"Don't you love fruit?" Dimitri asked, smiling like a Cheshire cat. Léopold had it bad, and it was even funnier that he kept saying that he didn't want a relationship. Maybe this wasn't exactly a relationship, but Laryssa was definitely having an effect on him.

"Tais-toi," Léopold scolded, annoyed that Dimitri and Jake were practically undressing her with their eyes as she ate. The more he told himself he shouldn't care, the closer he was to throwing her over his shoulder and taking her to his bedroom.

"Come on, man. You know I've got this thing about watching girls with food."

Laryssa looked over at Dimitri, hearing his comment and laughed.

"Come sit with me. Please. There's plenty here for all of us. Ya'll are making me self-conscious watching me stuff my face." She patted the seat of the chair next to her.

"I'd love to," Dimitri said and obediently sat down. "See how nice your girlfriend is. You could teach him some manners."

"I'm not his girlfriend. We barely know each other," she stated calmly with her eyes pinned on Léopold's.

"Really?" Dimitri inquired. He glanced at Léopold who stood smoldering across the counter.

"Really," Léopold agreed. He detected a flash of hurt in Laryssa's eyes as he confirmed her statement.

Laryssa glared at Léopold then forced herself to look away. There was no way she'd let him see how angry she was, at him, at herself. She'd known she'd set him up when she denied being his girlfriend. She'd told the truth, obviously, because he agreed that she wasn't. What was worse was that it was apparent that her shower had done little to tamp down her attraction to him.

"We have much work to do today. I'm going to go get ready. Can you two conduct yourselves like gentlemen around her while I'm gone?" Léopold asked, walking away toward the hallway.

"From where I'm sittin', I'm not the one she has to worry about." Dimitri laughed as the vampire spun around and gave him a scowl.

"Behave," Léopold ordered right before he slammed his bedroom door.

"He's got issues. Treats people like they're house pets. Seriously," Laryssa noted.

Jake and Dimitri broke up laughing.

"It's true," she smiled, taking another bite of her danish.

"Amazing how you can spend a short amount of time with someone and get to know them so well." Dimitri put some fruit on a plate and began to eat. "I understand you had a run in with a demon last night. How're you feelin', cher?"

"I'm good. The marks are gone." She rubbed her hand above her breast where it'd scratched her.

"Glad to hear you're okay. That's some pretty quick healing, though. Now I know you're not a wolf. Or a vampire. You seem a little like a witch but that's not it either. Maybe a fae?" he guessed.

"Didn't he tell you already?" Laryssa asked.

"No. Despite spitting tacks and needles, Leo's got a sense of honor. He said he promised you that he wouldn't tell anyone."

"A sense of honor, huh?" Léopold had kept her secret. Why couldn't he have just betrayed her? She wanted a reason to hate him, to make her feel anything other than what she was feeling. Not only had he thought of her, getting her breakfast, he'd kept their conversation in confidence.

"He did tell us what happened last night," Dimitri told her, his expression growing serious.

"Everything?" she gaped. *What exactly had he told him?*

"Well, yeah, the bit about you going off to the lake."

"He was busy," she said coolly, recalling how she'd seen him biting his donor, her moans of pleasure. Foolishly, she had given into her own primal urges and she'd been the one making similar sounds hours later.

"Yeah, about that. You do know he's a vampire, right?"

"Hard to forget."

"I just want to make sure because I'm not sure what we're gonna be doin' today or where this is going to lead us, and he is what he is. You can't be runnin' off when he…" Dimitri's words trailed off as he took a few minutes to think of the best way to say what he was thinking. He didn't want to scare her, but not only did he turn wolf, Léopold was nothing short of deadly when he perceived danger.

"When he what?"

"When he becomes who he is. Obviously, you've seen the fangs and well, it just is in his nature. The women and men, the donors…he needs to feed. Now I'm not sure what you think you saw him doing with that woman last night, but he really does try to make his bite painless."

"And you would know this how?" Jake asked, grabbing a donut from the plate. He smiled and walked over to the windows.

"I know, okay?"

"But that woman…" Laryssa began.

"Let's just say that I'm experienced in the way of the bite," Dimitri explained.

"You let a vamp bite you?" Jake laughed.

"Yeah, I did."

"You let *him* bite you, didn't you?" Laryssa inferred, shocked at what he was telling her.

"It was out of necessity. Trust me. He was in bad shape and well, yeah. But believe me, he didn't want to do it. I guess I should've listened to his warning, because the way it felt…"

"Please stop talking," Jake urged. "My virgin ears don't want to hear this. You and Léopold. No."

"Fuck you. We didn't have sex. That is exactly the presumptuous attitude that causes problems. My point is," he turned to Laryssa, "that vampires have two ways to bite. Pain or pleasure. And he's gotta eat. So there ya go."

"I can guess which way he went with you," Jake jibed.

"Shut it, Jake. Can't you see I'm trying to clue Laryssa in on my vast knowledge of the vamp world so she doesn't freak out again?"

"You're a real doctor Phil."

Laryssa laughed.

"Seriously. The guy has to eat," Dimitri argued.

"If she didn't like the sight of his fangs, just wait until she sees yours, wolfman," Jake said.

"Jake brings up a good point….even if he's being kind of a dick." Dimitri glared at him and then continued talking to Laryssa. "I know you have kind of kept yourself out of the supernatural world and I'm sure you have your reasons, but he's right. At the first sign of danger, there's a good chance I'm gonna strip down and go wolf. I may not be able to respond with words, but I'll be able to understand you."

"Did you just say you're going to strip?" A huge smile broke across her face. She looked at Dimitri and then Jake, and couldn't help but picture them naked. Laryssa's face heated and began to turn pink.

"Yeah, we love to go nudie, baby." Dimitri laughed. "Seriously, though, you can't run off when you see my wolf. I won't hurt you. And neither will Jake, here."

"Thanks for letting me know. It's not every day that I see men taking off their clothes and turning into little furry animals," she giggled.

"Wolves. Big ferocious wolves," Jake insisted. "Jeez, this woman knows how to hurt a guy's ego. Maybe she wants a demonstration right now." He began to unbuckle his pants.

"No, no I don't." Laryssa covered her eyes and started laughing even harder.

"Easy, Jake. Keep your pants on. Leo's gonna kill us if he comes out here and sees you showin' your junk to his girl."

"I'm not his girl," she insisted.

"Yeah, whatever you say, cher. Okay we showed you ours…ready to show us yours?"

"Well, I didn't exactly get to see the show," she remarked with a grin. "But I do appreciate you telling me about your wolf thing you do…even if I didn't get to see you change. I will, however, take a rain check on that one."

"Hey, I can show you," Jake challenged.

"Not here. I'm tellin' you both, Léopold will freak. As much as my boy enjoys a good romp in the hay, he's just getting used to the nudity thing." Dimitri had seen the way Léopold was looking at Laryssa. Léopold could think whatever he wanted about his no relationship rule, but there was no denying the possessive way he was acting around her. What happened between the two of them remained to be seen, but if Laryssa was a bone, he didn't want to pick a fight with the big dog in the bedroom who thought it was his.

"As much as I'd love to see you change, and I really would, I think that maybe Dimitri's right on this. Léopold can get a bit cranky." In truth, she'd like to make him jealous, but playing games with his friends wasn't her style. She found herself drawn to Dimitri, though. His honesty was refreshing. It didn't take her but a few minutes to realize that she wanted to share with them what she'd told Léopold. "Okay, I'll show you mine. Ready, boys?"

"Hell yeah, let's go," Dimitri said.

Laryssa got up off her stool and moved toward the center of the great room. Dimitri stood and walked over to Jake, who was intently watching. She smiled at Jake and extended her hand to him, letting her energy focus toward her target. His donut flew straight out of his hand and into her own.

"Got it," she laughed and took a bite. "I'm a naiad."

"Damn, bro, she just took your donut." Dimitri clapped his hand on Jake's shoulder.

"Hey, now. Was that necessary?" Jake said, feigning indignation. He licked his fingers and grinned.

"She's amazing, isn't she?" Léopold appeared seemingly out of nowhere. *Goddess, she was showing them what she was and demonstrating her powers.* Either she was completely unaware of how powerful Dimitri and Jake were as wolves or incredibly brave.

Surprised to hear Léopold's voice, Laryssa jumped when he came up behind her and kissed her neck, his masculine scent spiraling into her senses. The man was dizzying and delicious. For a long minute, she felt herself melt into his embrace, closing her eyes. But Dimitri's cough reminded her that they weren't alone and that Léopold didn't want her. Her eyes flashed open and she turned to face him.

"You're beautiful," Léopold praised, his eyes drifting from hers down to her parted lips. Her alluring kiss lingered within inches. The temptation was so great, yet he knew he shouldn't.

"I, uh, I was just showing Dimitri and Jake what I can do," she stammered. Breaking free of his arms, she recoiled, realizing that she'd almost kissed him. Needing distance, she crossed the room and took a sip of her lukewarm coffee.

"A naiad, huh? Isn't that some kind of a water-being?" Dimitri asked, closing his fists. He resisted the urge to drag Léopold out of the room and have another chat with him regarding his intentions with Laryssa.

"A mermaid?" Jake guessed.

"More like a nymph," Léopold corrected. He brushed past her, twirling his finger into a curl of her hair, then let it drop. "A freshwater nymph."

"Not a mermaid. No tail or scales. Just me." Laryssa's skin tingled from Léopold's touch. She couldn't take her eyes off of him. He smiled at her as he popped a blackberry into his mouth. He wasn't playing fair. Shit, he wasn't supposed to be playing at all. *How am I supposed to ever forget him and our night together if he plans on flirting with me all day?*

"Nice trick with the donut, cher. Can you move heavier things?" Dimitri asked Laryssa.

"Yes, that and more, mon ami," Léopold answered for her, enjoying her eyes on him. Try as he might, he couldn't deny himself. Like a lure, she fascinated him. Watching her enchant the wolves with her engaging personality only made her more enticing. "We can discuss it on the way over to Ilsbeth's. We've got an appointment with a shrewd witch. Best not be late."

Laryssa shook her head at Léopold. The man was impossible. Larger than life, he exuded charisma and magnetism, entrapping her emotions. She glanced over to Dimitri who gave her a sympathetic smile. He knew, she thought. She couldn't decide whether she should feel embarrassed or relieved. Lost in thought, she gasped as Léopold took her hand.

"Come, ma chérie. I promise to look after you today," he whispered in her ear.

As she looked into his eyes, she knew she was in serious trouble. Her heart squeezed in her chest as he ushered her out of his home.

⚜ *Chapter Nine* ⚜

On the short ride into the city, Laryssa had carefully positioned herself as close to the rear side door as she could get in an effort to keep her leg from brushing up against Léopold's. Dressed in an Italian trim-fitting grey suit, he'd casually interject his opinion into the conversation, always giving her a sexy smile in the process. Taking time to undo the top button of his white fitted shirt was the only semblance of discomfort he displayed. Exuding confidence and strength, he'd insisted that he sit with her in the back seat for her protection. Neither Jake nor Dimitri had argued, but simply acquiesced to his demand.

Stealing glances at him, her eyes always found his. It was as if he knew when she'd look, what she'd say, making her feel as if he'd known her for a long time. Her thoughts drifted to the way he'd held her down, forcing her to admit she enjoyed her submission. If she'd allowed herself to think of what Léopold had done to her for even a second longer, they'd all know what she was thinking.

Quickly remembering she was in a car filled with supernatural men, she diverted her mind to a less sexually arousing memory: the demon. Its memory brought an unsurpassed surge of fear to her psyche, one that left her praying she'd survive what was to come. One week. It'd given her one week. She took a deep breath and blew it out, attempting to calm her nerves.

"It's going to be all right," Léopold assured her. He'd sensed her arousal, yet as quickly as it had begun, it was gone, replaced with anxiety. In response, he'd placed his hand atop her thigh, seeking to comfort her. The heat sizzled beneath his flesh. She was fully dressed, but she might as well have been bare to him. Léopold despised his growing need for Laryssa yet all he could think about was making her his.

"You sure you can trust her? Ilsbeth?" Laryssa looked into Léopold's eyes, searching for the truth.

"Ilsbeth and I have known each other throughout centuries. She's a difficult woman, but trust her? Oui, I do," he affirmed.

Léopold's touch warmed her leg, and Laryssa continued to have difficulty separating herself from her feelings toward the debonair vampire. One minute he was cruel, agreeing that she was nothing more than someone he'd met. The next, he possessively kissed her. His caring words, the caress to her leg gave her reason to suspect that he couldn't live within his own rules. She sought to squelch the optimistic thought, that he wanted more than just one night, but his actions spoke louder than his words. Unable to withstand the temptation, she placed her hand on his, completing their connection.

After driving through an ornate wrought iron gate, their car circled in front of Ilsbeth's home. As it came to a stop, Léopold exited first, then rounded the vehicle to open the door for Laryssa. Along with Dimitri and Jake, they made their way up a wide slate staircase that led toward the spectacular home. Its second and third floor windows, adorned in rock, stood watch over the meticulously manicured gardens. A pentagram, nearly eight feet in diameter, garnished the apex of a magnificent dormer that sat perched above the main entrance. As they passed through one of the seven enormous stone arches that led onto the porch, Léopold took Laryssa's hand into his.

Dimitri forged ahead of the group so he could announce their arrival. As he went to ring the bell, the door opened before he had a chance to press the button. Laryssa's friend Avery stood in the archway, smiling.

"You're here," she called. With a gleam in her eye, she spied Laryssa and pulled her into the foyer.

"Avery, I hoped you'd be here but I wasn't sure. This place is so…" Laryssa hugged her friend but quickly released her, taking in her surroundings.

"I know, right? It's amazing. Ilsbeth has a place in the Quarter, but this is where we come for special events. It's her home. No one else lives here," she whispered.

Rose-colored plastered walls with ornate crown molding gave way to a cathedral ceiling. Flecks of speckled light danced on the stone floors. Illuminated by daylight streaming through stained glass skylights, the foyer felt spacious yet it had been closed off from all other rooms and hallways. A corner staircase led to a balcony above, where a grand piano sat untouched. As the wooden front door closed, creaking alerted them of side doors being opened and an ethereal presence called Léopold's name.

Laryssa tightened her grip on Avery's hand as the panels disappeared into the walls and a beautiful woman with long platinum blonde hair glided into the room. Petite, dressed in a purple, crushed velvet jacket with matching pants, she exuded a preternatural aura. But as she began to speak, it was clear that she was very much of this world.

"Léopold, so very good to see you again." Ilsbeth gave him a smile, and waited patiently as he kissed the back of her hand.

"Ilsbeth, you're lovely as usual," he complimented, releasing her wrist.

"This is Laryssa," he told her. Laryssa let go of Avery's hand and reached for Léopold's. "Laryssa. This is Ilsbeth. Maîtresse des sorcières."

"Hello," Laryssa said softly, unsure if there was some kind of special witch protocol she should be following.

"The nymph?" Ilsbeth looked to Léopold for confirmation but Laryssa took the lead.

"A naiad. How'd you know? Did Léopold tell you?"

"No need to fret, my dear. Léopold has kept your secret. But as you will soon find out, I know lots of things." Ilsbeth sharply turned her head toward Dimitri and Jake. An imperceptible flash of fury glinted in her eyes. "Dimitri? What are you doing here? Léopold, you didn't mention that you've been keeping company with wolves."

"Hey, cher. I told Léopold you'd be happy to see me. Good to see you again, too." Dimitri grinned and gave her a small wave from a safe distance. He supposed that he should have told Léopold that he'd slept with the witch. Some things were better left as surprises. The witch was as gorgeous as he'd remembered. Their affair had burned hot, but fizzled out just as quickly. In truth, it had been more of an explosive ending. Quite the argument, as he recalled. His eyes darted over to Léopold, who glared at him. Offering a compliment, he sought to smooth over the awkwardness of the situation. "Ilsbeth, you're lookin' beautiful as always."

"I see you haven't lost your silver tongue," she remarked, turning away from him.

"Missed it, did you?"

"Hardly."

"As I recall, you seemed to enjoy my tongue." Dimitri regretted his words as soon as he said them, catching Léopold's look of disgust.

"Tais toi," Léopold chided. *Damn wolf.* Léopold made a gesture as if he was zipping his lips and nodded angrily toward the entrance, urging Dimitri to shut up and follow her.

"Come, we shall chat," she told them. Ilsbeth continued to ignore Dimitri, walking into the other room.

Dimitri shrugged at Léopold, giving him a devious smile. Léopold shook his head, trying to stifle a smile. The wolf didn't need encouragement to get in any more trouble, he thought.

Laryssa followed into the dimly lit room. Candles in assorted sizes and colors flickered atop the fireplace mantle while streams of light poured through thin rectangular floor to ceiling windows. Léopold took her hand in his, and they sat down in a chenille-covered love seat directly across from Ilsbeth, who reclined in a single high-backed chair. Dimitri and Jake made their way to an adjacent sofa. When they were all seated, Ilsbeth nodded over to Avery, who left them in the room, closing the doors behind her.

"What brings you to me today?" Ilsbeth began. "I'm delighted to meet a naiad. Very rare, indeed."

"There's a child, too," Laryssa told her. "I've only met one other like me."

"A child? Interesting." Ilsbeth raised an eyebrow at Léopold.

"Un bébé. I found her in the snow. In Wyoming. Yellowstone," he disclosed. His eyes met Dimitri's before returning to Ilsbeth's. "She'd been stolen from the Alpha's den. Someone tried to murder her."

"Hunter Livingston's pack?"

"Oui."

"Did you find her before or after she died?"

"Quoi? She's alive. Logan Reynaud is providing refuge. Kade and Luca are helping as well. We're the only ones who know of her existence."

"I asked, 'did you find her before or after she died'?" Ilsbeth repeated her question.

"I died," Laryssa told her, realizing that Ilsbeth had confirmed what she'd suspected to be true. "Why do you think Ava died?"

"Because, my dear nymph, this is how you're made. Naiads are not born. They are created, granted the gift of life through the water."

"The baby was alive when I found her," Léopold claimed.

"Touched by the lady, she awakens new. But as a child, she's not fully grasped her powers nor does she need water to survive. When she turns of age, she will blossom like a flower. Her price is water. But this cannot be why you've sought my assistance."

"We appreciate you sharing your vast knowledge, but we have a bigger problem. A demon. It seeks something from Laryssa," Léopold divulged.

"A knife," Laryssa added.

"A sacrificial knife. Tlalco Tecpatl," Léopold told her.

"Ah, I see. It seeks a relic. The Aztec civilization worshipped many different gods, you know. Throughout any given year, sacrifice came in many forms, but human blood was, indeed, spilled. No class of their society was spared in the rituals. Men, women, children, even infants, all died for the greater good," Ilsbeth lectured.

"Or so they believed. Mesoamerican history. It's a hobby," Jake made invisible quote marks with his fingers, "Let's just say not all the 'sacrifices' went willingly on the way up to get their beating heart cut out."

"They tore out their hearts? I thought that stuff was just in the movies." Laryssa cringed.

"'Fraid not. It was done at different times of the year, with specific kinds of victims as a way to give an offering so to speak, sometimes to help the gods do their job. They needed help with survival, their land, growing crops and such."

"What kind of gods would want death?" Laryssa challenged.

"There were many times during the year that human sacrifice was required. It was pretty much a monthly event. As for which gods? You know…the usual suspects. Rain. Sun. Wind."

"And water. Let's not forget the goddess responsible for water." Ilsbeth's mouth drew tight as the others anticipated her next words. "Chalchiuhtlicue. Some say she was married to the rain god. Some say she was the sister. Counterparts perhaps?"

"So with all this sacrifice going on, I imagine that brings about some bad juju," Dimitri surmised.

"Whether these ancient gods and goddesses exist or existed, is of little consequence. What is of importance is that there are beings who revel in death. Torture. Murder. Evil thrives on it. Like spores in a petri dish, the heat of evil cultivates the seed, it grows," Ilsbeth told them.

"Grows into what?" Laryssa asked her. A pregnant pause filled the room. "What does it grow into?"

"Demons," Ilsbeth responded.

"But I thought *demons* were kind of like fallen angels." Laryssa pensively pressed her lips together. She hated even saying the word.

"Indeed, they are lost to the underworld. But demons can be called to the surface by the nefarious intentions of the flesh, by man," Ilsbeth explained. "It is why we do not speak of the one they serve. The heinous act of the taking of innocent lives, through means such as human sacrifice, can summon forth a demon into our world, albeit temporarily. Even while in their netherworld, they seek to steal souls...often during death. More often than not, the soul does not belong to them."

"Death?" Laryssa asked.

"Indeed. Tell me, Laryssa," Ilsbeth stood from her chair. She walked over to an antique oak apothecary cabinet, which spanned an entire wall of the room. Its bottom half housed hundreds of square drawers, neatly labeled and organized, each with its own brass label finger pull handle. Bottles and containers of various sizes lined the five rows of wooden shelves. "What did you see when you died? A light?"

"No, nothing like that. It was peaceful but all I really saw was this lady. She was glowing and then she touched me, sending me back. But..." Laryssa tried to recall the experience. It sounded crazy, she knew. "I didn't see it. I just felt it. Something dark. Like when I see the hollow-eyed people that come after me…the dark ones. I don't just see them. I can feel them, the evil, down to my bones. I guess Avery told you about them. She's been helping me hide for so many years."

"The Lady stole you from the demon. Or at least this is what it perceives. It was there, trying to take you. You did not have a clear death. No, for naiads, they see the Lady."

"But who is she?"

"Some think she is Chalchiuhtlicue herself…giving life or taking it away as she sees fit. A deity of water, she rules the lakes, the rivers. Even childbirth. Or rebirth, perhaps? Others disagree with this hypothesis entirely, calling naiads daughters of Zeus or Poseidon. Whoever the Lady is, she grants life to young women who die within her arms. But there's a price that comes with the breath of life she breathes into her chosen ones."

"The water," Laryssa whispered.

"You can't live without it. Stray too far from her home and you will die."

"Why does a demon want an ancient Aztec knife? And why does it need her to get it?" Léopold inquired, reaching for Laryssa's hand. "It's given us a week to find it. It's threatening to kill the infant."

"All very good questions." Ilsbeth slid open a drawer and pulled out a clothed item. Setting it on the counter, she reached for a small clear glass bottle and uncorked it. "I'm very happy to help you, provide answers to what you seek, but as Léopold knows, I do not assist without remuneration. You see, as a witch, I cast many spells.

Spells which require ingredients. Some are quite common. Like castor oil, for example. Or yarrow root. There're things more difficult to acquire, such as, shifter hair. You know, like wolf hair, perhaps freshly ripped from its root." she gave Dimitri a cold smile and continued. "But it is the very rare ingredients that I treasure. Like a scale of a virgin dragon, perhaps. Or the fang of a vampire."

Dimitri's eyes darted to Léopold. He wished like hell his friend could read minds because he knew as sure as he was sitting in the room what Ilsbeth was going to ask...demand. He'd given her his own hair as a peace offering. He offered. She took. He was still waiting on the peace.

"You can see that when I'm presented with such a prize, I must have it. The blood of a naiad. Now that is very rare, indeed."

"No fucking way," Léopold told her, jumping to his feet.

Placing himself between Laryssa and Ilsbeth, he protectively guarded her. The wolves followed his lead, readying for attack. Shocked at the suggestion that Ilsbeth would ask for her blood, Laryssa clasped at Léopold's shoulders, hoisting herself to her feet.

"Tsk, Tsk, Léopold. You were always such an alarmist. Really, it's just a tiny bit of blood I need." She held up the bottle to the light and then set it down. Methodically, she unfolded the cloth, revealing a simple brass athame. "But it must come willingly or else it shall be tainted. It must be a gift. A gift in exchange for my knowledge and advice. I believe it's a fair arrangement."

"No. There must be another way," Léopold stormed. No way in hell was he letting that devious witch cut open Laryssa, slitting her like a chicken's throat.

"I'll do it," Laryssa volunteered. Her voice was soft but strong as she pushed past Léopold.

Dimitri fell back into the sofa, aware that Léopold was about to go ballistic. He nodded to Jake who followed his actions.

"What the hell do you think you're doing, Laryssa? No way. As in, no way in hell am I letting you do this," Léopold raged, blocking her way.

"I've got to do this," she told him firmly.

"No, you don't. We'll find another way."

"We can't afford to waste time. Ilsbeth can help us. You saw what happened to me last night." Laryssa's eyes brimmed in moisture as she raised her hand to him, gently caressing his cheek. "You must trust me. Please, Leo. I need answers."

Her pleading tore at his heart. *Goddammit.* He knew she needed answers, but why the hell did it need to involve knives and blood? Her blood? It was true; they had little time to find what the demon sought. Perhaps even less time to find a way to kill it. With his eyes on hers, he solemnly nodded in agreement.

"I'll be okay," she told Léopold as he kissed her palm. He held her wrist but she pulled away, walking toward Ilsbeth. "Let's do this thing."

"Naiads are known for their bravery. That is also why some see them as dangerous. Come give me your wrist," Ilsbeth instructed.

Laryssa pushed up her sleeve, allowing Ilsbeth to take her arm. Léopold came up behind her, surrounding her with his strength. She felt him support her forearm, his warm breath on her ear.

"I won't let anything happen to you, ma chérie," he whispered, with a kiss to her neck. His eyes caught Ilsbeth who was watching him like a hawk. "Be gentle with her."

"Léopold, darling. You act as if I'm a novice witch wielding a kitchen cleaver. Would you like a demonstration of my power?" She smiled while busily preparing the bottle with a glass funnel. Ilsbeth found Léopold's fascination with Laryssa interesting. Well aware of Léopold's limited capacity for expressing his emotions, she grew concerned.

"No, I don't. But heed my words. Be careful," he grumbled.

"Can we just get this over with? How bad can it be? Now that we're on the topic, why can't we just do it like they do at the doctor's office? Haven't witches heard of hypodermic needles? They hurt, too, but very efficient. Safe." Laryssa's eyes widened as Ilsbeth held the shiny athame up to the sky as if she were worshipping the sun. *Why the hell did I volunteer to do this again? Oh yeah, scaly demon from hell. Wants to make me his bitch.* Nervously, she bit her lip as the witch began to chant. "Hey, don't you think that you should use alcohol? I don't want to get some kind of an infection."

Laryssa tried to control her racing pulse, but lost her concentration. Her eyes widened as Ilsbeth seized her wrist. If it weren't for Léopold's calming presence behind her, she would have bolted out the door.

"Seriously, I think I might have an alcohol pad in my purse somewhere. Ahhhhh," she screamed as the blade sliced through her skin. Her natural instinct was to pull her arm away, but the damn witch was strong, holding the dripping wound over the funnel. "Shit, that hurts. Fuck. Fuck. Fuck. Okay, I think that is enough. You said you only needed a few drops."

"You're okay, mon amour," Léopold whispered.

Mon amour. Did that arrogant vampire just call me his love in front of all these people?

"Mon amour? Seriously? I thought we just agreed that I wasn't your girlfriend, mister 'I don't do relationships'?" she jibed. Laryssa tried to turn her head to yell at him but he easily held her in place. His laughter filled her ears. "Okay, look, the bottle is halfway full already. I hope someone brought orange juice. Or cookies. Sweet baby Jesus, that hurts."

"I must say, Léopold, this naiad is a live one. Spirited. She'd make a good match for you," Ilsbeth surmised

"Strong-willed. I think that is the term she prefers." The sweet scent of Laryssa's blood filled his nostrils, and Léopold struggled to ignore her bleeding incision.

"All done, now. See how easy that was?" Ilsbeth sang, delighted with her prize.

"Easy? Easy?" Laryssa's voice began to get louder. "What the hell? Alcohol, people. Band-Aids. Anyone here ever heard of first aid?" She looked over to Dimitri and Jake, who were snickering on the sofa.

"Yeah, laugh it up, wolf boys. It's not your blood."

"This," Ilsbeth held up a clear plastic bottle, "is river water. Why give you a Band-Aid when you can easily heal yourself?"

"No, no, no. I really don't think that's sanitary," Laryssa insisted. But as soon as it hit her skin, the energy spread throughout her arm, instantly ceasing the pain. Within seconds, the water flowing from her cut turned from dark red to pink to clear. "Oh thank God. My wrist is healing. I've never tried that. It's worked in the river, but that's just amazing."

"A little trust, please. I do know what I'm doing," Ilsbeth said, handing her a clean towel. "And that, my friends, is the magic of a naiad…among other things."

Léopold took the towel from Laryssa and gently dried her arm and fingers. She gave him a small knowing smile as he did so. *Mon amour. My love. What is it with this man?* For someone who didn't want a girlfriend, he acted differently. He'd been caring, protective. As his eyes drifted from her hands to her eyes, it was as if she could detect a hint of understanding. Whether he'd admit it or not, there was something developing between them. Her heart constricted as he placed a kiss to her small scar.

"I don't mean to interrupt whatever's going on between you two, but you do want to hear more about how to find the Tlalco Tecpatl. Or did you just spill blood to give me a hostess gift?" Ilsbeth put her hands on her hips and rolled her eyes, flicking her long fingernails.

Both Léopold and Laryssa snapped out of their trance, quickly moving to sit back down.

"Oui, let's hear it."

"Naiads have existed for centuries, as have demons. My theory is that this demon was initially brought forth to the surface of our world by the Aztecs. No doubt, there's been much evil and death over time, but since it seeks this particular artifact, it's tied to it somehow. The demon calls it by name as if it belongs to it. Unfortunately, for you," Ilsbeth looked to Laryssa, "it also calls you by name. I believe when you died, it was there. It claimed your soul for itself. It does not matter whether or not it was the demon's to begin with. Demons lie, steal, murder. The interesting thing about this Tecpatl, this knife, it is rumored to be able to destroy those who claim it."

"Why can't the demon just go get the knife itself?"

"Because it can't. It is hidden to the demon. Your sisters before you have documented instances of demons seeking artifacts from them. They've hidden them, cursed them so that even if the demon knew of its location, it could not get it by itself. It needs you to find it, bring it willingly."

"Why does it expect me to just hand over the artifact?"

"Because it will threaten you or kill someone you love, someone you care about. And if you want to destroy it, you'll need to get close enough to kill it by your own hand, Laryssa. Only a naiad can send it back to its creator. You must use the Tlalco Tecpatl to kill it. Do you understand what I'm saying? Only you can do this. No one else. That is the disadvantage of that particular weapon."

"Can we just do some kind of exorcism? Find a priest?" Laryssa asked.

"No, this demon is linked to you. It believes you belong to it. If it gets its way, not only will it get the Tecpatl, it'll have you too. A demon's courtesan, as you will."

Laryssa felt her face grow hot as panic swirled through her mind. How could this happen? She'd been so careful to hide, to keep her powers concealed from others.

"Are you saying that we have to kill this demon with the Tecpatl or it will take her...forever? There must be some other way," Léopold objected.

"She knew this. What did it say to you?" Ilsbeth pressed Laryssa for an answer.

Laryssa nodded slowly in defeat. "The demon...it told me I'd belonged to it since I died, but I just assumed it was crazy or something. It...it began to touch itself. It was horrible. Please, I can't say what it was doing."

"It's preparing for you. Its flesh to yours. It seeks you now that it's seen you're a woman...no longer the girl you once were."

"No, this cannot be happening. Léopold, please tell her. Tell her she's wrong," Laryssa pleaded.

"I wish I could but I tend to agree with Ilsbeth. I saw what it did last night. We must find the Tecpatl and kill it." Léopold wrapped an arm around Laryssa, who fell against his chest. "I swear, I'll protect you."

"We need to find it," she agreed in defeat. In all her life, Laryssa hadn't ever killed anything. Sure, she'd fished, but that was the extent of her great hunting ability. And now she was expected to kill a demon in hand to hand combat? It seemed an impossible feat. Yet she had no choice. Do or die. She'd choose do. She'd kill the beast.

"Your sisters before you and those who remain with us have hidden their keys and secrets away from the rest of us. I do believe that naiads would be stronger as a whole if you'd gather strength together as one. But because naiads are often unaware of their past, they're afraid to come out in the open. Fear can be very motivating. Despite all of this, your sisters have documented what you need in books." Ilsbeth paced the room and picked up a silver candle snuffer off the mantle. "ιστορίες του νερού. Tales of the Water."

"A book? What? Are we supposed to go to the library to find it? Or do you happen to have a copy?" Dimitri asked.

"Not that I was talking to you…because I wasn't," Ilsbeth sneered. "But there are several copies that have been written and rewritten over the years, going back to ancient Greece. To answer the question, a copy of the book always finds its way to a naiad."

"Not me. I think I'd know, right?" Laryssa remarked.

"You own an antique store. Perhaps it's found its way into your hands that way? Is it possible that the book's in your collection and you don't recall it?"

"I guess anything's possible, but I know that I've never seen it. That being said, Mason takes care of most of the smaller items. Books aren't my specialty. I guess I could ask him."

"Within its pages, you will find the key. If you're tied to this demon, then you're linked to its artifact in some way. Only the book will tell you how to find it."

"I can't believe this." Laryssa fell forward and placed her head in her hands. Terrified as she was, she refused to cry. Léopold's hand, rubbing her back, erased some of her tension. When she finally looked up, everyone in the room was looking at her. "What?"

"Laryssa, what lies ahead is not already written one way or another. We shall fight this together. I will not leave you," Léopold promised.

"The vampire is correct. Your destiny is now allied with the men in this room. I'm certain of this fact." One by one, Ilsbeth began to extinguish the flames. "I'm afraid that is all I can tell you for now. Given your extraordinary gift, I will meditate to see if there is any other way I can assist you with your dilemma. Now, if you all would excuse me, I need to speak to Léopold. Alone."

"I think I should stay with her," Léopold began.

"Alone," Ilsbeth repeated, sliding open the hidden doors.

"I'm fine. Really, Leo. You go. I'll stay with Dimitri and Jake. I want to say goodbye to Avery."

"Don't worry, man. I've got her. Come here, cher," Dimitri encouraged, opening his arms.

"Really, you guys. I'm fine. Sure, I got a bit of bad news, but I can handle it," she joked lamely.

"Come on, now. You know you want a piece of the wolf," Dimitri teased, hoping to lighten the mood. Despite Ilsbeth's glower, he suspected she knew that he was only trying to cajole Laryssa.

"I'll wait for you out here," Laryssa reassured Léopold, whose face was drawn tight in concern. She walked over to Dimitri and hugged him. Together they walked out of the room.

"We need to have but a brief chat, old friend," Ilsbeth stated, sealing the room so that she could speak privately.

"Although the mystery is killing me, I do believe we've had enough excitement for one day. Get on with it, then. Say your piece." Léopold crossed the room, staring out the windows into the courtyard.

"The naiad. She's very beautiful, isn't she?"

"Oui, she is. Somehow I don't think you wanted to speak to me about Laryssa's appearance." He spun around, resting his hands on the back of a chair.

"We've known each other a long time."

"Oui."

"I would not exactly call what we have a friendship but more of a mutual respect, would you agree?"

"I believe that accurately describes our arrangement. At times, we've been soldiers for a cause. Warriors in arms, I suppose. Luckily, we've never been on opposing sides."

"The naiad is very special. She does not realize the implications of her powers, a neophyte in a dangerous world. Although she's lethal in her own right, she's vulnerable." Ilsbeth spoke with her back to Léopold as she busily organized her ingredients and cleaned the athame. "She'll need your guidance. The security of your experience. She must be able to trust you in all ways."

"Agreed." Léopold grew weary of the ambiguous conversation. There was much work to be done to find the book. "What is it, Ilsbeth? The day is short. Tell me your concern."

"I see the way she looks at you. And," she turned to face Léopold, catching his eyes, "the way you look at her. You're not yourself. You may fool her and perhaps, even the wolf, but you do not fool me."

"Stop with the cryptic words. What is it that you wish to tell me?"

"You care for her. And she for you. The seeds of love have been planted in that cold dark cavity inside of your chest where you used to house a heart."

"You don't know what you're talking about. It's not possible," he asserted. "Besides, if you've been paying such close attention to me the past several hundred years, you'd know full well that I don't have mistresses or girlfriends. What you suggest is preposterous."

"Deny it all you want, vampire, but I do know you. And I know what I just saw. Frankly I don't care if you ever fall in love. But actions do not lie. A caress. A look."

"This is ridiculous. Is this really why you wanted to talk to me?"

"Do not hurt the naiad," Ilsbeth warned. "You are a bastard, Léopold Devereoux. A trustworthy one, but I still stand by my statement. This woman, she cares for you already, despite not knowing you very long. I don't know what you've done, but I can feel it in her energy, and I can damn well see it in her eyes when she speaks to you. Now, if you want to sit there and tell me with a straight face that you feel absolutely nothing for her, that's your business, but I'm warning you not to play with her emotions. She needs you to survive this quagmire. And above all else, she must be able to trust you. If you plan on hurting her, you might as well slay her yourself, because the demon will have her and her soul."

"You do know that there's part of me that wants to take you by your broomstick and send you off? You're altogether maddening." Léopold blew out a breath, frustrated by the witch's insight. He shook his head, unwilling to make eye contact with Ilsbeth.

"Yes and yes," she laughed. "But I'm right."

"I will not concede your point, but I promise not to hurt Laryssa. This'll have to be enough for now. I fear that is all I'm capable of doing."

"It's not that bad, you know."

"What?"

"Opening your heart. Caring again. Loving someone. You may not think you deserve this gift, but you do. We all do."

"Are we finished?" Léopold smiled, refusing to engage her further. More than anything, he'd love to give in to his desires and believe what Ilsbeth was saying. But at the end of the day, it couldn't be. Because the witch was wrong about one thing; he didn't deserve Laryssa. And she didn't deserve the death and despair he'd bring to her life.

"Be well, Léopold."

"Be well, Ilsbeth." Léopold slid open the doors to find Laryssa laughing with the young witch, Avery.

Oblivious to him, she brimmed with a resilience and confidence that he hadn't expected to see, given the challenges that lay ahead. He gave her a quick smile as she hugged her friend goodbye. Praying he could keep his promise to Ilsbeth, he resolved to protect her from not only the demon who sought her death, but the beast within himself, who yearned to take her for his own.

❧ Chapter Ten ❧

"Mason," Laryssa called as she entered her store. Bells rang, alerting her manager that someone had entered the building. "We have a room full of books in the back that we've been working on cataloguing. Got them in an estate sale a few months back. Trying to determine which are worth anything. Most of them we'll end up donating to libraries and schools. The ones we've already determined we'll sell are here in this display. As you can see, there's only a couple hundred."

"Just a couple of hundred," Jake joked. "There's nothing better than spending time going through some dusty old books."

"Good stuff, right?" Dimitri laughed.

"You said the others were in the back?" Léopold asked.

"Yeah, but let me ask Mason first if he knows about it."

A tall handsome man wearing an apron pressed through the swinging doors, polishing a silver ashtray.

"'Bout time you got in. Whatcha been doing, girl? Can't you see how busy we are around here? You're gonna get your ass fired."

"Stop it, Mase." Laryssa slapped his arm. "I, uh, need to talk to you…in the back."

Mason let his eyes wander over the men before raising both his eyebrows at Laryssa. She tugged on his arm, dragging him back behind the doors.

"Stop looking at me like that," she said.

"Like what? I didn't say a word. Not one word." He pushed the shutter open an inch to peek out at them. "Really, Lyss. Didn't know you were so kinky? Three men at once? Or did you save one for me?"

"Mase, I need you to focus. But in the interest of time," she quietly pointed to each of them through the small crack and whispered, "that one there is Dimitri. Beta of Acadian Wolves….as in 'do not mess with him'. I haven't seen it yet but he told me that he strips down and turns into a big bad wolf. So hands off."

"Did you say strip? Oh baby." Mason whistled, and Dimitri turned his head toward the door.

"Stop it. They can hear you," she shushed. "That one there. Also wolf. Military wolf, I think. Again, he falls into the danger category."

"Nice too. Did he show you his gun, girl?"

"No. No he hasn't. Would you knock it off?" She sighed and bit the end of her thumb, looking to Léopold, who'd begun actively looking through the books. "And that one…"

"You mean mister tall, dark and mysterious. Sexy beast," Mason growled. "Sharp dresser. Love the suit. I can see that one's got expensive tastes."

"Yeah, he does." She glanced at Léopold and then snapped back to her conversation. "He's off limits. Vampire. One with very sharp fangs. Extremely dangerous. As in approach with caution."

"He's totally hot."

"Yeah, I know. They all are, but Léopold's…he's really just…I don't know… like no one I've ever been with."

"Oh my God. You didn't!" he exclaimed with a broad smile.

"Would you be quiet? They'll hear you…as in freaky supernatural hearing. Probably have heard every single word we've said." She blew out a breath, leaned her head back against the wall and closed her eyes for a minute.

"Hmm…hmm…hmm…you've got it bad, don't you? Not that I can't see why. He is yummy."

"Please. Don't say anything else, okay? I'm an idiot. And yes, before you even ask…yes…I did what you're thinking. But it can't happen again, okay?"

"Why not? What's wrong with him? No motion in the ocean? Hey, what about that bite? I've heard that's a surefire way to…" Mason studied her neck for marks.

"He didn't bite me."

"Let me get this straight. Bed but no bite?"

She nodded.

"What kind of a vampire doesn't suck blood?"

"One that's into one night stands, that's who." She shrugged, bending her head from side to side, trying to ease some of the tension in her shoulders. "It's complicated."

"I just bet it is."

"Listen, there's something I need to talk to you about…I'm in trouble."

"What kind of trouble?"

"The kind of trouble that can get a girl killed."

"What are you talking about? If you're in danger, you need to call the police, Lyss, not waste time chattin' it up with me."

"No, what I need is for you to run things for me for a few days…a week tops. Please. I promise to give you a raise if you can just keep the wheels turning while I'm gone." In a week, she'd be dead or have killed the demon. Mason shook his head in refusal but she knew he'd help her. He was a long time trusted employee and friend and could easily keep things afloat in her absence. "And I need your help with one more thing. I'm looking for a book. A rare book. Something that may have come into the shop during one of our estate runs."

"That, I can help you with. Got your back on the shop, too, but I'm tellin' ya for the record that getting involved with vamps and wolves isn't the best idea you've had in a while, no matter how good-lookin' they are."

"Yeah, not much choice. I need them. They're helping me…stay alive that is. Come on, I'll introduce you. I want them to hear what you've got on the book…if anything."

Laryssa pushed through the doors, not waiting for his agreement.

"They're helping you? Is that what you call it? Helping you my ass," he mumbled under his breath.

"Hey," Laryssa called to get their attention. "This is Mason. He's my assistant manager. Handles all small store items. Silver. China. Clothing. Books. Mase, this is Dimitri, Jake and Leo."

The men exchanged nods but Léopold never took his eyes off Laryssa. She'd known that he'd be able to hear her conversation, but she didn't care. All of what she'd told Mason was true.

"So I hear ya'll need a book," Mason began. "We've got all kinds here. A whole room full of them in the back as a matter of fact."

"I promise to help sort them all when I get back," she offered, knowing she wouldn't. They each had their own jobs and worked well to stay out of each other's hair. "The title of this book is, 'Tales of the Water' or 'Stories of the Water'...something like that."

"It's most likely written in another language. Greek. ιστορίες του νερού," Léopold added. "Maybe an ancient language such as Latin. I suspect it won't be very special in appearance."

"Well then, why would someone have kept it?" Mason asked, searching through the records on the computer.

"I don't know, really. I just know that it would have come to me...sometime since we first opened the store," Laryssa said.

"That's a long time. You sure it's not upstairs at your place?"

"No, I'd remember if I had kept one of our books…especially a book like that."

"Well, hello there…look at this." Mason moved to the right so that Laryssa could view the screen. He pointed to an entry. "That one there. 'Foreign text' is how it's listed. Looks like we sold it three months ago."

"That might be it. Did they use a credit card? We need an address. A name." She watched as he selected the book and brought up the information.

"Nope. Paid in cash."

Laryssa pinched the bridge of her nose. "Okay. Do you remember who sold it? To be honest, there're days I can't remember what I had for lunch let alone what I sold a couple of months ago."

"Or I could have sold it."

"True. Hey, you have a date on it?"

"Looks like December nineteenth." He tapped on the keys. "Nothing says Merry Christmas better than a book about water."

"Tales of the Water. And I don't think they bought it for the holidays. Any other books sold that day?"

"No, mostly big items. A few knick knacks."

"Let me use the computer a minute, Mase." She moved into position and began typing. "Video. Hold on a sec. I just need to pull up the security video from that day. Here we go….let's see what we've got. Lots of furniture movin' in and out."

"What are we gonna do? Put out a missing person's report? All they did was buy a book. Not exactly a crime."

"If I need to. I met a cop yesterday, and she seems pretty motivated to help us." She smiled over to Léopold and continued, "Maybe we know the person. We get lots of repeat customers. Or maybe these guys might know…wait, there's you and there's a book. Leo, Dimitri, Jake. Come take a look."

As she stepped back, Mason leaned in to study the picture. "Yeah, I do remember that dude. Kept asking what other old books we had. That's pretty much all we sell."

"I know this man," Léopold stated. *Martin Acerbetti.*

"Why does this not surprise me?" Dimitri said, stroking his beard.

"Martin doesn't live in the city. He's got a place outside of Baton Rouge."

"How well do you know him?" Laryssa asked.

"Not very well. He's a bit idiosyncratic. Has a temper." While the eccentric vampire had violent tendencies, Léopold had never known him to actually commit murder within the city limits. Kade had very little tolerance for those who broke his rules. "I don't keep company with him. No matter, though, I'll call him and how do you say…like the Godfather…make him an offer he can't refuse, no?" He smiled over at Dimitri.

"See, I knew you liked that movie," Dimitri laughed, patting him on the back. "That's my man."

"Do you think he knows about the book? About me?" Laryssa inquired. It seemed strange that a rare book meant for her actually made it into the store and then was bought by another supernatural.

"Maybe. Maybe not. It doesn't matter, though, because we need it. It's not like he's a demon. He's a vampire. One I can easily manipulate, kill if necessary." Léopold brushed lint off his sleeve, unaware that both Laryssa and Mason had gone quiet. When he looked up, he caught them both staring. "What?"

"Hey, man, do what you gotta do." Mason held his hands up defensively, shaking his head with a smile. "Um, yeah, I guess I better start working on those books in the back. You need anything else, Lyss?"

"Leo, I know this is who you are. But some of us," Laryssa pointed to her chest and then to Mason and gave a small laugh. "We, uh, don't go around talking about killing people or demons...got me?"

"Humans, always so sensitive," Léopold sniffed. "I speak nothing but the truth. This vampire is not to be trifled with, Laryssa. I'll do what needs to be done to get the book."

"Well, this human has got to get back to work. You take care, Lyss. One week and you better get your fine ass back here." Mason hugged and kissed Laryssa on her cheek, never taking his eyes off of Léopold.

When he'd gone through the swinging doors, Laryssa turned to Léopold with her hands on her hips.

"Really? Did you have to go all 'I'm a vampire' just now? You freaked Mason out," she informed him. "And to think he thought you were hot!"

"Oh, he's hot all right," Jake jested. "Nothin' like baptism by fire."

"I think Mason will survive. Besides, if you...Lyss," Dimitri drawled out her nickname that he'd heard Mason use, "are gonna hang out with vampires and wolves, he's got to get used to it sometime."

"How to make friends and influence people....yeah, that's what comes to mind when I think of ole Léopold here," Jake jibed.

"He's got the influencing part down right. Don't worry 'bout that," Dimitri teased.

"I swear you've all gone mad," Léopold remarked with a grin.

"Hangin' out? Is this what we're doing? I'll make sure to invite ya'll to book club. Although with the way Mason reacted, I don't think any of you would last ten seconds around them," Laryssa said, walking toward the door. *Did they really expect to become friends when all was said and done?* She couldn't tell, but she had to admit that she did like both Dimitri and Jake. Léopold, she liked way too much. Unfortunately, he'd made it clear that he had no plans to be with her afterwards, let alone have a friendship. "Leo, you scared the bejesus out of him."

"Hey, does this mean you think we're 'hot' too, Lyss?" Jake winked, knowing he was poking at the bear with the fangs. "Because ya know I'm single."

"Yeah, me too," Dimitri weighed in with a broad smile. "You know us wolves are okay with kinky, right?"

"More than okay," Jake added.

"Ya'll have big ears. Didn't your mamas ever tell you it was rude to listen to other people's conversations?" Confirming what Laryssa had suspected, they had heard every word of her conversation with Mason.

"If you're finished, we've got a book to go find. Come on, let's go. I'll make the call in the car." Léopold held the door open. As Laryssa went to pass through, he wrapped his arm possessively around her waist and nuzzled his nose into her hair. "For the record, wolves, I think it's best you understand that the only 'kink' Laryssa is going to be having is going to be with me."

Laryssa looked over her shoulder and her eyes met with his. She sought the hidden meaning behind his seductive words, but he merely smiled, leaving her without answers. Her heart caught, remembering their night together. She wanted so much more than he'd ever conceive of giving her. Yet every time he touched her, excitement flickered deep inside her belly. She knew better than to listen to her heart, but with his arm solidly around her, she was lost in all that was Léopold.

⤜❧ *Chapter Eleven* ❧⤛

Laryssa stood in front of the art deco mirror, contemplating why she'd insisted on going with Léopold to get the book. In the car ride back to his home, he'd called the vampire, who'd agreed to give them the book in exchange for an undetermined amount of money. Léopold had steadfastly refused to tell her how much. Even though she figured he could afford it, she still felt indebted to him. He'd brushed off her concerns, maintaining that he was doing it for Ava. The manipulating vampire had given Léopold one condition in addition to monetary compensation; he'd asked him to attend at a soiree at his home.

They had quarreled when he'd told her he planned on bringing a blood donor with him to the party, as it would be expected for him to do so. Angrily, she demanded that she accompany him to find the book, arguing that it was her life on the line, not some mindless blood bag. After nearly an hour of going back and forth on the issue, Léopold had conceded her point.

The red satin evening gown she wore clung to her curves, streaming to the floor. The V-neck accentuated the swell of her breasts, and the diamond-studded spaghetti straps, gathered into a singular strand, exposed the creamy skin of her shoulders. The revealing contours of the low-backed dress incited both a sense of nakedness and sensuality. Her makeup was subtle and refined. The matching coral lipstick made her lips appear swollen, as if they'd been kissed.

She glanced at her upswept hair and absentmindedly touched her neck. She wondered what it would feel like to have Léopold pierce her flesh. To allow him to drink from her while they passionately made love. A tear threatened to fall as melancholy struck. Léopold, while provocative and flirtatious, had made no sincere attempt at continuing what they'd started. Their connection felt as strong as steel yet he denied any hint of a relationship.

The sound of a door opening stirred her from her reverie. Léopold's reflection stared back at her, his dark eyes piercing her own. She brought a finger to her lashes, hoping to conceal her emotion, but deep down she knew he could sense even the smallest change in her mood. It bothered her that she felt as if he knew her better than she knew herself. The intimacy was too invasive, too seductive.

With the threads of Léopold's restraint growing thin, the spectacular sight of Laryssa left him reeling. *Goddess, she is enchanting.* He'd planned to keep her safely by his side all evening, but he couldn't fathom how he'd be able to stop himself from making love to her. Did she know how much he wanted her? How he'd secretly lost control? The realization that he was considering breaking all his rules, to make her his own, slammed into him like a train. Centuries of never loving another, and out of the blue, he'd become obsessed with his little naiad.

Concern furrowed in his brow when he thought of the implications. Tonight at the party, he couldn't dare let the others know of his intentions. Like a rare exotic flower, she'd attract the attention of the other vampires, leaving them thirsting for her nectar. If they knew what she meant to him, it would further expose them both. They could use her to get to him. He'd never forget that his wife and children were dead because of his actions.

"You're stunning." His dark suave voice left no room for argument. Gently resting his hands on her bare shoulders, he stood behind her.

"Thanks. You look incredible in your tux. So handsome. Like a prince," she said. A hint of sadness tinged her voice.

"Are you worried about tonight? It's not too late to change your mind, ma chérie." Léopold gave into impulse, and brushed his lips to her nape.

"No. I'm going. I was just thinking, that's all."

"I've brought you a gift." Léopold knew he should take her into his arms, refuse to let her go, but they couldn't afford to lose time in discussion. He reached into his jacket and pulled out a velvet box.

"What is it?" *Jewelry?* The man ran hot and cold. He must have an ulterior motive. She knew better than to

243

think he was wooing her with presents. Besides, he didn't have to do a damn thing to draw her to him, she was already captivated. The more time they spent together, the more she desired the impossible. Reaching for the box, she simply held it.

"Open it. It completes your role," he told her.

"My role?"

"As my date. My donor."

"I play my roles well. Don't you remember the first night you met me?"

"Oui. Calm and cool. Your leathers said biker chick, but you did have a difficulty maintaining your balance if I recall correctly."

"It was you," she said.

"What do you mean?" Léopold had to hear it for himself, her reaction to meeting him. His had been the same, he knew.

"You really don't know?"

He smiled, but said nothing.

"God, Leo. Are you really going to make me say it? Okay, fine. I was rather infatuated with this really sexy guy who had just walked into the bar. I became so nervous that I lost concentration and slipped. Those seats are dangerous, you know?" Laryssa paused, feeling the heat rise to her cheeks. She cleared her throat and continued. "You affect me. I think I've lost a good amount of brain cells just being around you the past few days."

"A guy, huh?" He laughed. "Sounds like I have some competition."

"No, I'm afraid that you've already won." Uncomfortable with her admission, Laryssa looked away from him, breaking eye contact.

"Open the box," he insisted, changing the subject.

"It's beautiful." Laryssa did as he asked and gingerly trailed the pad of her forefinger over the diamond-studded bracelet and its matching earrings.

"It's yours. Put it on." Léopold watched as she inserted the earrings. Gently, he took her wrist and fastened the bracelet. He thumbed the clasp. "This here, this little button. Depress it and it'll release a hidden silver chain from its interior. It's a small weapon, but it can be effective."

"Silver?"

"Yes, that's one rumor about us that's true. Like the wolves, we don't do well with silver. I know you can move objects, but this is one more layer of protection in case things go south."

"Thank you. It really is lovely."

"Perhaps we should discuss the rules," he suggested, continuing to touch her.

"You've already told me that I need to pretend as if I don't mean anything to you. I'm a donor, not a girlfriend."

"Mais oui. If they suspect anything more, you'd essentially be exposed as a weakness of mine."

"Are you telling me that none of the people going tonight are lovers?" she asked. What kind of people took someone to a party but acted like they barely knew them? None of it made sense.

"Depends on the definition of lovers. I'm sure there're others in the same predicament but you must understand, it is the nature of the affair that dictates our actions. Martin is a purist. Some would say he's orthodox."

"How do you mean?"

"Take me, for example. Contrary to what you may think, or the wolf," he rolled his eyes, "I'm social with humans, wolves, witches, etc. I conduct business and pleasure with little regard to who is a vampire. But Martin, he leans toward socializing only with vampires. He does this because one, he wishes to be with his own kind, those who understand his needs, and two, because he believes that he's far superior. Tonight, you will see only vampires and humans. His tastes run dark, so while I expect he'll bathe his guests in decadence, you may see things that surprise you. You must remain calm."

"What kind of things?"

"Whatever happens, stay focused. You must act as if it doesn't bother you, understand? As a guest, I'd be expected to bring a well-trained donor or human with me who isn't easily offended. Preferably, I'd bring someone who'd want to participate."

"Participate in what?"

"Feedings. Sex. Games. All out in the open, of course. It's his home so he'll be altogether impossible. You must be wary of Martin and the other guests. He surrounds himself with those of like minds."

"He sounds delightful," she mused.

"I cannot stress the importance of following the rules," he told her. "The rules are for your own safety, mon lapin."

"Please don't call me that. You know I looked that up online, and I'm not a…"

"The rules," he continued with a small smile, ignoring her protest. "First and foremost, never leave my side. Not even to use the bathroom. Female vampires will also be in attendance and have no qualms about taking another woman. In their presence, you must be subservient. I know this isn't something that comes naturally to you….or should I say, you submit when you choose." He caught her gaze, referring to how she enjoyed being restrained. "You'll be my guest. And I'm your master. As such, you will address me as master or sir. You will not address me by any other name."

"Master? I…I…don't," she began to argue but decided against it. All she wanted to do was get the book. "That title sounds pretty vampish to me. Or like some BDSM club thing."

"Oui. It's a bit of both. All you need to know is that you are expected to behave a certain way in order to blend in."

"Is this how you treat all your dates? Or is this just because we are going to this party?"

"This is why I don't attend his parties very often. But since you asked, I don't do dates. And secondly, I think you doth protest too much when it comes to your own sexual preferences. Let us not forget last night. I do recall how hard you came."

"Just because of what happened last night, it doesn't mean that I'm like your donors. Don't get used to this persona we're making up," she insisted, hating that he knew what she fantasized about in the bedroom.

"With that sass, you'll earn yourself a spanking."

"Promise?" She wished she was joking but she'd love the feel of the sting of his hands on her bare bottom. Trying to distract herself from the ache that grew between her legs, she bit her lip and flashed her eyes up to him.

"If you talk to me like that at the party, I'd think nothing of bending you over my knee in front of everyone. I'm sure Martin would enjoy the display. I know I would. Hell, maybe he'd give us the book for free." He watched intently as her face flushed at the mention of a spanking. The scent of her arousal nearly caused him to tear off her dress.

"As if," she teased. *In public, that'd be a no. In private, hell yes.* "Not happening."

"Now that's not very submissive, ma chérie. You must play the role. If not, that kind of behavior will get you in trouble tonight. No, correction, that'll get us both in trouble. On the other hand, if we do this right, we can get in and out…. make an appearance, corner Martin, get the book and leave."

"Easy peasy."

"Hardly. Although Martin has agreed to give it to us, who knows what he'll say when we get up there? He could try to manipulate me further, to hurt you. He cannot be trusted." Léopold's face grew serious and his eyes darkened. "Laryssa, I meant what I said earlier. I'll kill him if he tries a game, puts his hands on you. We must get that book in order to get the Tecpatl, to kill the demon."

Laryssa nodded quietly.

"You need to be prepared for this possibility. At the end of the day, it's my nature to kill. This is who I am, who I've always been, who I always will be. Do not ever think of me otherwise."

She turned in his arms, caressing his freshly shaven cheek with her hand.

"Leo, you're so much more. How you have gone all these years thinking like that, I don't know. I may not have known you for very long, but that isn't you. Last night, I felt you deep inside me…that man is caring and passionate. And that's what's inside your soul. If you're forced to kill tonight, I'll be there standing right beside you. I'm not scared of you or anything you're capable of doing. I can do this. I'm not a helpless damsel in distress. I'm not human, either."

Laryssa rose on her tiptoes, and pressed her lips to his. *I could love this man*, she thought. He was tough, yet incredibly compassionate. Confident but self-deprecating. Vampire did not equate to monster, no matter what he'd seen or done in his lifetime. Resisting the urge to deepen the kiss, she eased back onto her heels and gave him a small smile.

"I'm not worthy of you, mon amour," he whispered, his eyes remaining closed.

"You are," she disagreed, laying her palm to his chest, knowing she'd never be satisfied with one night. Consumed by him, she wouldn't give up on breaking through to him. His battle hardened exterior seemed impenetrable, but she had the will of a thousand warriors. He just didn't know it yet. "Leo, when this is over…It's just that I… I want us…we need to talk."

"Oui. But we can't afford to get distracted now." His eyes opened, burning with fire.

"Later then? Promise me."

"Oui." With a shake of his head, he shoved the emotion back into his chest and returned to discussing the plan. "Tonight, it'll be just you and me."

"What about Dimitri and Jake?" It wasn't lost on her that he'd again changed the topic of conversation.

"I told you, Martin's a purist. No one but vampires are permitted to step foot onto his property. Arnaud will drive us. Dimitri and Jake will follow, but stay parked down the street. I pray they don't have to intervene, but I'm not foolish enough to take you there without backup. Jake inserted a bug into my collar. I'll call on them if needed, but only if we're in dire straits."

"Anything else?"

"When we walk through that door," Léopold glided his hands over her shoulders and down her arms, "you'll belong to me and no one else. You'll be mine in every sense of the word. Your actions. Your body. Even your blood."

Laryssa's eyes widened and her pulse raced. She considered his words, aware she'd no choice but to give in to his will, his rules to stay alive. But for a second, she wondered if she'd do it for him even if her life wasn't on the line. Deep within, she knew the answer, but would never admit it. She'd already gone far over the line, giving him too much power over her heart and he didn't even know it.

"I can do this, Leo. I'm not a fool. I wouldn't be going if I thought you'd hurt me," she told him, holding her chin up high. *My heart, however, is already aching.*

Léopold gave her a small smile and shook his head. She intrepidly trusted him, and he couldn't conceive how such a gentle being could have such faith in him.

"Are you going to bite me?" she asked, catching him off guard.

"I'll avoid it at all costs. I can assure you that we won't make love at the party, so there is virtually no risk of creating a bond if I was forced to bite you. I honestly don't see that happening, but I can't rule it out." Léopold felt the sting of rejection emanating off of Laryssa. *Does she want me to bite her? To bond with me?* As much as he wished to contemplate her wishes, he needed to focus on their imminent task, one he was certain was not going to be as easy as it appeared. "You can back out of this at any time. But the second we step out of the car, there's no going back. Do you understand? I'm going to need you to give yourself over to me without reservation. Tell me, Laryssa. Do you agree to the rules?"

"Yes. For tonight, I'm yours." The words fell naturally from her lips without hesitancy. She'd give him more than one night, a lifetime if he asked. As they walked to the car, she'd never been more confident of anything in her life.

The affair appeared entirely civilized at first glance, but Laryssa knew otherwise. She fought to maintain control of her breathing as she took in the gala's atmosphere. A sensuous blues song filtered throughout the antebellum mansion. As the band played on, couples milled about the ballroom, drinking and laughing. While some guests were dressed for an evening at the opera, in ball gowns and tuxedos, others looked as if they were going to a fetish club, wearing leather and corsets. All eyes fell on them as they entered.

"This way," she heard Léopold say, and gladly followed, terrified to be left alone.

"Drink," he told her, handing her a champagne-filled flute. She hesitated, concerned it could be poisoned. As if sensing her apprehension, he took a sip of his own and coaxed her. "It's delicious."

Remembering her role, she nodded in agreement and placed the rim to her lips. Taking a tiny amount into her mouth, the bubbles danced over her tongue and down her throat. She sucked a deep breath, and she willed herself to calm down. Her temporary tranquility was soon replaced with fear as an imposing man with exposed fangs approached. She struggled to keep the liquid down and squeezed Léopold's arm.

"Léopold Devereoux, my old friend. How've you been? I must say I was surprised to get your call this afternoon, but I'm thrilled I did."

"Merci beaucoup, Martin. I certainly wouldn't pass up such a fortuitous opportunity to enjoy your company and do business all at once." Léopold supposed he was laying it on thick, but he was well aware that Martin enjoyed having his ego stroked, especially in a public forum. "Your home's magnificent. The restoration is impressive."

"Thank you for noticing. But of course, someone of your stature would appreciate the finer things. I've personally overseen all of the architectural detail work," he boasted, his eyes feasting on Laryssa. "You must introduce me, Léopold. Who is this lovely little choice you've brought with you tonight?" He held out his hand to her.

"This is…" It occurred to Léopold that they hadn't discussed whether or not to use her real name. Thinking quickly, he chose a name that he knew would draw her ire, making her focus on him, not her fear. "Jessica. Jessica, this is our gracious host, Martin. Go on, mon lapin. Don't be shy. You have permission to shake his hand."

"Yes, sir," she answered submissively. Her heart raced as she extended her palm toward the imposing vampire. As it occurred to her what Léopold had called her, Laryssa's eyes flared. *Jessica? Jessica freakin' Rabbit?* She caught the smile on his face, realizing he'd done it on purpose to distract her. Tamping down her reaction, she embraced her role. Laryssa lowered her eyes and placed her hand in Martin's, praying he couldn't feel her fingers shake.

Martin gave a devious smile, before capturing her hand and placing his lips upon it. Rather than release her, he held onto it, engaging Léopold in conversation.

"Oh my, she is striking," he crooned. "You must let me taste her."

"Ah, I'm afraid that's not possible. You see, she's in training with the agency. I'm working very hard to teach her the proper manners required of a donor. Please forgive her in advance as she's a novice." Léopold possessively wrapped his hand around Laryssa's waist, pulling her away from Martin, forcing him to release her hand.

"Well, I must say it is very generous of you to do that for them."

"Considering the short notice, it was acceptable. Your observation is correct, though, mon ami. She's quite fetching. I plan to use her in every way possible this evening, make sure she's thoroughly disciplined." Léopold maintained a deadpan tone to his voice as he commented, as if it were nothing more than business.

Martin released a hearty laugh. "Practice makes perfect. But do let me know if you need any help with her. I'd be happy to give her a go."

Laryssa kept her eyes on the floor. *Give me a go? Is this guy serious?* Martin's voice made her feel as if thousands of spiders were crawling over her skin. She rubbed her arms as nausea threatened.

"Merci. Your offer is very generous, however, this one is entirely my responsibility. On another note, I've brought what you've asked regarding our business."

"Very good. We can make the transfer in a bit." Martin grew distracted by a large crowd of new guests filling the foyer. "Will you please excuse me? I'll be but a minute and then we can go to my office." Martin looked again to Laryssa and blew a kiss at her before turning his attention to his new arrivals.

As he walked away, Laryssa felt herself sag against Léopold in relief.

"You're doing very well for a novice," Léopold noted, sipping his drink.

"Thank you, sir," she answered.

"Jessica," he paused and chuckled. "Are you enjoying the party?"

"Yes, sir." *Enjoy the party?* Laryssa wasn't sure if he was serious or not. She briefly considered breaking character but judiciously decided against it. Martin had looked at her like a shark who was about to snap up a seal and she wasn't about to test her theory.

Léopold took Laryssa's hand in his, leading them onto the dance floor. As they stepped out onto the parquet floor, he took her glass and his, and handed them off to a waiter.

"Come," he ordered.

At his demand, the smallest flicker of irritation flashed in her eyes and she lowered her lids quickly, concealing it as she remembered her role. It had only lasted a second. No one gave her a second look, but Léopold had noticed.

"Manners, pet," he warned, reaching up into the back of her updo. Tugging slightly on her hair, he exposed her neck while pulling her flush against him with his other hand. "Or would you like that spanking I promised you?"

Yes. Arousal flooded between the juncture of her thighs at the thought of him doing so. As he pulled her against him, Laryssa's body came to life against his as if they were the only two people in the room. His clean male scent enveloped her as he took control. Her hands fell to her sides, allowing him to guide her to the driving beat of the music. She felt the hard length of him brush against her belly. Involuntarily she released a small moan.

"You are a very dirty girl, aren't you, ma chérie? My, my, my. You do want me to do that to you, don't you?"

"Yes, sir," she breathed into his shoulder. Closing her eyes, she couldn't look at him, to see his rejection as she confessed her desires. "I want it…I want that and so much more…but only with you."

"Jesus Christ," he swore as his cock hardened against his zipper. *Fuck, she's going to kill us both.* She may have been playing a role, but he was certain she meant every single word she said. They were only supposed to seek the book, get out safely. Instead, her actions were ripping him from the inside out. His teeth ached for her skin, for her blood. Any remaining doubt he held that he'd be able to get her out of his mind and his life disintegrated like he'd taken a sledgehammer to a piece of chalk. Once he took her blood, he suspected he'd create the kind of bond that would ensure his centuries of solitude were truly finished.

With furor, he spun her in his arms, slamming her back into his chest. Like a vise, he held tight to her waist, gliding his other hand over her chest until he'd wrapped it around her throat. But the struggle didn't come. No she merely fell into his erotic embrace, digging her nails into the side of his thighs.

"Mon amour, we cannot wish for the inconceivable. Be afraid. Fight me. See me for who I am," he demanded as he ground his erection up into her bottom.

"If it is what you wish, sir," she replied. Lost in the rhythm, she gave into Léopold's demand. No longer playing a role, she reveled in his strength. "But it is you who I seek. Be assured, I see only you."

"Look around you, pet. They all feast upon the sight of your skin, coveting what I have. This, this is my world." *Goddammit. When will she finally see me for what I am? Can't she see the grotesque and treacherous world into which I've brought her?* Léopold may not have been Martin's friend, but these vampires walked within the precarious circles of his life.

Laryssa opened her eyes and noticed that no longer were the other guests dancing. If not otherwise engaged in sex or feeding they had stopped to stare, to observe their impassioned dance. Consumed by the moment, she shook it off, unwilling to care what they thought. This was what vampires did, impulsively acting out their deepest desires, exhibiting their lust and anger.

"Let them look," she challenged, bending at the waist and writhing against his swollen flesh. "Master, I'm here to serve you, not them."

With a jerk, he'd righted her, against him. Was she insane? The charade had gone too far. Léopold considered taking her out to the limo and fucking her senseless, when she placed her hand over his, urging him to take her breast. He slipped his hand underneath the silky fabric, cupping her soft skin. Teasing her nipple into a taut point, he pinched gently until she sucked a breath. But she didn't stop him. No, her arousal filled the air, not a soul in the room misunderstood her intentions.

"Yes, sir."

"How far would you go? Would you let me strip you, fuck you here, in front of everyone?" He couldn't stop himself from pushing her. When would she realize that she was falling for a lethal vampire, who lived off the blood of humans? When would she wake up and see that no matter how badly he wanted her, a life with him would be fraught with vulnerability and danger?

"I would go as far as you needed me to go. Can't you see that? None of it matters unless I'm with you." Laryssa almost lost her composure as she became aware that she'd just professed how she felt about Léopold.

It was not lost on her that others in the room had heard, had been watching. Underneath the cover of her role, she safely revealed her feelings. She'd known that she wasn't supposed to give the impression that she cared for Léopold. He'd be angry with her, she knew, for putting them at risk. She stopped dancing and slid out of his hands, and bowed her head, attempting a recovery of the situation.

"Please forgive me. I have taken advantage of your kindness in training me by letting my physical attraction, my personal lust toward you take priority. I understand if you wish to report me to the agency," she said in a meek voice.

Léopold stood firm, his feet rooted to the floor. If he could have his way, they'd leave right now, but they had to get the book. Cognizant of their errors, he appreciated her effort to rectify what they'd done. As he looked around, the other guests had once again begun dancing, ignoring them.

"See that it doesn't happen again. While I intend to make sure you receive the punishment you deserve for calling spectacle to us at this affair, we shall make the best of it, no?"

Léopold went to usher Laryssa off the dance floor when he spotted Martin making a beeline toward them. No doubt he'd been alerted to their sensual tryst on the dance floor. Going on the offensive, Léopold widened his strides, dragging Laryssa by the hand behind him.

"Martin, I must apologize that my training got a tad out of hand on the floor. This one," Léopold nodded over to Laryssa, whose eyes fell to the floor, "must be reprimanded as soon as possible. She may have difficulty learning to be a donor as it's apparent she confuses the attention of a master for affection."

"Dear boy, I do know the issues involved with finding suitable donors. Like you, I prefer a flavor of the week. Variety is the spice of life so they say. Relationships with donors are an inherent pitfall to the process. Don't worry a minute about the display. My guests," he gestured around the room to several couples who begun publicly having sex, "they do enjoy a good show. Come now, let's attend to business before the party goes into full swing."

Laryssa felt as if the wind had been sucked out of her. Swirling emotions made her feel as if she'd just ridden a roller coaster. But unlike the carnival, there was no respite from the jarring descent. Perhaps she had been confusing her own emotions with the role, but from her head to her toes, her skin burned for his touch.

Breathing deeply, she summoned all her strength, letting the power of the naiad flow through her blood. She forced herself to focus on their mission, the reason why they were at the party. Like a forest animal, she sensed the hunter. Instinctively preparing for the attack, she appeared calm but her storm of energy built. Soon they'd have the book and they could finally leave.

Holding tight to Léopold's tuxedo sleeve, Laryssa followed him down a long hallway. When they arrived in Martin's office, she glanced up and caught an eerie gleam in their host's eyes. She pretended not to notice, hoping he didn't have a death wish. Léopold, sharp and cunning, hadn't survived centuries by embracing naivety. Martin knew this. He'd anticipate the great difficulty involved if he planned on trifling with Léopold, but he'd think Laryssa a weak victim. She could tell by the way Martin eyed her, that he secretly planned a coup. He stalked his prey, luring them into his trap.

Tense, Laryssa went on alert. She strode across his office with a subtle grace, ready to spring at the first inkling of danger. She observed how Martin circled Léopold, engaging him in conversation, his eyes darting over to her every now and then, aware of his quarry. Laryssa scanned the room for objects that could be used as weapons. She approached a plaster statue sitting on a pedestal and was running her fingers over the smooth surface, when she heard Léopold say her name.

"Jessica, we'll be but a minute. Please stand over near the doorway," Léopold ordered, never taking his eyes off Martin. He wanted Laryssa near the exit, far away from the devious vampire.

"Yes, sir," she answered on cue.

Léopold retrieved his cell phone from the inside pocket of his jacket and began to tap the surface. Within seconds, he'd transferred the funds into Martin's account and returned the device. Laryssa's energy slammed into him, and he realized she was close to snapping. With her back against the wall, she stood submissively with her hands at her sides, yet he knew she was ready to strike. They needed to get out as soon as possible.

"The transaction's complete. The book?" Léopold inquired. "I'm afraid we have another engagement this evening and must get going."

"Leaving so soon? How disappointing," Martin commented as he checked his phone, making sure he'd received the payment. Satisfied, he put it on his desk and slowly made his way toward Laryssa. "The book is there on the shelf behind my desk."

Léopold observed the vampire's actions. He spied a single book, which sat next to a crystal vase.

"That one there, with the black spine. I had it rebound. It was a tattered mess."

"Tell me, Martin. How did you come about the book? You never did say."

"I didn't, did I? Not much to tell. A bird put a bug in my ear at a party once. Told me about rare books and mentioned that the ones written in Greek are quite the fetch. I discovered it in this little antique store on Royal, buried with dozens of other old books. I couldn't be sure it was real, of course, but nevertheless I snatched it up for pennies. Stole it, really, considering the profit I just made." Creeping closer to Laryssa, he stopped to lean on the back of a leather chair.

"Lady Luck was with you." Léopold slowly rounded the desk.

"And you as well. This donor you've brought. I beg you to let me show her our unadulterated ways." In a flash, he stood before Laryssa, gripping her chin in his hands. A man of short stature, he buried his nose up into her hair. "Her skin is radiant, like a virgin. Smells pure. Tell me, are you?"

"Am I what?" she asked, her voice filled with feigned tranquility. Laryssa fumbled with her bracelet. Her finger found the nub and tugged at the hidden wire.

"Do not touch her!" Léopold demanded, reaching for the book.

"She's special to you, Devereoux? You've gone soft, I see. After all these years, I wouldn't have believed it. You may fool the others, but not me. Tell you what…I'll keep your secret…in exchange for a taste of the virgin." Martin hooked his fingers around one of Laryssa's spaghetti straps and yanked it downward, exposing her bare breast. With a hiss, his fangs descended and he lowered his head to his prize.

Laryssa screamed as Martin attacked. She'd been certain he would bite her, but instantly, Léopold had leapt to her rescue. He wrapped his arm around Martin's neck in a stranglehold. Enraged that Martin had touched Laryssa, Léopold growled and tightened his grip. But Martin held strong, refusing to let go of her shoulders. Sliding the silver chain taut, Laryssa managed to bend her arms and jammed the chain upward into his throat, scoring his skin. The smell of burnt flesh filled the room and Martin howled in response, allowing her enough time to kick his shin. With a grunt, he released her and Laryssa slipped aside.

"Let this be a lesson to others. Never, ever touch what is mine." Léopold seethed, and sunk his razor-sharp fangs deep into Martin's shoulder.

Léopold held tight as Martin flailed, unsuccessfully trying to dislodge him. He extended his fingernails into claws and pierced them into the soft flesh surrounding Martin's spine. Léopold bore down on his grip, tearing away at the tendons and muscle until Martin's head rolled onto the floor. Within seconds, the vampire's body disintegrated into ashes, leaving nothing but silence in his wake.

The door flew open and one of Martin's guards ran into the room. Laryssa reached her hand toward the statue. Calling on her power, she flung it across the room, catching him in the head. As he fell to the carpet, she slammed the door shut. Léopold, in his furor, realized he'd gone feral in front of Laryssa. He'd revealed the beast. Now, she'd finally see him for what he was…a savage animal. The loss of her in his life would break him, but he'd executed Martin with no remorse. Unable to stomach the taste of him in his mouth, Léopold spat on the floor. As he swiped his forearm across his mouth to clear the blood, he forced his blazing red eyes back to black. The truth of what he was had come to light, and he found it impossible to look into Laryssa's eyes.

"The book? Where'd it go?" Irritated, Léopold focused on the business at hand.

"There." She pointed. In the melee, it had fallen under the desk. Her heart pounded in her chest, expecting that any minute a deluge of vampires would break down the door, seeking revenge for what they'd done.

"Let's get out of here," Léopold calmly said, picking it up off the floor. He slid it under his coat and looked down, disappointedly, to his bloodstained shirt. "Ready?"

"But Leo? What about the others? What if they…" *Kill us.*

"They won't touch me. Or you. Don't be afraid." Not after he'd just killed Martin. Every single vampire on the premises had heard his words: *Never touch what is mine.* They didn't have to see what had happened behind closed doors to know Martin had been killed. But Léopold would not be held at fault. Martin should have known better, did know better. He'd knowingly challenged Léopold and lost. "We're going to walk out of here right now. Our business is finished. Take my arm."

Laryssa wrapped her hand around Léopold, confused as to why she felt no sadness over the death of another human being. But Martin hadn't been human. *Vampire.* If Léopold hadn't stopped him, he'd have bitten her, drained her. As her foot brushed through his dust, she silently wished him good riddance.

⤚⧉· *Chapter Twelve* ⧉⤚

Léopold threw his head back against the seat in disgust over what had transpired. After making their way safely to the limo, he'd taken off his shirt and jacket, throwing them in the trunk. Arnaud had provided him with clean towels so that he could make quick work of removing the blood and ash from his face and hands. But as he sat bare-chested across from Laryssa, there was nothing that could be done to cleanse his soul.

She'd seen him kill. Not only had he killed, he'd decapitated Martin. He sighed and closed his eyes so he didn't have to see the disdain on her face. Or worse, she'd fear him. Jesus Christ, this was why he didn't fall in love. All he ever did was bring pain to those he cared about. Laryssa was no different. No matter how much he wanted her, they had no future.

When Laryssa had finally reached the back seat, she'd hoped they'd celebrate their victory. Exhilarated that they found the book, she soon found her spirit deflated like a balloon. Léopold had seated himself as far away from her as he could possibly get. A chill settled over them like a layer of frost as Léopold retreated within. Laryssa wondered what was wrong with him. She'd seen his beast, and it had been magnificent. Like a great warrior, he'd taken down his opponent in battle, saving them both.

After fifteen minutes of mind numbing reticence had passed, Laryssa could no longer bite her tongue. Falling to her knees, she crept up between his legs and pressed her forehead to his belly. His hand slid to her hair, teasing out the pins, softly tugging the tendrils free. Still, not a word passed from his lips.

"Leo, please. Let me in," she whispered, rubbing her face into his warm skin.

He shook his head and closed his eyes. *Too much pain.* He couldn't bring this death to her feet, not ever again.

"I won't give up on you. Talk to me," she continued, unwilling to relent.

"I can't," he hissed. "What I did…"

"I saw you tonight. I saw everything. And I'm here. I'm not leaving you." She raised her chin and looked into his eyes. "No matter what you think, I'm not afraid. I'm not repulsed. You were…you were amazing."

"Amazing?" he scoffed. "How can you say that, Laryssa?"

Laryssa reached up to his shoulders, gliding her fingers gently down over his pecs, forearms, finally taking his hands within her own, then pressed his palms to her cheeks.

"Because it's the truth. You're the strongest man I've ever met. Ferocious when threatened. But you're gentle. Protective. Courageous." She kissed the tips of his fingers. "And I want you in my life. One night will never be enough. You've ruined me. There's no one but you."

"Don't you see what I'm capable of?" he asked. His voice faltered. "So long ago...I fought...to keep my family safe. But they killed my wife. My daughter. My son. I left them vulnerable to my enemies. It was no different than if I had sliced my own sword into their necks. When I became vampire, there wasn't a soul inside my chest to be taken. It died with them. For centuries, I've done nothing but kill, ruthlessly climbing my way to the top of the food chain. Those people you saw tonight at the party...this is the danger that surrounds me."

"It wasn't your fault. You cannot continue to think like that, to die this way. What you do is not living...it's experiencing without really knowing, tasting life." Tears brimmed in her eyes, empathizing with the guilt he carried. "I've lived with danger in my life ever since my own death. Every. Single. Day. You are the first good thing to happen to me since I've been reborn. I'll fight for you in my life. But you have to choose me, not guilt. Choose. Me."

"Laryssa," he croaked. For the first time since he'd been turned, someone was offering him the keys to the shackles he'd willingly worn since he'd found his family slain. His prison walls began to crumble. Freedom beckoned. All he needed to do was take it. Goddess, he wanted to open his heart to Laryssa, never let her go.

"Do it, Leo. Believe my words. I saw you tonight. You did your worst. And I am still here…offering myself to you. All you need to do is say yes. You can do it. Just choose me."

Léopold's heart exploded. With her knelt before him, she'd taken an ax to the centuries-old barrier he'd erected. She was everything he'd desired for a thousand years but nothing he'd ever had. Demanding and seductively submissive, at times, she'd witnessed the very darkest he'd become and still sought his attention, his heart.

"Yes." He buried his lips into her hair, raking his hands into her locks. "Goddess, please forgive me, I choose you."

Laryssa let the tears fall as he pressed his lips to hers, pouring all her love and passion into her kiss. Never would he think he was undeserving of her in his life. She'd make sure that he'd know, with no room for doubt, that she was his and he was worthy.

Léopold shattered, releasing the fire he'd held back for so long. Embracing the craving he'd held at bay, he claimed her with his mouth. Sweeping his tongue against hers, he sucked and teased at her lips. His little nymph had torn away his defenses, leaving him splayed open for her bidding. An urgent hunger built in his chest as she moaned into his lips. Tonight, Laryssa would be his.

"Leo," Laryssa panted.

Her hands frantically tore at his buckle and within seconds, she'd unzipped his slacks, taking his swollen flesh into her hands. Stroking his smooth taut skin, she gave him no warning before capturing his cock with her warm mouth. She sucked him hard from the root to his tip, plunging him in and out of her lips. Opening her heavy lids, she caught his eyes and smiled. Swirling her tongue over the plump head, she darted it over its slit, tasting his seed. Twisting his shaft at its stem, she sucked him once, twice then moved her lips over his tightened balls, suctioning them into her mouth.

"Fuck, yes. That feels so good," he grunted. "If you keep doing that, I'm going to…ah, no, no, no."

Unwilling to come in her mouth, he quickly grabbed her by the shoulders, bringing her upward. Recapturing her lips, his hands found her zipper and ripped at the material. He slipped the straps over her shoulders, letting the dress sag at her waist. With a final tug, the fabric left her bare save her panties, garter belt and stockings. Reaching for her breasts, he gathered the soft flesh together. Gently kneading them, he parted his lips catching a nipple, licking and biting at its ripe tip until she screamed with pleasure. Moving from the right to the left, he took his time, lavishing attention to her body.

"You're the most beautiful creature I've ever known," he breathed into her skin.

"I want you so much, Leo," Laryssa managed. As she writhed against his growing arousal, she could feel the length of him through the thin silk barrier. "Fuck me now. I can't wait. Please."

Léopold extended his claws, ripping at her panties until only her stockings remained. Laryssa put her hands on Léopold's shoulders, slowly impaling herself. She threw her head back, thrusting her breasts forward. Léopold held her waist, taking in the glorious sight of his nymph riding him hard. Cupping her breast, he caressed it, altogether aroused by the way she'd got lost in the passion, undulating on him.

"Perfect. You're so goddamned perfect." Léopold whispered as he slid his hand down between her breasts and over her belly.

His fingers descended between their bodies, until he found her slick pussy. He brushed his thumb through her lips, finding her aroused nub. Léopold felt her shiver in response and he knew he'd captured her attention. Letting his other hand slip down her back, he took her ass into his hands. She moaned, rocking against him, surging into his touch. His fingers trailed down the crevice of her bottom.

As his grazed his forefinger over her puckered skin, her eyes flashed to his, but she didn't say a word. Instead she raised her hips, sliding upward, and then rocked him back into her.

"Yes, that's it, mon amour," he reassured her. "Let me have all of you."

Laryssa took only a minute to adjust to the new sensation. She'd never been touched there, but as he continued to circle her anus, she found herself arching her back so he'd increase the pressure.

"Goddess, you're so responsive. I'm going to make love to you in every way possible, Laryssa. There'll be no part of you left unexplored by my touch, my lips," he promised.

"I'm yours to take." She'd given him permission, she knew. Having done so, she trusted him with her pleasure, her life. As he slowly pressed his finger into her tight hole, she quivered, stilling her movement. "Ah."

"Mais oui. Your lips." He kissed her. "Your pussy." He kissed her again. "Your heart. I'll take all of you… as mine. But do you want this, ma chérie? Are you certain?"

"Yes," she cried, as he plunged his finger all the way into her ass. Enveloped in all that was Léopold, she clung to him, her nails dragging down his pecs. Rocking into her orgasm, her chest heaved, desperate for air. "So full. So close. Don't stop. Don't fucking stop. Please, Leo. I'm coming…I'm coming…"

The moment her pulsating contractions took hold of his flesh, he drove himself up into her pussy again and again. Infatuated with her loss of inhibition, Léopold's fangs descended, scraping her neck. Only a whit of suppression kept him from transforming into his naturally feral state. *Feed.* The urge to pierce her sweet skin flourished in his chest. He had to have her. The need for her blood grew unbearable.

"Leo, yes. Do it!" she screamed, her body shuddering upon his. Raptured in climax, Laryssa knew he desired to take her essence. Yearning to have his fangs buried deep in her flesh, she clawed at him, drawing his blood with her nails, becoming the wild mate he rightfully deserved. "Do it. Make me yours."

With an animalistic growl, Léopold exploded, sinking his teeth into her neck. He could feel her buck underneath him in release as her nectar flowed down his throat. It was as if her blood had been created solely for him, and the reality shook him to his core. There'd never be another woman for him but Laryssa. His emotional celibacy had been shattered within days of meeting her and this final act had destroyed the possibility he'd ever return to solitude. The bond he'd fought so long to prevent registered immediately. The memories in her cells meshed with his. He knew she couldn't possibly feel the bond, for it was he who was destined to her for eternity. Waves of ecstasy from her energy filtered into him, and he'd never been more certain of anything in his life. This magical being he held in his arms was forever his.

~⊰⊱· *Chapter Thirteen* ·⊰⊱~

Dressed in nothing more than their bathrobes, Léopold and Laryssa sat in silence staring at the pages. After making love in the limo, they'd come home, changed and immediately started working on the book. As much as each of them would have preferred to linger in the afterglow of their lovemaking, the demon's words and the threat of Laryssa's impending death pushed them onward.

For over two hours, each of them had taken turns looking through it, yet they'd found nothing that'd tell them where to find the Tecpatl. Even though Laryssa was unable to understand the Greek language, she'd hoped that because it was her book, it would reveal its secrets to her. Frustrated, she flicked her fingers through the pages one more time before slamming it down on the table.

"I don't get it. Are you sure this is right? There're chapters on sand? Ocean temperatures? Crustaceans? Fish? Even mermaids? But nothing about naiads? Nothing about Aztecs or Tecpatls? It doesn't make sense. Listen, I know you haven't read it page for page yet, but I don't have a good feeling about this."

"You must have patience. There's close to a thousand pages here, all in Greek. You have to give me time to read through the details."

"I guess I just thought that if it was supposed to be my book," Laryssa stood and began to pace, "that it would just…I don't know…that something would just come to me. But no. I put my hands on the pages and guess what I feel?"

"What?" He gave her a small smile.

"Nothing. Absolutely nothing. Zip. How can that be? Shouldn't I feel something? A spark? A tingle?"

"Not sure. Do you always feel something when you touch inanimate objects?" He grinned again, trying to get her to relax. Seldom were things in life as easy as they appeared.

"Well no, but it's supposed to be written by my people, right? If I saw this book on a shelf, I'd have no idea it was meant for me. No wonder it sat there in the store. Hell, I let Mason sell it."

"You've gotta give it some time. We just got home. Apparently, whatever answers it holds, we just haven't found them yet."

The front door opened, and they both looked up at Dimitri. After getting notice that they'd retrieved the book, he'd driven Jake back to Logan's so he could help keep watch over Ava. Dimitri took sight of their grim expressions and crossed the room.

"Hey," he said, sensing the tension.

"Hey, yourself," Laryssa commented. She walked away from the table and threw herself into one of the large chairs and propped her feet on its ottoman. Exhausted, she closed her eyes and put her arm across her forehead.

Léopold looked at him, raised his eyebrows and shrugged.

"So, uh, I see ya got the book. I'm afraid to ask how it's going," Dimitri said.

"Ma chérie expects immediate results, but as you can see," Léopold picked up the book and handed it to Dimitri, "it's a bit of a read. We've paged through it. At first glance, the table of contents reveals nothing unusual, makes no mention of naiads."

"Greek, huh?"

"Oui. Do you know how to read Greek?"

"I know a bit. I'd be happy to look at it." Dimitri glanced at Laryssa. "So what else is up? Is she okay?"

"She needs to go to the water. We ran into some trouble at the party."

"Trouble, huh? Things get rough?"

"Yes," Laryssa mumbled.

"You could say that my offer wasn't sufficient compensation." Léopold's blood boiled with a new surge of anger, remembering how the vampire had attacked Laryssa. "Martin touched her."

"Jesus, Leo. Laryssa, are you sure you're okay?"

"Yep, just tired. Leo's right. I have to go in the water."

"She was spectacular. Gave him a good fight. Then, she hit one of his lackeys with a statue. Sent it straight through the air without touching it."

"That a girl. Damn vampires can't keep their hands to themselves." Dimitri smacked his palm to the table. He raised an eyebrow at Léopold and gave him a small smile. "No offense."

"None taken." Léopold stood and walked behind Laryssa's chair and began to massage her shoulders. "She needs water. And rest. We can look at the book tomorrow."

"What else can I do to help?"

"I want to give Arnaud a call and check on him. He was supposed to bring us food, but he's not here yet." He felt Laryssa tense, but continued. "Laryssa won't feel right until she goes in the lake. When she flung that statue, I'm afraid she used up her energy. Tonight was pretty intense. Would you mind seeing her to the dock? I'll only be a few minutes. I'll come down after I'm done."

"Sure thing. You ready, Lyss?" Dimitri asked with a wink.

"Yeah, thanks," Laryssa responded, thinking about Léopold ordering his *food*. The mere idea of him taking another woman or man's blood, giving anyone the gift of his bite riled her.

Laryssa understood that he needed blood to survive. He was a vampire after all. But the brutal honesty of their intimacy in the car, getting him to accept her, it had led her to believe that they'd agreed to have a relationship. She realized, though, that they hadn't discussed exactly what that meant. Her mind told her it was wrong for her to only know him a few days and expect fidelity, but her heart told her differently. She reflected on why she was so irritated with him and whether it made sense. Rational or not, she knew that she couldn't share him. Not with women or men. Not for sex or food. She wanted a future with Léopold, one where he belonged to her and only her. Stewing in jealousy, she pushed up out of the chair, hiding her face from Léopold. If she caught his gaze, she feared she'd rip into him.

Léopold watched as Laryssa trod down the hallway with Dimitri, refusing to look him in the eye. Like a switch, she'd gone from passionate and loving in the car to seething under his touch in the living room. Though she had no idea, he could feel her jealousy and anger toward him as if it were his own. *Interesting.* But why she was jealous, that he didn't understand. It wasn't as if he'd so much as mentioned another woman. Picking up his phone, he selected Arnaud's number. As the tone rang in his ear, it occurred to him that she may have misunderstood his intentions. *How could she think that I'd feed from another woman after my confession to her? I chose her over all else.* But rather than sharing her concerns, Laryssa became withdrawn, concealing her thoughts from him.

He impatiently tapped his foot as he caught sight of her out the window, walking hand in hand with the wolf. His little rabbit was going to have to learn to trust now that she'd committed to him. *What fun it would be to teach her a lesson,* he thought. He supposed she also was due a reprimand for her behavior on the dance floor. Smiling, he licked his lips remembering the taste of her, anticipating the devious punishment he'd deliver, one they'd both enjoy.

Laryssa's spirit flared to life within the dark abyss. Naked to the cold, she'd stripped in front of Dimitri, no longer worried about being discovered. Like a gentleman, he'd turned his head. In truth, she hadn't cared if he'd seen her. Now that she'd confessed her nature, she felt liberated. Nude and slippery, she breathed in the water, letting the healing begin.

Dimitri sat on the dock with his jeans rolled up and his feet in the water, watching Laryssa swim. Gloriously bared, she dove, exposing her bottom. But when she didn't resurface, he panicked and began to tear off his shirt.

"It's okay," he heard Léopold say.

"No it's not. What the hell? She's drowning. Come on, help me," he snapped.

"Elle va bien. She breathes in the water." Léopold laughed. Still in his robe, he sat next to his friend. "She's amazing, no?"

"Scary is more like it. Dammit, Leo. You could've warned me," he said, blowing out a breath. "Jesus, how does she do that? She's been under for almost five minutes now."

"It's the way of her species. The lake…it heals her. Keep watching."

"Watching for what?"

"Ah, there," he pointed to a faint glimmer, which soon began to illuminate the water within a ten foot diameter. "See. She glows." Léopold chuckled.

"Now that's something you don't see every day. She's like one of those fish…you know, the kind that lights up to lure their prey."

"She's captivating."

"You do realize your girlfriend is lit up like a light bulb, right?"

"Oui."

"Goddamn," Dimitri exclaimed, punching Léopold lightly on his shoulder.

"What's your issue, wolf? I assume you have some good reason for flailing your arms at me?"

"You like her…she's your girlfriend," Dimitri sang.

"Oui, I suppose she is." Léopold's eyes darted to Dimitri, enjoying his shocked expression but quickly focused on the lake again.

"What happened?"

"What are you talking about?"

"Okay, what happened to my dark souled friend, Léopold?"

"My soul has never been dark," Léopold informed him in a serious voice. "My soul died. The day my family died, I died."

"Hey, I was just joking, man. Come on. Lighten up." Dimitri looked to the water and tried not to laugh. "Listen Leo, I'm sorry. Really. And I'm sorry you lost your family all those years ago. But I've always known your soul is in there. And it's never been dark or anything like that. Don't forget, I was there when you saved Wynter. You've just been…I don't know…hurt bad. So you went with tough and alone. Could be worse. You survived."

"Oui, I survived. But as Laryssa pointed out to me this evening, I haven't been living. She makes me want to do that again."

"So, uh, what's the story?" Dimitri asked. "She seemed kinda pissed at you when we left. But look at her now."

"She flourishes. But she must learn that we cannot have secrets," Léopold told him with a smile.

"Can't argue with that….but what happened?"

Before Léopold had a chance to answer, Laryssa broke through the surface with a cry of victory and began laughing. Caught up in her self-induced electrifying pleasure, she'd forgotten about Dimitri. As she glanced over to the dock and saw the men watching her, she rolled onto her back, exposing her breasts. Floating in the water, aglow with energy, she knowingly teased them.

"You've got yourself a live one, bro," Dimitri commented.

"That I do. She's devilish." Léopold shook his head and grinned. "And very disobedient. Look at her taunting us. She knows what she's doing."

"Oh, I'm lookin'."

Léopold gave Dimitri a glare.

"What, man? You know me. I'm not one to pass up the beauty of a nekkid water nymph," Dimitri teased.

"Naiad," Léopold corrected.

"Whatever. Say listen, you mind if I go wolf for a while? I'm planning on stayin' the night given the whole demon business, but I've been crammed in the city for weeks."

"Run wild, mon ami." Léopold's expression was one of pure delight as he watched Laryssa kick her legs and frolic. "You may want to stick around for a few minutes."

"Why's that?"

"Tonight, my little Laryssa came alive on the dance floor," Léopold began.

"I thought you guys were trying to remain inconspicuous?"

"Yeah, we kind of lost sight of that. Let's just say that I do believe she enjoys an audience."

"Really, now? She should be your perfect match, then," Dimitri snorted, recalling how the first time he'd ever met the vampire, he'd been deeply engaged in a public display of affection, having sex in the middle of Mordez. "Well if you're puttin' on a show, I'm down with that."

"Ah, here comes our little fish," Léopold commented, never taking his eyes off Laryssa.

Rejuvenated, Laryssa swam toward the dock, deciding that it was time to talk with Léopold. Taking in the sight of him and his delicious smile, she'd have to resist tearing off his robe and pulling him in with her. As she approached, she kicked her feet up into the air, spraying them both.

"Come in," she called, laughing as they wiped the water from their faces.

"You know, Dimitri, Laryssa and I came to an agreement this evening." While Léopold spoke to Dimitri, he smiled at Laryssa, his eyes locked on hers.

"Yeah. Hmm…what's that?"

"Well you see? I've been quite stubborn about keeping a certain little naiad out of my mind."

"Stubborn? You? Never," Dimitri chuckled.

"Oui, it's true. Our agreement was that I let go of my past, my guilt and choose her. Which I did. Yet for some reason tonight, she thought I betrayed her," Léopold said, his tone growing serious. "But I didn't do any such thing. You see, I was merely ordering food for us…as in human food."

"A girl's gotta eat," Dimitri added with a grin, knowing Léopold was about to do something he'd enjoy.

"Yes she does. But Laryssa thought I was bringing another woman into my home…for me. Now tell me, why would I do that when I've told her she's mine, when I've recently fed from her?"

"Leo, I…" Laryssa stammered. Her heart began to pound as she heard Léopold calmly tell Dimitri what had transpired between them in the car. *Why is he telling him what happened?* Even though she momentarily looked away, she was unable to take her eyes off Léopold. He was smiling. Damn him, he knew. He knew she'd been jealous. "You said you were ordering a meal. You just did that last night and a woman showed up. How am I supposed to know what you mean?"

"Because, mon amour," he crooked his finger at her, drawing her to him until she brushed against his calves, "I made you mine. And you must learn how to trust... to communicate."

"I'm sorry, but I..."

"So you see, Dimitri, she's very naughty." Léopold reached into the water until he'd fitted his hands underneath her arms. Easily lifting her out of the lake, he brought her upward so she straddled him on her knees. He kissed her lightly and continued. "Tonight on the dance floor...she teased me mercilessly, enjoying their eyes on her."

"She did?" Dimitri asked, raising his eyebrow at them.

"Tell me Dimitri, how do you feel about spankings?"

"I do like a good spanking." Dimitri flattened his hands behind him, leaning backward onto the dock.

Laryssa's eyes widened and she tried to push away from Léopold, but he held her firmly about her waist. Slowly he kissed her neck, placing his parted lips underneath her ear. As much as she wanted to struggle, the heat of him wrapped around her caused her to melt. A moan escaped her lips and before she knew what was happening, his lips had found her nipple. Her body lit on fire, and though she caught a glimpse of Dimitri, she soon refocused on Léopold's touch.

Abruptly he stopped and flipped her on her tummy, settling a towel under her head. She knew instantly what he planned to do. Torn between running away and encouraging him, Laryssa squirmed in his lap, putting pressure on his growing arousal.

"Take her hands," Léopold told Dimitri who smiled and turned to oblige. "Now, pet, shall we see what new heights we can reach?"

"Leo, don't do this," she said, feigning protest. Her pussy clenched in arousal as his hands glided over her inner thighs and caressed her bottom.

"I'll stop if that's really what you want. The truth is all I ask. In return, I'll be honest with you. Tonight, after all I'd confessed, you didn't trust me."

"I'm sorry, you know that…"

"Mon amour. Did you enjoy being watched tonight as we danced? Did you like it when I caressed your breast in front of all those people?" Léopold trailed his fingers down the crevice of her ass until he reached the heat of her core and then just as quickly removed his hand. "No lying, now. Tell me the truth."

"No, of course not," Laryssa insisted. She cried out as a sharp slap landed on her bottom. She clutched Dimitri's hands as the erotic sting sent a bolt of desire to her pussy. "Leo, no."

"Did you enjoy being watched? Do you enjoy Dimitri here, watching?"

Laryssa moaned as her hips writhed into Léopold's lap, seeking relief. Her nails dug into Dimitri's palms.

"Please," she begged as another slap landed on her flesh.

Léopold rubbed her reddened cheeks, smiling at how much she enjoyed it yet still refused to admit her penchant for exhibitionism. He slid a hand up her inner thigh and glided his fingers through her wetness.

"Oh God, Leo." Laryssa's orgasm built as his fingers found her clit. She looked up to Dimitri, who was smiling. Embarrassed, she buried her face into the towel and wondered how Leo knew her every fantasy. Things she dared not say. How could he know these things about her after only a few days? He was destroying the secrets she'd kept cached in her own conscience. Suppressing, hiding...it was what she'd learned how to do, but within minutes, he had left her soul unmasked.

"Do you see how difficult she can be, Dimitri?"

"She does seem to enjoy the spanking...but she looks like she wants to come."

"All she has to do is tell me the truth." Léopold slapped her cheeks twice more then plunged a thick finger inside of her, circling her clit with his thumb. Easing off the pressure, he removed the stimulus she needed to come but still held her tension tight. "Do you like this, Laryssa? Being spanked? Being watched? You're safe. All you have to do is say the word."

Laryssa shook her head, refusing to look at either of them, her hips gyrating into his hand. Dimitri played with her fingers and she finally raised her eyes to meet his. With his warm gaze upon her, her excitement escalated. She gasped as Léopold's palm landed on her bottom, causing a renewed gush of her own juices to flow between her legs.

"Say it, pet, or I'll stop," Léopold warned. "I'll let you go right now."

"Don't stop," she pleaded, giving in to his demand. "Yes. Goddamn you, yes."

Tears brimmed in her eyes, her body was shaking, readying to come. At her confession, any last remnants of angst about how she'd felt on the dance floor fell away like seeds in the wind. It killed her that Léopold could make her feel so incredibly open, knowing exactly how to bring her to the precipice of pleasure. Like a ball of string, her darkest dreams were coming unraveled.

"That's it, mon amour. Do not be ashamed. We are what we are." Léopold massaged her ass, while continuing to fuck her with his fingers. Goddess, he wanted to bend her over and make love to her right here on the dock, but he didn't think she was ready for that level of exhibitionism yet. Increasing the speed and pressure, he added a third finger, pushing her over the cliff. "Let go."

Rocking into his hand, Laryssa lost all touch with reality as her climax claimed her. Soaring high, she shook violently as he stroked the thin strip of nerves inside her core. Unrelenting, his fingers strung out every last spasm. She closed her eyes, gasping for breath, when she felt herself whirl into a thousand pieces. Materializing inside Léopold's bedroom, she fell into the sheets with him.

"What the hell, Leo?" She slapped at his arm, gasping for air. "You have to warn me when you do that. How do you do that anyway?"

"Like your magic, mine is my own," he responded.

"Can other vampires do that?"

"None I've met. But then again, I haven't met any others as old as I am. I wasn't able to do it right away. I suppose I perfected it sometime in the fifteenth century. Nevertheless, I prefer to keep it a secret. The element of surprise is an excellent weapon."

"So why'd you bring me back here? You seemed to be having fun on the dock. I know I was." She winked, still trying to catch her breath.

"Just thought it best we retire in private. As much as I know Dimitri enjoyed your performance, it's not very fair to leave him wanting more. I care for you both, but I'm afraid I won't share you." Léopold disrobed, and pulled Laryssa onto his chest.

"Let me get this straight. Giving me a spanking and getting me off in front of him is perfectly acceptable, but you don't want him to join in? Seems awfully selfish." Laryssa glided her palms over his bare chest, wrapping her leg over his waist.

"Oui. I'm very selfish. Dimitri knows this," he agreed. "I also have my limits. You're mine, no one else's."

"But he just watched you do that to me."

"Spank you? Make you come?" he said with a smile.

"Yeah, that." She rolled her eyes, still coming to terms with what just happened and how incredible it had been.

"It's different. That was for your benefit, not his, mon amour. Exhibitionism, even voyeurism I enjoy. But another man making love to my woman? No. That's not going to happen. Besides, what's the protest? Is this something you want…to make love with another man, a ménage? Because if it is…I don't…"

"I'll admit Dimitri's attractive, but no, I don't want a threesome. Still… about what we just did. Well, that may be normal for you, but for me…I don't do those things. I'm not like that."

"But of course you do and you are exactly like that. Did you not learn a thing from your spanking? You will do those things with me and you'll love it. You're beautiful when you come…so uninhibited. It's an honor to witness."

"It's just so embarrassing. God, Leo." She hid her face in his chest, pressing her lips to his skin. "It felt so good, though."

"No shame. I won't hear of it. Just tell me how it felt."

"When you spanked me, it was just a small sting, but then all the nerves inside me contracted. It made me so hot."

"Go on," he encouraged.

"I don't know. I just loved it. When you put your fingers in me…it felt so good. And I looked up and saw Dimitri watching, knowing he enjoyed watching us. The whole thing was crazy…but liberating." Laryssa pushed up on her arms so she could look at Léopold. "Leo, how do you know these things about me? I've never in my life done anything like that before."

"I may not be able to read auras, but I've had the benefit of time. I'm good at reading people, even when they don't make their intentions explicitly known to me. And now," he stroked her cheek with his fingers, gazing into her eyes, "the bond has begun. Your blood. It's as I told you it would be when we made love and I drank from you. I can feel your emotions projecting at me. Like tonight with the food thing…"

"So that's how you knew…"

"Oui. And if we choose to complete the bond someday, you'll be able to do the same with me." Léopold ran his thumb over her bottom lip. "I have to ask, though, why is it you felt so ashamed tonight? I could feel that too. Even when you came, you still wouldn't just let it go all the way."

"I guess it's just a hang-up. I've been hiding for so long…who I am, how I feel. When I came back from that pond that day, after I died, I had the biggest secret in the world. And when I finally told the people I trusted…my family, they freaked out on me. I mean, look at the lesson I learned when I shared what I was. Pretty much any fantasy, sexual or otherwise, that I've had, I kept to myself. Besides, I already felt like some kind of freak. Being naiad, I can't trust anyone. No one knew about me except for Avery, and even with her, I've kept closed up about all kinds of things. Believe me, it's made for some very lonely nights. My last boyfriend called me frigid. He was right. I just can't open up. It's not easy." Laryssa sighed with the realization that even though she'd accused Léopold of not living, she was guilty of the same. "So then you come along and just kind of sweep me up in this tornado, exposing my fantasies about being watched or held down. I hate it that you can do that. But I love it, too. You are the first person to ever really know all my secrets and accept me for who I am."

Laryssa took her eyes off of Léopold and noticed the room was lit up with candles. What had he done? On a rolling serving cart next to the bed, there was a large plate of sandwiches, cheese and fruit. Two flutes had been filled with champagne. The bottle sat in an ice bucket along with several bottles of water.

"Oh my gosh. The candles. They're beautiful…but how?"

"Arnaud. It's why I had to call him. You need to eat, Laryssa. Especially if I'm going to be feeding from you."

Laryssa turned back to Léopold and pressed her lips to his. "I'm sorry. I should have told you how I was feeling. I just…I don't want to see you with another woman. I know you need to eat, but after having you bite me today…what we shared was so intimate. I know it's not fair of me to ask."

With ease, Léopold flipped Laryssa onto her stomach and she squeaked.

"Oui, I cannot say if our roles were reversed that I'd ever let you do it to another man." Léopold rubbed her shoulders and spoke softly into her ear. His semi-erect cock brushed along the cleft of her bottom. "But we're just getting to know each other, as you've pointed out, and what we are proposing is a…"

"Commitment?"

"Oui. Of sorts." Léopold reached over to a small silver bag next to the food. He pulled out a small bottle, opened it. Pouring the aromatic oil into a palm, he warmed it with his hands before applying it to her skin.

"What is that? Ah, you have magic hands," she groaned with a smile. "Hmm…smells like cinnamon."

"You like? I have more surprises for you, my little naiad. Just wait." Glad she wasn't able to see the devious grin on his face, he worked down the muscles of her back, smoothing out the knots.

"Should I be scared or happy?" Laryssa knew Léopold was up to something. He hadn't even mentioned the food aside from saying she should eat.

"We need to talk," Léopold said, gliding his fingers over her soft globes.

"Hmm…about?"

"Us…how we're going to proceed with our relationship."

She giggled. "Relationship. Yes, Leo, I think that's definitely what we're doing."

"But first, let's talk about toys." Léopold continued to massage her, letting his thumb circle her puckered hole. With his other hand, he dripped oil onto her bottom.

"Toys?" Laryssa tried to lift her head, but as soon as she felt his finger probing, she sucked a breath and dropped her forehead into the sheets. She was afraid to ask, but managed to mumble the question through the linens. "Hmm…what kind of toys?"

"Laryssa, I want to know everything about you from your favorite color to what makes you scream the loudest in bed. I like to play. And I…want to play with you." Léopold pressed his thumb into her anus. Feeling her clench underneath his touch, he held it still, allowing her to relax. "That's right, mon amour. I want to explore all of you. Will you let me do that?"

Laryssa knew what he meant. She hadn't ever done what he was suggesting. Never had a man known her body the way he did, and he was just getting started.

"I've never…I know in the car you touched me there, but I…I'm not sure, Leo," she hesitated.

"How does this feel?" He removed his thumb and inserted two fingers into her, gently pumping in and out of her back hole.

"Tight, so full…but, oh God, why does everything you do to me feel so damn good? You'll be the death of me," she teased. The more he stretched her, the more she wanted him in her. She began to move her hips against the sheets, trying to get leverage as the ache between her legs grew stronger. But as the energy began to build, she felt the loss of his hands. "Don't stop."

"Toys. Remember? I'm going to take you here, too, but we've got to have patience. See?" Léopold held up a bulbous pink device to her eyes, but pulled it away quickly so she didn't have too much time to think about its size. Liberally applying oil to the rubber, he replaced his fingers with its slippery point.

"Leo, I'm not sure that's going to…ah, yes…fit." *God, what is he doing to me?* She was close to coming undone.

"Push back onto it. See, there it goes." Twisting it gently, he pressed it past her tight ring. "Just a bit more."

"Leo, Leo," she cried. A sting of pain was followed by the most delightful fullness that caused her pussy to flood in arousal. "Oh yes, please, Leo…"

"So beautiful. Look at you. I can't wait to fuck your ass." He massaged her bottom, spreading her cheeks apart, then adjusted the plug to make sure it was settled deep inside her. "But now, we must talk."

"What? Talk? Talk about what? Leo, you can't leave me…" she begged.

Léopold gently rolled her over, kissing her protest away. Letting his hands roam over her breasts and neck, he cupped her face and held her in place. Capturing her lips with his, he softly brushed his tongue over hers. Lost in their kiss, he speculated that she'd been created just for him. She was so adventurous. Passionate. He knew what he had planned next would unnerve her, but he was altogether certain she'd come alive when it was done. Sliding his hands over her shoulders, he spread her arms outward, toward the headboard.

The sound of Velcro tearing alerted Laryssa but not nearly soon enough. As she sought to move her arms, she found that Léopold had secured her wrists.

"Leo, what are you doing?" she asked calmly. Strangely, the restraints only served to ramp up her desire. Tugging her arms, she tested them to see if they'd come loose.

Léopold slid his body down hers, placing a kiss to her belly as he went. Securing her ankles, He slid his fingers into the cuffs to make sure they held without being too tight. He pushed out of the bed to admire his work, grinning as he caught the look of annoyance on her face. The glorious sight of Laryssa lying spread-eagle on his bed sent a rush of blood to his cock.

"Do you like it? I think it works quite nicely. It secures underneath the bed, so I don't need to damage the furniture," he grinned.

"Uh, yeah, very nice, Leo. Look what you've done to me," she laughed. "Okay, fun's over. Let me go."

"Come now, ma chérie. Must we have this conversation again?"

"The one about me saying no?"

"The one where I test your limits. You seemed to enjoy it very much last night, not to mention what we just did on the dock." He leaned over her breast and blew a warm breath on her nipple, smiling as it beaded in response. "And I do believe you are enjoying it now."

"Hey, what about safe words mister fifty shades of fangs? Safety first." She gave him a broad smile, continuing to test the straps.

"You're supernatural, Laryssa. Any confines I place on you are merely ones you allow. At any time, we both know you could move the straps out of place, freeing yourself. Go ahead, do it," he challenged. "I'll take you any way I can get you...I'm not picky. Tie me up, tie me down. Whatever."

She threw her head back against the pillow and groaned out loud, aware that he'd called her out on another one of her fantasies. The subtle feel of surrender felt natural, freeing. "How do you do that?"

"Last night. Your response to me. Every second I'm with you, I know you even better. And right now, I'm thinking that maybe you're hungry. Do you like brie?" He smiled. Naked, he sat on the edge of the bed and prepared it.

"Brie? You're kidding. Please tell me you're kidding."

"No. We need to have a discussion about feeding. So I feed you...open," he ordered with a smile. She made a face, but complied. He popped the tasty cheesy toast into her mouth. "See? It's good, no?"

"Yes. Okay, yes. Once again you are right. God, this really is delicious." She eyed him, noticing that he appeared deep in thought while he was slicing the cheese. "Talk to me, Leo. Why exactly am I tied up while we eat?"

"Because...if we're going to exclusively see each other, which I believe we are, then I'll need to feed from you." Léopold turned to Laryssa and gave her a devilish smile right before he started to spread brie on her nipple. "To be one's food...well that is how you say...a serious commitment. But for us, Laryssa, it is so much more. Not only will the bond grow deeper," he stopped to place a slice of cheese in the valley between her breasts and continued, "you'll begin to crave my bite. Eventually, I anticipate that we'll want to fully bond. And if that happens, you'll want my blood as well."

She opened her mouth to speak but Léopold popped a bite-sized finger sandwich into her mouth. She rolled her eyes in response, but soon made a subtle noise of contentment as she chewed it.

"So before we go any further, we should have a discussion. And I thought…what better way than to use food to demonstrate to you what it is like to be food?" Spreading a small amount of brie on her other bare breast, he smiled. Léopold snatched a couple of grapes and placed them down her belly in a line, clear to her pelvis. Then he lifted a glass of champagne, and brought it to her lips, careful not to spill any on her skin. "I believe in full disclosure. There haven't been many people in my life that I can trust. I need to be able to trust you…to know this is really what you want."

Laryssa swallowed and looked at the food covering her body.

"You're unbelievable, you do know that?"

"So I've been told." He fed her a slice of apple, smiling as she ate it.

"Leo, I do want this. I want to give us a chance. I know normal people…they take months, years to make these kind of decisions. But I also know I'm not normal. And you? Well, just look at me. Far from normal. You helped me to accept myself...to admit it...to be free. And even this," her eyes fell to her brie-covered nipples, "it's a little unconventional, but I know I'm gonna like being dinner."

She wagged her eyebrows at him and laughed.

Like a panther, Léopold stalked around the bed, carefully climbing up her body on his hands and knees until his face was inches from hers.

"You're certain?" he asked, looking into her eyes.

Laryssa nodded as her heart began to pound in her chest. The sight of Léopold, devastating and commanding, made her shiver in excitement. Like a dark prince, he cloaked her in his erotic shadow. As his lips descended on her breast, she sighed in relief that he'd finally touched her. The sweet pain of his teeth caused her to give a ragged gasp. Arching her back, she pressed herself up into his mouth.

"Goddess, woman, you have the most delicious skin." Using his tongue, he cleaned her rose-colored areola of the creamy white cheese. "My hunger for you is insatiable." Capturing her other pink tip, he sucked and laved until it was rigid with need. "Your magical essence is like no other blood I've had. I've never tasted anyone like you." Léopold crawled downward, placing his lips over each grape, replacing it with his tongue.

"Oh my God, please, Leo," she pleaded. Each time he kissed her flesh, the wetness between her legs increased, aching for his attention. As her core pulsated, her bottom tightened around the plug she'd forgotten was there, causing a vicious cycle of arousal to ensue. She attempted to clench her legs together but was unable to move. The cuffs on her ankles held her thighs far apart.

"One must take his time when eating. Savor the flavor," he mused. Rising above her, he reached for the bottle of champagne, letting the ice cold water drip across her chest.

Laryssa thrashed at the sensation, biting her lip. Her body was on fire and the contrast of the icy splash only surged the energy she'd held at bay. She knew that if she wanted to she could release her bindings, yet she resisted. Being at Léopold's mercy was immeasurably erotic and addictive. Being unable to anticipate his actions only added to the excitement of being under his spell.

Settling his knees between her legs, Léopold took his time licking her full peaks, making sure he'd eaten all the cheese and fruit from her body. His tongue glided downward, and he laughed as she bucked beneath him, trying to get him to move faster. Kissing below her belly button, his fingers separated her folds.

"Patience, pet." His lips touched her mound ever so lightly as he spoke. His voice vibrated against her soft flesh, but he didn't go any further.

"Please, Leo. I can't take it…I need you to touch me," she cried. He was torturing her with his lips, she thought.

"Did you know that champagne goes well with just about everything?" he commented blithely, spilling it over her clitoris. He heard her moan in sheer bliss as he licked over her swollen nub, sucking the effervescent delight.

Letting the bottle drop to the floor, he plunged two fingers into her satiny core.

Laryssa felt as if she would fly out of the bed as Léopold took to her pussy, making love to her with his mouth. As his fingers pumped in and out of her, she stiffened as her climax splintered throughout every cell of her body. Driving her hips against his mouth, she cried his name out loud, seized by the orgasm. As she tipped the scales, her wrists and ankles wrenched at the unyielding straps.

Léopold held her hip tightly with his hand as she reared up into him. Forever lost in the taste of her, he knew he'd never again drink from another woman. As she tightened upon his fingers, he relished the pleasure he could bring her. The thirst for her heightened and he could no longer deny himself of her heavenly blood. He reared his head up, his fangs distending from his gums. With a savage cry, he pierced the soft skin of her inner thigh,

A scream tore from her lips as she felt him slice into her soft flesh, biting her. A profound wave of ecstasy ripped through her as another orgasm slammed into her. As she gasped for air, she felt her legs and arms release from their bindings.

"Laryssa," Léopold grunted, relinquishing his bite.

Pushing up to his knees, he hooked his arms underneath her legs. With his eyes locked on hers, he fully sheathed himself in her warmth. He watched as Laryssa balled the sheets up in her hands, bracing herself as he retreated and then slammed into her heated channel. Feral with passion, he held onto her hips, pounding into her over and over again. As he felt her contract in climax around his swollen shaft, he screamed her name. Succumbing to his own release, Léopold willingly submitted to the unfathomable rapture, his seed erupting deep inside her.

As the last spasm tore through him, Léopold fell forward onto his forearms, careful not to crush Laryssa. Her flushed face smiled back at him, and he tried to hide the vulnerability that crept into his chest. So many years alone had kept him impervious to heartache. In a few short days, his entire life had evolved. She'd be his weakness, but also his strength. Given no choice but to come to terms with his emotions, he'd protect and cherish her. Laryssa was a gift he'd never expected, a dark horse who'd tame the monster inside.

He eased himself out of her, rolled onto his back and brought her with him so she lay upon his chest. Pulling the comforter up over them, he felt his body meld into hers as they snuggled together. Léopold and Laryssa quietly held each other not saying a word. They'd just committed to each other, all the while knowing they needed to find the artifact. With or without it, she could be dead by the end of the week.

It had been nearly a thousand years since Léopold had last prayed. But as he stroked his thumb along her wrist, he found himself asking for forgiveness and mercy, appealing to the Goddess to give him the power to save

Laryssa. It may have been too little too late, he knew, but he'd move heaven and hell to keep her in his life....forever.

Chapter Fourteen

The demon's hot breath singed the hairs on the back of Laryssa's neck. Its talons dug into her arms and its acrid stench filled her nostrils. Struggling, she tried to move, but couldn't. Her sticky eyelids blurred her vision. She blinked as tears began to clear her eyes. Red scorched earth cracked beneath her feet, and she knew she'd been taken somewhere far from New Orleans. A bloodcurdling scream tore from her lips. The terror gripped her mind, seizing her muscles. The echo of her voice filled the barren terrain, leaving no doubt she was in hell.

"Welcome home, princess," it growled into her ear.

Hysterical, Laryssa gasped for breath. Dizzy with panic, her knees buckled but the creature held her upright. The hardness of it pressed into her back and the bile in her stomach rose. *Oh God, how did I get here?*

"Tell me, did you find it yet?" Its claws moved from her arms to encircle her waist, reaching under her breasts.

"I don't…I don't have it. Let me go," she yelled. Jabbing an elbow towards its gut, she attempted to wrench free of its hold. Fear boiled over to anger as she realized it'd somehow taken her from her bed. All too real for a dream, her senses told her she was no longer on Earth. It'd somehow managed to extricate her from the warmth of Léopold's arms.

"You'll never escape me now, Laryssa. I broke through your wards...into your mind. Once I have the Tecpatl, I'll travel to the other plane whenever I want. But you," it extended its tongue and gave a hiss, "you shall remain here with me...forever."

"I'm going to kill you," she stated calmly. Numb to her terror, she had no other choice but to fight it. If death was inevitable, she'd face it like a warrior. "I'm going to find that Tecpatl and destroy you."

The demon's dark laughter filled the cavernous space.

"You just do that, princess. Just remember that your king is waiting on you. Tic toc. Tic toc. Do it or the baby will die. Perhaps I'll take a few others if I get the chance to leave here before it's found," it threatened.

"You're nothing to me," she snapped.

"Rylion. My name's Rylion. Say my name, because I'm your master. Soon it's my blood you'll crave. Because I'm generous, I'm going to give you a little gift...something to remember me by." It squeezed her tightly and dragged its claws deep into the smooth skin of her belly until her blood spurted onto the ground.

Laryssa cringed as its long forked tongue wrapped around her neck and traveled down her chest. A new surge of horror speared through her psyche. Thrashing wildly, she screamed and kicked to get away from the barbed fingers that eviscerated her abdomen. Her feet cut into the sharp gravel, tearing up the flesh. She bit it with her teeth and dug her fingernails into its scaly arms. All at once, the ground broke and she tumbled into oblivion. *Falling. Falling. Falling.* Her deafening screams went unanswered.

The ear-piercing sound of Laryssa's voice launched Léopold into action. Sprinting out of the shower, he found her tangled in the sheets. Her eyes were closed into reddened circles, her whitened face stained in tears.

"Laryssa," he whispered. Gently, he rubbed her arm, and lifted her body into his embrace so that he cradled her like a child. She continued to flail her arms and legs as if she were fighting an invisible enemy. "It's okay, ma chérie. Come now, it's just a dream."

A final scream escaped her lips before her eyes flew open. Seeing Léopold, she clutched at him, gasping for breath.

"Leo," she wept. "It was here."

"No, it was just a nightmare. See, look around you. No one's here. Just us."

Footsteps grew louder and Laryssa jumped as Dimitri flung open the door to the bedroom.

"What's wrong?" Confused, Dimitri looked around the room, finding only Léopold and Laryssa in each other's arms. "What the hell just happened up here? I could hear the screaming all the way downstairs…and it wasn't the good kind, either."

"A nightmare," Léopold told him. But as he adjusted Laryssa on his lap, he noticed a bright red stain blossoming in the linens. "What the…"

"Ow!" Laryssa cried out. Coming down out of her shock, a searing pain pierced her abdomen. "Something's wrong."

"Help me cut this off her. Use your claws," Léopold told him, tearing at the fabric.

Dimitri helped to rip away the fibers until they reached her skin.

"Careful," he said. Her belly, fully exposed, was covered in blood.

"Jesus Christ," Léopold exclaimed. He shot Dimitri a look of concern and then kissed Laryssa's head. "How did this happen?"

"I don't know…somehow…it was here. No, I was there. It…it had me, touched me." She shivered, remembering the feel of its scaly skin upon hers, the smell of it, the wetness of its tongue.

"Dimitri, come here. Take her," Léopold insisted.

"No, don't leave me. Please, Leo."

"The lake. Let me get water. If I take you with me, it'll hurt too much. I'll just be a few seconds," he promised. Remembering how Ilsbeth had used it to heal her wound the day before, he reasoned it would work again.

"Okay," Laryssa grunted as Léopold lifted her into Dimitri's arms. "You promise?"

"I promise." Léopold grabbed the ice bucket and instantly disappeared.

"Hey cher, we're gonna find this son of a bitch. Don't you worry." Dimitri stroked her hair and gently patted the five-inch incisions that dotted her tummy, trying to clot the blood. "Just listen to me…Leo's got this, okay?"

"It hurts." She sucked a breath, trying to focus on Dimitri's voice

Léopold appeared within minutes, and knelt before them. Cupping his hands, he drew up the liquid into his palms.

"The water healed you before. This'll work. Here we go…" Léopold let the water dribble over her open wounds, wishing he could be the one to take her pain. To his relief, his assumption was correct. As it hit her skin, it began stitching her back together. "Look, it's working"

"Oh God," she sighed as the pain began to subside. "We've got to find it."

"The Tecpatl?" Dimitri asked.

"Oui." Léopold knew what she'd meant. He couldn't agree more considering the demon had almost killed her in his own house. If it'd come to her here, it'd be able to find her anywhere.

"I'm going to kill it." Laryssa's face grew serious. A dim sadness flickered in her eyes, but they no longer held tears. The seed of hate had been planted and she planned to let it grow.

"Maybe you need to rest," Dimitri suggested, looking to Léopold for support.

"No, I need to find it. Now." Laryssa paused, glancing to Dimitri and then to Léopold. Her voice never wavered as she spoke with conviction. "I'm going to find that knife and drive it so deep in its heart that it'll never be able to dislodge it. When it's relegated to the pits of hell, it'll spend an eternity wishing it never met me."

Léopold and Dimitri let the silence fill the room, not responding. Everyone knew the situation would come to a head soon. They also knew Laryssa was right. She was the only one who could kill it. They had to spend the day reading the book, researching every last possibility in an effort to locate the artifact. If the demon had found a way to make itself tangible, worldly, able to strike at flesh, Laryssa's days were numbered.

⤙ *Chapter Fifteen* ⤚

Three days had passed since the demon had attacked Laryssa. Yet as she ran her fingers over her bare stomach, it was as if she still could feel it crawling all over her. Even though Léopold had read the book from beginning to end, he'd found absolutely nothing to indicate where the Tecpatl was located. She'd spent hours on the internet researching both naiads and the Aztec civilization. Calls to experts at the Smithsonian, the Metropolitan Museum of Natural History and several other prominent institutions proved futile. While they all knew of Tecpatls or kept them in their collections, none had been specified as the Tlalco Tecpatl. Even more disheartening, most denied its very existence.

Exhausted, she and Léopold had made love only a few times since the night they'd committed to each other. Laryssa suffered insomnia, worried the demon would call on her again in her sleep. As depression set in, she considered how unfair it was of her to insist that Léopold only feed from her. It was likely that she'd be dead by the end of the week. She'd asked that he choose her, yet what right had she to give herself to him when she knew she would die? The guilt made her want to push him away so he wouldn't care for her, wouldn't miss her when she died. After the devastation he'd endured from the death of his wife and children, she refused to be responsible for killing him a second time.

Returning to the lake had been Laryssa's only refuge. The more time she spent in it, the more she wondered what it'd be like to just live there like a mermaid in a sea. Rising through the water, she glided along the waves, pretending not to notice Léopold sitting in his chaise longue on the dock. She hated the book, the very one glued to his hands. Like a worthless newspaper, she wished she could throw it in the fireplace and light it up in flames. She let the satisfying fantasy float around in her head for several minutes before gathering the nerve to approach Léopold. It tore her apart to suggest that he call on a donor, but she resolved to talk with him....to prepare him for her death. Terrified of his reaction, she swam slowly toward him, keeping her eyes lowered to the water.

"How are you, my beautiful naiad?" he asked, never taking his eyes off the pages.

"I'm okay...I'm wet. Anything new?"

"'Fraid not. Just more of the same jumbled mess of water facts...insane, really. I know this was written several hundred years ago, but seriously, it's nothing but babble."

"Garbage in, garbage out," she muttered.

"Hmm?"

"I said, garbage in, garbage out. Did you ever consider that Ilsbeth just, I don't know, got it wrong? Fucked up? Maybe she's full of shit too," she seethed.

"Temper, temper, ma chérie. We'll figure this out." He took a deep breath and sat the book on his lap, adjusting his sunglasses.

"Yeah, well, you're not the one destined to become the bride of Satan in a few days. No, that'd be me. Lucky, lucky me." Laryssa flopped to her back, moving her hands and legs back and forth, floating on the surface.

"A demon," he corrected.

"What? Did you just seriously say that?" Laryssa lifted her head to yell over at him. "What the fuck difference does it make whether it's a demon or the real king of hell, or not? It told me it was a king. Believe me, where it took me, it was hell…hell for me anyway. Do you know what happens when I don't have water?"

"Oui, I do. And I'm well aware that you're scared. I don't blame you. Don't you think that I'm pissed off that we can't find anything in this damn book? That I'm scared to death that I'm going to lose you? Jesus Christ, Laryssa, I just found you…I need you. But we've gotta keep focused. Keep our eye on the proverbial prize. We can't get distracted. You're letting your fear blur your thoughts." Léopold hadn't adjusted to the trepidation Laryssa had projected since she'd been attacked. No amount of cajoling had helped to alleviate her spiraling descent into hopelessness.

Léopold decided that he was done being nice. He'd push her to the edge, incite her anger. He needed her to fight. Leaning over, he placed his forearms on his knees, holding the book with both his hands.

"Did you hear me? Are you listening, nymph? Because I need you to stop feeling sorry for yourself. This is far from over. I'm telling you that you need to shove all that woe-is-me crap down deep and get with the game. I don't know what's going on in that pretty little head of yours, but whatever you're getting ready to tell me, I know I'm not gonna like it. So what's it going to be? Are you going to just lay back and die? Because if that's the case, we might as well just call the demon now." Léopold thought he may have gone a little too far, but he was getting desperate to shake her out of her funk.

"You, you…" Laryssa saw red. Did he really think she'd given up? Mad at him, angrier at herself, she went on the attack. Her voice got louder as she swam toward him. "You condescending ass! Do you really think I survived all this time to just roll over and let some fucking demon take me? God, I hate this," she screamed. Hauling her palm back into the water, she shoved it forward.

A deluge of cold spray splashed over Léopold. He jumped up and threw off his sunglasses, wiping at his face and hands. In the process, the book fell to the deck.

"And there ya go. That's the spirit," he laughed. Unfolding a towel, he wiped his face.

"You're mean," she spat back at him, finding it difficult not to laugh. The sight of her debonair vampire, hopping up and down as if he'd been doused in holy water brought a smile to her face.

"I prefer the term, 'motivational', no?" He shot her a broad smile before searching for his shades. They, too, had fallen to the ground. As he reached to snap them up, he noticed the book. Its brown leather cover was covered in a speckled glow, similar to the color that Laryssa emanated when she submerged.

"Laryssa, come here," he called, his voice tense. "The book."

"Yeah, yeah," she sighed. But as she pushed up onto the warmed wooden planks, she, too, saw what had captivated Léopold's attention. "What is it? How? It's sparkling."

"No, ma chérie, it's glowing. Glowing just like you. Don't you see? It's the water," he exclaimed. "We should have known."

"What should we do?" Laryssa asked excitedly. Reason quickly set in and her mind began to turn with possibilities. "If it's the water, maybe I should take it in with me. Wait. No. We can't just throw it in the water. The pages are paper. I'm certain of it. There's no way that would work. Maybe brush it on there…carefully or something. But look at it. There're a thousand pages. I mean, how would we know where to start?"

"Come." He patted the dock. She gave him a look, raising her eyebrow at him. Realizing how much she disliked being bossed around, he corrected his words in a sweet tone that told her he understood her perfectly. "Would you please join me?"

He laughed as he said the words aloud, aware of how ridiculous he sounded. Léopold Devereoux didn't ask. He ordered. Sometimes nicely, sometimes, not at all. Being with Laryssa was changing all of that, teaching him a set of manners he wasn't entirely sure he wanted to learn. But as her laughter filled the air, he shook his head, knowing he'd done the right thing. The sound of her joy was becoming the most delightful part of his day.

"Yes, darling," she drawled, smiling up at him. "I do love sitting next to you."

"Mais oui. I'm a catch." He winked and gave her a lopsided grin, chuckling as she shoved on him gently with her shoulder. "Look, it's starting to fade."

Leaning forward, he captured a bit of the water in his hand and flicked it over the cover, but the spots continued to vanish. He blew out a breath.

"Wait. Let's just think. It's my book, right? If anyone could make it work, it would've been discovered already. So maybe," she hesitated, then dipped her fingers into the basin and ran them across the cover. Instantly, it lit up again. A broad smile broke across her face at the victory. "I'm the one who has to do it."

"Excellent. Now….we start at the beginning," Léopold said, flipping the cover open to the first blank page. "The table of contents. Fifty chapters. I'll hold it. Go ahead, touch it," he urged.

Laryssa did as he said, carefully brushing her wet finger across the paper. She shook her head, disappointed nothing was revealed. Léopold carefully pulled over another sheet. Half way down, a line began to appear.

"Leo, look," she whispered, astonished it was working.

"Lucky number twenty-seven." Léopold took out his cell phone as the writing appeared on the page. When she lifted her hand, he snapped a picture. "Calle del Arsenal de las Ursulinas? Mères des filles. La clé."

"The historical signs? Rue des Ursulines. Ursuline Avenue. What does the rest mean?"

"Mères des filles translates to mothers of girls. La clé. The key."

"I was hoping for something along the lines of: 'follow this map to get the knife'. Guess I knew it wouldn't be that easy." She blew out a breath and looked out to the lake, deep in thought. "Mothers. Girls. I don't know. Is there a school on Ursuline? Maybe it's hidden there."

"Filles du' Casket."

"What?"

"Filles du' Casket. The casket girls. The convent on Ursuline."

"You mean the one that tourists visit? Rumors of scary vampires?" She laughed.

"Oui. That's the one. But as you know, my pet, vampires have been around for the millennium. The Ursulines came over in the early eighteenth century. Perhaps the good sisters protected the Tecpatl? They were known to take in young girls, the poor and the like.

Maybe a naiad sought safe harbor and hid the relic within the convent walls?"

"But where? I guess we could get in on a tour, but where would we even begin to look?"

"Not worried about how we'll get in...I've got that covered." He shot her a knowing smile. "It's the where that's a problem. The place's fairly large, and the item is probably small. Maybe we should try chapter twenty-seven...to see if there's more."

Laryssa turned the pages, her anxiety rising. *Two days.* It was all she had left to find the Tecpatl. Why couldn't the naiad who wrote the book be direct about its location? She had an inkling of worry that the enigmatic words would only lead them on a wild goose chase, but they were out of options. She shrugged and shook her head in frustration, searching for the chapter. *Let the chase begin.* Again, she dipped her fingers in the water, running them over the wafer thin folio, her eyes widening as more letters surfaced.

"Le waterleaf tombe donne la clé," Léopold read.

"What's it mean?" she asked.

"The waterleaf falls bestows the key...which makes absolutely no sense at all." He sighed and plowed his fingers into the hair on the back of his head.

"Maybe it'll make sense once we get there?"

"Maybe." *It fucking better*, he thought. He'd just spent time trying to convince Laryssa they'd find the Tecpatl, yet the text made no mention of it. "Try the next page, there's got to be more."

She repeated the process, but this time a primitive drawing appeared. A series of lines hovered above what looked to be scales, a fish. Below the fish was a key. Laryssa sighed, unsure of how it tied in with the Tecpatl. Immediately she pictured the river.

"Un poisson," Léopold commented, looking at the picture. "Like you, no?"

"Did you just call me a fish?"

"Oui. But in a good way." He laughed and placed a kiss to her cheek. "Surely this is tied to you? It's a fish. And water. I'm not sure what it means yet but at least we have a clue."

"So, uh, how do you feel about breaking into a convent later?"

"Sounds good. I take all my dates there," he teased.

"Thought you didn't date?" she countered.

"Touché. That was true, but I do now."

"A convent, huh? You sure vampires don't burst into flames at the sight of a cross?"

"Easy there. You're going to insult my delicate ego."

"Delicate ego? Now that's a good one, Leo," she jibed.

"Come now, we must get ready to leave. Sun will be down in an hour. We'll take the car then, you know, pop in," he suggested.

"About that…you promised to warn me first, right?"

"Promise, mon amour," he purred, kissing her neck. This woman would break him, he knew. He had to figure out a way to save her. If she died, he might as well stake himself.

~&· *Chapter Sixteen* &~

"Nice wheels. Can I drive it?' Laryssa asked, trying to distract herself from the fact that they were about to break into a convent. *Yep, if there is a more direct path to hell, I can't think of one....well, aside from the damned demon.*

"You know I'm very fond of you, no?" Léopold deflected her question, staring at the cream-colored plastered wall that surrounded the old convent.

"So you'll let me drive it?"

"You're the most beautiful little naiad I've ever met."

"I'm the only naiad you've met. Can I drive home?" She smiled at him, realizing he was avoiding answering.

"Well, aside from Ava, that's true. You ready to go inside?"

"I've never been in a Lamborghini before. How fast does it go?" she continued.

"Do you recall me telling you that I don't share?" he countered.

"Yeah, that was about me, not the car. I promise to be careful. Besides, it's just a car."

"Just a car," he sniffed. "You do realize how much this car…"

"No. Don't care. And why's that? Let me see… yeah, that's right, I could be dead in two days. Just checking…no, I don't care how much it costs. But I would like to drive really, really fast." Without equivocation, she reached over and took his hand in hers. Their easy conversation had filled her soul, allowing her to forget, albeit only for seconds, the sobering reason why they were sitting in the car in the first place.

Léopold glanced out the window with a grin and shook his head. He'd give her the damn car and anything else she wanted to make her happy. He knew she was worried…worried they'd fail, that the demon would kill her. Maybe he couldn't change the situation, but he could lift her spirits.

"We'll see, mon amour. I'm not going to let you get us killed speeding before we have a chance to make love again."

Laryssa made a sad face, sticking out her bottom lip and then quickly smiled. "Please…."

"Okay, okay. I'll let you drive it. On one condition." He took the keys from his pocket and held them out to her.

"What is it?' She raised a curious eyebrow at him.

"When all this is done, I want you to move in with me."

"It's kinda soon for that, isn't it?"

"Shall I tie you up again when we get home?"

"So it's just my blood you want?"

"No. It's you that I want. I want you in my home. I want you in my bed. And I want you there forever." Léopold had deliberately let the bond grow stronger each day, aware that it would only be a matter of weeks before he sought to complete their bond. It had been a conscious choice that at one time he'd thought preposterous, yet he'd never felt more satisfied or alive. Laryssa recognized the serious tone of Léopold's voice. No longer engaging in easy banter, he'd pinned her in place. Her heart sped with the realization that he was genuinely asking her to move in with him. Her mind warred over what she wanted to do versus what she'd been conditioned as a human to think she should do, what was socially acceptable. Despite knowing she was immortal, she had led her life very much as a human. But having a demon slice open her midsection, one who planned on dragging her into its horrific underworld, forced her to set priorities and face the reality of her situation. There was a very good chance she'd die in two days. With no time for a bucket list, agreeing to move in with the man she was falling for seemed to be the most rational choice in the world.

"Yes," Laryssa replied softly.

"Excellent," Léopold exclaimed, pleased with her answer. He extracted the keys from the ignition and dangled them in front of her. "Ride home. You drive."

"Really? You're serious?" She extended her palm and he dropped them in her hand.

"A man never jokes about his car." The corner of his lip curled upward, his eyebrow raised.

Laryssa wrapped her arms around Léopold and hugged him. She could tell she surprised him as he slowly returned her embrace. Biting her lip, she realized that she'd almost told him how she felt. How embarrassing, she thought, that she'd almost used the *love* word. Aware of why they were sitting in the car, emotion welled inside her chest. Fighting the tears she knew would come all too easily, she pressed her face into his shirt. Inhaling his masculine scent, she sought to sear the memory of him into her psyche. From the way he smelled to the way he firmly held her in his arms, she'd never forget him. Whether in heaven or hell, he'd always be hers.

"This is creepy," Laryssa whispered, carefully walking through the darkened convent.

"I promise to protect you from the vampires," he teased, keeping his voice quiet.

"Maybe we should've told Sydney we were breaking in. Or even better, asked if we could come in…you know, legally." She shone her flashlight toward the floor, hoping no one would see them and call the police.

"The police know nothing of our ways," he said with disdain.

"But what about Sydney? Hello? She lives with a vampire, right?"

"Oui. But she's new in town. Besides, she needs to keep Ava safe, not babysit me."

"I'm just sayin'. Would be nice to be able to just flick on the lights and look around."

"I can see perfectly fine. Come this way," he told her.

"You do remember that I'm not a vampire or wolf? I'm very close to being human. Do you think you're going to be able to accept being…" She'd almost said 'married' and immediately swallowed her words, shocking herself that she'd even had the thought.

"Being what?" he said, unaware of what she was thinking. He gestured toward her. "This way, into the living quarters."

"Are you going to be able to accept that I'm kinda human? I know I have some abilities, but I've been less than effective in helping with finding this knife. Look at how long it took us to figure out what to do with the book. For crying out loud, I had it in my shop for two months and didn't even know it," she huffed, following him down a long hallway.

"You're naiad. You just haven't had time to strengthen your powers yet. And eventually," *with my blood…when we bond,* "you'll be able to do even more things. Don't sell yourself short."

"Maybe…if I actually live long enough. Do you see anything? What was the saying again? Something about a leaf."

"Le waterleaf tombe donne la clé. The waterleaf falls bestows the key." Léopold studied the artwork, hoping there'd be some clue or picture of a leaf.

"Ugh, damn cryptic naiads. Waterleaf. What do you think that even means? Are we talkin' lilies or maybe ferns?"

"Not sure. Maybe the book referred to an actual waterleaf. It's a species of plant. Flourishes in the water. Little blue flowers."

"I have to admit that I'm impressed with your knowledge of horticulture." Catching the small laugh he gave, she pressed him. "What? How'd you know that?"

"Wikipedia. Even an old man like me can use the internet, ma chérie," he grinned. "But look around here, there's no plants at all. I still think that it must be in one of the paintings."

"Look at this staircase…it's incredible," Laryssa commented, flashing the light over the wood. The three-story-high spiral staircase curved upward so that you could look down to the floor while you ascended. "You know this is one of the oldest buildings in the city?"

"Oui. The architecture, it's…"

"It's waterleaf," she interrupted, taking notice of the underbelly of the staircase, which had been inlaid with an intricate cream-colored molding.

"Where?"

"Here." She pointed to the edges that were carved with tiny leaves. "This pattern. It's waterleaf. I can't believe I didn't put it together. I've been in so many mansions…see this pattern. Usually it's carved in the crown molding. But this is rare. I mean look at it, it's a huge area. It covers the entire back of the staircase going up to the ceiling."

"Oui." Léopold sighed, assessing the situation. Taking off his suit jacket, he handed it to Laryssa. She took it from him, giving him a look of confusion. *This is not going to be pretty.* As much as he appreciated fine woodwork, it had to go. *Pity.* Without warning, he balled up his fist and punched it directly through the molding. He heard her gasp as splinters flew into the air.

"Jesus, Leo, what the hell are you doing?" she shouted, bringing her hands to her mouth. "You just totally wrecked that wall. This is a historic building. Oh my God…Lord, please forgive this vampire. We're in a fu…freakin' convent, for God's sake."

"Oui, I'm aware of the fact, but we don't have a lot of time. And I don't have patience. I'll be sure to send a generous donation that more than covers the damage." Léopold began to peel the wood away from the back of the stairs.

"But…but…" she stuttered. Altogether aghast with his actions, she shook her head. But as she shined her flashlight into the empty space, curiosity took over her actions. Intrigued, she searched the cavity. "Leo, Leo…do you see that?"

"See what?"

"Stop for a second. Look, that there." She pointed to a small shiny object on the floor. "That's not a key. What is it?"

"Stand back," he ordered. Reaching into the chamber, his fingers brushed over the piece of metal. Leaning a bit further, he was able to collect the small item. Lifting it to the light, they both studied their find. "Un poisson?"

"A fish," she confirmed. "It's brass. It doesn't look like any kind of key that I've ever seen, but that has to be it. Can I see it?"

Léopold deposited it into her palm. The cold bumpy ridges of its scales were rigid, and she couldn't tell if it was an ornamental piece or something else. But as she flipped it over, she noticed the small round bar that ran from its tail to its head.

"Hey, I've seen one of these. Well, not this exact one but a tiger. An antique tiger lock. This one's similar. I think it's a puzzle, though. The key must be inside it." She shook it and it rattled. "There's something in here."

Léopold brushed the dust off his hands, retrieving his coat from the crook of Laryssa's elbow, where she'd been holding it. He slid his arms into the sleeves, and smoothed down the wrinkles. Laryssa glanced up at him, reminded that behind his refined supermodel looks, lurked a ferocious warrior.

"We've gotta go," Léopold said, hearing sirens in the distance.

"But what about this?" Her eyes darted over to the shards of wood covering the floor.

"As I said, I'll make a donation." Léopold put his arms around her waist, attempting to prepare her for their departure. "Ready?"

"Léopold, you can't just leave..." Laryssa lost all thought as he transported them back into the car. They fell into the passenger side seat together. As her head stopped spinning, she took note of her positioning. She sat atop of him with her legs straddling his. She gave him a small smile, and brushed her breasts into his chest.

"Now this I like," he quipped, pressing his erection up into her.

"You are a very bad vampire. Making a mess like that," she scolded, her voice husky. "Naughty boy."

"Is that a challenge? 'Cause you've got no idea how bad I can be," he replied, letting his fangs drop.

"Léopold," she feigned protest. Being so close to him caused her body to flare in heat. "We've got work to do."

"It's true." He nuzzled his nose into her neck, pressing his lips to her skin.

"Why does breaking and entering make me horny? You're corrupting me," she laughed.

"All day long, ma chérie, all day long." He laughed, but knew he was seriously close to tearing off her clothes. Realizing that if they went further, they'd be having sex in a parked car, with the police soon to arrive, Léopold gripped her by the waist and lifted her into the driver's seat. "Now be careful with my baby. Treat her gently. Avec amour."

"Nothing but love, baby," she said with a wink.

Léopold braced himself as Laryssa inserted the key into the ignition, and the engine roared to life. His stomach flipped at the sight of his gorgeous naiad with her hands wrapped around the steering wheel. As she shot him a sexy smile, Léopold knew for certain the experience would be something he'd already guessed. In more ways than one, he was in for the ride of his life.

⚜ Chapter Seventeen ⚜

Sydney patted Ava on the back, while rocking her in the chair. The sweet smell of the baby warmed her from the inside out, and she wondered if she'd ever change her mind about not having children. Even though she and Kade couldn't get pregnant, the possibility of adopting had always remained an unspoken option.

She had to admit to herself that the past four days, living with the Alpha and his mate, hadn't been even close to a hardship. Both Logan and Wynter had shown her what she'd always imagined to be southern hospitality at its finest. Strangely, she found herself becoming close to Wynter. From sunup to sundown, they chatted about everything from recipes to television shows. Granted, their cloistered existence was beginning to wear thin in that they both yearned to get out of the house, but Sydney knew that by the end of the week, something was going to break in the case. God help them all, she prayed that it wouldn't involve death.

Daily, she'd checked the interior and exterior, ensuring that there were no weak links in the physical structure of the house. Samantha had seen to spells, making sure that no demonic forces could cross over into the home. Unbeknownst to the wolves and the vampires, she'd ordered increased police patrols to be set up within a five block radius. Despite having taken every safety precaution, Sydney knew all too well that if a supernatural force wanted to get to a person, they'd never give up on a plan of attack. Even if they had to wait it out, eventually they'd make their move and strike.

Sydney smiled at Wynter, who'd entered the room. She'd thought it was interesting how the Alpha and his mate had taken to the baby. Even if they never found Ava's biological father, Sydney was certain the baby would have a good home. Between Léopold and the Alpha, there was no question she'd be raised with love.

"How's our baby doin'?" Wynter asked Sydney, drying her hair.

"She's good. It's amazing to me how she sleeps so well after her bottle. She's just so adorable," Sydney said. She got up from the chair, and walked to the crib. Carefully laying Ava on her back, she pulled the baby blanket over her.

"She really is, isn't she? You know, I never thought I'd want pups so quickly. But having Ava here…it'll be really hard to let her go." Wynter's eyes teared up as she spoke. She turned back to the mirror and toweled at her hair, attempting to hide her emotion.

"Have you given any thought to what might happen if they can't find her father? I know the priority's been on killing this demon and keeping everyone safe, but at some point, we're gonna have to have the conversation."

"Logan's said he's put out feelers to his contacts…to packs around the country. Léopold. Well, you know him. He immediately hired an investigator. But they've turned up nothing."

"And what happens if that's the answer? There's a chance the guy may have offed himself, ya know. I see it happen all the time."

"The only thing I know is that she'll be raised as pack. Ilsbeth said that Ava's naiad. Even if she's a hybrid wolf, she'll go through the change. She'll shift. She needs to be with pack," Wynter insisted.

"Hey, you'll get no argument from me. I just wondered if you'd thought about maybe adopt…" Sydney went quiet as the hairs on the back of her neck stood up.

"What was that noise?" Wynter whispered loudly. "Did you hear that? It was something…I don't know…It sounded like a wind chime maybe."

Sydney caught Wynter's gaze and held her finger to her lips to shush her.

Wynter nodded as Sydney went to the dresser. She slipped on her holster and gun she'd removed earlier so that she could hold baby. Wynter quickly crossed the bedroom, scooping Ava up into her arms. Sydney looked out the window, noticing a few people walking down the street. Nothing appeared unusual, but she knew better than to believe what her eyes told her. The noise sounded again and she knew something was wrong. She looked over to Wynter and silently mouthed, "Stay here."

Sydney heard Wynter click the lock on as she shut the door. She quietly padded down the stairs, bumping into Jake, who was running toward his Alpha's bedroom.

"Where's Logan?" Sydney asked, her voice barely audible.

"Logan and Dimitri are on their way here. I just texted them. Did you see anything?"

"Nothin', just a few tourists. I'm goin' to go outside and see what's going on…make sure things are still locked up. Cover me?"

"I'll take the second floor and spot you," Jake told her.

"Come lock the door behind me," she responded. "Don't let anyone in this house."

"No one gets in," he agreed, taking out his gun.

"Seriously, no matter what happens, do not leave Wynter and the baby."

Sydney watched as he bolted it shut then went through the archway toward the gate. Even as she walked toward the exit, everything appeared exceedingly calm. The fresh night breeze blew through her hair, and she wondered if maybe one of Logan's neighbors had installed a wind chime. When she reached the gate, she peered through the wrought iron. Seeing nothing, she pushed the handle and guardedly exited the property to check the gate's lock from the exterior. Looking up the street to her left, she caught sight of a pedicab traveling away from her and reasoned that maybe the noise they'd heard could have been caused by it. Glancing to the right, she noticed a well-dressed man standing on the corner, checking his watch. Even though he looked harmless, she kept sight of him in her peripheral vision as she double checked the gate. Then without warning, he turned to walk in her direction.

"Excuse me," she called out using her professional tone of voice, and lifted her badge from the chain around her neck, so that she could easily identify herself as a police officer as he approached. The stranger appeared not to hear her, looking the other way.

"Sir," she said loudly.

Her second attempt caught his attention and he turned to her with a smile. Although the man looked exceptionally handsome, something about him seemed off, not quite right. His smile was too friendly, as if he'd recognized her as a long lost friend. A flash of creepiness clutched at her chest, the kind she'd get when arresting sex offenders. While his looks appeared benign, her instincts told her otherwise.

"Sir, stay right there," Sydney ordered. She reached for her gun and raised it. He deliberately approached her with his arms outstretched. Bracing the weapon with both hands, she held the barrel upward, looking around her to make sure there weren't any bystanders.

"Sir, if you don't stop right there, I may be forced to shoot," she told him. Out of the corner of her eye, she spotted Jake standing behind an open second story window with his gun aimed downward.

"Sydney," the man trilled. His voice sounded freakishly low, as if he'd been using an electronic device to disguise his identity.

She watched in astonishment as his body flickered, revealing an unearthly form. *Scales. Horns.* Without hesitation, Sydney fired into the night. The bullets hit its chest, but sailed through its body without injuring it.

"What are you?" she whispered as it came toward her. By the time it had reached her feet, it had transformed into its true hellish form. Its long talons snapped together on the pavement, the stench of its breath saturating the air.

"I'm your worst nightmare. And I want you to deliver a message," it hissed.

"A message?"

"A message for the naiad. For the wolves. Tell them I was here and I'll be back for the baby if she doesn't return the Tlalco Tecpatl to me by midnight tomorrow. I'll find her."

"Yeah, okay. Well, here's my message..." Sydney unloaded an entire clip into the demon, praying to God it would take him down. When the dust settled, she gasped as it lurched for her, laughing as it did so.

Grabbing her by the throat, it lifted her off the ground. Sydney could hear Jake firing off his weapon yet the creature held tight. Extending its claws, it sliced its entire fist into Sydney's abdomen. Like a red hot poker, its nails pierced clear through from her belly to her back. She released a horrific scream as her organs burst apart at its touch. Blood spewed onto the street as it threw her to the ground. Gasping, her throat filled with fluid. The demon leaned over her wound and spat its acidic saliva into her before dissipating into the night. As the circle of darkness surrounded her, thoughts of Kade danced in her mind. Although she tried to fight, the sweet sensation of death called to her, lulling her to sleep.

❦ *Chapter Eighteen* ❦

Laryssa's stomach lurched with the news that Sydney had been attacked. By the time Dimitri had called Léopold, they'd already driven to the lake. Laryssa had remained silent the entire trip back to the Quarter, her thoughts spinning with dread. Even though it was good news that the demon hadn't breached the wards, it had viciously assaulted the detective.

Laryssa couldn't fathom why they hadn't taken her to a hospital. Léopold insisted that there were no human doctors who would have been able to save her. Her organs had endured systemic trauma and the resulting injuries were catastrophic?. No human should have survived. The gash to her abdomen had sliced her open clear through to the other side. Dimitri had relayed that Kade had arrived within minutes of her being slain on the street. Kade's blood had been the only hope, keeping her alive. It should have healed her completely, but she hadn't fully recovered. Still unconscious, she clung to life.

As Laryssa and Léopold slid open Logan's back door, they were met with somber faces. The Alpha's eyes met Léopold's, but he made no move to release his mate from his arms. Samantha sat, holding the baby and glanced up to Léopold with reddened eyes. Rather than engaging in conversation, Léopold merely nodded and waited as Dimitri approached him.

"Hey man," the beta said, putting his hand on Léopold's shoulder. "Laryssa. How's it goin'?"

"We found something. It's some kind of a lock, maybe a puzzle," Laryssa offered. Earlier, they'd filled Dimitri in about the book and how they'd discovered the hidden writing. "We were on our way back to see if we could get it open. We think it'll tell us the location of the knife."

Dimitri nodded. "You'd better not stay long then."

"How is she?" Léopold asked. "Kade?"

"She's alive. But something's not right," Samantha answered from the sofa. She kept her voice quiet as she brushed her fingers through the baby's hair. "The vampire blood should've healed her."

"Jake saw the whole thing. He covered her from the window. Shot it several times…I mean over and over. Nothin' worked." Wynter paused, shaking her head and considering her words. "After it gutted her, it…well, Jake said it spat into her. Blood or something. I don't know. I was in the room with the baby and didn't get close to the window."

"Why would it do that?" Laryssa wrapped her hands around her midriff, recalling the burn of its claws. "There must be a reason."

"Kade thinks the demon did it to tie her to it somehow. It said something about taking her and the baby if it didn't get that knife." Wynter broke free of Logan's arms and nervously walked into the kitchen. She pulled several cups out of the cabinet and checked the pot of coffee she'd brewed earlier. In an effort to keep busy, she arranged the mugs in a row. "Can I get ya'll some coffee? Cream? Sugar?"

"Yeah, thanks." Laryssa felt as if she'd been sucked into an alternate reality. *Would you like cream and sugar with that demon?* Here they all were calmly and politely discussing Sydney's attack as if it was completely normal, a day in the park. Having lived her whole life away from the supernatural world, it was like immersion therapy gone wild.

"You know, it, uh, talked to her before it attacked," Dimitri added. Noticing that Wynter's hands were shaking, he took the pot of coffee from her with an understanding smile and finished pouring.

"Oh God," Laryssa said. She pushed her fingers through her hair in worry.

"It talked? What did it say?" Léopold approached Samantha and ran his hand over the baby's forehead. Ava smiled up at him and cooed in response.

"Same ole with a dash of more. It wants the Tlalco Tecpatl…by tomorrow night. Said it's comin' to you.

You're running out of time, Leo." Dimitri's eyes fell on Laryssa. They all knew the consequences if they didn't find it, and they had less than twenty-four hours to do so. "There's one other thing I forgot to mention. This time, Jake said it looked like a man. A human. It didn't last long, but that's how it appeared at first. I don't remember Ilsbeth sayin' anything about that."

"It needs Laryssa to be whole, to cross over to our world whenever it wishes. It's possible that since it attacked her, maybe her blood did something to augment its power," Léopold surmised.

"Gave it extra mojo," Dimitri guessed.

"Oui, made it stronger. Or it may have been able to do it to begin with, no? It's not like a demon's going to tell us its abilities. No, it's going to lie, conceal. It'll do what it needs to do to get the Tecpatl, but it wants Laryssa. That night at the lake…it's more than just her soul. It wants her."

"I agree with Leo. That night…the way it looked at me. This won't end until I kill it or it takes me." Laryssa's voice was shaky as she spoke the words aloud.

"I'll never let it have you," Léopold told her, his eyes meeting hers and then falling to Dimitri.

"Hey, maybe you should go see Kade? We didn't want to move Sydney too far so we kept her here…took her upstairs. Figured the wards on the house are workin' since the demon couldn't get in. But I gotta warn you that Kade doesn't seem to be takin' this so well."

Léopold opened his mouth to tell Dimitri that he would visit, when he heard Luca trample down the stairs and into the great room. With his fangs protruded, Luca rushed toward them. Instinctively, Léopold moved in front of Laryssa, protecting her from an attack. Already aware that Luca disliked her, Laryssa kept quiet and clutched the back of Léopold's jacket out of fear. While she knew that Sydney's mate, Kade, would be devastated by her attack, she hadn't anticipated the ill-tempered vampire's violent reaction.

"Goddamn you, Léopold. This is your fault. You brought that baby here. You knew Sydney would try to protect the child. If she dies, it's her blood on your hands. Yours and that nymph you're fucking," Luca roared. "If you'd just given her over to the demon, none of us would be in this mess."

Before Laryssa or Dimitri had a chance to stop him, Léopold lunged at Luca. Shoving him against the wall, Léopold seized Luca by his throat with one hand. Luca struggled to get free, but his effort to dislodge Léopold's grip was futile. Everyone in the room froze at the sight of the two vampires engaged in battle, one nearly killing the other. Neither Dimitri nor Logan made a move to interfere, as they knew it wasn't their place as wolves to get involved in the dispute.

"Stop it!" Samantha screamed. The baby began to cry, and she quickly handed Ava to Wynter. Despite wanting to break up the fight, she, too, knew not to get close to the vampires. She was pregnant and wouldn't risk the life of her own child.

"This…this…is what separates us from animals, "Léopold seethed, his fangs descending in anger. "If we cannot protect a child, then we are no better than the demons. The detective knew what she was doing. She accepts her oath."

Dimitri caught Laryssa's gaze. He shook his head at her, warning her not to interfere with their argument. Ignoring him, she surged forward. Dimitri caught her hand but she shook him off, running to intervene.

"You will submit, son of Kade. Do it," Léopold growled as Luca choked for air.

"Léopold, stop. You're going to kill him!" Laryssa cried, pushing her way in between the two vampires. She trembled in fear as she did so. They'd both gone feral yet she couldn't let Léopold kill the vampire. She knew that Luca disliked her, but she couldn't imagine that a man expecting a child would be callous enough to kill her in cold blood in front of everyone. Squeezing in so that her back was to Luca, she placed her palms on Léopold's chest. "Please. Stop."

"Get out of the way, Laryssa." Léopold's eyes fell to her, and the sight of her face weakened his fury.

"No, Leo, I won't. Please…for me. Just stop." Laryssa's voice went soft, trying to reach into his soul.

"This doesn't concern you." Léopold pinned Luca with his eyes, letting a renewed rush of rage flow through him. "What say you, Luca? Would you like to die today? Or would you do the right fucking thing and try to save this child?"

"Ssss…orry," Luca hissed, but still Léopold refused to release him.

"Look at me, Leo. Luca could kill me right now, but he's not even trying." Laryssa glanced over her shoulder at Luca. He may not have been able to bite her but he could have snapped her neck. "Don't do this. He's got a family…he's having a baby. His friend's hurt. He's just upset…like you. Let it go. Please don't let the demon win."

"Merde," Léopold huffed, tossing the vampire to the floor.

Luca stumbled over to Samantha, who caught him in her arms. The tension in the room simmered to a slow boil.

Léopold grabbed Laryssa by the waist and pulled her against him, whispering in her ear. "Tu es folle."

"I don't know what you just said, but thank you for letting him go," Laryssa replied. Her forehead fell to Léopold's chest, relieved he hadn't killed Luca.

"Don't ever do that again," Léopold demanded.

"Someone's gotta make you see reason," she responded. The low dominant tone of Léopold's voice registered in her mind. He wasn't making a suggestion, rather he was ordering her.

Léopold grasped the back of her hair, and tugged her head backward. He loved her bravery, yet it would get them both killed if she didn't listen to him. Looking into her eyes, he felt her shiver against his body. Retracting his fangs, he observed the slight waver of her lips as they parted just for him.

"Never again, Laryssa," he told her. Giving her no time to argue, he kissed her. Deepening his hold on her, his lips took hers, in a show of passion and possession. Satisfied he'd made his point, he reluctantly pulled away. Leaving her breathless, he gave her a smug smile before releasing her from his embrace.

Laryssa panted quietly, trying to catch her breath. Unsure of how Léopold had so quickly turned the tables on her, she tried to slow her heartbeat, which felt as if it was pounding through her chest. Her face flamed and she wished she could run out of the room.

"We're going upstairs to see Kade," Léopold announced as he nodded at Luca.

"Maybe you should go with them," Wynter suggested to Logan. Kade had been despondent, sitting at Sydney's bedside and refusing to talk to anyone. They all knew his blood should have cured her, but her pulse remained erratic. "Laryssa, why don't you stay down here with us?"

Laryssa nodded, feeling as if she needed space from Léopold. The man had a way of compelling her, paralyzing her thoughts and turning her body into fire. As if she couldn't get enough of the drug she was addicted to, she stopped him before he left to go upstairs, and lovingly touched her palm to his cheek. She gave him a sad smile, and then briefly touched her lips to his face. With nothing else to be said, he tugged on a lock of her hair before turning back to Dimitri, disappearing down the hallway and up the stairs.

"Go ahead, Laryssa, sit down. I forgot the coffee," Wynter said.

"No, really, I can get it. You want some?" Laryssa asked.

"Thanks, I'd love a cup." Wynter sat carefully into a recliner and held Ava against her chest, patting her on the back.

"None for me. My little one, here, doesn't do well with the caffeine." Samantha took a deep breath. "Laryssa, thank you…for stopping Léopold just now. I would never recommend getting between two vampires, but if Léopold had…you know, had hurt Luca…" She rubbed her stomach with tears in her eyes. "I just…I know Luca can be difficult, but we're close to Sydney. And he and Léopold have never gotten along well. I'm not trying to make excuses. Well, maybe I am. He's just upset."

"I get that Luca's not my biggest fan, Samantha. Ya'll hardly know me. I can't blame him. But I'd never stand by and let Léopold kill him without trying to stop it." Laryssa picked up two mugs of coffee, set one in front of Wynter and then sat down.

"True. We don't know you. And that's why it means even more that you stopped him. Wynter and I both know Léopold and he's…" Samantha looked away, unsure of what to say.

"You don't have to say anything. Really. Léopold is lots of things, but he cares and he's helping me. He saved that little baby girl right there. He didn't have to but he did. And now the demon. He won't stop until we find the knife."

"The demon. I know Ilsbeth doesn't mind speaking of it but maybe we shouldn't," Samantha suggested. "The wards are strong but it knows where we are."

"I have to kill it." Laryssa took a sip and swallowed. When she looked up, both Samantha and Wynter were looking at her as if she'd sprouted an elephant's trunk. "What?"

"How can you say something like that and be so calm about it?" Wynter asked while she played with Ava's toes.

"Léopold's not going to let you go after a demon," Samantha asserted.

"Léopold doesn't have a choice. Neither do I." Laryssa took another drink then continued. "Not sure if Dimitri mentioned it but that thing…that creature…it came after me the other night. It, uh, it scratched me up pretty bad. Somehow, with me dying all those years ago, it thinks I belong to it. The knife that it wants…it's the only thing that'll kill it. Unfortunately I have to be the one to do it, because only a naiad can kill it. Léopold knows. I don't think he wants to face the fact that I may die, but deep down, he knows that it has to be me."

"Speaking of Léopold, I guess that chat we had the other day didn't make any difference," Wynter commented with a small smile.

"I saw it too," Samantha added. "Never thought I'd see the day."

"Me either. The way he looks at her…" Wynter began.

"What?" Laryssa had an idea of what they were talking about but she couldn't bring herself to discuss her feelings for Léopold when Sydney was upstairs fighting for her life and her own life could very well be gone by tomorrow night.

"Like an ice cream sundae with whipped cream on top?" Samantha smiled.

"You really are preggo, girl. No, he looks at her like…you know, like a lion who's about to find his mate. Leo the lion finds his lioness." Wynter's voice became sultry as if she were trying to really sell her story.

"Yeah, I guess that does sound better. You'd think with me being mated to a vampire, I'd know a bit about what he really wants…and I can tell you it's not ice cream."

"I know you warned me about him, Wynter, but we…I'm…let's just say that I care about him a lot. But none of it really matters…I could be dead tomorrow. It's not fair to him." Laryssa set the cup of coffee on the table and raked her hair up into a ponytail, nervously twisting it into a bun. "We probably shouldn't be talking about this when the detective is so sick."

"You've been feeding him," Samantha noted quietly. Her eyes darted over to Wynter and then back to Laryssa. "Have you bonded?"

"Léopold? Bonded? No way," Wynter blurted out, shaking her head. Even though Léopold seemed smitten with his nymph, she found it hard to believe that he'd commit to anyone, given his proclivity for solitude. One glance to Laryssa told her that she'd made the wrong assumption. "Hey, I'm sorry. It's just that Léopold…I never thought he'd bond with anyone. It's nothing personal, it's just that he's, pardon the pun, a lone wolf….vampire."

"He's not how you see him. He's had his reasons. But to answer your question, I have been…feeding him, that is. He said that we've started the bonding. I don't know what to say about it. It's complicated." Laryssa rose to defend Léopold. Her fingers absentmindedly flittered over the bite mark on her neck. With Sydney nearly dead, the realization that she soon would have to face her own mortality was not lost on her. She smiled at Wynter and Samantha who waited for her to finish her thoughts. Her eyes began to brim with moisture, and she pressed a fingertip to her bottom eyelid, in an effort to catch a tear. "I'm sorry. It's just that I don't want to hurt him."

"You? Hurt Léopold? Sweetie, I really don't see how you could do that. Not sure if you noticed but he's usually the one who does the hurting…" Wynter's words trailed off, as she realized how upset Laryssa had grown.

"Listen, I know he's arrogant. Bossy. He's really bossy." Laryssa gave a small laugh. She stood and walked over to the kitchen sink, placing her cup inside it. "But he's caring and he doesn't deserve to lose someone else. Look at what just happened to Sydney. Let's face it, there's a very real possibility that I may die tomorrow. The bond…for his sake, I have to try to stop it."

"A bond with a vampire cannot be broken." Samantha felt Laryssa's pain. Having bonded with Luca, she knew how it felt to have that intense connection with a vampire.

"No it cannot," Léopold asserted, having walked in on their conversation.

Laryssa's face flashed to his, and an overwhelming barrage of guilt surrounded her, knowing what she planned to do. With the bond already set in, it was as if she could feel him touching her soul, reading her innermost thoughts. She attempted to think of something unrelated, altogether pleasant, like how she enjoyed reading a book at the outdoor café while listening to live music. As she did so, the guilt worsened. *Liar.* The word rang in her mind. No, she wasn't really lying, she told herself. Masking private thoughts was her right. Yet as he strode over to her and caressed her cheek, her stomach clenched in shame. She averted her gaze, unable to look him in the eye. They'd talk soon enough, she reasoned.

Stupidly, she'd mentioned her concerns to Wynter and Samantha. Blaming it on her naivety, she'd take responsibility if the conversation went further. Pasting on a passive expression, she glanced to the women who cautiously eyed them from the sofa. She wished she didn't care what any of them thought, yet they'd known her secret and hadn't rejected her. Talking with a wolf and a witch had felt natural, as if she'd finally found other women who were like her. Even though she'd always felt that way with Avery, their hushed conversations were intended to eradicate the evidence of her naiad origins. No longer in the shadows, she could finally openly engage with others.

"How's Sydney? Kade?" Laryssa changed the subject. "That was fast."

"Not much to be said. Sydney's resting. Kade is stronger than people give him credit for. He'll be her rock while we do what we need to do. What he doesn't need is people fussing over him. He can handle this." Léopold crossed the room to Wynter, who stood with the baby. "Ava? She's doing well?"

"Yes. She's adorable. Just the sweetest little girl," Wynter gushed.

"Oui. She's loved here. I never doubt my actions," Léopold observed. "Sometimes the best things in our lives are unexpected, no?"

"True. I swear Logan and I will do everything we can to keep her safe. Promise me, Léopold that you'll get rid of this beast that's after her. Please," Wynter pleaded.

"We," he looked to Laryssa, "will do our very best." He ran his fingers over Ava's back and then turned to Laryssa. "We need to get going."

"Is Dimitri coming with us?" Laryssa asked.

"No, I've asked him to stay here. Where we're going, we'll be safe until we meet up tomorrow. Ladies," Léopold nodded at the women, and walked to the sliding door, opening it, "Good evening."

"Thanks for the coffee," Laryssa said with a small knowing smile, appreciative that Wynter and Samantha hadn't pursued the discussion about her breaking the bond with Léopold.

As Léopold ushered her out the door, she purposefully jammed her hands into her pockets, resisting the urge to touch him. Like a magnet to steel, her body and heart was drawn to him, but if she was ever going to break the bond, she'd need to stay strong, keep herself at a distance. She caught Léopold's eyes roaming over her posture, and suspected that he'd detected her deception. Laryssa had never been in love, really loved another person with all of her soul, enough that she'd sacrifice everything to make him happy. It was in that moment that her heart crushed with the reality that she'd fallen for Léopold. She'd never be able to take away the agony he'd suffered watching his wife and children die, but she'd be damned if she'd torture him all over again. If she could break the bond, he'd survive her death with little consequence.

She looked down to her phone for the time. In less than twenty-four hours, her life would most likely be over. Even if she somehow managed to find the knife, she didn't trust the demon not to take her anyway. Closing her eyes, she shuddered, recalling its tongue on her skin. No, it'd never be satisfied with some little trinket that promised it a free pass to the other side. It wanted what it had tried to take once, what belonged to it. Her body. Her mind. Her soul.

~❧· *Chapter Nineteen* ·☙~

"Where're we going?" Laryssa asked. The sign to the Lake Ponchartrain marina alerted her that they weren't returning to his home.

"We're getting off the land, ma chérie. This demon. It's grounded to the earth. The water. Now that's where we'll find a bit of peace." Léopold pulled into the yacht club and drove up to the valet parking. Shifting the car into park, he opened his door as the attendant arrived.

Laryssa fumbled the fish puzzle in her fingers. She ran her thumb over the cool metal fins, and tugged, hoping that for once, something would just magically happen...that it would open, revealing its secrets. As she expected, nothing happened. Swirling clouds of worry passed through her mind as she stared mindlessly at the rows of boats. The door hinge clicked, jarring her contemplation, and she jumped in her seat.

Léopold towered above Laryssa, studying her. Before he had a chance to reach for her, she leapt out of the car and wrapped her arms around her waist. She'd been acting strangely ever since he'd returned downstairs to find her talking with Wynter and Samantha. Whispers of broken bonds were all he'd heard, but it was enough to tell him that his little rabbit was readying to flee.

He thought it interesting that although he'd never bonded to another person in his life, how naturally he'd taken to the experience. With her blood in him, he could sense both her thoughts and feelings. Reading Laryssa was becoming as simple as reading a menu. She'd deliberately tried to deceive him, shielding her true emotions with false ones, but he'd known all the while what she'd been doing.

"You okay?" Léopold inquired. He tapped his finger on the top of his car.

"Yeah, I'm fine. Just a little tired."

"I guess breaking into convents will do that to you," he joked.

"A museum. We broke into a museum…to keep evil out of the city. That's my story and I'm sticking to it." She gave a small laugh.

"I knew you'd see it my way. Come, pet. We must get to the boat." Léopold strode down the docks, taking care to make sure Laryssa was in step with him. Whatever storm brewed inside her pretty little head, he planned to calm it and make sure she never lied to him again.

"Here we are," he commented, unlocking the chain. "Ladies first."

Laryssa went to take a step and stopped, realizing the 'boat' was not a simple fishing skiff. In line with everything Léopold, the sixty-foot yacht sparkled underneath a flood of lights. Rolling her eyes at him, she shook her head and smiled.

"Is this yours?" she asked, stepping onto the boarding ramp.

"Mais bien sûr, mon amour," he replied.

"You know I don't speak French, Leo. But I'll take that as a yes."

"Oui. And I do believe you do speak un petit bit. I recall that you don't appreciate being called mon lapin." He smiled and winked.

"So, um, how'd you learn to steer this huge boat of yours?"

"Ah, my sweet Laryssa, you'd be surprised at all I can do. When you're immortal, you have much time on your hands, no? I usually employ a captain to sail it for me. This, however, is not one of those times. We need to be alone." Léopold retrieved a small stainless steel flask from his bag and handed it to her. "There's some water in here. Go ahead inside. See if there's anything you can find in the book to get the puzzle to open, to show us where we need to go to get the knife. Remember, this fish was meant for you, a naiad."

Laryssa heard the anchor drop and was certain that Léopold would soon be down to check her progress. After an hour of looking at the puzzle, she hadn't come any closer to finding the solution. Tracing the pad of her thumb down its underbelly, she could feel small bumps, but they didn't move. *Remember, it was meant for you.* The track of Léopold's words played in her mind. *The water.* Everything, since the day she'd drowned, came back to the water. It was who she was, how she thrived, how she'd continue to survive as an immortal.

Opening the flask, she dribbled the water onto the fish, expecting to see it glow. Disappointed when it didn't, she flipped it over. Trying again, she waited patiently but nothing changed. Only wet metal lay in her hands.

"Come on, dammit. I'm running out of time," she gritted out. Furious and frustrated, she lost her temper, and hurled it across the room. The fish smashed into the wall and tumbled onto the floor.

"It's going well, no?" Léopold said, entering the cabin. He shook his head and picked up the puzzle. "Come now, you must concentrate."

"I can't, Leo. Can't you see? It's not working. Nothing is going to work," she replied.

"You can't give up," he scolded. He tossed the fish in the air and caught it. As it landed in his palm, he felt movement. "Perhaps a little anger goes a long way?"

"What?" She sighed.

"It's moving. It has to be the water. Look…the scales, they're peeling."

"Really?" She jumped to her feet and ran over to Léopold, watching as he thumbed away the scales. Like a fan, they began to spread, until the cavity was revealed.

"A key," Laryssa breathed.

"Yours." Léopold held out the copper object and offered it to her.

Laryssa hesitated, and then reached for the key. As soon as she touched it, her body quivered as if she were a tuning fork that had been struck against metal. The resonance of the key shocked her, searing into the layers of her skin yet her hand wouldn't release it. Tears ran down her face as it burned her palm, her eyes widening with the realization that they'd discovered something horrific. *Death. Torture. Blood. Screaming.* Flashes of the demon flickered through her mind. Laryssa fought for breath, her chest heaving in pain.

She faintly heard Léopold's voice but was unable to respond. Driven by its diabolical energy, she staggered out onto the deck. Evil coursed through her veins and she was helpless to stop its commands. Léopold lunged for her as she teetered on the edge of the stairs, but she thwarted his efforts to catch her by effortlessly causing a chair to fly through the air, nearly cracking him in the skull. Scrambling over the seats, she reached the ledge of a railing. In the recesses of her mind, she fought to stay sane, but the drumming of evil propelled her over the edge into the deep abyss of the lake.

Like water on a hot oiled pan, her body sizzled as it hit the lake. Convulsing, Laryssa lost herself to the dreadful coil of death that had taken her as a child. The water, typically her savior, rejected her as the evil shroud ensconced in the key held her under, searching for its target. She gasped for breath, and her throat flooded with water. Choking, her eyes bulged in terror, but she was helpless to resist its compelling draw. Shackled to the key, she gave in to its will.

By the time she hit the lake bed, she'd embraced the cold darkness that sought to take her. The metal in her hand burned like fire, forcing her to consciously experience the slow torture of drowning. With the demon dancing in her head, she prayed for God to take her, yet she remained awake in her nightmare. As her fist hit the rocks, a single chasm illuminated a few feet away from her. Laryssa's attention was drawn to the small hole. Unable to move her body, she slid her arm toward it. Feeling as if she was ripping the skin from her hands, she pried her fingers open and jammed the key into the rock. The last thing Laryssa saw before she drifted off into oblivion was the brilliance of a white stone blade.

Léopold lay naked in bed, skimming his finger over the flint edge of the Tecpatl. The primitive stone had been chiseled into a razor-sharp point. Bound to the rock with cord, its ornate handle had been carved into a warrior. Decorated in black and red, the soldier bowed on his knees, its hilt bore his horns. Léopold wasn't entirely positive how she'd found it, but was certain her power had somehow summoned it forth. She'd invoked the magic, and it had responded. It made no sense that it would be in the location where he'd anchored the boat, but as he fingered it, he surmised the object was otherworldly in nature. Perhaps at one time it had been of the earth, created by man's hands to slice open the chests of fellow humankind. But at some point, it had taken on meaning to the demon. For however long it had existed clandestinely in the depths of the lake, the enchanted knife had finally returned to a naiad.

Léopold contemplated how Laryssa had been possessed by whatever evil was infused into the key. After she'd fallen into the water, he'd dove in, frantically searching for her. By the time he'd found her at the bottom of the basin, she'd lost consciousness, but still glowed in the blackness of the waves. Curled in her hand was the Tecpatl. As they'd reached the surface of the water and the midnight breeze brushed her face, her eyes flew wide open in horror. He'd tried to comfort her, but she'd batted him away. Wrapping her shaking hands around the ladder, she'd climbed out of the lake, leaving him to hold the knife. Her fear and foreboding was palpable and while Léopold continued his attempts to assuage her, she'd rejected his company. She'd insisted on showering alone, so against his better judgment, he'd ceded to her wish.

Léopold had caught onto her strategy to camouflage her feelings by forcing unnatural thoughts. From desperation to determination, he'd sensed her emotions fluctuating across the spectrum. Even though he'd given her a temporary deferment, allowing her solace in her bath, he quietly calculated his next move. The sound of the water ceased and his heart raced in anticipation of their discussion. He looked forward to enlightening her about having faith in their bond.

Laryssa stood nude in front of the mirror, drying her body. When she'd been torn out of Léopold's home into the demon's pit, ripped apart, she'd told herself that she could survive anything. But the sheer evil that had possessed her entire body left her reeling. It shook her to her core, leaving her numb. Lost in the sensation that had suffocated her in the lake, she closed her eyes and took a deep breath. Slowly opening them, she toweled her hair, taking in a glance at the pearly bumps on her neck. *Léopold.* She'd fallen hard for him. It was as if she could literally feel her heart splintering open, knowing she'd be gone within hours. Never would she be able to have a life with the one man who'd selflessly given her the freedom to be herself, who'd shown her pleasure she'd never known, and the one man on Earth who she'd gladly lay down her life for without a second thought.

He'd fight her, she knew. Their argument would come and go, but it had to be done, she'd made the decision. Regardless of the outcome, it didn't matter. Once the demon had her in its claws, she'd never see Léopold again. She'd put off talking to him as long as she could. Wrapping the towel around her body, she sighed and opened the door.

The spectacular sight of Léopold sprawled on the bed caused her heart to stop. His lips curled upward, as if to warn her he'd gone on the offensive. Perfectly masculine, his powerful frame laid waiting for her. From his well-defined chest down to his steel-hard abs, he defined virility at its finest. His thick cock lay heavy upon his thigh, growing ever larger with each breath he took, his eyes feasting upon her.

Laryssa fought the gooseflesh growing on her skin that was caused by the sight of him. She forced herself to look away from the distraction that was his beauty, but she could still feel his presence surround her in its erotic snare. She pressed her lips together as tears rose in her eyes. *Let him go*, her conscience screamed. *I must break the bond.* It wasn't fair to deny him, to crush him with the loss of her soul.

"Leo," she began, "I know we found the Tecpatl, but the death…the evil, tonight it was in me. It's not going to let me go."

In one continuous movement, Léopold was up off the bed. With deliberation, he set the Tecpatl on the dresser in front of her. He stood close behind Laryssa, mere inches away, but didn't touch her skin. Like the stealth predator he was, he waited for his prey to make her first move.

"We must break the bond. Tomorrow…today, he's going to take me. The knife. He'll use it somehow." Laryssa stilled as she felt Léopold wrap his arm around her chest. Her eyes glanced up to his reflection in the mirror and her breath caught. With his eyes pinned on hers, his mouth tightened in a firm line. Her pulse raced as his fingertips skimmed her chest, her body strung out like a live wire ready to be struck by lightning. "It's not fair to you. You already lost your wife, your kids. The bond, it'll make it worse when I go. Maybe you could get a donor or…"

"Laryssa," he growled. Laced with domination, Léopold's voice filled the room. "Never will I have another's blood. The bond cannot be undone. More importantly, you don't want it undone."

"But Leo, you deserve so much more than what I can give you. I can't bear to hurt you." Her chest heaved as she spoke with despair. "And tonight…what I felt in that knife. In my mind. No, through my entire being. I may kill the demon, but there's a good chance that it's going to kill me."

"So you quit? Jesus Christ, woman, don't you understand how much you mean to me? Who you are to me?" His eyebrows furrowed in frustration.

"What am I? I'm a naiad. And yeah, Leo…I care about you. Can you see how much I care? I don't want to hurt you. It took you a thousand years to get over the death of your wife and just when you decide to live again, to bond with me," Laryssa shook her head, lowering her eyes and whispered, "I'll be gone."

"You have to fight, goddammit. Do you hear me? Fight!" he yelled. Goddess, she was giving up after all they'd been through. Denying their bond? No fucking way would he let her bow out gracefully. She was his and he had no intention of letting her go. "Listen, I don't know what happened tonight with the key, but it's over. It. Is. Over. We did it. At every turn, we've figured it out."

"But, Leo…"

"Look at me," he demanded, his fingers gliding over her throat. "You pushed me when it was impossible to do. Now I expect the same from you. I'm telling you to fight. Fight for your life. Fight like hell for us."

"I can't," she choked. Her eyes flashed to his. "It's impossible. I've felt it...the evil."

"I know you were shaken up today, but you're stronger than the demon. We're stronger. You need to make the choice to trust. Trust me. Trust what you feel inside. Trust us." He took a deep breath, cradling his other arm around her waist. Lowering his voice, he spoke to her heart. "Be mine, Laryssa...always. Choose me. Choose us."

A tear ran down her face as Léopold threw her words back into her face. *God, how did this happen? Doesn't he realize I've already chosen him? That I love him?*

"Mon amour. Choose us," he repeated.

"Yes," she whispered, her eyes closing as she trembled.

"Yes," he repeated, kissing her neck. There was nowhere the demon could take her where he wouldn't find her. "I'll never leave you...ever. Never again will you be alone. Have faith...in us."

"Leo," she breathed. "I want so bad to believe you."

"Bond with me," he suggested. Léopold had thought long and hard about asking her to complete the bond. He sought to mark her as his own, to take her as his mate. The instinct to do so was overwhelming. Denying the urge had become increasingly difficult. He'd known it would happen the first time he bit her. But now with her possible death looming over them, it gave him the excuse to take what he wanted. No regrets, he'd bond with her eternally. "You're mine, Laryssa. You'll never belong to another."

"I…I," Laryssa stammered, unsure of what to say. Forever binding her soul to his was certainly irrevocable.

"No matter what happens, I'll come for you. You'll never belong to another. You've already given your heart to me," he challenged. *Amour.* He'd heard the words that played in her mind, ones she'd never confess aloud. He knew he wasn't playing fair, but there was no other choice. He tugged on her towel until it fell to the floor. His cock brushed against her back.

"You're mine, Laryssa. Say yes."

Laryssa swayed in his arms, his smooth voice like a melody in her head. *Say yes.* Her instincts roared in response, telling her to accept her soul mate. Though their ages spanned centuries, their connection felt older than time itself. Impulsively, she embraced the truth in her heart.

"I'm yours," she said, without hesitation. With her heart in his hands and his skin touching hers, desire flared. She drew a deep breath, inhaling the smell of him into her psyche. A maddening ache grew between her legs.

"Oui, mon amour. That's it," Léopold praised. *Goddess, she is magnificent.* Like an angel, she'd taught him to live again. He smiled as the scent of her arousal filled the room. Satisfied with her submission, he sought to devour her.

"From this day forward, we'll be together. No fear shall befall us. No demon will separate us. This," his hand moved to her chest, over her heart, and lightly tapped, "is mine only. And my heart is yours. Your body." He slid his hand down over her belly. Gliding his finger into the warmth between her legs, he pressed his middle finger up into her tight channel.

"Ahhh," she cried.

"You give to me freely. Mais oui, ma chérie. Your body blazes for me, no?"

"Leo," she managed, groaning as he withdrew his finger.

Léopold brought his hand to his mouth, licking her cream with his tongue, then cradled her chin with his hand, pressing his coated fingers through her lips. Laryssa moaned in response, tasting herself on him.

"You belong to me...and I," he took her hand and brought it to his cock, "belong to you."

Laryssa's mouth went silent, as she immersed herself in the sound of Léopold's voice. Talking hold of his swollen shaft, she stroked her thumb over its silken skin. As she went to pump him with her hand, he spun her around to face him. Breathless, she reached to put her palms to his chest and Léopold backed her into the dresser until her bottom edged against its cool surface.

"You have no idea how much you mean to me, the gift you've given me," he told her, his voice dark and smooth. Raking his fingers up into the back of her hair, his lips descended on hers. Delivering all the intensity his heart held, he kissed her, his tongue sweeping against hers. No matter what happened, he wanted her to feel the love that was growing inside him, the emotion he could not yet put into words.

Laryssa fell into his arms, consumed by his intoxicating kiss. His lips, soft and strong, claimed hers. She could taste his passion for her as his seductive tongue invaded her mouth, seeking and probing. Losing control, she matched his pace, with the need to have more of him. Biting and sucking, she moaned into his mouth.

She gasped for breath as he pulled his lips away, watching as his eyes went wild with lust, and he fell to his knees. She braced her hands on the bureau as he placed his hands on her inner thighs. Slowly and deliberately, he widened them. She panted in anticipation of how he planned to take control of her body.

"Open your legs," he demanded.

Never taking his eyes off of hers, he dragged the tip of his tongue through her swollen lips and smiled up at her.

"Your pussy is so wet." He licked her again and she moaned. "So sweet." Using his fingers to spread her apart, he lightly sucked her swollen clit. "And mine." Using his other hand, he plunged two fingers into her satiny flesh. Continuing to make love to her with his mouth, he skillfully brought her to the edge.

"Leo!" she screamed, shaking as he pleasured her. Her inner walls clamped around his fingers, and she fought to hold her release at bay. Letting go of the dresser, she plowed her fingers into his hair, drawing his face further into her pussy.

Unrelenting, he flicked his tongue lightly over her clitoris, gradually increasing his tempo and pressure. Reaching his hand behind her thigh, he clutched her hip. She bucked against him. In rhythm with his fingers, she drove her hips to his mouth. As he felt her inner walls begin to quiver around his hand, he took her protruding nub between his teeth, softly biting and then sucked her hard until she moaned in release.

"Yes. Fuck, yes. Oh, God. Leo, Leo!" she screamed as her orgasm slammed into her. Ripples of endless pleasure ran through her, and she felt him lift her onto the bed.

"Hands and knees, now," Léopold commanded, easing her belly upward. In one smooth stroke, he thrust into her.

"Yes!" she cried, adjusting her weight so that her legs were spread for him.

"Merde, you're so tight. Don't move," he grunted as her pussy quivered around his cock. The tingling sensation drove him toward his own climax. With a deep breath, he fought the urge to come.

"Fuck me!" she cried. Her forehead fell forward onto the pillow. She wiggled against him, trying to make him move. A sharp slap to her bottom, intended to punish her efforts, only served to further arouse her tender flesh. "Ahhh…yes."

"You're a naughty, girl, no?" He spanked her again on her other cheek, aware of how much she liked it.

"Please, Leo…" she begged.

"You really have learned no patience, have you? How I look forward to teaching you, ma chérie. Tonight, I will own every part of your sweet body," he promised. Clutching her hips, he began to move an inch at a time. The torturous pace he set would make them both want for more.

"Leo," she repeated as she felt him retreat, then enter her ever so slowly, making her mad with need. "Faster."

"You feel so good…yes," he growled. Filling her to the hilt, he stilled himself yet again. He reached for the bottle of lube under the sheets that he'd planned on using on her tonight.

"Don't stop," she protested. As the cold slippery gel hit her bottom, she'd expected he'd brought the plug with him. Laryssa arched her back into his caress of her bottom.

"I'm going to fuck you here tonight," he warned. "Your ass is so beautiful."

"But…ahhh." Her pussy clenched down on him as he inserted a finger into her back hole. Unlike the time before, it slipped in easily, with little pressure.

"That's it." Léopold smiled, hearing her moan as he pressed in a second finger. He began to pump his hips once again, gritting his teeth as he sheathed himself inside of her.

"Yes, yes, yes," Laryssa rambled, adrift in the sensation. Nothing else existed but their two bodies, joined as one in pleasure.

With a final thrust, Léopold pulled his cock all the way out of her, then coated himself in the lubrication. Circling her puckered flesh, he teased her with his fingers, and pressed the firm tip of his cock into her anus.

"Ah yeah. Take me," he encouraged.

"Leo," she panted. "I don't know….I, yes, don't stop." She shook her long mane back and forth, adjusting to the fullness.

"Yes, yes…feel me in you, see how we're made for each other. Push back on me," he instructed, running his fingertips down her shoulders. Responding to her long draw of a breath, he slowly entered her until he was all the way in, his hips flush against her bottom. Gently, he fisted her locks into his hand. Her tight muscles gripped his cock, massaging every inch of his manhood. "Oh yeah."

Relaxing into his dark intrusion, Laryssa opened herself to him. By the time he'd eased his shaft all the way inside her, she'd exhaled a breath and tried to move. As if reading her thoughts, he gently began to rock back and forth, letting her become accustomed to the sweet pressure. Laryssa rose to meet his thrusts, urging him to go faster, but he took control, forcing them to immerse themselves in the ecstasy of every long stroke. Together, they moved in sync, losing themselves to the moment.

Laryssa moaned Léopold's name over and over again as he stretched her in the most satisfying way. She'd never felt so delightfully out of control in her life. Yet, all the while, she was aware of her power dancing through her blood. With his hand pulling her hair, the delicious sting on her scalp caused her to groan aloud. She felt his other hand slip from her hip around to her waist. Letting him direct her, she arched her back as he pulled her torso upward until she was only on her knees.

Holding her firmly around her midsection, he increased his pace. As his primal need grew, Léopold's fangs descended and he released her hair, letting it fall to the side, revealing the long curve of her neck. Wrapping both arms around her, he found her clit once again. As he surged into her ass, he continued to stroke her hooded pearl.

"Mon amour, so fucking close," he hissed.

"Bite me now," she insisted, asserting her dominance. Her swollen nub pulsated as he applied more pressure and she could not keep from coming. "Leo, please."

So near to his own climax, Léopold released a chuckle at his mate's demand. He'd known all along that her submission would come only in the bedroom, and even then, she'd do so on her own terms. Powerful in her own right, she'd push his limits to places he'd never imagined. Yet that was why he was falling in love with her. She captivated him with her adventurous sexuality and courageous spirit. As he heard her groan in displeasure that he hadn't heeded her, he brought his wrist to his own mouth. A quick slice of his fangs sent his blood dripping onto her back.

"We've chosen each other...my sweet Laryssa...." His words trailed off as he held his arm to her lips. Instinctively, she clutched it, drawing in his sanguine essence. Hissing in ecstasy, he reared his head back and sank his teeth deep into her shoulder.

Laryssa clung to Léopold, her body convulsing as her climax ripped through her. From the second his potent blood touched her tongue, she was slammed with a tsunami of foreign emotions. Centuries of memories and feelings poured over her like a massive waterfall, cleansing her, making her anew just for him. As if his thoughts were her own, they ripped through her mind. *Serenity, that he'd finally found his soul mate. Lust, his mind consumed by an insatiable hunger for only her.* She smiled as his love filled her chest. Hidden behind all of it was rage, simmering below the surface. No one would touch his mate.

Tears streamed down her face. Positively possessed by the intimacy of their bond, she quaked in his arms. Overwhelmed, Laryssa let go of her fears, embracing his warmth. The fibers of their bond tightened around her and she knew that from this day forward, she'd never be alone again. The charismatic vampire had stolen her heart, and she'd always be his. *I love you.* The words flittered through her mind before she could even stop the thought. *Je t'aime de tout mon coeur,* she heard in response and smiled. Even though she didn't understand his words, she knew he loved her, enough to commit to her for eternity. No matter what they faced, she knew with certainty he'd go to the ends of the Earth to keep her at his side.

Chapter Twenty

After making love in the wee hours of the morning and sleeping all day, Léopold's mind turned to killing the demon. He'd called upon both Dimitri and Ilsbeth to meet him at his home. As soon as dusk settled in, they all stood waiting by the docks. The grass was scorched from the last time the demon had shown its ugly face in his yard, and he expected that's where it'd come again looking for Laryssa. While Ilsbeth had suggested summoning the demon where it had last surfaced in the city, Léopold refused to put anyone else in jeopardy. With the Alpha's home warded and well-guarded, the confrontation had to occur where there were no other innocents. Above all else, he sought to keep Ava hidden.

Ilsbeth reiterated to their small group that only Laryssa, as the owner of the Tecpatl, could send the demon back to its hellish origins. Any other attempts to kill it would be done so in vain. The naiads had hidden the knife, knowing the demon could use it to break the veil of the underworld at will. Only a naiad could send it back to

Satan. The witch speculated that at some point, the demon had bargained with the Aztecs, attaching its entity to the knife. Relishing in the human sacrifices, the demon used its influence to feed the killings, possessing the thoughts of those who stabbed the Tecpatl's jagged edge into the sternums of its victims, tearing out the beating hearts of men, women and children with their bare hands. They wouldn't be the first or last civilization to do so. But the demon, whose name was Rylion, had infused its evil into that particular weapon.

It terrified Léopold that the demon sought to take her. Since they'd bonded, he'd felt every memory she'd retained of her attacks and Laryssa was convinced that it wanted more than the Tecpatl. *Rylion.* It had called itself her master. Yet no matter the demon's delusions, Léopold knew for certain no one, not even he, was Laryssa's master.

Léopold gave a small smile to Laryssa, who nervously fingered the Tecpatl's hilt. He was unsure of her ability to utilize the bond, to sense more than his emotions. *No matter what happens, I'll come for you, mon amour,* he thought to himself. Instantly, she smiled in return, letting him know she'd felt him. After years of allowing the loss of his family to define him, to entomb and paralyze him in grief, she'd set him free. Falling for her had been an unanticipated gift. Admitting he loved her, however, saying the words out loud, would not come easily. Slipping his hand into hers, he brought her palm to his lips, accepting that he'd gladly give his life for hers.

Thunder rumbled in the distance, and he glanced down to Laryssa whose expression had grown serious. *Rylion,* he heard Laryssa whisper. Lightning struck, crackling across the atmosphere into the lake. Out of the corner of his eye, he heard Dimitri arguing with Ilsbeth and shot him a glare, warning him to cease their conversation.

"It's here," Laryssa said. She looked side to side, expecting Rylion to materialize out of thin air.

"Behind you," Dimitri called to Léopold.

"Laryssa," the demon snarled.

Both Laryssa and Léopold spun on their heels. The demon cackled, tasting her fear like a fine wine on its tongue. Its long forked tongue slithered out from its parted lips as if it were a snake, scenting its environment. Léopold shoved in front of Laryssa, shielding her from its line of vision.

"You brought it," Rylion continued, boring its eyes into Léopold. "Come to your master, Laryssa. The ancient one cannot protect you."

Laryssa felt her face blanch. Its cold voice sank its icy claws into her mind. Even though she'd spent hours mentally preparing, her fear crept up, causing her stomach to lurch. She pressed her forehead into the back of Léopold's shirt, focusing on their bond. Like a band of steel, it tied them together. Nothing, not even this heinous creature, could tear it apart.

"Rylion," she said. Her voice was soft yet firm as she stepped around Léopold. If she had any chance of killing it, sending it back to hell, she had to get close enough to use the knife. "I have the Tecpatl." *I'm looking forward to giving it to you. Tearing you open with it.*

"Let me see it," the demon demanded. Its form flickered briefly into a human male and then quickly transformed back to its scaly self.

As Laryssa raised the flint blade to the sky, her determination began to amplify. *Fuck this thing. This ends tonight.* Her eyes darted over to Léopold who nodded, sensing her intentions. Instead of him seeking to hinder her, she felt his confidence in her powers. This incredible man would die for her tonight, she knew. But he'd support her independence to fight a battle that only she could win.

"Ah. So many memories....the screaming. Children dying, feeding me their souls," Rylion reminisced. "It's beautiful, isn't it? Bring it to me, my sweet naiad."

Laryssa approached the demon, aware that Léopold had her back. She heard mumblings in the air, and caught a glimpse of Ilsbeth chanting.

"The witch has no say here. The Tlalco Tecpatl is mine, has always been mine. That bitch stole it from me, and now it's back," Rylion told them, falling to its knees. Holding its hands out toward Laryssa, it began to speak in tongues.

Laryssa's heart pounded so hard it felt as if it would break her ribs. The hilt began to vibrate in her hands. At first it was merely a tingle but within seconds it burned the skin of her palm. The excruciating pain only served to focus her on her task.

"Liar!" she screamed at the demon. "This is mine, asshole. If it were yours, you'd be able to get it yourself. But you can't. You need me."

"You must give it to me of your own free will. Do it now." Its red palms curled, calling it. "We make a deal."

"You get the Tecpatl in exchange for renouncing your claim to my soul. Take it or leave it," she told the demon.

"We're not negotiating," Léopold growled, in an attempt to support her. "Laryssa's mine. Surely, even a son of Satan like you can feel the bond. She'll never be yours to own...not her soul, not her body. Take the deal, Rylion. Then disappear." A cloud of uneasiness fell over Léopold as he spoke to the demon. If Laryssa gave it the knife, Rylion would have the ability to pierce the veil of the underworld whenever it wished. It was no secret that demons and other underworldly creatures lied. He glanced at Laryssa, trying to get her to strike the demon first. But her innocence washed over him, reminding him of her naivety. Léopold pricked at her mind again, urging her to stop, but he could feel her unbridled fury as it took over. The agonizing years she'd survived, plagued both in hiding and shame, played in her head. No longer would she succumb to that weakness.

"Say it. Say it. Renounce me," Laryssa demanded, her face hot in rage.

For the first time in Laryssa's life, she summoned every ounce of her power. She held out her hand and tunneled her energy towards a huge oak tree. It ripped from the ground with a thunderous roar, and flew across the yard, landing next to the demon. She hated the creature, hated everyone who had ever made her feel like her life was less than living because of what she was. Now that she had Léopold and had embraced her origins, she refused to relinquish her new life.

"As you wish," Rylion falsely conceded. It nodded toward the ground, concealing the deceitful smile it wore. "Your soul was rightfully mine. It was stolen. But I want the knife."

"Say. It," Laryssa spat. She sensed Léopold's concern for her through the bond. It almost felt as if he was trying to warn her, to discourage her from her mission. *I have to kill it, Leo. Please.* As her hatred for Rylion flooded her psyche, she pictured Ava, the demon trying to kill the baby. Laryssa, certain in her decision, shook off any doubts.

"I have no claim to your soul," it vowed, continuing to claw the air with its fingers. "Your turn. The knife. Give it to me."

A flash of deceit in the demon's eyes was all the warning Laryssa had that Rylion was going to take the knife. She couldn't allow him to stop her. The creature had to be sent back to hell. Lunging at the demon, she aimed at its abdomen. As she did so, Rylion latched its talons around her wrist. Crushing her flesh, it forced her to drop the Tecpatl into its own hand.

"You treacherous bitch. Now, you will know death like you've never known," it jeered, yanking her against its chest. The power of the knife splintered through Rylion, and it convulsed in electrifying force. With a whisper, the demon materialized into nothingness, taking both Laryssa and the Tecpatl with it.

Laryssa's cheek slammed into the acrid dust as she fell to the ground. She didn't need to open her eyes to know where it had taken her. She protectively curled into a ball, flattening her palms onto the ground and pushed up on her knees. She shook her head to break loose of the trance she'd been in, so dead set on killing the demon.

Léopold. She'd felt his concern for her while she'd argued with the demon. It almost had been as if he hadn't wanted her to give Rylion the knife. But he'd known that only she could kill it. It didn't make sense. Confused, she rubbed the bridge of her nose trying to think clearly. Wiping the sweaty dirt from her eyes, she caught sight of Rylion stroking the knife as if it were a baby. *Baby.* She vaguely remembered an image of the baby. Had Léopold tried to communicate a picture through their bond? *But why?* She felt dizzy as her mind attempted to solve the puzzle. The sickening truth began to set in as she coughed out the red particles that had stuck to her tongue. The demon had renounced its claim to *her* soul. But not Ava's.

Muttering to itself, Rylion finally took notice of Laryssa and smiled. Oddly, to her surprise, it didn't approach her. Standing tall, it transformed into a man. Its gorgeous features didn't hide the evil that lingered in its soulless eyes. It smiled, moving its gaze to the hollow-eyed soldiers that hovered on the outskirts of the barren land where it lived. Like a desert horizon, the rocky terrain seemed to go on forever, blocked only by the hundreds of ghosts who stood waiting on its orders. Laryssa's skin crawled as she saw them slithering about like zombies. For years she'd seen them in the streets, stalking her like predators, yet now she understood them for what they were, mindless drones that Rylion had created of its own being. Like a hallucination, they were part and parcel of the demon.

"Do you like my new shell?" the demon asked, stroking its fingers over its pecs and admiring its mortal form. "Finally, after thousands of years, I'll be able to walk again on the Earth. And it's all thanks to you."

"I hate you," she sputtered. Her chest heaved as the hot air burned her lungs.

"Hate. Lust. Deceit. All admirable traits as far as I'm concerned. Don't forget how many deaths I had to bring with this knife to earn this honor." It smoothed back its shoulder-length, jet black hair and then stretched its arms. "I've earned you as well, Laryssa. Or have you forgotten that I'm your master?"

"Fuck you. You gave up your rights. Leo, he will come for me," she asserted.

"Very true. But you see, I didn't give up the right to Ava's soul," Rylion informed her. Its eyes lit up in excitement as it continued. "Your vampire tried to warn you, but your hate burned brightly like a torch. A little trick of mine that always seems to work. You do know that Ava's death came at my hands. And like yours, her soul was mine…stolen."

"No, no, no," Laryssa repeated. She glanced away for a second and it disappeared. Screaming into the vast expanse, she searched for it. "Where are you, you bastard?"

"I'm here." Laryssa felt the air gush from her chest as she heard a baby's cry. *Ava.* She closed her eyes, willing it not to be true. *No. Oh dear God. Have mercy. Not the baby.* Forcing her neck to straighten, she turned toward the sound. The demon stood cradling Ava in its arms, laughing as it did so.

"Behold. My daughter has arrived."

"Open the goddamned veil," Léopold demanded of Ilsbeth.

"You must be patient." She raised her head and shot him a glare as she held her hands to the dirt where the demon had last appeared.

"Leo, man. Just give her a second. We'll find her," Dimitri said.

Léopold felt Laryssa even though the demon had abducted her. As soon as Ilsbeth opened the door to

Rylion's lair, he was going after her. His gut had told him that the demon would take her, if not for her soul, then to use as a bargaining chip for something else, someone else. *Ava.*

Suspecting it was true, Léopold pulled out his phone and texted Logan. He sucked a heart wrenching breath as he read his reply.

"Jesus Christ. It took her!" Léopold yelled, throwing his phone across the yard in a rage. "It fucking took her."

"Yeah, it took Laryssa. I know. We'll get her back," Dimitri replied.

"No. It took Ava."

"How the hell..?"

"I don't fucking know."

"The knife. It used the knife," Ilsbeth responded, as she sliced her palm open with the athame. "Stand back. When it opens, you must leap through. Do not hesitate. I'll keep it open."

Léopold stormed in anger, knowing that after all his efforts, the demon had taken Ava. Still, for the life of him, aside from Ava being naiad, he couldn't make sense of why Rylion wanted her so badly. He blew out a breath as the ground began to shake. Dimitri stood at his side.

"You don't have to do this, wolf," Léopold said.

"Yeah, I know. But you throw a good party. You know I love to dance," Dimitri tried to joke.

"Dance with the devil."

"They're playing our song."

"You ready to go kill this thing?"

"Yeah, let's do this shit."

The ground began to shake as Ilsbeth chanted louder and louder. A crack in the earth formed slowly before them, opening to a fiery chasm below. Léopold gave no warning before he hurled himself off the edge into the deep abyss. Dimitri gave Ilsbeth a wink and jumped in after him.

Léopold landed on his feet, bracing himself with his hands. A gust of wind kicked up, and through it, he heard the cry of a baby in the distance. A hundred yards north, he caught a glimpse of Rylion dangling Ava like a carrot, his little rabbit stood lost in consternation. Léopold struggled to hear their conversation. *Laryssa, I'm here. We're coming.* As soon as he'd thought her name, the ground began to swell with whirls of red dust. Slowly, the particles circulated upward into the air, escalating into an opaque wall of gritty earth.

"Follow me," Léopold called to Dimitri, who tore off his clothes and transformed into his wolf. Stumbling through the gusty sheets of soil, they ran forward.

Laryssa felt Léopold in her mind, but kept her eyes on the infant. Forcing an impassive expression, she fought to conceal her shock. *Ava is Rylion's daughter?* She quickly tried to make sense of the ambiguous relationship, but there was no reconciliation. As Léopold grew closer, she sought to distract Rylion with questions.

"How can Ava be your daughter? She was born of a wolf," she challenged.

"Possession is a tricky business, especially seeing as I had little control over my access to freedom. But I was owed a soul... you were stolen from me, after all. The wolf was weak and I happened to get lucky, breaking through and possessing him. I'd had plans for the wolf, but that night with his mate changed everything for me. It was my seed that fertilized the bitch's womb. A soul. A brand new soul...just for me."

"You're sick." Laryssa coughed as Rylion brought forth clouds of debris. She shielded her face and took a step toward it. "So you killed her in the woods...."

"Oh no, I killed her mother with my own hands while she bore the child ...a wolf's hands. Ava died that night too. But that goddamned bitch who creates you water whores stole her from me. Like you, all she needed was the water to do it. Of course, the wolf...well, that didn't turn out so well for him," Rylion explained.

"He knew." Laryssa wiped her eyes, aghast with the revelation.

"The beauty of possession is that they don't know they've been possessed." The demon laughed, and began to pace with Ava crying in its arms. "All Perry knew was that he'd killed his own mate. He left and killed himself." Rylion stopped and paused. "What's so perfect about this is that like the Aztecs, I'm willing to sacrifice my own child. Don't you see, Laryssa? It's always been about you."

"Me?"

"I've watched you all these years and then you hid from me, keeping me from your home, your life. Even when I sent my ghosts to watch over you, you spurned me. Why, Laryssa? You've always known I'm there."

"I don't belong to you. You're wrong," she yelled through the wind.

"Even though you reek of the vampire, you're still mine. And you're going to come to me….willingly."

"Are you fucking crazy?" As shock set in, Laryssa began to shake her head. Catching the sight of movement out of her left eye, she attempted to refocus on Rylion. She suspected that the demon had sensed that Léopold was in its world but she wouldn't give it an inch of help.

"Ava's soul for yours. I'll hand over my only daughter to the vampire and his wolf. I know you're here," it called out into the storm. "All you have to do is say yes. Say the words. Accept your place at my side. Look at me now…I'm a man. I can satisfy your earthly cravings. Tell me…tell me that I'm your master. Give me your soul."

"Put the baby down…over there!" she screamed through the din, pointing to the rock where it'd left the Tecpatl.

"Say it. Accept me as your master. Give me what is mine, Laryssa, and the vampire can have the baby. Reject me and I'll murder her. It'll be on your conscience forever."

"Put her down first," Laryssa insisted.

Slowly, she approached him. The Tecpatl rested only a few feet from her hands. If her abilities worked in the underworld, she could have called the knife to her hand. But no matter how hard she tried, the energy wouldn't respond to her summons. She held her hands upward, exposing her palms to him. *Get the baby. Leo, get the baby.* She prayed like hell that throughout the chaos, Léopold could hear their discussion.

"You accept my conditions?"

"Yes," she whispered, spying the knife.

Rylion moved quickly to set the child upon the dirt, never taking its eyes off of her. Once it'd surrendered the child to the earth, it strode toward Laryssa, a broad smile breaking across its face.

"Say it Laryssa. Say you're mine," it ordered.

Laryssa nodded, feigning submission to its will. *Move.* The command came strong, filling her chest with dread. *Move. Now, Laryssa.* Without thinking, she sensed Léopold was coming for her.

"I'll say it...you are my mas..." Her words fell apart as she dropped to the ground and rolled out of the way. Léopold flew from behind her, smashing into the demon. Dimitri cut through the dust and scooped up the child into his arms, tearing back into the tornado of filth. On her knees, Laryssa crawled toward the rock, to the Tecpatl.

"You're dead," Léopold grunted, shoving his fist into Rylion's face.

The demon's human form disappeared at first contact, allowing it to dig its savage claws into Léopold's arms. Léopold pinned it to the ground and hit it again, but Rylion just laughed, and rebounded out of the vampire's grasp. Continuing his assault, Léopold extended his own claws, slicing a gash across the demon's chest. Rylion stumbled backwards, but never faltered. With his fangs descended, Léopold charged at it, tearing his fangs into its flesh. As he bit into it, he curled his fingers into a point. Spearing his hand into the demon's chest, he perforated its gut, clear through to the other side. Closing his fist, Léopold ripped out the demon's entrails from its cavity.

Rylion careened backwards as Léopold released it. The demon's laughter grew louder, even though its legs threatened to fail.

"You can't kill me, you fool," the demon boasted, its wounds healing before their eyes. "No one can kill me."

"I can, fucker." Laryssa screamed as she charged it from behind. "Go to hell!"

Using all her strength, she plunged the Tecpatl into Rylion's back. The sound of its scales splitting open echoed into the air. The demon screamed and hissed, flailing its arms, but she continued to use every last ounce of her strength to ram the knife through its thick skin. She leveraged the knife to hoist herself upward and wrap her legs around its waist. Laryssa held tight and twisted the blade into its flesh. Rylion staggered back and forth as she plunged the blade up to its hilt. Rylion's soulless warriors swirled into a vortex, returning to the demon's body, but it wasn't enough to save it from the destiny of the Tlalco Tecpatl. Blood gushed from its wound, splattering onto the cracked dirt. As the demon's essence drained from its body, it was sucked back into the infernal netherworld from where it had come, its body toppling over, face-down onto the ground. No longer of this world, it had been sent to hell.

Laryssa screamed for it to die, over and over, obscured within her task. She felt Léopold's hands on her shoulders, heard his voice calling her name, but continued to lie atop the scaly shell of the demon. Afraid to release the knife, she rejected Léopold's touch, shoving a hand at him.

"It's gone." Léopold spoke softly to her, aware that she'd come unhinged. His little naiad was no killer…until now. The storm ceased, allowing him to nod over at Dimitri, who held the baby. The shimmering veil remained, but he needed to get Laryssa to move. "Come, ma chérie. You did it."

"No, no, no," she mumbled, terrified that the demon would return. Laryssa felt Léopold brush her mind and whispers of his soothing words caressed her heart, allowing her to open her eyes.

"That's it. You're okay. It's me. It's Leo." For the first time in his life, he'd referred to himself by the shortened name his mother had called him as a child. Even though Dimitri also addressed him as such, it had been Laryssa, alone, who'd made him own it. The name represented the revolution she'd caused within his soul. Her love for him and his for her. "I've got you."

Gently, he slid his hands under her arms, peeling her off the corpse. Through their bond he sent her all his strength and calm, communicating how incredibly proud he was of her. He almost had her extricated when she tensed. With her hands still frozen around the stone hilt, she refused to let go. Léopold reached around her, placing his hands over hers and jerked the Tecpatl from the crackling epidermis. Once released, she clutched the knife to her chest as if she was protecting a cherished treasure. Aware that she'd been traumatized, Léopold scooped her up into his arms, cradling her. His rabbit was a warrior. But now that the battle had been fought, she'd crumbled into his embrace.

Chapter Twenty-one

A week had passed since they'd permanently banished the demon from their world. Laryssa had begun working again in her store, with Léopold insisting she take it easy. While she hadn't told many people yet about her newly owned supernatural status as a naiad, she no longer hid it either. Working to train Mason to take over day to day operations so that she could travel with Léopold was going well and she looked forward to her future.

As Laryssa locked the door, she recalled how ecstatic Logan and Wynter had been when they'd returned Ava to their home. A wolf, the child needed to be raised by wolves, in a pack. A naiad, she needed the guidance to learn how to survive and thrive in the water and to hone her abilities. Hunter Livingston had given his blessing to the New Orleans's Alpha and his mate, granting them rights to raise the child. Laryssa and Léopold had been designated godparents by Logan. Laryssa had been honored and humbled, grateful for the opportunity to be a presence in Ava's life.

Laryssa contemplated the only unresolved matter, which had been Sydney's recovery. While her soul had not been lost to the demon, Sydney would never be human again. It had been true that her injuries from the demon would have killed her if it hadn't been for Kade's vampiric blood. While it had gone unspoken on the night of the attack, Kade had turned her. Léopold had known it but hadn't told Laryssa until a few days after she'd killed the demon. Sydney, although engaged to a vampire, had steadfastly wished to remain human. But what was done could not be undone. Despite Léopold's repeated visits to Kade's house, Sydney had reportedly not accepted her fate, remaining depressed and isolated in their home.

Since Laryssa's terrifying experience in the underworld, she'd been working with Ilsbeth to locate information about how to return the Tecpatl to the water. Ilsbeth, still unsure of how to return it, promised she'd assist her. In the meantime, Laryssa had locked and buried it deep within the lake bed for safe keeping.

True to his promise, Léopold had moved most of Laryssa's belongings to his French Quarter townhouse, where they spent the week. They planned on spending weekends at his home on the lake. In either location, she had open access to the life-giving waters she required for her existence. Earlier in the day, they'd made plans to meet for dinner at a quaint outdoor restaurant a few doors down from his home. As she walked along the sidewalk, she realized that she was no longer scared of seeing the eyeless warriors. They'd been a mirage all along, designed by Rylion to keep her under its watch. Even as the night fell, no longer would she fear darkness. No matter where she was, Léopold was with her, supporting her, loving her.

The only thing that concerned her was that despite the bond, they still hadn't said they loved each other. Three little words seemed like a minute detail given their bond, yet it was becoming tremendously important to her. She loved Léopold. Not only did she want him to know, she wanted everybody to know. Whenever they made love, she could feel his love slice through her, and while he'd whisper sweet nothings in French, she wanted to hear that he loved her.

Bells rang overhead as she opened the door to the restaurant. The maître d' motioned to her, gesturing with his hand for her to come to him. She giggled and looked over her shoulder, unsure of how he'd recognized her. *Léopold.* Rolling her eyes, she politely smiled at the man and walked toward him.

"Ms. Theriot?" he confirmed.

"Yes."

"Mr. Devereoux is waiting for you. Please follow me." He turned, and walked through the busy restaurant.

Laryssa followed him, complying with his wish. Lilac lights illuminated their path through the darkened restaurant. The host pushed through a glass door, holding it open so she could go first into the open courtyard. Ensconced in bowed branches above their heads, hundreds of tiny lights twinkled in the trees. The candlelit tables were decorated with small vases of fresh flowers. As she walked through the romantic dining garden, she spotted Léopold seated in a back corner.

Her stomach fluttered as Léopold gave her a sexy smile. The twinkle in his eye told her she was in for a surprise. As she approached the table, he stood, briefly touching his lips to hers. Waiting for her to sit down, he signaled for the waiter to pour her a glass.

"Mon amour. Lovely as always. How was your day?" He casually swirled his wine and studied its legs against the light.

"Great. Mason's doing well."

"How soon do you think he'll be ready to take over?" he asked nonchalantly. As the waiter passed, he nodded.

"Maybe another week. I think all that alone time without me really helped prepare him." She picked up her glass and sipped her drink. "Did you get to see our baby girl today?"

"Oui. She's doing well. And Logan and Wynter…let's just say even though I don't think they were in any way expecting a new pup, they'll make wonderful parents. I'm sure they're going to be quite busy."

"I still don't understand how Ava can be Rylion's," she stated with disgust.

"She's not. I believe that, like you, the demon thought it had claim to her."

"Delusions of grandeur is more like it."

"Possession is possession. Even witches can sometimes achieve it. But one thing is certain; it was Perry's body that created Ava with Mariah. After Rylion had killed Mariah, though, and then the baby, it claimed her soul or should I say, tried to. The water of the womb is perhaps the most vital water any of us will know in our lifetimes. The Lady saved her from the demon. No evil taints Ava," Léopold confirmed. "Our little one's going to be just fine. She's going to be the belle of New Orleans someday."

"Do you ever wish...I mean, you're a vampire..." Laryssa's voice went soft and she looked away. His hand on hers caused her to glance up to him.

"I won't lie to you. I've always wanted children, but this life of mine, you see...it all died. And now that I have you, that's all that matters." Léopold sensed her sadness. They'd never discussed children. It was never an option....until now.

"You're all that matters to me, Leo. It's okay, really. I mean I never thought I could have kids, so it's okay."

"But if you could...would you?"

"With you?"

"But of course with me," he laughed.

Laryssa took a deep breath and sighed. "Yes." She hoped he wouldn't be mad at her.

"Luca and Samantha are having a daughter."

"I thought you said that she was a witch. They're very lucky."

"Ilsbeth believes it is a possibility." Léopold gave her a small smile, waiting for her to put the pieces together.

"Us? No," she replied, shaking her head. Getting her hopes up for something that was impossible would crush her.

"Oui. Us. Apparently, like witches, naiad can bring life…with vampires."

"Don't joke about this. It's not funny."

"Not joking."

"I'm not ready to have kids yet but oh my God, if you're serious, I'd love to have your children someday," she confirmed. *I love you so much.*

"You'd make a wonderful mother, ma chérie." He smiled, pleased with her response.

Laryssa was his perfect soul mate. The vision of her swollen with his child nearly brought tears to his eyes. She simply had no idea how much he'd fallen in love with her, but he planned on telling her tonight. The waiter approached the table, setting their appetizers in front of them.

"Leo, I…" Laryssa began. The love in her heart felt as if it was going to burst if she didn't tell him how she felt. She needed to say the words.

"You look very sexy tonight," Léopold said, changing the subject. "I love when you wear skirts, do you know that?"

The dominant tone of Léopold's voice sent chills up Laryssa's spine. She licked her lips and gave him a small smile.

"Well, I do enjoy making you happy." Laryssa felt his hand on her leg underneath the table and she jumped in her seat. The heat of his palm sent desire singing through her body. Knowing he'd sense it immediately, she picked up her fork and stabbed a piece of lettuce in an effort to act normally.

"So very glad to hear that, because I thought this would be the perfect place to continue our lessons." Léopold let his hand drift to her knee.

"Lessons?" she croaked. "What lessons?"

"Perhaps I've used the wrong word. Experimentation. Oui." His devious grin told her she was in trouble.

"Experimentation? With what?" Beyond her enjoyment of being restrained, they'd discussed how she'd enjoyed being spanked in front of Dimitri. *Oh God, not that. Not here.* Before she could protest, she felt him nudge her knees open, the cool air wafting up her dress. Looking around at the other patrons, she straightened her back as he began to tug up the hem.

"Um, Leo. What are you doing, darling?" She laughed as his fingers trailed up her inner thigh. Looking around the restaurant, she hoped no one could see what he was doing. Even though the white tablecloth obscured the view, Laryssa couldn't stop the rush of heat that filled her cheeks.

"Saying hello."

"Um, hello to you, too. You do realize we're in a restaurant...a very busy restaurant?" she whispered.

"Oui, I'm acutely aware of our location. You know, I've been thinking about that day on the dock." *The spanking.* She projected her arousal at him and his cock jerked in response. He grinned and gave her a knowing look. Léopold couldn't wait to test her limits. "I see you do remember."

"Yes, I remember clearly. It was…" *Embarrassing. Erotic. Hot.* "interesting."

"So I thought, why not experiment further?" Caressing her soft skin, he edged her panties with his fingers. He could feel the heat emanating from between her legs and sought to tease her mercilessly.

"But Leo," she began, but was unable to finish as he slipped his forefinger underneath the flimsy fabric. He brushed through her slick lips and pressed a single finger up into her. She closed her eyes and grabbed onto the cloth napkin. Trying not to let anyone know what he was doing, she opened her lids and sighed. "Please."

"Shhh…you wouldn't want everyone to hear you now, would you?" He laughed "You're wet, mon amour. So nice."

"Leo," she breathed as he pumped into her core, circling his thumb over her clit. Biting her lip, she shot him a sideways glance. *Is he crazy? Someone's going to know. We're going to get thrown out of the café.* As if he could read her exact thoughts, he upped the ante.

"Don't worry your head about what's going to happen next. I got you a gift." He gave a broad smile and winked. Withdrawing his hand from her underwear, he swiftly reached into his pocket and retrieved the pint-sized silicone horseshoe-shaped device he'd bought her. He easily concealed the toy, which was no more than two inches long. When his hand fell back to her lap, she'd closed her legs. "Open, pet. Or would you prefer a spanking?"

Laryssa shook her head back and forth, completely shocked that he was pressing her with this game. Overwhelmed with her own lust, she vacillated between doing as he said and running away from the table. Dear God, the man tested her. It was frightening and exhilarating, but all the while, he had a way of tapping into her darkest thoughts.

"What'll it be?" The side of his lip curled upward, but his tone told her he was completely serious.

Laryssa took a deep breath and blew it out. Her heart skipped a beat as she complied with his instruction. She resisted the urge to leap off her seat as the smooth outer layer of the toy brushed over her pussy. As he slipped the tiny vibrator inside her, she rocked from side to side on her bottom, causing the overlapping design to brush her clitoris. From her swollen nub to the thin stretch of nerves inside her, she was tantalized every time she shifted in her chair. With no area left untouched, she swore she'd come by the end of her appetizer.

"Leo…Oh my God. What is that?" She watched intently as he withdrew his hand from underneath the table, licked his fingers and then proceeded to drink from his wine glass.

"Hmm…you are much tastier than any culinary delicacy." He picked up his fork and began to eat his salad. His eyes caught hers and she frowned. "Just a bit of fun.

Sweet torture for both of us, I expect. You're not eating. Come on now, don't waste your dinner."

"Are you kidding?" she responded, trying to keep her voice down.

"Do I ever?" He continued eating with a glint of amusement in his eye.

By the time their entrees arrived, Laryssa was nearly undone. As she scooped a shrimp out of her étouffée, the device pulsed inside her and she muffled a squeak. Her eyes landed on Léopold who grinned.

"What are you doing?" she asked, keeping her voice steady. The vibration ripped over her clitoris, deep into her pussy, causing her to drop her utensil. She gripped the edge of the table as desire rolled through her. She studied Léopold. "How are you doing that?"

"Not a witch, I'm afraid. A man must keep his secrets. Now remember, dear Laryssa, don't make too much noise. You'll have an audience."

"You're evil." A spasm of pleasure rolled through her again, and she coughed, trying to disguise the loud moan that threatened to escape her lips. Deciding fair play was in order, she picked up a breadstick and seductively slid it into her mouth, never taking her eyes off of Léopold's.

"I prefer to think of it as doing you a favor…expanding your horizons and such." Léopold's cock hardened to steel at the sight of her trembling with need. The scent of her arousal saturated his nostrils. He didn't think he could get any harder until the little temptress plunged the rod into her mouth. Sucking his breath, he adjusted his erection. At this rate, he'd be the one coming at the table. "The food's delicious, no?"

"Leo," she groaned.

The vibrations increased in intensity, bringing her closer to orgasm. The room turned hotter and hotter as the assault on her pussy continued. Reaching for the buttons on her shirt, she undid one. She grabbed at his pant leg and dug her fingernails into his thigh. Stifling her panting breaths, she tried to figure out how he was operating the device. With one hand on his fork and the other on the table, the mystery only continued. Her eyes quickly roamed the room, terrified that someone would hear her, discover the tremors racking her body.

"Come for me, pet. Come in front of all these people," he encouraged, loving how uninhibited she was. While it was true he'd instigated their exhibitionistic play, she'd embraced it with passion. As her orgasm began, he offered her his hand. The only thing that would have made the moment any better was if he'd been inside of her himself.

"I…I…Leo…Oh my God…I'm…"

"Shhhh….just let go."

As her release slammed into her, she crushed Léopold's hand and dropped her head. Small high-pitched grunts escaped as she let the climax shudder through her body. Sweat beaded on her forehead, and she closed her eyes. As the convulsions began to cease, she panted for breath.

"You are the most stunning woman I've ever met in my life," Léopold praised.

"Home. Now," she gritted out, unable to control her thoughts.

"But you haven't finished…" he laughed.

"Oh, I finished. We're leaving. Now," she demanded forcefully, pushing out of her seat with the palms of her hands on the table. Brushing her damp hair out of her face, she strode across the room, aware that Léopold was following in her wake.

Léopold threw money on the table, and hurried after his wanton naiad. *Absolutely spectacular,* he mused. He'd never met, nor would he ever meet again, a woman like her. He hurried in front of her, opening up the door so she could pass through it.

Laryssa, blazing in desire, couldn't get home fast enough to make love to Leo. Striding through the courtyard, she hardly noticed anyone around her. The only thing that mattered was getting out of the restaurant. As she brushed by the maître d', who attempted to flag down Léopold, she caught sight of Dimitri at the bar, grinning like the cat who hadn't just eaten the canary but its whole nest. *Fuck. What is he doing here?* Certain it had something to do with Léopold, she spun and saw the broad smile on his face.

"Hey cher," Dimitri said, letting his eyes roam over her.

"What are you..?" she began but was interrupted.

"You have something of mine?" Léopold asked his friend.

"Why yes I do," Dimitri drawled, continuing to smile at Laryssa.

"Merci beaucoup, mon ami," Léopold said, opening the palm of his hand.

"Any time, bro," Dimitri laughed.

Laryssa's eyes widened as Dimitri dropped a quarter-sized remote control into Léopold's palm. *Dimitri had been controlling the toy?* Too aroused to be angry, she feigned indignation.

"You…" she stammered and pointed to Dimitri. "I cannot believe you let him talk you into this. Bad, bad, bad wolf."

"And you," she pinned her eyes on Léopold who looked sexier than ever. With utter dominance, she approached and grabbed him by the tie, forcefully yanking him toward her, "are a very naughty vampire….one who deserves his own little punishment. You had best get me home…I believe you owe me."

"You heard your woman," Dimitri laughed. "Time's a-wastin'"

"That it is," Léopold responded. Without giving Laryssa warning, he scooped her up into his arms and shoved through the front door with the back of his shoulder.

Giggling, Laryssa kicked her feet and pressed her face against his white dress shirt. As Léopold kissed the top of her head, she began to undo his buttons, gliding her hands underneath the crisp fabric, caressing his chest. Within ninety seconds, he'd rounded the corner of the block and was frantically punching his finger at the security pad.

With a light buzz, the door clicked open and he captured her lips with his. Using his foot to slam it shut behind him, he stumbled into the foyer with her in his arms. He heard buttons sprinkle all over the floor like little discs doing a tap dance and realized she'd split his shirt wide open. A bite on his shoulder sent a jolt to his cock.

Laryssa couldn't get enough of him. Aggressively, she tore at his clothes, biting and licking at his skin. Her feet landed shakily on the floor, and she ripped his shirt all the way off of him. Lifting her arms so he could bare her, she moaned at the loss of contact. She was hardly aware that he'd undone her bra until it slipped to the floor. Reaching for him, Laryssa speared her fingers up into his hair, clutching at his head.

His lips found hers again. In frenzy, they passionately kissed, his tongue sweeping up against hers. Seeking, questing, he stroked her mouth with a hungry urgency. Laryssa savagely returned his kiss, fiercely claiming him for her own. Immersed in each other, their bond flourished, escalating their intimacy.

Léopold's erection pressed into her belly as he backed her into the living room. He gently pushed her onto the floor, and she moaned into his mouth. She kicked off her shoes, reaching her hands down to his pants, and unbuckled them. Laryssa freed his iron-hard cock and stroked it, gliding her thumb over its glistening head.

With her other hand, she gently massaged his tightened balls until he groaned in pleasure.

Léopold couldn't wait another second to be inside her. He shoved up her skirt, tearing off her panties with his claws. Reaching between her legs, he cupped her mound. He'd considered removing the u-shaped vibrator, but decided to leave it in place. Fingering the top of her folds, he depressed a barely visible button, activating the sultry vibrations. Laryssa moaned in response, guiding his shaft toward her entrance.

"Leo, the toy..." she spoke into his mouth. The engorged head of his arousal pressed against her entrance and she fell back onto the floor, widening her thighs.

"Oui," Léopold guided his swollen flesh into her wet pussy. The slick surface buzzed against his erection as he drove into her.

"Too much... yes, Leo," she breathed.

"You're taking me, all of me. Ah yeah, that's it." He plunged in slowly, allowing her to stretch as he rocked inward.

From his root to his tip, her quivering pussy and the slow trembling of the device stimulated him, sending shockwaves throughout his body. He wouldn't last very long inside her this first time, he knew, but he planned on making love to her all night long. *Goddess, I love this woman.* As his pelvis settled into hers, he leaned onto a forearm. With his other hand, he cupped her breast. Caressing her ripe flesh, he took to her rosy peak, teasing her nipple with his teeth.

"Leo, oh God. Fucking yes." Laryssa saw stars as the pressure on her clit resonated deep into her core. Writhing up into him, she whimpered under the glorious sensation.

"Look at me, mon amour," he grunted, staving off his own orgasm. When she refused to comply, he took her chin in his hand. He smiled as her eyes slowly met his.

"Leo, I...I..." *love you.* Her heart felt as if it would shatter. No one had ever broken her down into such a basic state, holding her life in his hands. He'd infiltrated every fiber of her being, wrecking her for anyone else. And her soul rejoiced that he had.

"Can you feel me?" *I love you.*

She nodded, panting as he slowly rotated his hips against hers.

"You are my blood and flesh...my reason for living, my sweet naiad."

"Leo."

"I love you, Laryssa. You've stolen my heart. Forever. You and I. Hear my words...feel my words." He closed his eyes, funneling the swirling vortex of love he'd held back.

The emotion in Laryssa's chest bubbled over at his words. *I love you.* Her eyes began to tear, but he gave her no time to adjust. A wave of his memories, thoughts and feelings crashed over her, reverberating down from her head to her toes. She felt his pain as if it was her own. *The death of his children and wife. The loneliness he'd hidden throughout the centuries. And finally, the tremendous love and respect he held for her.* And then she heard the words again as if he was speaking them aloud to her; *I love you. My love, my life.*

"I love you, too. You mean everything to me. I love you so, so, much…" her words trailed off as he began to thrust deeply inside her.

Even though Léopold had heard her project the words in her mind many times, he'd never acknowledged them. But now, as the words spilled from her lips, he sought to claim her. He'd never be able to show or tell her how much she meant to him. Like his own personal savior, she'd torn apart his shallow existence, giving him a new life.

With each surge of his hips, Laryssa arched up to meet him. Looking within the deep abyss of his eyes, she opened her soul to him. Nothing short of his possession of her would satisfy her desire. The craving gripped at her chest. Reaching upward, she brushed her hair to the side, submitting, offering him her neck.

At the sight of her surrender, Léopold's fangs descended. Her pussy contracted around his cock, tightening like a vise as her climax teetered over the edge. The sound of flesh meeting flesh filled the room, as he pounded his shaft into her warm center. He felt the barrage of her emotions, ones filled with sheer contentment, filter through him. Soaring over the edge, Léopold lost control. Like a cobra, he struck, his sharp teeth piercing through her milky skin. Her exquisite blood flowed down his throat, weaving itself into his cells.

A sharp prick to Laryssa's neck was quickly replaced with the exhilarating ecstasy that only Léopold could deliver. She cried his name, embracing the furious climax. Wrapping her thighs around his waist, she snared him to her pelvis, undulating up into their simultaneous release. Together they moved in rhythm as their orgasms tore through them at the same time.

Laryssa's cries subsided once Léopold retracted his bite. Shivers ran down her spine as he licked the sensitive skin that ran from behind her ear down between her breasts. She felt him remove both himself and the toy from between her legs as his lips latched onto one of her tender nipples. The delightful sensation brought a smile to her face and she giggled softly.

"No laughing in bed, woman," he growled, giving her a nip.

"Ah…hey, no more biting," she teased. "I need to recover."

Léopold crawled up to her so that he could meet her eyes. Filled with love and dedication, he gently kissed her. Their tongues fluttered softly with each other's.

"I love you," he asserted once more. Rolling onto his back, he brought her with him.

"I love you too," she whispered. "You do know I plan on getting you back for what you did today."

"I'm looking forward to it." Léopold kissed her head and closed his eyes.

In a thousand years, he'd sought to suppress every emotion and experience that would lead him toward a relationship. Yet it was that very connection he'd avoided that now brought peace and tranquility into his life. As he held his mate in his arms, he smiled. It may have taken him centuries, but he'd finally achieved the nirvana he'd sought. His life, once latent with obscurity and death, had been transposed into one of tenderness and love. With Laryssa at his side, nothing would ever be the same.

❧ *Epilogue* ❧

As the waves rolled in, Dimitri considered his decision to take a vacation by himself. With Logan and Wynter busily adjusting to their new family situation and Léopold and Laryssa ensconced in their bond, he had needed to take a break from New Orleans. Since Jake had promised to fill in on his role of beta, he'd left town, content that he'd wrapped up loose ends.

As he looked up at the spectacular panorama of the night sky, he marveled in the expanse of the universe. While it was altogether stunning, it caused him to pause, wondering how he'd gone all these years with no real purpose. His role as beta had been important to the pack, no doubt. But aside from assisting Logan, he wondered what else was out there and if maybe, in his absence, they'd never miss his presence.

A nagging itch plagued Dimitri as he sat on the wide expanse of beach, looking out over the Pacific ocean. Ever since he'd returned from Rylion's pit, he couldn't shake the feeling something had gone awry. As he'd risen from

...e baby in his arms, he could've sworn
...ng had latched onto his wolf. He'd felt Ilsbeth's
...yes on him, but she'd denied anything was wrong when
he'd questioned her. He hadn't expected that Léopold
would have noticed anything wrong with him, but his
Alpha felt every emotion that ran through his veins. Yet
when Dimitri had withdrawn, Logan hadn't said a word.
He should have mentioned it to him, he thought. But
every time he'd gone to approach Logan, the house was lit
up with the coos and giggles of their princess.

Even though he'd tried to shake it off, Dimitri felt
dirty. Tainted. Bringing his personal angst into their warm
and loving home wasn't something he would do. No,
running had been the only option. San Diego wasn't the
furthest he could travel on his bike, but it sure as hell was
the place with the nicest weather.

He'd known better than to go into another pack's
territory without giving fair warning, but he'd lost focus.
When the moon rose, he planned to seek out the Alpha.
But until then, he planned to sit his ass on the beach.
Maybe he'd learn how to surf. Maybe he'd drive up Pacific
Coast Highway. Maybe he'd stop by La La Land, get
himself a new tattoo. It didn't really matter as long as he
felt his skin tingling as if it was crawling with lice.
Whatever it took, he had to get his shit together again.

Dimitri had lived a hundred and fifty years on the
bayou and aside from Jackson Hole and New York City,
he hadn't left his Cajun roots…until this week. Trying to
shake off his guilt for leaving the pack, he took off his

shirt, and laid his bare skin on the sand. Praying that his suspicion wasn't true, he dug his toes into the sand and breathed in the sea air. Since he'd left seven days ago, he hadn't gone wolf. He was lying to himself, he knew. Something...something insidious...evil had touched him. His wolf had gone silent, and he was terrified to test his suspicions.

Tonight, though, he'd face his fears. He'd run in the desert, maybe kill a meal by himself. As one with his brothers in the Acadian wolves, he'd never once considered going off as a lone wolf. But the voice that he'd picked up in hell told him to run from New Orleans, to flee. And flee he had. He stared up at the stars, hoping his silent meditation would rouse his inner wolf, the fighter that had gotten him through life. In his mind, he called the warrior to the surface and for the first time in his life, no howl of existence responded. He clutched at his chest with his hand as panic set in, and he choked to catch his breath.

Even though his wolf went silent, his preternatural hearing picked up the patter of paws along the shore. A yip in the distance alerted him to the danger. Leaping to his feet, his eyes honed in on a dozen pairs of eyes. As they attacked, their teeth sinking into his flesh, he cried out for his wolf, who as if in a coma, lay sleeping in his mind. Sounds of his own screams reverberated as he was dragged to the ground. Kicking and punching, he tried in vain to fight off his attackers. A final blow to his neck, took him into the sand. As the blood drained from his mortal body, he screamed out to his wolf to wake.

*Dimitri's story coming fall 2014
(Immortals of New Orleans, Book 6)*

The Immortals of New Orleans

Kade's Dark Embrace
(Immortals of New Orleans, Book 1)

Luca's Magic Embrace
(Immortals of New Orleans, Book 2)

Tristan's Lyceum Wolves
(Immortals of New Orleans, Book 3)

Logan's Acadian Wolves
(Immortals of New Orleans, Book 4)

Léopold's Wicked Embrace
(Immortals of New Orleans, Book 5)

Dimitri's story coming fall 2014
(Immortals of New Orleans, Book 6)

About the Author

Kym Grosso is the author of the erotic paranormal romance series, The Immortals of New Orleans. The series currently includes *Kade's Dark Embrace* (Immortals of New Orleans, Book 1), *Luca's Magic Embrace* (Immortals of New Orleans, Book 2), *Tristan's Lyceum Wolves* (Immortals of New Orleans, Book 3), *Logan's Acadian Wolves* (Immortals of New Orleans, Book 4) and *Léopold's Wicked Embrace* (Immortals of New Orleans, Book 5).

In addition to romance, Kym has written and published several articles about autism, and is passionate about autism advocacy. She also is a contributing essay author in *Chicken Soup for the Soul: Raising Kids on the Spectrum.*

Kym lives with her husband, two children, dog and cat. Her hobbies include autism advocacy, reading, tennis, zumba, traveling and spending time with her husband and children. New Orleans, with its rich culture, history and unique cuisine, is one of her favorite places to visit. Also, she loves traveling just about anywhere that has a beach or snow-covered mountains. On any given night, when not writing her own books, Kym can be found reading her Kindle, which is filled with hundreds of romances.

• • • •

Social Media/Links:

Website: http://www.KymGrosso.com

Facebook: http://www.facebook.com/KymGrossoBooks

Twitter: https://twitter.com/KymGrosso

Pinterest: http://www.pinterest.com/kymgrosso/

Made in the USA
Middletown, DE
31 March 2016